deadkidsongs

deadkidsongs

TOBY LITT

HAMISH HAMILTON
LONDON

HAMISH HAMILTON

Published by the Penguin Group
Penguin Books Ltd, 27 Wrights Lane, London W8 5TZ, England
Penguin Putnam Inc., 375 Hudson Street, New York, New York 10014, USA
Penguin Books Australia Ltd, Ringwood, Victoria, Australia
Penguin Books Canada Ltd, 10 Alcorn Avenue, Toronto, Ontario, Canada M4V 3B2
Penguin Books India (P) Ltd, 11 Community Centre, Panchsheel Park,
New Delhi – 110 017, India
Penguin Books (NZ) Ltd, Cnr Rosedale and Airborne Roads,
Albany, Auckland, New Zealand
Penguin Books (South Africa) (Pty) Ltd, 5 Watkins Street, Denver Ext 4,
Johannesburg 2094, South Africa

Penguin Books Ltd, Registered Offices: Harmondsworth, Middlesex, England

First published 2001
1

Set in 11.35/14 pt Monotype Garamond
Typeset by Rowland Phototypesetting Ltd, Bury St Edmunds, Suffolk
Printed in England by Clays Ltd, St Ives plc

A CIP catalogue record for this book is available from the British Library

ISBN 0–241–14070–6

For Luke, Guy, Mark, and John

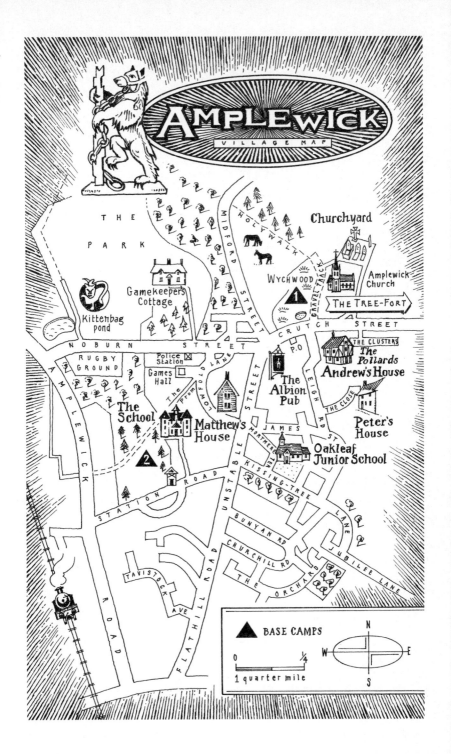

The bottom drawer of the filing cabinet in the far corner of my father's study was labelled TOP SECRET. I had always been furiously curious about this, a fact my father was not unaware of. He hanged himself the day before my fourteenth birthday. On the day after his funeral, I snuck into his study, found the key and unlocked the filing cabinet. Inside the bottom drawer was a single Lever Arch file marked CLASSIFIED. I clicked it open, slouching back into my father's swing-chair. Inside the file was a neat stack of about 500 sheets of going-brown A4 paper. The top page had these words typed across it in red ink underlined with black: SECURITY CLEARANCE REQUIRED: LEVEL ONE. To this, in my father's beautifully controlled legal script, my own name, Matthew, had been subjoined. Hoisting my feet up onto his oh-so-sacred desk, I flipped the first page and it began –

SUMMER-AUTUMN-WINTER-SPRING

SUMMER

CHAPTER ONE

Matthew

Nun will die Sonn' so hell aufgeh'n
Als sei kein Unglück die Nacht gescheh'n!
Das Unglück geschah nur mir allein!
Die Sonne, sie scheinet allgemein!

Now will the Sun as bright ascend
As if last night Unluck did not descend.
The Unluck fell upon me alone,
The Sun, it shines on everyone.

(*Translated after the* Kindertotenlieder *of Friedrich Rückert*)

i.

When we looked upwards we saw beneath us a sky of rosebushes, gravel paths, equipment and thick, healthy, but slightly too-dry grass. (Not that it would ever go razor-edged and cut you. It was too purely English for that. Tensed between thumbs, it would give a farty vibrato like that of a badly beaten-up cello.) The ground above us, on the other hand, was blue, blue as the deep end of a very wide swimming-pool. A swimming-pool seen not from the diving-board, but suspended motionless above it. Suspended so that no shadow is projected down, and there is no idea of edge at all. A swimming-pool splash-virgin, quite unruffled. At the horizon, a rough line of oak trees was interrupted half-way along by the leap of pylons and wires.

This was how we saw the world. The four of us. Gang. Not The Gang. Just Gang. Andrew, Matthew, Paul and Peter. Hanging upside-down from the highest branches of the tallest spruce in Andrew's father's garden.

"Can you see them yet?" asked Peter, who dangled on the lowest branch.

"No," said Matthew. "Shut up."

Matthew had the binocs. They were matt-black steel, with an extra-grip texture where your hands held. A strap of old flaky brown leather hung from them. They were his grandfather's binoculars and they had seen action with him (and he had seen action with them) on the beaches of Normandy.

"Still no sign?" said Andrew.

"Nothing of consequence to report," Matthew replied.

We were too old to admit taking a great pleasure in our upside-downness, yet not too old to have lost a boyish love for all bodily disorientation: shakings, fallings, submersions, blindnesses, stretchings, giddyings . . .

The hair on our heads floated up (down) as if we were conducting an experiment with static electricity.

The highest up the tree was Andrew, because we were all agreed that he had the best father. Then came Paul, whose father was a teacher. Then Matthew, whose father, as well as whose mother, was dead. Last and lowest of all was Peter, whose father came home late every day except Friday.

We had a command structure, because Gang had to have a command structure. But there was no other and no better reason for it than that. Andrew was Sergeant. Matthew, Sub-Lieutenant. Paul and Peter Corporals. Yet between us there were no innate inferiorities. (Or none at this time apparent.) Each had his skills, each his points of refusal. For example, Andrew always balked at water. Matthew was genius at all firecraft. Paul knew Morse, German and a smidgin of Russian. Peter had to wear spectacles.

We dressed efficiently, in a way that prepared us for every eventuality. Especially, War. Also, we wished to identify ourselves as Gang. We therefore favoured Army Surplus. Our uniform was based upon a grown-up version of the Scouts. We wore khaki shirts and shorts. We carried our equipment around with us in knapsacks. This equipment included: Swan Vesta matches (their tips dipped in wax so they would still light even after being immersed in water), twine, Bowie knives, water canteens of aluminium sheathed in leather, white wax candles, kindling in an oilcloth bundle, Kendal Mint Cake, soft-lead pencils and papers, a First-Aid kit (carried by Matthew), torches, a billy-can for boiling water in, tea bags (in a freezer bag with a twist), chocolate bars, hard tack biscuits, a thick tarpaulin, aluminium plates and cutlery, metal cups enamelled in white and blue, catapults, a compass, maps. We also had a good sturdy canvas tent. This was for camping out in whilst off on expeditions, but never under a tree, where it would get wet after a rainstorm.

We all of us had blond hair. Hair blond as winnowed, crushed, sun-blasted straw. We sometimes doubt whether we would have formed Gang if all four of us had not been so blond. Matthew's hair was slightly darker and redder than ours. However, it lightened up during the early Summer months. It was no basis for exclusion. We were a shock-headed sight to see go by, and there was no doubting that. If we were out on a route march, cars would slow down to marvel at us. Four. All in a line. (Quadruplet boys?) Perhaps the singing also caused some surprise. We sang any number of songs, "Keep the Home Fires Burning", "There'll be Bluebirds over the White Cliffs of Dover", "The Ovaltineys Song" (that is, until our voices started to break), "Hang Out Your Washing on the Siegfried Line", "It's a Long Way to Tipperary", "We'll Meet Again", "The Internationale" (Paul's father had taught him all the words by the time he was ten), "Gin Gan Goolie", and others.

Just mentioning these things makes us feel an incredible nostalgia for Midfordshire, for our shared boyhood, for a time when life was that rarest of all things: truly good.

Walking along, early starting, well equipped, beneath the thick boughs of an English wood. Out on manoeuvres. Doing a recce. Locating a suitable base camp. Sunlight bright above the leaf canopy, hot when it hits your face, surprising the eyes so they close, but mostly cool in the mossy quiet. Our only communication, the prearranged hand-signals.

Between us, we felt as if we could cope with just about anything that might come along. This confidence didn't make us complacent, however. Gang-life was a constant preparation for the unexpected. The greatest fear we had was that the coming war would be nuclear right from the start, and that we would none of us get the opportunity to perform the glorious actions we had so often imagined.

Imagined like this:

Midday. August. The countryside is quiet. We are waiting, silently. The War has been on for eight days or so. The Russians have begun their invasion. Already they will have taken London and the Southern Counties, and now they are heading remorselessly Northwards. Soon they will be with us. Matthew is acting as look-out, up a tree on top of Amplewick Hill. He hears the tank (a Soviet T-64) before he sees it. He flashes a quick Morse message towards the rest of us. (We will all have learnt Morse by this time.) Then he climbs down the tree and springs to join us. We have requisitioned several rooftops for sniping activity. All those years of preparation are finally paying off. We have recced this village from top to bottom. It is quite clear to us the way it should be defended. From somewhere (this aspect of the scenario was never clearly defined, but no doubt Andrew's father would be involved) we have managed to assemble an impressive arsenal of weapons: Polish sub-machineguns, ammo, hand-grenades, mines. Just at the crest of Crutch Road, we have set an explosive tripwire. It should take out the first tank. If that doesn't work, the TNT can be set off manually. Three of us are hiding upon the three most strategically important rooftops. After the mines have gone off, we take out as many of the Russkis as we can with a synchronized volley of hand-grenades. Next, we pick off the retreating soldiers one by one (we assumed that, by now, having met little resistance since before Newton, the mighty Soviet Army would retreat). Then we meet back at base (the Nissen Hut in Andrew's garden) to plan how to cope with the Russkis' inevitably more savage second assault.

All this was clear in our minds. Clearer by far than the jobs and careers our schools were supposedly preparing us for. War

12

was coming, and we must ready ourselves for its arrival. Little did we know that our War, when it did come, was to be fought not on the roads and streets of Amplewick, but within our very homes, our kitchens, our bedrooms. It would be glorious, all right. But there were to be no marvellous explosions. No medals, parades, cheering, freedom. There was to be glory, indeed. More than enough glory for all, had all been inclined to take it. And before the War was over, two of us would be dead.

ii.

Perhaps we have given the impression that our life during this period was one of constant anxious preparation. But it would be wrong to imagine we spent so much time preparing to save our country that we left ourselves none in which to appreciate its many brittle beauties. Sometimes we did nothing more (yet what more important activity is there?) than sit and watch the gentle progress of things about us. The uphill struggles of overburdened ants. The blossom-flight of butterflies. The darting skiff of river-boatmen. From clouds to cedar trees to cows to creepy-crawlies, we had a profound respect for Nature in all Her various manifestations. Whether consciously or not, we learned from Her all the most important lessons in life. About perseverance, about grace, about camouflage, about adaptation. It is no use fighting against Nature's adopted order. The power that properly belongs to Her, the awesome force, can only be directed, never opposed. Mother Nature was our Schoolmistress. Hers was a classroom that we ever approached without dawdling, a classroom contained within a couple of scrubby acres called Wychwood. Here, our real education took place, and here we conned the textbooks which are not textbooks: fires, stings, punches and weather. The sky was our blackboard. A patch of soft grass our desk. Our pens were sticks and Bowie knives.

It was our closeness to everything around us that we most remember. For example, our intimacy with the very ground itself. The almost-concrete hardness of a well-beaten path (such as the one running up the green vortex of Holy Walk). The soft loaminess of a woodland floor. The too-deeply-gravelled path in front of Paul's house. The lifelessly gray sand-paths of The Furze, around which we were forced to run, always stepping in someone or other's just-made footprint, the ground twice as wearying as grass, by the Games Master, Mr Spate. The wide wet green grass of Amplewick Park, mined with divots hidden to trip the non-high-stepping runner-across. The combed-back baldness of the grass on Crackback Hill, months after the snow had melted and sledges had been replaced by sniffing dogs and screaming children.

We knew these different grounds intimately. We spent our lives so close to them: always lying down on, squatting behind, digging into, picking up to examine.

This was our natural habitat.

The delights of the earth's various smells: acrid, cow-patty, decay-sweet, decay-sour, alcoholic, honeyed, old-flower-vase-water-like, powdery, sulphurous, dank, petalled. And above all, the heavenly odour of grass new-cut. A Purcell smell, so delicate it is, so laced, so graced with the immanence of nostalgia. Every child should be told to breathe deep of the effluvium of grass and hay, and all cut-stalks. This, they will remember always. And by preparing for their decrepit futures, by deliberate memory-making, they will know they did justice to their childhood, whilst living and loving it.

"Well?" asked Andrew.

"I can't see anything," said Matthew. "No, wait a minute. It's a blue pram, isn't it?"

"Yes," said Paul. "With silver wheels."

By now we could all see, but Matthew shouted out anyway. "He's in the lead! He's in the lead! Look, he's in the lead!"

We cheered loudly. The luck of hanging upside-down had worked.

It wasn't just Andrew's father, though. It was also his friend from the Albion pub, Roger. They had taken turns pushing the pram all the way from Flathill. And now, at the steep top of Amplewick Hill, they had come into sight, emerging from the small forest of oaks. All they had to do, in order to win, was canter down the smooth tarmac road, past the turning into Gas House Lane, then push themselves (and the pram) up the more gradual incline in front of Andrew's house. Crutch Street, in other words. (See Map.) Once over the crest of this, they would be only a few hundred yards from the Market square, the finish-line, the glory and congratulations.

We watched in silence, breath held, to see how big the gap was until the next pram, the challengers.

We counted like parachutists tumbling away from a Douglas C-47 Dakota. One one-hundred. Two one-hundred. Three one-hundred.

Another pram came over the hill, four falling seconds later.

It took a moment for us all to recognize Paul's father. We were very surprised. We hadn't expected to see him this far up the field. He had never entered the Pram Race before. Running alongside him was Mr Grassmere, husband of the Headmistress of our school. We all gave another cheer, though a quieter, more formal one.

These were the only two of our fathers to be taking part in the Annual Amplewick and Flathill Pram Race.

A couple more teams crested the brow of Amplewick Hill, neck and neck. We didn't know the men, which meant they were probably from Flathill.

The breeze picked up slightly. The tree-top queeved back and forth.

"Let's climb down and cheer them home!" shouted Andrew.

Now that we knew victory for one or other of our fathers was almost assured, we wanted to be certain we were there to celebrate with them.

We started to clamber down: from branch to branch, choosing carefully our hand- and footholds.

We had descended half-way, and were no longer able to look over the roof of Andrew's house, when something happened: Andrew, by mistake, stepped on Paul's fingers. Paul, with a cry of pain, let go, and seemed about to fall. He didn't. He dropped a foot or so, before managing to catch hold of an outstretched branch. But, after doing this, he swung a little back and forth, and one of his feet kicked Matthew in the teeth. It wasn't so much the strength as the surprise of the blow which caused Matthew to lose his grip. He began to fall, and as he did he grabbed out for something to hold onto. The only thing within reach was Peter, Peter's arm, the arm with which he had been holding onto the tree-trunk, just starting to look up towards the commotion above him. With the combined weight of Matthew and himself now upon it, Peter's grip was broken. The two of them, from a height of about ten feet, fell away from the tree, and down onto the ground below. Luckily, it wasn't on the cobbles of the drive, a few feet further to the left, that they landed. Instead, immediately at the bottom of the tree was a small bed of Antique English roses: Vanguard, Sir Walter Raleigh, The Countryman, and The Knight.

Andrew's father was a devoted gardener, and so the earth beneath the rosebushes was soft with dark, fragrant manure, bought by the quarter ton from the Farm. (Many was the time that we'd plucked the thorns off the larger, hoarier bushes and lick-stuck them upon the bridges of our noses, turned ourselves on the instant into fearful mutations of the human form: dinosaur-boys.) And so Matthew and Peter's landings were about as soft as they could possibly have been. Neither fell directly onto a rose-bush. Some of the older bushes were hard-stemmed enough to have near stabbed a body through. But, even so, they had tumbled a fair distance, and hit the ground pretty damned hard. Peter had been lucky enough to be falling feet-first, and was therefore able to absorb most of the impact with his legs. We watched as he crumpled and rolled over, in perfect imitation of the parachutist we'd seen at last year's Air Display. Matthew, however, had been yanked away from the trunk by Peter's pull, and so he landed, almost inevitably, smack on the flat of his back.

By the time Andrew and Paul reached the ground, Peter was already up on his feet and starting to brush himself down. But Matthew, his eyes open but glassy, his skin turning pale, just lay there without moving.

iv.

At that moment, Matthew was totally convinced that he was dying. He looked up at the swimming-pool sky, through the dark-swaying branches of the tree. His glance passed over our downturned faces, the faces of his three greatest friends. These, he thought, will be the last sights I will ever see, the last in the world. He felt paralysed. In a panic, he tried to move everything, every limb and every muscle, at once. But nothing moved. He couldn't even force his eyes closed. Then he realized that he wasn't breathing, that, really, he wasn't able to breathe. All he

17

wanted in the world was to take another breath, just one more breath before he died. But his paralysed, dying, stupid, stupid body was stopping him. He was drowning in the sweet fresh air of an August afternoon. Oxygen was all around him. He could feel the breeze between his fingers. But something blocked his mouth, stopped up his lungs. He wasn't in control of his body. His body had abandoned him. "I'm so stupid," he thought. "I'm going to die." And then he noticed one final thing: the world was entirely silent. Not only was he unable to break through to breath, he was also cut off from all sound.

Looking down at Matthew, to where he lay, aquiver on the earth, we could see his mouth twitching.

"Shouldn't we do First-Aid?" said Andrew.

For some reason, Matthew's head began to fill with thoughts of his dead parents.

When we used to ask Matthew what his father did before he died, he gave us a different answer every time. Matthew's father had variously been fireman, coal-miner, lion-tamer, oil-rig worker, astronaut, spy, Prime Minister and Eskimo. (Matthew had Eskimo corners to his eyes.) His mother, curiously, throughout all her husband's metamorphoses, had remained entirely constant. She was a housewife. She had never done anything apart from stay at home all day in the kitchen, roasting the most marvellous joints of beef anyone had ever tasted. But we all knew, and in his heart of hearts Matthew knew, that his parents had been ordinary people, ordinary people who had died only slightly less ordinary deaths. They had been killed in a car-crash on the way home from the pub when he was five years old. His grandparents had been babysitting that evening for him and his younger sister, Miranda. When the policeman had left and the tragic news had sunk in, they realized that they would have to bring the two orphaned grandchildren up themselves.

Matthew always hated living with his grandparents. They were very, very old: he sixty-five, she sixty-three. Almost everything Matthew did confused them. He lied to them even more than he lied to us. (Because with us he knew there was always a chance, a good one, usually, that we were going to find him out. But with his grandparents, he could get away with just about anything.) His lies ranged from the pointlessly small to the insanely vast. Sometimes he made up new words, stupid words, nonsense words, and told them it was the latest slang. Every school holiday began a few days early and finished a whole week late. Most impressively, Matthew could always get money out of his grandparents. He said it was easy, because they felt so guilty about being alive when his parents, who had been so much younger than them, were dead. He said they were desperately trying to make up for the fact that he'd never had anyone to play football with, or jump and climb on.

"I don't love you," he used to say to them. "You're not my parents. My parents are dead. You're spack."

Spack meant spastic.

Matthew tried to use this incantation as infrequently as possible, so that it didn't lose its thaumaturgic power.

Miranda, unfortunately, had a little sister's tendency to copy him, in this as in all other things.

At one stage, she was saying "My parents are dead" so often, particularly to teachers at schools, that she was taken to see a special doctor who, she later told Matthew, asked her lots of questions but never once listened to her heart with a stethoscope. (This meant that she was probably mad. If you went to a doctor and they didn't use a stethoscope, that's what it meant.)

"We get worried about you when you stay out after it gets dark," Matthew's grandparents said. "We start to think something terrible has happened to you."

Matthew knew they meant "Something like the terrible thing that happened to your mum and dad."

But he just answered, "Don't be such a pair of old spackers. I'm with the others. We always stick together. No-one's going to get us."

Matthew began to think about what he would miss, if he were to die right at that moment. He knew his grandparents were planning one of their dreaded quiet evenings in. After the excitement of the Pram Race, he was meant to go straight home. Everything that happened after that was entirely predictable.

First, around four o'clock, came tea. Matthew's grandparents always drank Earl Grey, which he thought tasted like cat's piss. This was accompanied by a lemon-sponge cake and sponge fingers for "the children". The grandparents would ask Matthew and Miranda question after question, about school, about playtime, about homework. Miranda tended to babble on and on about which of her friends was saying what about which of her other friends. (She was only a year younger than Matthew, but it was the longest year in the world.) In clear contrast, Matthew treated the evenings as a training exercise. He tried to imagine that he'd been captured behind enemy lines and the Russian Kommandant and his wife were trying to charm details of Allied operations out of him. He must give nothing at all away. The torture would start later, he knew. But for the moment he must be tight-lipped and resolute. (Name, rank, number. Nothing more.)

At around five, on quiet evenings in, Matthew and Miranda would accompany their grandmother into the kitchen, and help her to prepare supper. Supper usually consisted of boiled ham, boiled potatoes and broad beans in white sauce. Matthew hated all of it, and Miranda was scared of broad beans. (She thought they were beetles with their legs cut off.)

Around six, the whole family would sit down on the sofa. It was at this point that the torture really started. Matthew's grandfather would fetch the photograph album out of the sideboard. There was only one album. The family had never been great ones for owning cameras. The word "Memories" was embossed in gold italics in the middle of a fawn leather-effect cover. The volume began with the two sacred portraits of Matthew and Miranda's great-grandfather and -grandmother, on their mother's side. They were Victorians, and Matthew was certain that he had nothing at all in common with them. He didn't really believe that the photograph was really of his great-grandmother. He believed his grandmother's mother had been another exact copy of his grandmother, and so on, and on, back through time. Always the same, never different. Then came the photographs of Matthew's grandmother in her pram and his grandfather on his bike. A lot of the slightly later shots of Matthew's grandparents had been taken by photographers on seaside piers. There seemed to be three snaps for every year, one for each of the major Summer bank holidays. Some of the photos had edges that were strangely crimped. Then came the faded images of Matthew and Miranda's mother, as a child. The black-and-white photographs were a quarter the size of proper modern ones, and had a silly border of white. Matthew would watch as his mother slowly stopped looking quite so much like Miranda. School. Hockey team. In a park. Then Matthew's father appeared, standing beside a sports car. Almost immediately, there were the wedding photos. Matthew hated these, especially the one of his mother grimacing as she tried to cut through the hard icing of the wedding cake. Then, completely out of sequence, was the only photograph Matthew cared anything about: his father in his National Service uniform. His grandparents never paused at this, always thinking that Matthew and Miranda were dying to get on to the baby photos of themselves. Of course, there was almost nothing in the world that Matthew wanted to see less. After a few pages of baby, toddler and birthday-party images, there were the small, square newspaper

Matthew, lying breathless on his back, had a new thought: I want to say something before I die. I want to pass my last words on to the other members of Gang. He didn't know exactly what it was he wanted to say. But he knew that it would be momentous, life-changing for all three other members of Gang.

The three of us began to attend very closely to his goldfish mouthings. Each of us had a different interpretation of what he was trying to say. Andrew thought he said "Dead", Paul "Dad" and Peter "Did".

Our trance was broken by loud cheering from down the bottom of the drive. All of a sudden, we knew exactly what to do.

"Stay there," said Andrew, at the very same moment Paul and Peter said, "We'll stay here."

Andrew zig-zagged off between the rosebushes and sprinted down the cobbled path.

We knelt beside Matthew and spoke what words of small comfort we could.

When Andrew dashed out onto the road, his father's pram was about twenty yards away. The gap between it and the second-place pram, pushed by Paul's father, was now only a dozen feet, or perhaps even less.

As Andrew ran towards him, he saw his father looking as red-faced and furious as he'd ever seen him. His eyes were sternly fixed on the finish-line, even though it was hidden behind the brow of the last low hill.

In any other circumstances, Andrew wouldn't have dared approach his father when he was so explosive-looking. For a moment, but only for a moment, he thought about merely standing aside, and cheering his father on. If he did that, his father wouldn't be annoyed with him. Afterwards, he could go back to see if Matthew was really all right.

There were about twenty people on the pavement. A dozen more stood at open windows or on doorsteps. Most Amplewick-ians, including Andrew's mother and Matthew's grandparents, were standing in the Market square near the roped-off run-in to the finish-line. But Andrew overcame his momentary terror.

"Matthew's hurt," he shouted when his father got within shouting distance. "You've got to come. I think he may be dying."

Andrew stopped in the road, to emphasize his seriousness. His father swerved past him without a glance. The man's focus upon winning could not be broken quite that easily.

Andrew, overtaken, now started desperately after the lead pram, and found, somewhat to his surprise, that he was just about able to catch up.

"Dad!" he shouted. "Matthew fell out of the tree! He's not moving!"

"What was that?" gasped a voice behind him.

Andrew knew without looking that it was Paul's father. Still, he kept pursuing his own father.

"Dad! I think Matthew's paralysed."

This time Andrew's father heard his son, who was by now running along at his side.

"Don't touch the pram," he shouted. "If you do, we're dis-qualified."

They were now pushing up past the entrance to Andrew's garden.

"Where is he?" shouted Paul's father.

"In our garden," Andrew called back over his shoulder. "He fell out of the tree."

For the first time, Andrew's father seemed to take in the import of his son's words.

"I'll be back after I finish," he gasped. "Straight away. Can't lose now."

Paul's father had meanwhile slowed to a jog. "Come on!" he shouted. "We have to go and look!"

But Andrew's father was now forcing himself and his pram up the final incline. "We can do it, Roger," he urged his running partner.

Andrew kept up with him for twenty paces more, looking sideways into his father's anguished and sweaty face. Then he, too, peeled away, and dashed back towards the garden. He swooped past Mr Grassmere, who was standing with his hands on his pink knees. Paul's father's pram, forgotten, was gradually picking up speed, beginning to roll back down the hill.

vi.

Paul's father dashed between the paint-flaky white gateposts and up the cobbled path into the garden of The Pollards. The scene which greeted him when he came in sight of the bottom of the tree was in no way ambiguous: Matthew was standing there, hands on hips, a manlier pose than he had ever assumed before. He had had a brush with death, and that brush had left behind upon him the tint of melodrama. He knew that for the next few hours at least he was to be the centre of attention. Already he was dreading the worry of his grandmother, and how hard he would have to fight to resist it. It was as if his nose was being positioned within the handkerchief, and he was being ordered to blow. His freedom of movement would be taken away. Tree-climbing, for the next few weeks, at least, would have to be top secret. Which wouldn't be difficult, as all our activities were of necessity covert. Anything we did within sight or hearing of our parents was a deliberate deceit, intended to convince them that we weren't a deadly fighting force. Only Andrew's

25

father had any inkling of the kind of life we led whilst un-observed. As for the others, we always did our best to preserve their innocence. Without having to be told, Matthew knew exactly the line he should take. Nothing of any substance must be revealed; everything revealed must be untrue; the untrue revelations must give no indication as to the truth; all indications must suggest that there was nothing of any substance to be revealed. In other words: name, rank, number.

Paul's father ran up to Matthew and put his hand on his shoulder.

"Fine," said Matthew, before the question was even asked. "Just a bit winded. It was nothing."

"Sit down," said Paul's father.

"I'm fine," said Matthew. "I really didn't fall that far."

"Does your head hurt at all?" Paul's father asked.

"No," said Matthew.

"Are you sure?"

"Quite sure."

"Walk around," said Paul's father.

Matthew executed a perfect circle.

"I think you should go back to the race," said Matthew.

We were standing to one side, letting Matthew get himself (and us) as far out of trouble as he could. Just then, Andrew ran round the corner and skidded to a halt beside Matthew. He was about to speak, but then he saw the look in our eyes. He knew that to show any concern would be to undermine Matthew's feigned nonchalance. In a situation like this, the danger was always that we'd end up being kept apart by our parents. Some of them, most particularly Paul's father, but also Peter's mother and Matthew's grandmother, believed that we were a bad influ-ence upon each other. Their problem was that, taking each of us individually, and examining our behaviour, they couldn't locate any origin to this maleficence. If they had been able to locate a leader, a leader-astray, then they would have been closer to their ultimate goal: destroying Gang. But more than anything else we were careful to keep Andrew's higher rank secret from all outsiders. We were Gang. Gang was four. Each took conse-quences for all. No-one knew these truths better than Andrew. And so, he said to Paul's father: "I seem to have made a bit of an unnecessary fuss, don't I?"

"That's all right," said Paul's father. "I'm glad you did. It's only a race. It's not that important."

"But you might have won," said Paul.

"And for all I knew your friend might have been seriously injured," his father replied.

"But I wasn't," said Matthew. "Nowhere near."

"Shall we go and see who won?" suggested Peter.

"You don't get away from it as easily as all that," said Paul's father. "There is an issue at stake here. An important one."

"Let's go," said Andrew, pretending to speak as if Paul's father weren't there. "Matthew is obviously all right."

We turned away from Paul's father, and started walking towards the road. Matthew bravely led the way, so as not to show any weakness. Afterwards, however, he told us it was all he could do not to puke, right then and there.

"Don't you see?" said Paul's father, pursuing both point and us.

"Thank you," said Matthew, stopping, "I really appreciate it that you thought you were coming to save me."

At this Paul's father became annoyingly irate. "Do you boys care more about a sodding pram race than the life of one of your friends?"

By now we had all stopped.

"But I wasn't injured," Matthew repeated.

Paul's father gave us a despairing look.

"All right, then," he said, "let's go and see if the bastard won. I expect he did."

Quickly, we walked up Crutch Street, over the hump, and down towards the finish-line in the Market square.

A couple of middle-aged men dressed in white nappies with safety-pins on the front trundled past. Inside their pram, they were pushing along about twenty big-eyed dolls.

"Go on, Clive!" shouted Paul's father, who had recognized one of the fat, hairy babies. It was Mr Butcher, the Geography teacher.

Matthew was having some trouble keeping pace with the rest of us. He was feeling very dizzy, and couldn't see quite as well as usual.

Whilst we walked, Paul tried to keep as much distance as he could between himself and his father. There was the terrible possibility that his father might put his arm round him or even kiss him on the cheek. Paul's father believed that parents should be more demonstrative towards their children. This now led to a situation, both absurd and embarrassing, of father trying to hug son, son trying to elude father. The chase sped up. Eventually, when they were about ten feet ahead of us, and still accelerating, Paul's father managed to grab hold of Paul's left arm. He pulled him to a stop, and held him there. The other three of us could do nothing but walk past on either side of them. Paul's father was whispering furiously. None of us, not even Paul, against whose ear the mouth was pressed, could make out everything he was saying. But the gist was that Paul should be in no doubt who had made the correct decision, morally.

The rest of us overtook Paul's father's running-partner. He was now disconsolately wheeling the pram along. This was hardly surprising: they'd had a chance to win, a good chance, and Paul's father had put the kybosh on it. Hoping to rescue Paul from the ticking-off, we drew the man's attention to Paul's father.

"If you go now, you can still avoid coming last," said Andrew, truly.

The man looked back at Paul's father. "Come on, you idiot!" he shouted, gruffly.

When Paul's father looked up, the man beckoned him onwards towards the line.

Paul's father ended his lecture, adding only that they would speak more later. He then trotted past us, took hold of the pram and began to push it the thirty yards to the finish-line.

Paul himself caught us up, and we commiserated with him over the bollocking he'd received.

"I bet your father went ahead and won," said Matthew to Andrew. "I'd have hated to have stopped him."

"How many years in a row is that?" asked Paul.

"Five," said Andrew. Then added, "Come on. He'll be wondering where we are."

At that, we all started to sprint for the finish. After a couple of seconds, it became clear that we could have only one objective: to overtake Paul's father, and to do it before he reached the line. This would be our small revenge. He would understand what us beating him meant, but wouldn't be able to get us for it. We ran and ran, fists punching the air.

"Come on," shouted Paul, to whom winning was most important.

On hearing Paul's voice, his father glanced back, saw us coming, and started to accelerate.

Peter overtook him first, then Paul, then, almost immediately, Andrew. Matthew fought hard all the way, and it looked at one point like he wasn't going to make it. But just at the last moment he put on a heroic spurt to prove that he was really right as rain.

Andrew's father stood in the middle of a small crowd of admirers, his proud wife beside him. His hand was being vigorously shaken by the Mayor, who had yet to put on his red robes and gold chain for the awards ceremony. (He was in shorts and vest, having been a competitor in the race.) Matthew's grandparents were among those waiting to say a word of congratulation. Miranda and her best friend from school, Trisha, stood off to one side, completely uninterested.

Paul's father barged straight up to him. "What the hell do you think you were doing back there?"

Paul's father was very out of puff, and his words came gasp in gasp between gasp-gasps.

"I don't know what you mean," said Andrew's father.

The Mayor stepped aside to let Paul's father come closer.

"Your son informed you that Matthew had been injured, possibly fatally, and you just ran straight past, straight past."

"What? What's that?" said Matthew's grandfather, pushing his way closer.

"I'm – I'm fine," said Matthew, his voice for some reason at least an octave higher than it ever was when he spoke to us.

"Are you?" said Matthew's grandfather.

"Was a sodding pram race more important to you than the life of a boy?"

Paul grimaced. Like all grown-ups, his father was repeating himself.

"Are you all right?" Andrew's father asked Matthew.

The crowd which had grown as more people gathered to watch the argument looked at Matthew.

"Yes, I am, really," replied Matthew, just before his grandfather began embarrassingly to touch him.

"There you are," said Andrew's father. "Nothing to worry about."

Andrew was standing as close to his father as he could, hoping people would notice how alike they looked.

"But what if he hadn't been all right?" shouted Paul's father. "How would you have felt about it then?"

"Listen," said Andrew's father, pretending to talk only to Paul's father, but actually addressing the crowd. "I could see you'd gone to take care of the situation. What more could I do?"

"That's a lie," said Paul's father. "You're lying. You didn't even bloody look back."

Matthew's grandfather looked at Andrew's father, waiting for his answer.

"He did," piped Andrew. "I saw him."

The crowd noticed the family resemblance.

"You're his son," said Paul's father. "Of course you're going to back him up. If you didn't, he'd –"

"Why don't we sort this all out later?" said the Mayor. "Down the pub."

(Paul's father never went to the pub.)

Matthew's grandmother had now joined her husband, suffocating Matthew with unwanted comfort.

Miranda stood listening and watching at the edge of the crowd.

Andrew's father stood face-to-face with Paul's. He knew that Paul's father was weaker than he was, and he also knew that Paul's father hated violence. (Probably because he wasn't very good at it.)

The silent confrontation lasted a full minute.

Then Paul's father grabbed Paul by the hand. "I hope you choke on it," he said to everyone. "I really do." And with that he dragged his reluctant son away.

Paul's father never understood anything important.

31

CHAPTER TWO

Andrew

**Du mußt nicht die Nacht in dir verschränken,
mußt sie ins ew'ge Licht versenken!**

Within thyself fold not the Night,
Instead bedrown it in Everlight!

The Battle of Britain was taking place about six feet above our heads. The Allied Air Force, represented by two Spitfires, and two Hurricanes, was surrounded by a swarm of twelve or thirteen Messerschmitt 110s and 109bs. Despite their overwhelming numerical inferiority, our boys were putting on a damn fine show. Several highly exciting dogfights were taking place. One of the Messerschmitts was going into a tail-spin, trailing behind it a long cloud of black-painted cotton-wool. The second of the Spitfires had sustained some serious damage. Wrapping-paper flames of orange and gold gushed from its right aileron. Above each plane, a transparent fishing-line or two stretched up towards the ceiling. Brass-topped drawing-pins held in place the most important air-battle in History.

Andrew and his father had constructed these Airfix models together, sitting, elbow-to-elbow, at the kitchen table. None of the rest of us had anything like as many. Paul, in fact, wasn't allowed War-type toys, at all. His father, who drove a Volkswagen Beetle, and was therefore highly suspect already, didn't like War in any form whatsoever. Matthew had a cardboard box containing about twenty aeroplanes of various scales. His pride and joy was an Avro Lancaster B.III Dambuster. But his grand-father insisted they were kept in the box, rather than displayed all over the place. (The only thing Matthew owned which had come from his father wasn't an Airfix model but a Teddy Bear called Teddy. He'd been given this on the day he was born.

Teddy embarrassed him. He wished his father had bought him something more actionous. But, even so, he still slept with the bear upon his pillow, though this was a fact he kept secret from the rest of us.) Peter had about five aircraft of various descriptions. However, he was more interested in dinosaurs, and had a large collection of model ones, parading the width of his bookshelf.

We were sitting round in Andrew's eyrie (which was what we called his top-floor bedroom), drinking thick milk out of extra-cold glasses. It was the afternoon of the day after the Annual Amplewick and Flathill Pram Race. In the morning we had called round on bicycles at Paul's house, only to be told that he wasn't allowed to play with us any more.

"I'm sorry," said Paul's mother to Andrew. "But after what happened yesterday, we don't really feel very happy about him coming round to your house."

"Can we see him, just for a minute?" Matthew asked, politely.

"No, you can't," said Paul's mother, and shut the door on us.

We had kicked about The Park in a collective gloom. After going home for lunch, the three of us reconvened at Andrew's again. Andrew and his parents had long ago come to an agreement, which we all massively envied: they would never come into his eyrie, if he promised never to burn the house down.

We also, of course, most of all, envied Andrew his father. He was quite clearly, the Best Father. But his mother wasn't at all bad, either. She was a religious woman, very preoccupied with the flowers in Amplewick Church. Before getting married to Andrew's father, she had been a Jew. Now she was nothing in particular, just like everybody else. When we went round, she often served us homemade lemonade (which we liked) or elderberry wine (which we poured into the gutter outside the eyrie window). Andrew's mother didn't make us take our shoes off in the kitchen. She had grey hair even though she wasn't as old as she might have been.

"Well, this is bad," said Andrew, after knocking back the last few drops of extra-cold milk.

"Very bad," agreed Peter.

"Paul will tough it out," Matthew said.

"We must make preparations for his return," said Andrew.

"I will make a note of it," Peter said.

"Operations should continue as normal," Andrew asserted.

"It's what Paul would want," said Matthew.

"But we will make no great excursions. Nothing Paul would regret having been absent for," stated Andrew.

"Exactly," said Peter.

"And we will get back at Paul's father," said Andrew.

"How?" asked Matthew.

"That's what we have to decide," said Andrew.

We talked for a while longer in a similar fashion. Eventually, we came up with a plan of action. We agreed that the easiest way to hurt someone is to attack something they own, something they love. With Paul's father two obvious targets presented themselves: his garden and his cat Tabitha. We would begin with a few sorties in amongst the flowers and vegetables. Starting small, we would uproot this and that, at random intervals, as if we were badgers or deer. Then, later, when we had accomplished enough damage there, we would escalate to the cat. It was all highly satisfactory. Though, of course, we would have preferred to have had Paul with us, and not been having to come up with such revenges. Yet we were left no choice. Negotiation with the enemy was effectively impossible. We couldn't go in there and start kowtowing to the Commie demands of Paul's father (the worst father). All we could do was hope our friend was being accorded his full rights, as stated in the Geneva Convention.

Under Andrew's leadership, we decided not to act before the POW's release had been effected. Until then, it was best for us just to lie low. In this way, no obvious connection would be made between Paul's incarceration and the destruction of his father's pride and joy. We were cunning like that.

Our impatience in the mean time would have been unbearable had it not been for a blest intervention.

"Fall in!"

It was Andrew's father, calling up from the first-floor landing. (How we honoured him for respecting his son enough to do this!)

We clambered down the narrow staircase, and lined up in front of the Major-General (aka Andrew's father).

Sometimes he was the Major-General, and sometimes he was just Andrew's father. It was easy to tell which was which: the two characters had completely different voices.

"And how are the troops today?" he asked. "Bearing up, I hope. Not just lying rotting in your pits."

"No, sir," we barked, together.

We were standing stiffly to attention, as we always did when the Major-General was present.

"At ease, men," he replied, "at ease."

We leaned back against the banisters, looking, no doubt about it, as glum as glum can be.

"I have a difficult mission for you," said the Major-General. "But I'm not sure if a bunch of lazy layabouts such as yourselves are quite up to it."

"Ready, willing and able, sir," said Matthew who, lacking a father of his own, adored Andrew's father even more intensely than the rest of us, Andrew himself included.

"We need to put down some supplies for the coming Winter campaign," said the Major-General, strolling up and down, hands behind his back, just like Monty in the films. "We've had a quick recce done, and we believe that we have located a rich source of fuel near by."

We knew what he was talking about, we'd pulled off this kind of caper many times before, but such was the charisma and authority of the man, he never failed to enthuse us anew.

Once our participation was agreed (of course, it had hardly been in doubt), he briefed us in detail. The greatest danger to successful completion of this operation was presented by enemy snipers. If we did not exercise extreme caution, we could end up being picked off one by one. (In this, he did not know how prophetic of future calamity his words were to prove.)

We ran noisily down the stairs and out of the house, leaving the Major-General to pace anxiously about. At least, that's what we liked to imagine he was doing.

ii.

The fallen branch was exactly where the Major-General had told us it would be: hidden behind a pall of ivy, half-way up Holy Walk, a few paces off to the right of the path.

Holy Walk is perhaps the loveliest of all Amplewick's quainter corners. A continuation of Gravel Track, the track that passes between Amplewick Church and Wychwood, the Walk gently sways up a soft incline towards The Park. (See Map.) At points, the huge hollybushes on either side, the bushes which must once have given it its now-corrupted name, meet above one's head in a prickly canopy. The sides of the Walk are banked, like those of a low stream. Underfoot, the path is soft with leaf-fall and clicky with stick-fall. No-one not a local would ever find their way along Holy Walk.

The branch was large and heavy, and two of us were needed to shoulder it. This proved slightly awkward, as the bough was far from straight. The mission with which we had been entrusted was to get the branch all the way back to The Pollards, without being spotted by a single person. Neither dog-walker nor policeman, mother nor pensioner must see us and our loot.

There were, we now see, two quite distinct reasons for this. The one given to us at the time by Andrew's father was that it was all good training for us in covert activities. The other, more prosaic, and only realized later, was that the land bordering Holy Walk was privately owned. Technically, we were trespassing on somebody's property and stealing their timber. It would seem, therefore, from this, that the people most to be avoided were the land-owners. But in all our years of living in Amplewick, we'd never once caught sight of them. They were a reclusive couple, whose Weimaraner dogs ran around on the lawn outside their cottage. Smoke rose from the chimney, and a radio could be heard playing classical music. Peter, who played violin, identified it as Russian, probably Stravinsky or Shostakovich. All, of course, highly suspicious, if not downright incriminating. In our hearts, we were convinced they were spies. And so, we enjoyed getting one over on them, by stealing their wood, and thereby diminishing their resources.

Perhaps we should mention that, as part of the exercise, the Major-General would sometimes assume the part of an enemy patrol, and attempt to intercept us. As the Major-General knew all of our routes and evasion tactics, an element of bluff and double-bluff was introduced.

It is hard, if not impossible, to convey how important this mission, and, in fact, all missions set us by the Major-General, appeared to us. During the time we were engaged upon them, they took over our entire world. The single-mindedness of young men is beyond all adult concentration. Our vision was as tunnelled as Holy Walk itself, a swirling vortex of obsession with, at the centre, a single fixed point: the wish not to appear, in the eyes of the Major-General, to have dodged it, to have failed. As long as he was satisfied, we were satisfied. And none more so than Andrew.

The first bit of the quarter-mile journey back was easy. We picked a path through the brambly undergrowth running parallel to Holy Walk. We weren't particularly quiet, sticks cracked beneath our feet, birds were disturbed above our heads, but this didn't matter. If we spotted someone coming along Holy Walk, we could always fall flat on our faces and wait for them to stroll past.

iii.

Once we came to the end of the Walk, things became trickier. There were now three routes open to us: Churchyard, Gravel Track, or Wychwood. Each had its advantages, each its perils.

The Churchyard lay to the left. It could be reached by a short sprint over exposed ground. We were almost certain to pass unseen once amongst the gravestones, certain, that is, unless we were unlucky enough to happen upon one of Amplewick's numerous funerals. (There were four separate Old People's Homes in the village. In fact, the village was crammed with old things. It had six or seven antique shops.) When we had skirted round the far side of the church and made our way through the Lych-Gate, it would only be a simple matter of crossing Crutch Road. However, the Major-General was well aware that this was our favoured route.

To take the Gravel Track was the most brazenly daring tactic of all. We would merely be retracing our footsteps, back towards The Pollards. There was no chance of concealment, should anyone be coming in the other direction. Because this seemed such a tactically dangerous move, the chances of our meeting the Major-General were decreased by just as much as those of meeting anyone else were increased. It wasn't a sensible route,

43

therefore he wouldn't expect us to take it. And so, sometimes, very rarely, we did. Bluff and double-bluff.

Today, Andrew decided, it was unlikely that the Major-General was an active threat. He had been otherwise occupied for the morning and early afternoon, mending something out in the Nissen Hut. He had seemed slightly distracted whilst issuing our orders. However, the man was a master of tactics. He might simply have been treble-bluffing us. However, having taken all these factors into consideration, Andrew ordered us to take the third and most circuitous route: Wychwood.

At the end of Holy Walk, we turned right and scaled a wooden five-bar gate. This took us into the bottom of a field full of rather flighty horses, horses which had, on several occasions, stampeded us. To-day, though, they were up at the top end of the field, grazing beside a hedge of hawthorn. We were able without too much anxiety, to make our way along the brick wall that formed the northernmost boundary of Wychwood. At a certain point, this wall became low enough for us to climb over, although the ground dropped away on the other side, quite severely. Matthew peered over the wall to ensure the coast was clear, then jumped the eight or so feet down to the ground. After passing the branch quietly over to him, Peter and Andrew followed.

Our confidence began to increase. Wychwood was fairly safe territory, or so we believed, and thus we moved with less than usual caution, down a well-beaten path. The sun was high in the sky and our shadows were fairly definite on the nettly ground beneath us. Cow-parsley was all around us, fragrant and almost above head-height. The grasses on either side of the path were already golden and straw-like. There was a madness of birdsong going on in the tree-tops: worried chaffinches, sour-tempered crows, irksome cuckoos. The air inside Wychwood seemed heavier than outside. It was certainly laden with all manner of flying things: there were bees, decadently fat and cumbersome, even though it was still only early August, flies making fizzing excursions to and from the horse-turds in the field above, dandelion clocks wafting slowly past on the syrupy, heat-saturated breeze.

Peter, who was one of the branch-bearers (the other being Matthew), stumbled a little off the path, and a cluster of burrs stuck to his ever-rumpled socks.

"Come on, chaps," said Andrew, "we've got to get a move on."

None of us could remember who had first discovered Wych-wood, and led us there, though it seemed likely that Andrew's father had had something to do with it, as he did with almost all the best things in our lives. If so, then it must have been he who first told us the place was called "Wychwood" and that nobody seemed to own it and that the little pond was called The Lake and that once upon a time an Edwardian lady had drowned in it. The name Wychwood suggested to us that this was the place where the mediæval townsfolk of Amplewick had come to ditch their witches. Wychwood was also known as Base Camp #1.

Andrew led the way, thrashing at stray stalks with a stick he'd picked up. Neither of us felt brave enough to shush him, though he was making a hell of a lot of noise.

As we walked, two of us carried the branch on our shoulders. We could have been Zulu tribesmen, back from a hunt, an antelope suspended between us, food for the evening's feast. The other one, in this case Andrew, strode a little ahead, scouting for mines, tripwires, ambushes and other dangers.

At a turn of the path, we came within sight of The Lake. This was the only vestige of Wychwood's former life as an Edwardian pleasure-garden. Once, there had been a white wooden bridge across The Lake, but that had a year or two before rotted and submerged.

After this, we made our way as deep into the foliage as we possibly could. It was densest towards the South, where there were a dozen or so rhododendron bushes against which we waged a constant battle. No matter how viciously we slashed them with our Bowie knives or thrashed them with sticks, they kept invading. Their bright purple flowers were particularly distressing to us. Like having very, very bad wallpaper put up, against one's will, in one's bedroom. (Matthew had very bad wallpaper in his bedroom. Trains, it was. Steam trains. His grandparents had insisted upon it. For his eighth birthday. By that time, Matthew hadn't liked trains for at least two years.)

"Maintain radio silence," ordered Andrew.

The Lake was now clearly visible. White rotting stumps poked out of the glutinous, fart-smelling water. That's where the ornamental bridge had once been. A rowing-boat, which hardly had room to turn about, so small was The Lake, was moored to one of the stumps.

Suddenly, just as Andrew was passing a particularly dense rhododendron bush, we saw him trip up, falling sideways into a patch of nettles.

"Agh!" he screamed.

We could see him trying to scramble away, to pull himself free, grabbing at nettle-stalks, at anything. But the rhododendron bush was shaking. It had already consumed Andrew's legs and was now dragging the rest of him in, as well.

"No!" cried Andrew. "No!"

iv.

We dropped the branch and dashed to help. Matthew grabbed one arm, Peter the other.

Our combined strength was sufficient to halt Andrew's absorption into the undergrowth, but not enough to pull him out.

"On three," said Peter. "One . . . Two . . ."

At which point, the rhododendron suddenly let go of Andrew, and we all tumbled back together, back into the nettle patch.

There we lay, stung by soft leaves, stung by humiliation, as the Major-General emerged from beneath the rhododendron. He was a fine sight to see, his whole face and his forearms blackened with boot-polish.

Andrew started to laugh. Foolishly, we joined in.

"That was far too easy," shouted the Major-General. "What in Christ's name were you thinking of?"

Andrew stopped laughing as suddenly as if he'd been pinched, slapped, stabbed, shot.

"You're a disgrace to the entire regiment," the Major-General said. "I suppose it's you who were in charge of this mission?"

"Yes, sir, I was," said Andrew, eyes lowered.

For a moment the Major-General's countenance seemed to brighten, thunderclouds passing. But then, eyes flashing lightning, he reached down, and picked his son up. With ease, he put him over his shoulder. Andrew's head hung down his father's back, his legs kicking uselessly in the air in front of his chest.

We stood up from the nettle patch.

Andrew's father had turned away from us, and was carrying his son down with unmistakable intent towards The Lake. He had reached the bank before we could catch up. He bent forward, and flipped Andrew, still upside-down, off his back and into his arms. Then, almost cradling him, almost tenderly, began to swing him back and forth. It was both a parody of the earliest days of fatherhood and the ultimate fulfilment of fatherhood's deepest essence: to punish. "On the count of three," he shouted. "One . . . , Two . . ."

Of course, we knew what was going to happen. No-one could have been surer of it than Andrew, and than him, no-one could have approved of it more wholeheartedly. Yet we needed,

47

once again, even after so many times, to have our faith in fatherhood reconfirmed. We needed to see there was Justice, and that Justice would exhibit a clemency far beyond the immediate incidence. "I am being harsh with you now," this was what Andrew's father's actions all implied. "Because the world will be far harsher with you, later. You must be prepared for this harshness, so that you may be able properly to withstand it."

We saw Andrew's blond hair, so like our own, swaying, his arms dangling. We heard his screams of futile resistance.

"Three," shouted the Major-General, his father, and threw him far out above the dark-glassy surface of The Lake.

v.

For a moment the upwardness of the arc-swing seemed to hold him, Andrew, our friend, our leader, there, suspended, as if he had achieved something impossible: flight. But then he plunged. Fell, failed, flopped down into the black water, going completely under. All of us had been in The Lake many times, both voluntarily and against our will. The fetid slap of its surface therefore came as no surprise to Andrew, nor did the thick liquid wallow of it, the scrape, bump, slime and tangle of unidentifiable floating things, the sucky pond-bottom grabbing at his fingers.

Surprise, instead, came in the form of the water that filled his mouth, almost his throat. This was unmistakably the beginning of drowning. Andrew didn't taste the water that was flowing into him. All his senses were focused upon one question: Which way up? Hidden within this question was another question: Where is air? And then another: Will I live? And another: Will I die?

He opened his eyes under water, in half-hopes of seeing the sun, or light, or lightness. But the water around him was all equally, unequivocally black. His eyes stung on the instant, marsh harshness getting in them. (We were with him, as Gang, though we stood on the bank, alongside the man who had thrown him in. We felt his every thrash, as if from the inside. Yet at the same time, we saw his sandalled feet appearing and disappearing, as he cartwheeled around, never breaking out into the air. This image of his panic combined with our sense of his state.) Peter moved towards the edge of The Lake, intending rescue.

"No. Leave him," said Andrew's father. "It's a better lesson this way."

Peter was halted. Matthew stepped forwards to join him. We were as close together as we could be.

(Paul was at his desk in his bedroom, pulling an old and annoying scab off his right elbow. When finished, he would put it in one of his Savings Jars, the others of which were labelled Fingernails, Earwax and Snot. Even he, at this moment, felt an unattributable disquiet.)

Finally one of Andrew's hands sensed a difference between water and air. We saw it stick hopefully out of the water of The Lake, like a human Excalibur. He tried to hold it there, a fist grabbing hold of life. We felt how he next attempted to force the rest of his body to conform. The head, that was the most important thing. The mouth. The nostrils. Get the head where the hand was. Yet at the same time, the hand must not loosen its grasp upon the air. To do that might be to lose hold upon life altogether. And life is never more vivid than when most about to disappear. As we watched Andrew's contortions, it occurred to us for the first time that we might truly be watching his death. There was a terrible possibility of spasm in his latest movements. We could see them turning uncharacteristic, hinting at death-throes. In our thoughts, too, Andrew was fading, dying. The thing in the water was now pure animal bodiliness. Our wish altered from Live to Survive.

"All right," said Andrew's father, putting our thoughts into practical words. "This has gone on long enough."

He pushed past us, us feeling, in his size and strength, the surety that Andrew would be saved, returned to us.

As the water covered his father's shoes, we saw the back of Andrew's head hit the surface and stay there. He stopped thrashing so violently about. Now was the moment for us all to concentrate on him righting himself.

His father was in up to his waist, his chest.

Accounts differed as to what ensued. Andrew insisted, as did all the rest of us, including Paul, that, at the moment his father grabbed him, he had already independently taken his first breath of saving air. His father, ranked for once against us, maintained that his son would have drowned, had he not acted at the moment he did. (He implied the words, "My son would have drowned," never the words, "I would have killed my son.")

Andrew's mouth rises above the water, breaks the surface tension of the pond. From the bank, listening on, relieved, we hear Andrew's characteristic coughing. We know, as he is shouldered by his father for the second time that day, that our leader, our friend, Andrew is still with us. (Of course we know, as it was later proven, that any individual absence, of the permanent sort, not Paul's temporary incarceration, meant a total change to all Gang-Members.)

Dripping, with pond weed still clutching at his ankles, like witches' fingers, Andrew's father lifts his coughing son clear of the water into which he himself had thrown him.

Laid down on the ground of the path, Andrew clutches his stomach and turns on his side.

"Didn't I tell you always to hold your breath?" says his father. "Didn't I say to blow out when you hit the water?"

Andrew couldn't help but think of the time and place his father had given him this advice. It was during their family holiday, the previous August, on a beach, in Cornwall. He and his father were body-surfing in the fresh waves. The day was the epitome of Cornish Summers: bright, blowy, brisk, billowy. Up the water-swell flipped Andrew, up and upside-down, plucking his feet out from under him, also. Without time to take a preparatory breath, Andrew found himself all a-tumble in the most solid part of all parts of the wave. For Andrew could sense that he was at the mercy of a mighty whim. If the water decided to bury him for ever within blueness, it would. Churning over a couple of times, feeling his fingers tickled by undertow, as if by mermaids or grandmothers, he found himself the sea's toy. But the ocean was not interested in playing, in playthings, in interest, in ocean. The water was the water, moving just as it did, governed by gravity entirely, pushed and impelled and pulled. Luckily, the next submerged cartwheel brought him out, out of the face of a white wall, a tall wave. He was dumped, on his head, on the pebbles, on the beach. The backwash flicked some of the smaller stones against his eyelids. A final, unintended wave came along to shove him further up the beach, towards his embarrassingly running-crying mother, as if to say what it wasn't saying, *Begone*.

It very quickly became clear to us that Andrew was going to be all right. The paleness of his skin and the weakness of his cough, these might have suggested an imminent departure. But we continued to feel his presence within us. And, after a couple of minutes, lying on the path by the side of The Lake, Andrew opened his eyes. During all this time, the Best Father had knelt touchingly by his side. "Come on, lad," he'd said, "snap out of it." He'd also said, "Stop larking around." And once, just once, he'd whispered, "Kangeroo." This, we knew, was an almost prehistoric nickname for our friend, our leader. It dated all the way back to when Andrew couldn't properly pronounce his own name. Andrew's father hadn't called his son Kangeroo in years. We knew what it meant. We saw how terribly much he loved him. So much so that, for almost all of the time, he denied himself the greatest joy, the joy of expressing his love.

Andrew was our leader. He was our leader because he was strong. His father's denial of love, of the bland statement of love, out of a greater love, was the greatest force in our lives. Only later did we fully realize this. (Those of us that were still around to have realizations.) At the time, we merely felt awe, awe far greater than had ever been inspired in us by Hell or PC241 or the Headmistress, or Russia, even.

Andrew recovered enough first to sit and then to stand up.

"You're all right now, aren't you?" said the Best Father.

"I'm fine," Andrew replied, bending over to breathe, the palms of his hands braced against his kneecaps.

"Very rash of you to jump in like that," said the Best Father. It was in ways like this that Andrew's father almost managed to be one of us. Unlike most grown-ups, he recognized the absolute necessity of coming up with a lie every time something happened about which one might be questioned. This was to be our lie, Gang lie, for all other grown-ups, for all others full-stop. If asked, we would say Andrew had rashly jumped into The Lake. There was no need for the Best Father to add, "And especially don't tell your mother what really happened." Mothers, it was obvious, must never, on any account, be told what had really happened. This we had learned from the Best Father. Mothers simply could not handle the truth of things. Yet our devotion to the lie went far beyond the immediate: this lie, like all our lies, was to be universal.

Peter compiled the Archives. (We wanted to leave an accurate and truthful record of our achievements, for when the historians, as they inevitably would, became interested in the saviours of the nation. And so, at the end of every day, on narrow-lined A4 paper, Peter made careful note of our operations.) The entry for this particular day would read: "Andrew rashly jumped into The Lake and needed to be rescued by the best father, who just happened to be in the vicinity at that time." Even to Paul, when he was finally released, however late or soon, we would pass on the lie. But the miraculous thing was, Paul would detect that the lie was a lie. We would give him no clue. Nothing in our tone or our expressions would hint at deception. Yet he would somehow become aware of what had really happened. And if he ever had to pass on the universal lie, he would do so quite consciously. That was one of the things that being in Gang meant.

"Very rash of me to jump in like that," Andrew repeated, between shallow coughs.

"What were your orders concerning operations conducted in the immediate vicinity of water?" asked the Best Father, assuming once again his Major-General persona.

"Extreme care to be exercised at all times, sir," barked Andrew, immediately.

"Quite right," said the Major-General, allowing himself, one final time, to touch his son's damp head. "Now, carry on as you were. This operation is highly important, and must be completed by –" he checked his chunky wristwatch "– fourteen hundred hours." Then he winked at us all, and said: "Seed cake for tea. Over and out."

"Yes, sir," said Peter and Matthew, saluting.

The Major-General strode off towards Initiation. The early Summer light through the leaf-canopy dappled him at moments with patches of white gold. Initiation was the name we'd given to the secret door into Wychwood. Half-way along the fence, at a special place, two loose planks hang down, each of them

53

suspended by a single nail. By pushing them apart, like parting curtains, easy access to Wychwood was granted, with no climbing over or scrambling under.

vii.

As soon as the Major-General was out of sight, Andrew collapsed again onto the ground. At this juncture we should perhaps make it clear that he did not cry.

When Andrew was quite recovered, we carried on with the exercise. Although almost certain that the Major-General wouldn't ambush us a second time, we proceeded with exquisite caution. Andrew kept his position at the head of the detachment.

We moved off the path, creeping our way slowly along by the wooden fence. This was the approach we should have taken initially. We had learnt our lesson, all of us had. It may only have been Andrew who received the humiliation of the dunking, but it was the reputation of Gang that had truly been immersed in rankest ignominy. Through Andrew, the Best Father passed on his lessons to all of us.

Every few paces, Andrew silently signalled for us to stop, making our progress slower, but far safer than before. It was a measure of his bravery that Andrew in no way acknowledged the shivers which were starting to convulse his body.

As expected, we made our way through Initiation and out of Wychwood without encountering any further enemy forces. Andrew did a quick recce round the corner, then signalled for us to follow him. At a dash, we crossed the dangerously open ground of the Gravel Track and crouched down under the yew trees at the edge of the graveyard. Moving from headstone to headstone, we gradually progressed to the front of the church. It was a sound tactical move. We saw two sets of dog-walkers going down the Gravel Track towards Holy Walk. After another quick recce from Andrew, we ran out through the Lych-Gate and plunged into the rhododendron bush on the small traffic island. Now came the moment of greatest danger: Andrew's house, The Pollards, lay across thirty or so feet of open ground. This included the main road from Amplewick to Flathill, the road along which the Pram Race had come. It was Andrew's task to get us safely across to the other side. Here, there were some more dense bushes in which we could conceal ourselves. It would then be a small matter to find our way through the back door into the Pollards garden. Mission accomplished.

Car after car went by, some in groups of three or four, trailing after a slower one, some faster and on their own. We crouched there beneath the perennial bush, listening out for the approaching engines. Then, when it was finally silent, and Andrew had checked the coast was clear, he set off by himself at a canter across the road. It was a very close-run thing: Andrew was scarcely onto the opposite pavement before a car came over the crest of Crutch Road. Luckily, he was shielded from view by a tall spruce tree. By the time they'd flashed into sight, he'd dived into the undergrowth.

"Blinking flip," whispered Peter. "That was a bit of a squeak."

"Perfectly calculated," replied Matthew, his confidence in the Leader total, unshakeable.

From his improved location, Andrew was able to look up the road both ways. On his signal, two short whistles, we were to pick up the branch, and run like billy-o. We almost went by mistake, when we heard him sneeze, so alert were we, so on edge. But then the silence between cars deepened, the whistle came, and we were off!

The sound of gunfire reached our ears before we had made it even half-way across the road.

"K'chh, k'chh, k'chh, k'chh, k'chh, k'chh, k'chh, k'chh, k'chh, k'chh, k'chh, k'chh!"

We looked round as we ran, but couldn't locate the source. Then we heard the Major-General's voice coming from on high: "I don't know why you're still running, you're both very dead indeed."

We looked up and saw him, perched on the very highest point of the roof of his house. The Major-General was a deadly sniper. That was one of the positions we'd identified as perfect for attacking the Russkis from. One could climb out onto the roof of The Pollards through one of the attic windows.

We staggered off the road, dropped the branch and fell down. Dead. Yet we didn't feel too bad about having been killed. From his chosen vantage-point, the Major-General could cover approaches to the house from almost every angle. Through blades of grass, we watched squint-eyed with awe as he climbed off the roof, hand over hand, shinning down the thick black metal drainpipe. This was the first time we'd ever seen one of our parents truly risking their life. (Of course, our mothers risked their lives merely to bring us into this world. For which we both respected and despised them. Their importance had ended just at the moment ours had begun.)

Andrew cowered in the bushes. He was wondering whether or not the Major-General had called a halt to the exercise. Being wet through was all very well whilst one was moving, but once one had to stay still it became a different matter altogether. He was ashamed to find his shivering was getting worse.

"Bad luck," whispered dead Matthew to Andrew.

"It wasn't luck," said Andrew. "It was just stupid."

Andrew's father, who, whilst out of our sight, had changed from being the Major-General, opened the back door of The Pollards. "Come on, lads," he said, mock-impatiently.

We carried the branch inside and over to the Nissen Hut. The Best Father went inside the house. There were wood-chippings all over the ground, beside the wooden trestle that Andrew's father used whilst sawing. He rejoined us, and together we sawed the branch down into hearth-sized logs. These we stacked, along with the many others we and he had gathered, in the woodpile, underneath a slanting roof of corrugated iron.

"That's a job well done," said Andrew's father, who had kindly decided to let our military incompetence teach us its own lessons, later, in private.

Whilst we were sawing, stacking, Andrew stood to one side, shivering. He was merely damp now, rather than wet. His father would not allow him to take any part in the wood-sawing. Once, when he tried to pick up a rolling-away log, his father stopped, and pointed to a spot further off. Andrew obediently went and stood upon it. No other punishment took place. None that we saw, anyway. However, as Andrew was usually his father's most valued assistant, particularly in garden activities, this leaving-him-out was quite hurtful enough. We knew that the true and truly deserved punishment would come later that evening, and that Andrew would most likely be wearing trousers and long-sleeved shirts for the next few days.

CHAPTER THREE

Paul

Ein Lämplein verlosch in meinem Zelt!

A Lamplet dwindled in my abode!

i.

We did not see Paul for an entire month after the Pram Race. Confined to barracks: that, when he got out, was how he described it. Paul's father was a cruel and unpleasant man. We had known from an early age that he could not be trusted. Andrew's father had only confirmed this when he called him a bloody Commie. Paul's father drove a Volkswagen Beetle, the car that had been designed, on the orders of Adolf Hitler, for the people of his Third Reich. In the back window was a sticker which read 'Atomkraft? Nein Danke!' (He also had a badge: Nuclear Power? No Thanks!). Paul's father believed in unilateral nuclear disarmament. This despite the Soviet SS-20 missiles that were at that very moment pointed towards the Sticklands Airbase, not twenty miles from where we lived. We found all this information tremendously disconcerting. We worried that, whilst he was out of our sight, and away from our influence, Paul was being brainwashed. It would be a terrible thing if he came back and was no longer in favour of War. Better Dead Than Red, that was how Andrew's father summed up his position, and ours, too.

For the month of Paul's imprisonment, a surveillance operation was undertaken upon his house. We did our best to watch over him, and were prepared to spring him at a moment's notice. Paul's house was called the Gamekeeper's Cottage. It was located just at the south-west corner of Amplewick Park. (See Map.) Out back, it had a square lawn surrounded by unimaginative flower-beds and bordered by a tall privet hedge. However, by climbing one of the spruce trees in the adjoining woods, and focusing Matthew's binocs on the window of Paul's bedroom, we were able to re-establish contact. Paul had anticipated our procedure. It was fairly standard, for this scenario. Even that first night, as soon as it got sufficiently dark, he turned the light off in his room, and began signalling us with his torch. The flashes came almost too fast for us to write down and decode, so anxious was he to communicate. His message read: i/ hate/ my/ father/ am/ trapped/ will/ try/ escape/ asap/ p. The following night, it read, no/ way/ out/ watched/ constantly/ damn/ them/ take/ revenge/ p. They continued fairly unchanged for a couple of weeks, before the first sign of hope, mother/ weakening/ p.

For most of the month, Paul sat in his room. He read books. Anything he could find that had violence and death in it. His father drove him along to the Library in Midford. At night, after the rest of us had Morsed our final encouragements, Paul would lie in bed, looking up at the watery light on the bedroom ceiling. "The others are out there," he thought. "The others are free. I didn't do anything wrong. It's all my father's fault. He just hates Andrew's father because he knows he's a better father than him. That's why he calls him a monster. That's why he calls him a fascist. I wish Andrew's father were mine. I wish that we were brothers and had the same father. I wish my father were dead, like Matthew's."

Paul's mother was kindly, well-meaning, sensitive and utterly deluded, just like all females. Most of the time, she agreed passively with whatever her husband thought. This, of course, wouldn't have been a problem had Paul's father held the correct views. But, for the first fortnight at least, he wouldn't entertain the notion of Paul going to Andrew's, or Peter's, or even Matthew's house. Paul's mother was weak, and let her husband persuade her. Yet eventually Paul was able to turn her weakness very much to his own advantage. For the unhappier he allowed himself to appear, the more it affected her, and the more upset she became, the more she set to work upon Paul's father. Paul's mother became his secret, unwitting ally. Even though she did not understand why, she womanishly knew that he needed to be with us. And so she kept telling Paul's father that Paul needed to get some fresh air. And that he should be spending time with boys his own age. And that he was looking very glum at the moment. Gently, she tried to bring Paul's father round to the idea of Paul leaving the house unsupervised. But Paul's father was almost impossible to persuade. He had cruelly decided that they should use the Summer holidays, and Paul's constant presence, as what he called an opportunity, an opportunity to spend more time together as a family.

ii.

Paul listened in on his parents' conversations, creeping back downstairs after they thought he had gone to bed.

"He has to be able to choose his own friends," said his mother.

"You know I don't like the values he's picking up from them. They're all of them completely in thrall to Andrew's father. He's got just the kind of skewed logic that appeals to boys that age. It's all to do with physical strength. Nothing to do with compassion. Nothing to do with real friendship."

"What were you like at that age?"

"Nowhere near as bad, I hope. I grew up in a seaside town, remember. I just wanted to go fishing the whole time."

"Can't you see how miserable it's making him? They're his friends. They've been inseparable since the holidays started."

"That's what I'm worried about. How's it going to be later on? What if he gets some stupid idea in his head that he's not going to go to university."

"Isn't it a bit early to be thinking about that? I mean, he hasn't even taken his O Levels yet."

"They'll drag him down. All of this talk of war. He may actually go off and join the Army."

"It's a stage. He has to get it out of –"

"What would you think of that? The Army. Where have all your principles gone?"

"This isn't just about principles. I'm his mother."

"He's violent. It distresses me. He and his friends go rampaging round the place, completely out of control."

"I think you need to give him a chance. Hasn't he been punished enough? After all, he didn't actually do anything wrong."

"It's an attitude. He needs to learn a lesson. I've tried talking to him, but he just won't listen. It's as if he goes deaf every time I open my mouth."

They sat for a while, staring down at the kitchen table as if they were examining a map of the world.

Paul's mother was first to speak. "God," she said, "I'm really-really looking forward to his adolescence. It's just going to be so much fun."

They laughed, laughed some more, drank wine, chuckled. And then Paul's mother started kissing his father, and Paul hurried back upstairs in disgust.

iii.

When Paul returned to us, something had to be done. It was necessary to debrief him. What we were chiefly concerned about was finding out whether or not he had been indoctrinated by his father. There were military secrets he might have given away, in a moment of weakness. Although we were almost certain that Paul had remained true, and that he should therefore be readmitted to Gang, it was necessary first to test him, to let him know clearly what would happen if ever he did blab. We had a brief discuss of exactly what to do and exactly where to do it. Andrew made the final decision, but there was no demurral from either of us. The plan was set. The debriefing plan. Paul, of course, not being completely stupid, had a pretty good idea what would be coming his way. For the first few hours back among us, he was incredibly wary. As we talked, up in Andrew's eyrie, Paul kept picking, picking, picking at the old hard jewel of a scab upon his right elbow. He knew that, at any moment, on Andrew's signal, we might spring some torture upon him. He was also aware that we would view it as highly suspicious if he submitted to that torture without first trying to escape.

It was a sunny Sunday. We all went home for lunch, then met up back at The Pollards. Andrew suggested that we conduct a reconnaissance exercise on The Furze. This was the first part of the debriefing plan. We all of us, including Paul, perhaps especi- ally Paul, admired the composure with which he put it into action.

As we walked up Crutch Street, through the Market square, over Noburn Hill, and down the long, wide maple-lined arcade of The Prom, Paul constantly expected ambush, abduction, torture, terror. He chose to walk a few steps ahead of everyone else. By presenting his back to us, he was putting his trust on extravagant display. Or that was how we chose to interpret it. But, despite this trust, we could sense his underlying fear, and just how vast it was. We knew that he was employing all our special alertness techniques: slowing his breathing down as much as possible, scanning for movement in the corner of both his eyes, tracking our footsteps on the gravelly path. The intensity of his listening was such that it almost deafened us. We could hear nothing beyond the relevant sounds: our breathing, our footsteps, our jingling pockets, our laconic talk. The scab had now flipped off Paul's elbow, and the reopened wound was gently, sweetly bleeding: it was a sign. We were enjoying this moment. Paul knew the scenario. This was the slow walk towards execution. The victim must look for any opportunity to escape. But he mustn't make a move until the very last moment. Merely to try and run away was futile. And so Paul didn't make an escape bid. Yet. Our confidence in him was being rewarded. He walked pretend-casually, still a few steps ahead.

We walked to the end of The Prom, where stood the Ample-wick and Flathill War Memorial. It was a solid chunk of white marble, semi-surrounded by a crescent of holly bushes. We spent a minute standing there, in solemn, silent, bent-headed respect. Each time we passed this way together, we moved another name down the alphabetical dead. To-day we were honouring I. M. White, who, during the Great War, made the ultimate sacrifice for King and Country. One day, we hoped, in the not-too-distant future, young men rather like ourselves would be doing the same, at a similar memorial, in gratitude to us.

After the minute was up, we marched onwards, out of the holly-bush circle, and up a winding sandy path. The Furze was particularly beautiful that day, though none of us would ever have said anything to that effect. The gorse bushes to our left were in bright yolky-yellow flower, and the pollen-heavy bees were making the most of it. To our right, the dark green of the open heath was suffused with a rich purple. The sand beneath our sandals was dusty grey. All around us, the air was filled with the cracking, shifting, clicking sounds of natural dryness.

"Split up," said Andrew. "Rendezvous at Base Camp #2 at fourteen hundred hours."

We synchronized watches, then dispersed in different directions.

Seconds later, it was as if we had never been there at all.

We chose divers routes towards Base Camp #2. Andrew doubled back down The Prom, creeping along the stream that ran parallel to our school building. Paul went as far in the opposite direction as possible, skirting around the far edge of a field of bright yellow rape. Matthew and Peter chose different approaches again, though slightly more direct: Peter stealthily crept through rabbit-paths in the gorse, whereas Matthew sprinted cavalierly across open ground, banging his back against trees, diving into bolt-holes.

Base Camp #2 was a deep pit in the sandy earth, covered over by a sheet of corrugated iron, right in the heart of a particularly thick gorse bush, towards the western edge of The Furze. It was the most secure of our Camps. To our knowledge, no-one had ever compromised it, though someone must have discovered the small clearing in the first place, and dug the pit. We attributed the Camp's creation to the local Combined Cadet Forces. They, like us, sometimes carried out secret night exercises, around the wilder parts of Amplewick. Base Camp #2 had two ways in, Emergence Escape Route One, and Emergency Escape Route Two, aka Exits One and Two. To pass through either it was necessary to get down on one's belly and crawl through the narrow space left between the gorse and the ground. There were a couple of branches that the last person in had to pull across behind them, to render the Camp totally secure. Once, a year or so ago, Matthew had found a slow worm in the pit, and for a second his squealing had convinced us that it was an adder. Peter, however, calmly remarked that the so-called snake had none of the adder's distinctive diamond-shaped markings, and made Matthew feel very foolish for a while. We were sure, though, that Base Camp #2 was exactly the sort of place an adder would choose, were it looking for a location to set up its nest.

The trick and trap of Andrew's plan was that whereas Paul would get to Base Camp #2 at fourteen hundred hours exactly, the rest of us would deliberately arrive there five minutes late. Paul would have to sit and wait, probably down in the pit itself, suspecting everything, knowing nothing. And the best part of it was that Paul really couldn't not be there, because if he was, if he wasn't, he would have disobeyed a direct order. That would be a Court Martial Offence, and would result in immediate expulsion from Gang.

Silently, we divvied up the Exits between us: Andrew crept in through One, Matthew and Peter through Two.

When we emerged into the small central clearing, there was no sign of Paul: he was either a deserter, or was loyally awaiting us in the pit. As per the plan, Andrew quickly pulled the final shutter of corrugated iron across the mouth of the hole. Meanwhile, Matthew and Peter laid their weight upon the three other pieces of the metal roof. Paul was trapped underground. It was deeply exciting. We banged violently on the corrugated iron for a minute or so, to bring the rust down upon him and the dust up around him. A loud cough confirmed that he was where we thought he was. Underground, Paul had dampened his handkerchief, spitting into it, then had put it over his nose and mouth. However, despite this precaution, he wasn't able entirely to avoid breathing in some of the choking, smoky air. Andrew smiled. His simple plan had worked perfectly. Paul had been left with no choice but to imprison himself: to do otherwise would have been to lose our company, our friendship, and our respect, for ever. Andrew really was a master of all matters tactical. Why make a complicated plan when a simple one works just as well?

At a nod from Andrew, we stopped banging. We waited, tense, silent, joyful.

noise when those above beat upon the roof was unbearable, like the baying of maddened hounds. We all of us were acquainted with the terror of being buried alive. And although we didn't know it at the time, waking up alive in a coffin was one of Paul's particular nightmares. The atmosphere in the Gamekeeper's Cottage with his parents, imprisoned, browbeaten, had been claustrophobic enough. But on finally being released, Paul had hoped for a different kind of torture, something better, if only by contrast. He knew we couldn't automatically let him back into Gang. What he really believed was that we were punishing him for the crime of having the worst father. Which, in many ways, was true: had there been no initial exclusion, the issue of readmittance would never have occurred. Paul had been the last to join Gang. He sometimes thought that he'd only been allowed in so that Andrew would have one more subordinate to humiliate. Paul also believed that Andrew took things out on him in a worse way than on anyone else. Even as he was choking, he clung to the belief that, had it been Matthew or Peter in the pit, Andrew would already be letting them out. What Paul wanted most in the world was to smack Andrew right in the teeth. He knew that, in a stand-up fight between the two of them, Andrew would win: Andrew was stronger and didn't mind being hurt. He was well-acquainted with pain, his father had made sure of that. But all Paul wanted was the chance to plant a single punch. After that, he would take whatever else Andrew decided to lay upon him. He knew the duffing-up which would follow wouldn't be all that bad. Not as bad as this. And, anyway, afterwards, he was going to go home with filthy clothes and dirt all in his face and hair. Paul knew Andrew wouldn't want to risk his permanent absence by giving him a black eye or breaking his arm. If the others had been planning on kicking him out of Gang, they wouldn't have gone to all the trouble of trapping and torturing him. They'd just have walked away. At the moment he'd seen the corrugated iron closing over his head, Paul had felt relieved. It had been a good sign. But the dirty airlessness was becoming unbearable. Finally, Paul decided to fake capitulation. After the next question Andrew asked, he shouted, "Let me out! Let me out! I can't breathe!" Up on the surface, Matthew and Peter looked at one another, winked, then looked at Andrew. We all knew that it was up to him to decide when Paul's interrogation would end. As yet, Andrew was unconvinced as to the sincerity of Paul's surrender. He nodded, curtly. We beat again upon the corrugated iron. Down in the pit, Paul felt utterly despondent. He'd been able to breathe, before he said he couldn't. He'd been able to endure burial, before begging to be let out. Up to this point, Paul had been fairly confident of survival. Now, though, fifteen minutes or perhaps even half an hour into the interrogation, he was beginning to fear he would actually die down in the pit. He was feeling giddy, and had fallen back into the soft sand of the floor. He'd stopped bothering to answer Andrew's questions. His true toughness hadn't worked, and neither had his false pleading. Now, at one and the same time, he gave up on both, and began to plot his revenge. If he did survive, Andrew would pay. Not immediately. Paul decided to forgo the pleasure of the single punch. Not to-day. But one day. Soon. Suddenly, Paul realized what he should do. What he should have done ages ago. He would get his revenge on Andrew. The ultimate revenge. He would take over Gang. It was far from clear how he would achieve this, given Andrew's physical superiority, and the total loyalty he could command from Peter, and almost total loyalty of Matthew. Once or twice, Matthew and Paul had expressed some disloyal disgruntlement to each other, over Andrew's behaviour, or with his leadership. "Just because of his dad," Matthew had said, sullenly, "he thinks he can do anything that he wants." Yet despite all these obstacles, Paul knew that he would achieve his revenge. Because he was absolutely particular end to this situation. All that remained was a pyrrhic victory for Andrew. He scored this by saying, "Stand at ease, soldier." Paul relaxed slightly, though the urge to punch was still strong. Andrew held out his hand. Paul shook it. We all smiled. All was friendship again, on the surface at least. Yet even at this moment of apparent reconciliation, Paul was careful not to flop down onto the floor. The rest of us were standing, and he couldn't be seen to sit down before we did. In fact, he had to appear perfectly ready, willing, and able to take part in another exercise, if Andrew so chose. The situation was becoming dangerous. Andrew moved to a small open area of sand, slightly to one side of the pit. He threw himself down upon the ground, as if the interrogation had exhausted him as much, if not more, than it had Paul. Matthew and Peter joined him, leaving a space free for Paul to complete the familiar circle. Careful that he was last to be fully seated, Paul joined us. The danger, for the moment, at least, was averted.

vi.

Slowly, Andrew brought Paul up to speed on the various operations we had conducted in his absence. All the time, Paul could think of only one thing: the earlier he managed to get back home, the better chance he stood of sneaking in unnoticed. Andrew, aware of this, and wishing to exploit it, drew out all his explanations to their utmost length. Having just been granted readmittance to Gang, Paul could do nothing but show the most impeccable fascination with everything to do with it.

The day was getting even hotter. The sounds of dryness which surrounded us were easily mistaken for the low rattle of a nearby snake. After enough time had passed to allow the gesture to seem nonchalant, Paul unbuttoned his khaki shirt and sat there in his vest. His hands and forearms were dirt grey, whilst the rest of him remained a Summery gold. A little dust had seeped in through the spaces around the buttons on the front of his shirt, and a line of thin dirt diamonds ran down his vest from neck to navel. When he thought we weren't looking, he picked his nose to get the remaining gunk out of it. His hair, thick anyway, but further thickened by dust, stood up all over the place.

Andrew talked for almost an hour without once being interrupted. During that time he restated and re-emphasized the entire ethos of Gang. He made several savage verbal attacks upon Paul's father. He said that, if things had been left to men like him, cowards, then the Russian Bear would already be lording it over us. He confessed that Gang standards overall had recently dropped. He sketched out a plan for the coming weeks. We were to go into a period of intensive training. All of us, even Paul, still thinking of revenge, were excited to see this determined kind of leadership in action. It was what Andrew did best: digging Gang out from the Slough of Despond. "We'll pull through," he said. "Don't worry. And in the end we'll be all the stronger for it." Midway through this peroration, Paul's nose began to drip blood. Matthew was first to see it. He nudged Peter, to alert him to the entertainment. For quite a while, neither Andrew, concentrating on his disquisition, nor Paul, on appearing interested, noticed. It was only when Peter nudged Paul, and handed him a handkerchief, that either of the two flows, blood or talk, was staunched. By that time, Paul's vest was spattered all down the front. "Thank you, Peter," said Paul, mopping up. Andrew decided it would be wiser to conclude. Paul lay flat on his back, and the bleeding stopped.

"All right?" asked Matthew.

"Oh, he's fine," said Andrew.

When he had quite recovered, Paul finally told us about what had happened to him in the last month. (The main substance of what he said has already been given, above.) He urged strongly that we take revenge upon his father with the utmost haste. Andrew assured him that plans were already in hand.

"He won't know what hit him," Matthew confirmed.

"But we'll have to wait a while," said Andrew. "If we don't, he'll know it was us."

We all agreed to that, and set to establishing a schedule.

Andrew then spent a few infuriating, to Paul, minutes, summing up and reiterating and restating and re-emphasizing. When, eventually, he finished speaking, we got down onto our bellies, and crawled out of Emergency Escape Route One of Base Camp #2.

The day had grown even hotter, outside the confines of our gorse haven. As we walked past The Prom, we saw a group of younger boys having a game of French cricket on the school playing-fields. The desire to join them was strong in all of us, but we resisted it. Once we came out onto the road, Paul indicated that he had to get home before his father. He was still holding Peter's handkerchief in the general vicinity of his nose.

"We understand," said Andrew. "But if you can get away this evening, we're going to be round Peter's house."

Paul nodded, then turned and started to walk slowly away from us.

As soon as he was out of our sight, however, he started to run, as fast as he possibly could. He dodged off the tarmac road, full of pot-holes, making his way along the short-cut, a narrow lane between scrotty hedges.

He sprinted all the way home.

Once home, Paul entered the cottage as stealthily as he could. Like all of us, he was an experienced creeper-about. His mother was in the kitchen, standing at the sink. Paul slunk by very quietly. As he did, he noticed that, although his mother's hands were up to the wrists in the washing-up water, she wasn't doing any washing-up. In fact, all she was doing was staring straight out over the lawn. Paul thought he might have heard her sob, but he was too concerned with getting into the bathroom to pay it much attention. He managed the stairs with little difficulty.

After locking the bathroom door behind him, Paul quickly undressed. He emptied the supplies and equipment from his many pockets. He whipped his snake-belt out through the hoops of his khaki shorts. He wrestled himself out of his vest. All his dirty uniform, shirt, vest, shorts, and pants, went straight into the wicker laundry basket. He made sure, however, to bury them deep down, far beneath the embarrassing civilian clothing of his parents. He climbed into the bath, and only then did he turn the taps on.

The sound of the water clanking through the old lead pipes alerted Paul's mother to her son's return. She came to the bottom of the stairs and shouted, "Is that you?"

Paul called back, "Hello, Mum."

"Would you like some milk?"

"Yes, please."

"Did you find your friends?"

"Yes, Mum, I did."

She shouted back something that Paul didn't understand. "What?"

"I said, 'I'm glad!'"

The stairs went quiet.

The bath was now half-full, and Paul cupped handfuls of water over his dusty head. His bottom pressed down into the grit of washed-off sand. He reached for the shampoo, which came in a tear-shaped plastic bottle. The transparent orange liquid ran like syrup into his palm. Soon he was a frothy-headed waterbaby. With the lump of the beeswaxy soap that his mother always insisted on buying, he washed under his armpits and around his small penis. Paul much preferred the creamy Imperial Leather that he'd sometimes used when bathing round Andrew's house. It was much more lux.

Lux meant luxurious.

Even over the gargling of the taps, Paul's hyperalert senses picked up his mother's weight upon the stairs. He juddered slightly, for no apparent reason. His mother was going into his room, which stood just opposite the bathroom door.

"I've put it on your desk," she said when she came out. "And some choccy digestives, as well."

"Thanks, Mum," said Paul.

He made his penis into a Stegosaurus, pulling the foreskin towards him with one hand and plucking the testicle sac up into a fan-like shape with the other.

He peed into his foreskin, catching the urine so that it swelled up to look like the head of a ripe poppy. Then he let it burst and spread out, weakly yellow, getting weaker, across his flat belly.

Andrew had shown him both these tricks, the last time he'd stayed overnight at The Pollards. Now that Paul was allowed to take baths in private with the door locked, he performed them ritualistically. Andrew had also taken the top and bottom of his foreskin between index finger and thumb, and made it talk like a little mouth. But Paul hadn't liked that trick as much, and so refused to do it. "Come on," said Andrew's penis. "If I can, you can." Since then, Paul had discovered several things for himself. He could make his penis go heavy and stand up whenever he wanted. He could also, if he tried hard enough, for long enough, make it ooze primeval slime.

He sloshed the urine off his tummy with waves from both sides. Then he rinsed the shampoo out of his hair.

He yanked the plug up by its chain.

After clambering out of the bath, he grabbed one of the rough white towels from the drying rack.

There was a full-length mirror in the far corner of the bathroom. Occasionally, Paul used to stand in front of it, nude, with his penis tucked out of sight between his legs.

Paul's pubic mound was covered with a thin layer of sparse golden hair. In some lights, it looked a little like spun sugar. Yet this hair wasn't the same kind of hair, thick, woolly, that he had on his head. It was much more like the stray wisps under his armpits.

"This," he used to think, "is what I would look like, if I were a girl."

Paul would become distressed at how authentically girlish his appearance was. The downing of golden hair didn't help.

When he wanted to concentrate on his private parts, he used to sit down with his penis tucked back and pinch the skin above his pubic bone into two parallel ridges. He would look down upon his self-created vagina and wonder.

To-day, Paul did nothing of the sort. (In fact, after to-day, Paul never did that again, at all.) Instead, he walked to the door and said quietly, "Mum?" But he was right in thinking she'd gone back downstairs. He unlocked the bathroom door and raced across the landing into his room. From the chest-of-drawers, he quickly pulled out clean vest and pants. He was in such a rush that he put them on without bothering properly to dry himself. Then he picked the glass of milk up from his desk and carried it through into the bathroom. He locked the door again, tiptoed over to the toilet and poured the milk quietly down the sink. He then washed the remaining white drops off the porcelain.

The only real vagina that Paul had seen belonged to a younger cousin, whom his family had once taken to the beach in Cornwall. Emily hated her swimming costume, but ran about quite happily with no clothes on. Once or twice, although she was rather scared of him, Emily had brought Paul things to look at: a bucket full of orange seaweed, a spider crab's spooky claw. Paul had tried hard to concentrate on the things, and not on his cousin's vagina.

There had been some attempts among Gang to persuade Matthew to get Miranda to take her clothes off in their presence. Matthew was terrified of the possibilities of humiliation this offered. Partly for Miranda, but mainly for himself. He saw her nakedness constantly about the house, and it worried him how similar her body was to his own. He didn't want this knowledge transferred to the others. He was afraid they would think less of him for it. If she had thought it might help her get into Gang, Miranda would most probably have been prepared to allow a scientific examination to take place. She had curiosities of her own. Particularly about Paul.

When he was sure all trace of milk had been washed from the bowl of the sink, Paul unlocked the bathroom door and carried the glass back into his bedroom. He had nothing to do, and boredom overtook him the moment he fell back upon the yellow-covered duvet of his red-framed bed. Paul's bedroom was full of new furniture in bright colours. His parents had taken him to a big shop in London, and had helped him choose whatever he wanted. Only, what he wanted wasn't available in the shops they'd taken him to. Paul wanted a roof dangled with Airfix models of Spitfires, Hurricanes, and Messerschmitts, just like Andrew had. Paul wanted a cabinet of mineral samples arranged in matchboxes on cotton wool, like Peter had. Paul wanted a gas mask and a pair of antlers and a stuffed fox and a brass bedstead, like Matthew had. For a short time, in the big London shop, Paul had become enthused by all the plastic and glass, the simple shapes and primary colours. But the first time they came round to see it, the others sat there with obvious discomfort. His room felt too modern: it didn't have anything to do with War. They hated it. Very rarely since had they returned. Gang meetings were always held at one of the other houses.

Paul picked up one of his yellow pillows and started to duff its head in. Then he lay back and started to think about how things would be when he and not Andrew was leader. He imagined his own impressive generosity towards the others. He fantasized about allowing Andrew, on occasion, during unimportant exercises, to be joint-in-command.

viii.

Paul was still thinking these thoughts when his mother called up the stairs to him. "Paul," she cooed. "Can you come down and help lay the table for dinner. Paul?" Lay the table, she meant, lay it completely, not help.

Paul trudged down to the kitchen. His mother passed him on the stairs. He knew he was going to be in trouble when she went into the bathroom but did not lock the door behind her.

Dinner was fishfingers with baked beans and mashed potatoes. There was a jug of cheese sauce, to pour over whatever you wanted. For afters, there were mandarins in jelly.

Thirsty, Paul gulped down a couple of glassesful of well-run water.

Upstairs, his mother pulled his shorts out of the washing basket, then his vest, then his shirt. She brought them downstairs into the kitchen.

It was at this exact moment that Paul's father arrived home.

"Paul," asked his mother, "how did these clothes get so dirty? And how did this vest get blood on it?"

'What's this, then?" asked Paul's father. But he asked his son, not his wife.

"We were playing," said Paul. "And I got a nosebleed. That's all."

Paul's mother knelt down beside him.

"If anyone ever hits you, you must tell me," she said.

Paul's father drew up a chair. Paul was taller than both of them, for the time being.

"No-one hit me," he said. "I had a nosebleed. Really."

"Then why are your clothes so dirty? Are you sure you weren't rolling around in the dirt, fighting?"

Paul didn't answer.

Name, rank, number.

"Were you, Paul?" asked his father, gently. "You can tell us. We won't be angry. We just want to know."

"We care for you," said Paul's mother.

"You know we love you," said his father.

Only a couple of minutes through the door, and already his father was humiliating himself.

"I – I fell over," said Paul, hoping that this added detail would make his story more convincing.

"Did someone push you?" his father asked.

"Did they, Paul?" echoed his mother. "Did they?"

"I fell over," said Paul. 'I did. Leave me alone."

"I don't know if this blood will come out," his mother said.

"Why don't we sit down and talk about this?" said Paul's father.

His appeasement wouldn't work. Paul might sit, but he would never talk. He folded his arms and stared defiantly at his father.

83

The kitchen table was round. The three of them were seated equidistantly, but Paul always felt that he was facing his father with his mother somewhere far off to the left.

One day of freedom, one afternoon, and back he was again, facing the possibility of another month's imprisonment.

"What did you do to-day?" his father asked him, attempting to restart the conversation, clumsily.

Paul hunched over his plate and prepared himself for interrogation.

"Um, we played," he said, not yet being old enough to refuse entirely to reply.

"What did you play?" asked his father.

Paul looked up from his plate. "War," he said. "We played War."

Paul's father tutted, and his mother looked at him with mock-furrowed brow.

"Don't you ever play anything else?" Paul's father asked.

"We like playing War," said Paul.

This was all that Paul's father had hoped to avoid. As a young boy, Paul had never been allowed toy guns, tin soldiers, Airfix models or anything at all exciting. His father, probably because of being a CND and Greenpeace member, had refused, year after year, every single one of Paul's birthday and Christmas requests. His mother, whilst asserting her own independence as a woman, both in thought and action, largely agreed with her husband's pacifist stance. Something within her naturally recoiled when faced with anything violent. The mere sight of Paul holding a stick as if it were a Tommy-Gun was enough to make her cry. In the same situation, Paul's father became very angry. But because of his principles, he was unable to use overt aggression or measured violence to express this anger. And so, whenever Paul upset his father, he was not beaten, or berated. Instead, he was brought to the kitchen table, asked if he was thirsty, given a glass of milk or orange juice, asked if he was happy at school, offered cake or biscuits, asked if his friends would like to come round to play, told that both his parents loved him very much, asked if he knew what guns really did to people.

Paul hated his father more during these moments than at any other time. Paul hated him for his lack of strength. If pressed, Paul would say that he found War exciting. What he meant by exciting was that he understood the total importance of War, for making human life, all life, what it is. Life is War. Life is conflict. And to sit down all pretend-friendly at the kitchen table and act as if it wasn't . . . Well, that was the behaviour of someone afraid of conflict. And this was how Paul knew his father to be a coward. He could sense that, at moments, his father really wanted to hit him. Yet his father's cowardice was such that he could never face his own aggression. He would turn to his wife and say, "I really don't know what to do to get through to him. You have a go." For this, for admitting he was confused, unsure, Paul hated his father even more. In fact, the whole scenario was, for him, nothing more than a submersion deeper and deeper into contempt.

"Do you understand, Paul, why your mother and I, why we might not like you playing violent games?"

It was a conflict in which one of the sides was fighting against the very idea of conflict itself. Paul's parents, under their political delusion, were trying to make the world a better, less violent place, by bringing their son up in what they saw as a better, less violent way. Paul, like all of Gang, saw beyond his immediate circumstances, and out into the wider world, a world which was not improving, which, if anything, was becoming worse. Paul was readying himself for a situation he knew existed; his parents, manipulating him to be part of a situation they vaguely hoped could be brought about, if enough people like them did enough manipulating of their children. It is not difficult to see whose logic was the clearer.

"Perhaps we should move," said Paul's father. "Perhaps we need to live somewhere else. I'm sure it's his friends."

"But you saw how much he missed them when you kept him away from them."

"You know he hits his wife," said Paul's father. "Andrew's mother, he hits her."

"Paul," said Paul's mother. "Why don't you go upstairs. I'll let you off the washing-up this evening."

Paul could hear the conversation continuing as he left the room.

"You shouldn't say things like that in front of him," whispered his mother.

"Why not?" said his father. "Maybe it would stop him hero-worshipping him quite so much. He needs some perspective."

Rarely had the Worst Father's jealousy of the Best Father become so overt. He knew that his son loved Andrew's father more than he loved him. Paul's father believed that he was a better father, a better man, full stop, and more deserving of his son's love. But there was nothing he could do about this without becoming more like the thing he detested. One of his most deeply held beliefs was that one should not force one's most deeply held beliefs upon other people. Not even upon one's children.

"Have you seen the bruises she sometimes has on her face? When he lets her out, that is. My God."

"I know," said Paul's mother.

Paul walked back in the door of the kitchen.

"I heard," he said. "I heard everything, everything you said."

His father jumped up from the table.

"And I think it's good," said Paul. "Yes, good that he hits her."

"No," shouted Paul's mother.

Paul's father came at Paul, as furious as he'd ever been.

"Hit me," Paul thought. "Please, hit me."

But, of course, he didn't: he was too weak for that.

CHAPTER FOUR

Peter

Heil sei dem Freudenlicht der Welt!

Hail, the Lovelight of the Globe!

i.

We sat within the circle of the great green crown. It often seemed, on approaching it, on foot or bikes, that the whole landscape had here undergone coronation. From within the circle, we could look out towards Midford. The crown rested, slightly askance, about eight degrees, upon the highest point of Greysand Ridge. For miles around, it was the jewelled Summer eye-catcher. Yet the crown remained no dead ornament for Monarchy. We had lit a fire within its very heart. As it rose, the smoke was dispersed and rendered invisible by the upper branches of the trees. They were oaks. Some of the stoutest in all Midfordshire. A perfect circle of thirty perfectly equal trunks, branches, twigs, and leaves. Other, smaller trees, grew up, in the spaces between them. The whole copse was raised about five feet above the rest of the field. This was the place we always came to, when we had something of extreme importance to do or to discuss. But we didn't call it The Crown. We called it the Tree-Fort. Perhaps the Tree-Fort had once been encircled by a low stone wall; however, by the time we came to discover the place, no trace was discernible upon it of the man-made. In order to enter, one had to know the exact location of The Door. Otherwise, the Tree-Fort was entirely impenetrable. Once inside, however, the Fort opened out into a shady clearing, at the centre of which stood the bonfire. We were sitting in a circle around it. The sticks Matthew had used to construct the fire were a little damp, and so our talk was at first swathed in grey smoke and accompanied by a constant crackle. We were discussing our next move. Andrew's period of intense training had not been a roaring success. The problem, it seemed, was that Paul's enforced absence had ripped the heart out of the Summer, and thereby ripped some of the heart out of Gang. Anything we did now was as nothing in comparison to what we could have done, had Paul been with us the whole time. With all armies, there comes a moment when they have done so much training they are sick of it. The troops become torpid. What they need, in order to break out of this stagnant state, is some real action, some real danger. It was now two weeks since Paul had been released. Despite the nosebleed incident and the shouting afterwards, he had managed to avoid a second period of incarceration. Plans were well in hand to take our revenge upon Paul's father. But we could not put them into action quite as yet. Not enough time had passed. The destruction and death we were planning would too easily be attributed to us. In consultation with Paul, Andrew had decided we needed to let at least a month pass before we gave the go-ahead to Operation Badger. It was called that because badgers often ruin gardens, and sometimes kill cats. So, for the moment, and a heck of a long moment it was, we were playing a waiting game. No wonder the general morale of Gang was so low.

"Well, then . . ." said Andrew, trying not to admit defeat. For the past twenty minutes, he had been attempting to put some puff back in our flagging spirits. Usually so charismatic, to-day Andrew was hardly able to keep our attention. We just sat there, staring into the day-lit fire. However much we hated to admit it, we were bored: bored with ourselves, bored with each other, bored with the Summer, bored with Gang. Yet the intensity of this boredom was more to do with excess of energy than energy's lack. Had there been a War in progress, we would have been giddy with adrenalin. Of all emotions, the one that causes young men most suffering is boredom.

It was fifteen hundred hours on a beautiful August afternoon. The few clouds were high, half-hearted, and far, far apart from each other. The breeze was so infinitesimal that only Nature's most filigree creations found any reason at all to notice it. Spiderwebs trembled imperceptibly. Dandelion clocks moved slow as the second hands of real clocks. Midges, alone, probably, could feel the breeze as anything like a force.

"I think I'm going to go home," said Peter. He looked towards Andrew for confirmation that this would be acceptable. This was a brave move on Peter's part.

However desperately he wanted to deny it, Andrew knew in his heart that to-day was a day we should give up on. Some brooding inertia had inserted itself between the four members of Gang. To realize again why we were friends, we needed to separate, to go to our variously hateful homes, to become ashamed of ourselves for wasting so much time.

In retrospect, it seems likely that Paul's vengeful mood had a great deal to do with the voiding of the day. He had clung to his resentment. He would not yield. Andrew would not yield. Matthew and Peter could not bring themselves to admit that there was any yielding to be done, one way or the other. There had been no overt conflict. No issue had arisen over which either Andrew or Paul would have had to capitulate, one to the other. They sat back upon the dry grass, leaning away from the unnecessary heat and almost invisible flames of our sun-drenched Summer fire, quite as if there was nothing between them but friendship, a friendship so strong it didn't even require demonstration.

After Peter made his suggestion, Andrew hesitated for a moment. He was worried that the failure of the afternoon would be regarded as his failure. It was a forced retreat: a Dunkirk of the spirit. But he realized that to attempt to deny the defeat of the afternoon, to try and then fail to mount a successful counterattack, would make him appear an even worse leader, and would leave him slightly more vulnerable than before.

"I think you're right," said Andrew, "it's too hot to do anything to-day. Let's disperse, and rendezvous at Base Camp #1 at eighteen hundred hours tonight. I've just come up with a new plan."

He hadn't. He was bluffing. But he had a long afternoon in which to think of one. And he knew he would.

We got up from where we'd been lying. Because we were young and lithe, there was no need for the back-arching and neck-cracking of later life. We simply went about our pre-departure tasks, moving with the slow smoothness of muscles ready and joints unseized. We pulled the campfire apart, ensuring that it would extinguish almost immediately. A few of the earlier ashes flew up and adhered to our lower legs, grateful for the opportunity of even this pseudo-breeze.

Then, still apparently as Gang, but in our hearts perhaps further apart than we had ever been, we made our slow way out through The Door.

We walked towards the hedge, where our bicycles were hidden. Andrew took his frustration out by kicking all the pebbles off the path. Paul strolled along, head down, satisfied, a little smug. Matthew was impatient to be home, so that, once there, he could be impatient to be back again. Peter felt guilt, guilt at having been the one to suggest we might each prefer, if only for a few hours, being apart to being together, being individuals to being Gang. To all of us, the idea that being at home, inside, might be preferable to being outside together was a betrayal of our every principle, of, in effect, the principle of us.

There were two routes to the Tree-Fort, Hill and Road. When we wanted to get there quickly, we went Road, when being unobserved was a great priority, Hill. To-day, Andrew led us down the broad smooth tarmac of the faster route. Having struggled up a slight incline most of the way there, we were able to freewheel most of the way back. Only the climb up Amplewick Hill interrupted our acceleration.

On entering our familiar village, following the Pram Race route, we split off, each in a different direction. (See Map.) The Pollards was just on Andrew's left. Paul's journey back to the Gamekeeper's Cottage took him round the church, along Gravel Track, up Holy Walk and through The Park. Matthew, in heading towards his grandparents', kept straight on Crutch Street, and did not swerve until after it became Unstable Street. Peter turned left after The Pollards, and freewheeled the short distance to his house in The Close.

Our goodbyes were subdued. We cycled away from one another, none of us looking back, no final words shouted, our legs heavy and our heads bowed.

ii.

Although he may appear to have played only a minor part in our adventures so far, Peter is perhaps the most important participant of all. For Peter was the official keeper of the Archives. Not one of the rest of us was allowed to do so much as keep a diary. This was because we had agreed early on that no more than one record of our activities should be kept. In that way, we would avoid entirely the curse of conflicting histories. What had been decided, what had been attempted, what had actually happened, all these aspects of the past were to be faithfully recorded by Peter. After he had written them up, they would be checked and initialled by the rest of us. In this way, our unanimity would be maintained, impeccable, even posthumously. We were anticipating that not all of us would survive. What we did not foresee, however, was quite how soon the first fatality would occur, nor from which unexpectedly local quarter the blow would fall.

And so it is from Peter's testimony, a Lever Arch file full of narrow-lined A4 paper, now foxed and brittle, that we have drawn the bulk of our inferences. Peter was meticulous in his notation of dates, operations, climactic conditions and unusual phenomena of all sorts. In fact, in everything pertaining to the activities of Gang. It is thanks to his punctiliousness that we are able so surely to narrate all of these events, both past and to come. Without Peter, this enterprise would simply not have been possible. Though, perhaps, indeed, that could be said of each of us with equal truth. Even in absence, those who were unlucky enough to perish have played their part. Yet it is Peter's accuracy which underlies every word of this story, and that fact should never be forgotten. It is true, also, that at this particular stage of events, Peter is about to take a more central role. All the more so because, from this point on, until the end of the chapter, Peter will be separated from the rest of us.

iii.

As usual, Peter's parents weren't in when he arrived back home. Because his father didn't earn enough money from his job to support them entirely, both of them worked. His mother did the cleaning in other people's houses, which Peter found extremely humiliating, particularly when he had to go round and fetch her home, for one reason or another. This often happened when he'd locked himself out. To-day, though, he merely wheeled his bicycle down the alley into the back garden, and used his special key to unlock the kitchen door.

Although it had been Peter who had acknowledged that the day was voiding fast, and who had most wanted to get away from the Tree-Fort, now that he was home he found the reason for this keenness was no longer apparent, and he stood in the kitchen already regretting that he'd spoken up. He didn't have anything immediately pressing or unbearably enticing to get to work on. His one set task for the remainder of the day was the bringing-up-to-date of the Archives. He poured out a glass of well-run water and took it up into his bedroom. The Archives were kept in a secret compartment, the location of which has never heretofore been disclosed. By removing one of the two large drawers in the base of his bed, Peter gained access to a hiding space of considerable use and almost total impregnability. It was here that the Archives, along with several other items, which have yet to be declassified, were safely stored. Peter slid the drawer back into place, then sat down, as was his daily ritual, at his Victorian clerk's desk.

The optician had recently advised that Peter wear glasses whilst reading or doing other close-up work. It turned out he was a touch presbyopic. In other ways, too, Peter was possessed of a longer, deeper vision than the rest of us. But the revelation of the specifics must be left for later. Peter pulled a couple of books off the shelf above his desk, and removed his glasses-case from the gap that they had left behind. He did not keep his glasses with the Archives and other Top Secret materials. This was out of respect for the different levels of classification.

To-day's was to be a particularly dull entry, though not unaverage for August.

In longhand, Peter wrote: "Went round to Andrew's then up to the Tree-Fort on bicycles. A discuss. Schedule for Operation Badger. Unanimous. Paul suggested small amendments. Worse revenge. Rejected as too risky. Hot day. Few clouds. Cleaned equipment. Did nothing. Morale low. Voiding fast. Andrew ordered rendezvous: Base Camp #1 this evening 1800 hours. Wise move."

After he decided there was nothing more of use to be added, Peter pulled the drawer out from the bed-base and slipped the Archives back into the secret compartment beneath. He then went to his small bookshelf and selected his favourite book. It was entitled *The Death of the Dinosaurs*, and had been a Christmas present from his parents, who knew he was interested in the subject, and wanted to encourage him in his scientific bent. One of the posters on the wall of Peter's bedroom displayed the different pre-Historic periods: Jurassic, Triassic, Pliocine, etc.

We were all of us interested in the dinosaurs, and, more particularly, in their extinction. This had been the case ever since Primary School, where we collected PG Tips cards of them. But among all of us, it was Peter who was the true scientist. Already, he knew what his A Level subjects were going to be: Maths, Physics, Chemistry and Biology. He was also the only one of us who really could be said to have a private library. This proved to be a crucial source of information, particularly later on. The rest of us merely let our books lie where they fell. Peter kept his, mostly, apart from those concealing his glasses-case, in alphabetical order.

For an hour or so, Peter read about the possibility that some single catastrophic event, perhaps the impact of a vast meteorite, had caused the death of the dinosaurs. The author, Teddy Shawcross, Fellow of the Royal Geographical Society, suggested that the dinosaurs had been slow-brained and physically cumbersome. When the catastrophe came, they found themselves unable to adapt quickly enough to changed circumstances, and so had perished entirely, within a few milliseconds of evolutionary time. The world was left to smaller, fitter, faster, younger organisms. Eventually, *Homo erectus* came along, took over, and had dominated things ever since. Perhaps, Teddy Shawcross suggested, *Homo sapiens* would fare no better than the dinosaurs, were catastrophe to strike a second time. It was obvious to Peter that Teddy Shawcross was referring to the possibility of nuclear war. Some days, it seemed that this was all grown-ups ever talked about. Whatever else they pretended to be talking about, nuclear war was their hidden subject. Most books on the dinosaurs, at least in Peter's experience, mentioned the possibility of human extinction, usually in the final chapter. It was as if the writers wanted to suggest that the stupidity of the great lizards found a parallel in some stupidity of our own. Even the first time he read it, Peter instinctively knew that this was wrong. Not all human beings were stupid and slow. Gang members certainly weren't. The Prime Minister, the American President, the Soviet Leader, the Chinese Premier (whoever he was), these people might be stupid, but not us. There were others, too, closer to home, whom Peter suspected were equally deserving of extinction.

Although the War we were preparing to fight was for the benefit of those around us, it did not greatly pain Peter to think that there would inevitably be some serious casualties. His parents, no doubt, would walk in front of a tank, or go blackberrying in a minefield. Before then, he would have warned them of the dangers. Probably risking his own life to do so. Crossing behind enemy lines. Yes, he would be completely blameless in their deaths. But they would carry on just as before. Like the dinosaurs, they would fail to adapt, and like the dinosaurs, they would die.

In another chapter, Teddy Shawcross suggested a second possible explanation for why such a dominant phylum, or group of animals, should so utterly die out. There was a scientific phenomenon known as phylogeronty. This word meant the old age of a phylum. He compared the general ageing of the dinosaurs to the particular ageing of a human individual. There was a loss of energy and a diminution of the senses. The teeth fell out. Teddy Shawcross identified the symptoms of phylogeronty as gigantism, spinescence and the loss of the teeth. Peter had looked up the first two words in his dictionary, but had only found the meaning of gigantism. It meant getting too big. Spinescence looked like it meant getting a curvy spine. We now know, however, having had access to a bigger dictionary than Peter, that it means growing thorns. (Thorns not horns.) Teeth seem to have been very important to Teddy Shawcross. And to the dinosaurs, as well. And to their death. Because from this point on, the argument was very much like that in the catastrophic-event chapter. With no teeth, the dinosaurs were even less able to cope with environmental changes. And so the catastrophe didn't have to be particularly catastrophic to wipe them all out.

The book now lay open on Peter's chest as he himself lay back, gazing up at the map of the stars he had drawing-pinned to the ceiling of his bedroom.

iv.

A door banged shut downstairs, and Peter knew that his mother had returned to ruin his reverie. She had just done the weekly shop. He heard cupboards opening and closing as she put the food away. Peter was not going to announce his presence until he was sure there was no chance he would be asked to lend a hand. Shopping, cleaning, putting-away, that kind of thing was what mothers were invented for. Eventually, the louder sounds ceased, and Peter heard a tap clank, start to run. He knew exactly what was going on. It was the same every Friday. His mother was making fish and chips. At this moment the three pieces of plaice were lying whitely on a chopping-board. The whooshing sound he could hear was the washing and peeling of potatoes. His father was due back in about fifteen minutes. They ate supper early on a Friday, around five o'clock, so that his parents would have plenty of time to get ready to go out, always to the Albion pub. Next came the sound of the knife banging down onto the chopping-board. Peter didn't mind the fish and chips so much during the holidays, but, during term-time, we almost always had fish and chips for school dinner, as well. This was because of the Catholics, though none of us knew anyone at school who would admit to being a Catholic. After Peter heard the slicing stop, he decided it was safe to go downstairs.

When he entered the kitchen, his mother was at the sink, rinsing off the vegetable knife, and the chopping-board.

This was the way it always was. Our mothers stood always with a worksurface in front of them, at approximately navel height: a pan-crowded hob, a sink full of dirty dishes, a sink full of dirty clothes, an ironing board. Occasionally, they found a task which required them to sit down, or even to go outside: shelling peas, knitting, sewing, or darning; hanging the washing out to dry, scraping peelings onto the compost heap, bringing the dry washing in, tying bacon rind under the bird-table. But mostly their backs were turned towards us, heads bowed, hands moving, minds elsewhere. Once we had clung to them, pulled at their skirts, tried to get them to turn around, to pay attention. "Mum!" we had said. "Mum! Mum!" Now, we let them continue with their work. Now, we ignored them as much as we could. Slowly, we were forgetting their faces.

"Hello, Mum," said Peter.

She glanced round and said, "Where have you been hiding?"

"I was upstairs," said Peter. "I was sleeping."

"What about your friends?"

"They went home as well."

"Nothing to do, and on a lovely day like this?"

"We didn't feel like it."

The darkly stained aluminium chip-pan was bubbling away on the hob.

"I'm going to the shop," said Peter's mother, then added, by way of explanation, "to buy some lemons." And then, to gloss it even further, "You know how your father likes a lemon." And finally, when Peter did not in any way respond, "Can't do without it, really."

103

"All right," said Peter, finally.

"Don't touch it," said his mother. "Just turn it down if it starts to smoke." She looked around for something. "And don't leave it alone." In an attempt to be menacing, she pointed at his nose. "Not for one second."

She picked up her purse, opened the hall door and, with one backwards glance into the kitchen, headed off to buy a bag of lemons that no-one would ever taste.

It wasn't that this hadn't happened before. Peter had often enough been left in charge of something cooking. On quite a few occasions, the something had been a chip-pan. But, this time, however, Peter felt a peculiar resentment. He hated the idea of being confined to the kitchen, merely out of obedience to the order of his mother. There is a vast difference between wasting time and being forced to waste time. The latter, for young men, in particular, is at least twice as frustrating as the former. And so, in an attempt to mitigate both his frustration, and his sense of shame at allowing himself to be forced into doing anything against his will, Peter decided to leave the kitchen. This disobedience was also not without precedent. Before, however, he'd always got away with it, somehow.

Without turning the heat down on the chip-pan, Peter dashed out the kitchen door, swung himself round the banister, and was half-way up the stairs before he even knew it. To turn the heat down would have been to taint the purity of the disobedience.

His thighs banged against the edge of his desk as he belatedly tried to slow himself down.

While reaching for the copy of *The Death of the Dinosaurs*, he managed to knock two of the model dinosaurs off the shelf. Adrenalin was making him clumsy. He decided not to pick the dinosaurs up. There wasn't time. His mother was unlikely to return, but his father could arrive at any moment.

With the book held tightly in his left hand, Peter skedaddled back downstairs.

The chip-pan was smoking more than before. Peter went over to it, and looked down into the bubbling golden murk. He closed his eyes and smelt the smell, the heaviest smell in the world.

He sat down at the kitchen table with the full intention of re-reading the chapter on phylogeronty. But as soon as he'd opened it to the correct page, the model dinosaurs lying on the carpet upstairs began to trouble him. What if, he thought, my mother comes back, goes straight up into my room and sees them knocked over and discovers I went up there while she was out? An instant later, he realized what a huge tactical error he'd made in bringing the Dinosaur book downstairs. He could always try to hide it. Perhaps by placing it, spine in, somewhere on the mantel shelf, along with his mother's cookery books. But, no, she was just as likely to notice that, too.

Peter's heart was still a-thump from the rush upstairs and back. Adrenalin was making him stupid. This was a phenomenon we had often noticed. With some of us, with Andrew and Paul, adrenalin was a positive boon, clarifying our thoughts wonderfully. For others, for Matthew, and even more for Peter, any excitement whatsoever led them to make drastic miscalculations. In his heightened state, Peter began to credit his mother with supernatural powers of detection. He was expecting her, when she came back, to find some excuse to punish him, or rather to make his father punish him.

Peter decided the safest thing would be to return the Dinosaur book to its customary place on the shelf, and at the same time put the model dinosaurs back just as they were before.

Again, he ran out through the kitchen door. Again, he swung himself up onto the stairs.

This time, however, something was to be different, something of huge importance.

Peter had replaced the Dinosaur book, and was hurriedly picking up a Brontosaurus, when he heard the front door open and close, and then his father call his mother's name. It was the worst outcome anyone could have envisaged. Peter dropped the dinosaur onto his desk.

"Hello?!" his father shouted. "I'm back. Yoo-hoo."

Peter knew that he would have to make his presence known pretty damn sharpish.

"Anybody home?" his father shouted.

Peter went to the top of the stairs.

"Hello, Dad," he said. "I'm —"

"Peter," his father said. "Where's your mother?"

Peter came down the stairs slowly. He didn't want to give his father any cause for anger or panic. "She's gone to the shop," he said.

"Come here, son," Peter's father said. "Give your old dad a hug."

As he clomped down the last three stairs, Peter could envisage the chip-pan as clearly as if his father had been holding it. He knew that the moment his father found he'd left it cooking, he would be in serious trouble. Helpless, Peter delayed the moment of discovery, and took his father's love, which so soon would be withdrawn. His father took him in his arms and lifted him off the ground. It was at that exact instant that black smoke started to flow out from under the kitchen door.

As a consequence of their position, with Peter's father having rather dramatically swung Peter round, it was Peter who first saw the smoke, looking over his father's blind back. Here, he found himself faced with another momentary decision. Here, he decided to accept the heroism of punishment. "Dad," he said. "I think the kitchen — it's on fire." It was hopeless, his saying kitchen. As if his father wouldn't locate, in the chip-pan, and in Peter's neglect of it, the cause of the blaze.

His father dropped him, swivelled round. Five steps took him to the door. A swift turn of the handle and he was through.

v.

The sight that greeted Peter, under his father's outstretched arms, on either side of his father's body, was the worst imaginable. The top half of the room was black with smoke. The bottom, as clean and clear as he had left it.

"Oh Christ," his father said. Covering his mouth with his hand, he rushed into the smoke. Peter followed him.

All he could see of his father were his legs. The chip-pan, however, like the orange flare of a jet engine, was quite another matter. It blazed out brightly through the blooming black.

"Open the door!" shouted Peter's father. "Now! Go on."

Peter ran round him, bumping him as he passed. The smoke was making his eyes sting and his lungs feel heavy. His hand scrabbled up and down the ridgy glass of the door, until it grazed itself on the edge of the aluminium door-handle. Peter turned it, and pushed himself out choking into the garden.

He could see his father's plan, and could see the horrible flaw in it. For, just to the left of the kitchen door, where the guttering came to an abrupt end, there was a large rainwater butt. Peter knew the dangers of introducing boiling, burning oil into cold water. It was equivalent to the tin-cans full of melted candle-ends that Gang dunked into The Lake, to watch them fizzbang. "No!" he shouted. But his father was already backing out into the garden, the chip-pan going all Roman Candle in his dishcloth-covered hands. "Don't!" Peter shrieked. But his father didn't listen.

With Peter still holding the door open, his father dunked the chip-pan into the rainwater butt. For less than an instant, the blaze was quelled. The scorching pan splashed down into

107

the tepid water. In the next moment, a huge hoof of flame kicked out of the butt and slammed right into Peter's forehead. His reactions were quick enough for him to close his eyes, but that was all. He fell backwards, his blond hair already on fire.

His father saw the stupidity of what he'd done. "Peter," he said, and started to thwack his son's head, with the dishcloth.

The hoof of flame was dissipating into a whiff of smoke. A thinner, nastier smoke was coming from Peter's head.

His father dipped his hand into the rainwater butt, to try and sop some of its cooling wetness onto his son's head. The hand dipped up to the wrist into near-boiling chip fat. Of course, the oil had floated on the water. He pulled it out with the only real scream that Peter had ever heard.

Although a little shocked at the suddenness of the scorching, Peter was still astute enough to know how it must be resolved. He staggered into the kitchen, where the smoke, far from clearing, seemed actually to have thickened. He turned both taps on full. He dowsed his flame-head under their hot–cold streams. The stinging was extraordinary. It was as if the brightness inside him were trying to outdo the brightness above. The wallpaper behind the cooker was on fire, as were the white tiles of the ceiling. The net curtains on the window were just starting to catch.

"Peter!" his father shouted through the doorway.

It was at this moment that Peter's true heroism first came to the fore. The house, he realized, might really be compromised, might really burn to the ground. If it did so, the Archives would be lost for ever. All that we had achieved, all that he had recorded, would be consumed by flames, be lost to the future.

His father was crawling in through the back door, carefully keeping his head in clear air close to the floor.

Peter realized he had only a moment. The ceiling fire was dripping down on to the kitchen door, like a yellow waterfall. Eluding his father's grasp, Peter stormed forwards, pulled open the kitchen door, and burst out into the hall. The contrast was extraordinary. If it hadn't been for the smoke he brought in with him, the hallway would have looked as normal as anything. And yet behind him, when he closed it, was his scalded father, was a life-and-death situation.

He ran towards the bottom of the stairs. Just as he got there, the front door opened and his mother came in. She looked at his black hair and the terribly pink skin beneath it. "What?" was all that Peter gave her the chance to say. He swerved up onto the stairs, and dived practically the whole way into his bedroom.

Downstairs, Peter's father ran out of the burning kitchen and straight through Peter's mother. They both fell onto the hall carpet.

Peter yanked open the secret drawer and retrieved the Archives. After standing up, he went and grabbed *The Death of the Dinosaurs*, too. He wasn't sure whether the floor of his room, which was directly above the kitchen, really was heating up, or whether his heated imagination was responsible.

His father caught him half-way down the stairs. "What the hell do you think you're doing?" he said.

Peter didn't answer him. The Archives were in one hand, *The Death of the Dinosaurs* in the other.

Outside, Peter could hear his mother shouting, "Call the Fire Brigade! Somebody call the Fire Brigade!"

His father carried him down the last six stairs and out into the mid-afternoon street.

Neighbours had already called the Emergency Services. With their usual efficiency, the Fire Brigade arrived about five minutes later. Smoke was ruffling along the hallway and out the open front door. Peter stood with his parents, on the concrete of the pavement. After assessing the situation, the Firemen hauled a hosepipe down the alley and in through the back door.

They managed to save everything in the house except the kitchen and the hall.

When the fire was safely out, they took Peter's parents to one side. Peter knew that the blame was going to be terrible. This was the worst thing he had ever done. He bowed his burnt-up head in expectation of a real ear-bashing. The most important Fireman told Peter's father, very, very sternly, that a child should not be left in charge of a chip-pan of boiling oil. Peter tried not to smile. The Fireman accused Peter's mother of the grossest negligence. Peter had never heard anyone bollock his parents this way. It was great. Finally, the Fireman turned his attention to Peter. "And as for you," he said. Peter shrugged his head down into his chest. "You're a very fortunate young man, indeed."

Just then, the ambulance arrived.

The Ambulance Men took Peter's injuries much more seriously than he did.

Still clutching the Archives and the Dinosaur book, Peter was put on a stretcher, loaded onto a gurney, and shoved into the back of the ambulance.

This drove him, without a siren, to Midford General Hospital, eight miles away. His mother insisted on coming with him.

She sat next to him, crying, holding his hand, and trying to stop herself touching his head.

"I'm sorry," she said, "I'm sorry," over and over and over and over again.

vi.

We, during this time, were all at our separate houses, doing our separate things. But we reconvened, as prearranged, round Base Camp #1, at eighteen hundred hours. When Peter didn't turn up, we waited a while, then cycled down his house, to see if he wanted to come out.

110

The Fire Engine was still there. A neighbour had made them a second pot of tea. Peter's father was standing in the road, talking to the most important Fireman. They were friends now, with all recriminations over. At first, Peter's father didn't seem to notice us. He certainly didn't realize Peter's importance to us or us to him.

"Where is he?" asked Andrew.

He didn't ask was he all right, for none of us believed anything fatal, or even really bad, could happen to us. We were the heroes. Unless there was a War, we survived.

"They've taken him to hospital," said Peter's father. "In Midford, they say he's going to be all right."

"What's wrong with him?" asked Matthew.

"He burnt himself," said Peter's father. "But he's going to be all right, he is." Then he turned back to the Fireman and they resumed their conversation.

We thought for a moment about cycling into Midford. The distance was only about eight miles, most of it downhill. It could easily be done.

The journey back would present the greater difficulty. By then, it would be dark. Some of us would have to go home first, to fix lights to our bicycles. We decided that we had better leave our visit to the Hospital until the following day.

"What about the Archives?" asked Matthew.

We looked back towards Peter's house. His bedroom was at the rear of the building, directly above the kitchen. But as far as we could see, the upper floor was entirely intact. It was a terrible moment. How could we find out the Archives' present status without alerting Peter's father to their immense importance?

"Let me handle this," said Andrew.

Casually, he walked over again to Peter's father. We watched, aghast.

They spoke for a short while.

When Andrew came back, he was smiling.

"Peter rescued them," he said. "Heroically. He took them with him to the Hospital."

As one, we rode towards The Park. Although bicycles were not strictly allowed, we cycled blithely in.

Andrew led the way. Matthew followed, keeping his eyes resolutely on the green canvas and brown leather straps of Andrew's panniers. Paul brought up the rear, the rubber brake-pad of his front wheel rhythmically rubbing. It slowed him down, somewhat. He would have to fix it.

Andrew was leading us towards the crest of Crackback Hill, from where we could gaze panoramically out over north Mid-fordshire, towards Midford itself, where our friend lay injured.

vii.

At this exact instant, eight or so miles away, in the Children's Ward of Midford General, Peter lay sleeping on harsh white sheets. The entire top of his head, his left eye, and his left ear, were bandaged over. Peter, who usually slept balled up on his left side, hand under cheek, was forced to try his right. If it hadn't been for the sedative administered by the nurse, he would never have been able to drop off.

His mother had stayed, fretting, until about seven o'clock, at which time she was persuaded that she could do nothing further of use. (Although that, of course, had been the case all along, obvious to everybody but her.) They told her that to disturb Peter now might actually be harmful. (Although she had already done just about as much harm as she was going to do.)

After kisses, and more kisses, she traipsed off to get a taxi, still clasping the crumpled brown-paper bag containing the three lemons. During this difficult time, the lemons had been her mainstay. When there was nothing else to cling on to, no son, no husband, there had always remained the brown-paper bag. The top of it was by now entirely adapted to the fist of her right hand, smoothed off, curled round, like the grip of a pistol.

Walking out of the Hospital reception, she threw the bag of lemons away. She wanted to blame them, and not herself. At this moment, she looked very ugly, her make-up wrecked by crying, and her hair by tugging and twisting. She had difficulty finding a taxi driver prepared to take her home.

The doctors and nurses were glad to see her go. But not half so glad as Peter, who hated her for not insisting he be placed in an adult ward. Peter felt humiliated by the primary colours and general atmosphere of childishness which surrounded him. Upon the walls were kiddy paintings of animals that looked more like other animals than the ones they were meant to be. There were dogs that looked like cows and cows that looked like rats. The worst of these was a splodgy Brontosaurus, directly within Peter's line of vision. His mother had wanted to treat him like a baby. She had even called him Baby. He feared for his future. He worried that his parents wouldn't leave him alone ever again. He envisaged them talking to Paul's parents and forming together and making a pact and trying to break up Gang.

The ward wasn't particularly quiet. One or other of the real children was always crying.

A nurse, who was very black, sat at a desk in an office, occasionally looking out through her brightly lit window.

Peter slept soundly. Beside him, in the locker for his possessions, safely lay the Archives, secure for posterity.

viii.

By the time we crested the brow of Crackback Hill, the sun was almost horizontal. At this angle, it turned the grass beneath our feet the yellow colour of sick leaves. In nearby fields, the usual white-gold of the corn was divided up into the long blue lines of hedgerow-shadow and the vast russet squares of the still-shined-upon. The arc of the sky, from right to left, east to west, went from navy to violet to aquamarine to powder. Apart, perhaps, from the crimsons and vermilions of the last few instants of a seacloud-framed Cornish sunset, this was as melo-dramatic a palette as the English landscape ever dares. Aero-planes had left occasional jet-streamers high up in the stratosphere. In the middle distance stood the forty-two chimneys of the brickworks. As the sun slowly went down, the furnaces were lit. White smoke blew gently across Midford Road, invading the sprawled village of Lower Hilton. When the wind blew south, we could taste the brickdust in the air, in our food, in every aspect of our lives. Along the far west of the landscape ran the train line, Midford to London. In the furthest of the far north, Midford's yellow glow against the sky slowly became apparent.

That was where Peter lay, divided from us, but loyal, loyal in his heroic rescue and retention of the Archives.

A few late walkers passed us as we stood there, feet planted upon either side of our bicycles. Little could they have guessed the thoughts that we separately had, nor the single thought that bound together. Each of us wished that it had been ourself, rather than Peter, silly Peter, who had heroically been injured. Though each was glad it had been Peter, not anyone else. The setting sun seemed to us the glory of our friend, disappearing awhile out of our collective sight.

Night was placating the landscape, bringing with it quieter noises and swifter movements.

"We will go to see him tomorrow," said Andrew.

Paul silently blamed Andrew for Peter's injuries, whatever they were. Had the afternoon not been such a failure, Peter would never have suggested going home. Had Andrew been a better leader, Peter would have been with us at that moment.

Matthew was consumed with worry for the friend that, among all Gang, he felt most equal to, closest to. They often spent time together when we weren't around, reading and doing experiments. He hated and feared the thought that Peter might come back different: ugly, afraid, girlish.

Andrew wanted to be able to do more than just bring us to this good place. He wanted to turn the incident into a triumph, a triumph for which he could take some credit. Peter's training had paid off. The bravery, beaten out of him, beaten into him, had finally found a use. But until this had been confirmed by Peter himself, none of it could be capitalized upon.

Thus, the morale of Gang lay at a particularly low ebb. Our unity, our Ganghood, for the while, was fractured. It would return, of that, of that more than anything, we were certain. But as the stars came out above our heads, we felt ourselves, for once, as far-distant from one another as they from us.

AUTUMN

CHAPTER FIVE

Matthew

Nun seh' ich wohl, warum so dunkle Flammen
Ihr sprühet mir in manchem Augenblicke,
O Augen! O Augen!
Gleichsam, um voll in einem Blicke
Zu drängen eure ganze Macht zusammen.

Doch ahnt' ich nicht, weil Nebel mich umschwammen,
Gewoben, vom verblendenen Geschicke,
Daß sich der Strahl bereits zur Heimkehr schicke,
Dorthin, von wannen alle Strahlen stammen.

Now see I why such darkling Fires
You did flash out at me,
O Eyes! O Eyes!
As if, with one Look only
You might your Might summarize.

But I suspected not, whilst Mists did me bedize,
Darned by deceptive Destiny,
How this Beam had turned Homewards already,
Toward the Source from which all Beams arise.

1.

I was waiting in front of my grandmother's house when Andrew's mother drove up.

Paul and Andrew were already sitting in the back of the big black Rover 2000.

I didn't want to go in the front, and have to talk to Andrew's boring mother, so I got in the back, too.

It was a white-skied, blow-windy Autumn day. We sat and didn't say anything all the eight miles to Midford.

The hospital was a huge cube of a building, made of dark red Midfordshire brick.

The corridors inside were long and smelt of just-cleaned bathroom. We walked through lots and lots of wards full of old people. Some of the men winked at us and made the thumbs-up signal, just like Spitfire pilots do after they've shot down a Messerschmitt. We kept hurrying, hurrying along.

Eventually, we found the Children's Ward. Peter was sitting up in bed wearing his stripy blue and white pyjamas.

He looked fine. We were very impressed by the lopsided bandages on his head, almost covering his left eye. (He told us afterwards that the nurses kept trying to make him choose a colourful hat to wear, so no-one could see anything. He refused, of course. Looking heroic was one of the luxest things about being injured.) Underneath the dressings, his head was a bit manky.

We were told he had only First, not Second or Third Degree burns. The skin was runny and pink. Peter was not allowed

123

outside, in case his head became septic. He had to take medicines which made him feel really ill.

"Greetings," Peter said.

"Hello," I said.

"Greetings," said Andrew.

"Greetings," said Paul.

We were all desperately anxious to know for certain if the Archives really were safe. But, of course, we couldn't ask anything with Andrew's mother sat there.

On his side, Peter wanted to know what would happen to our plans for revenge upon Paul's father.

We stood there, not enough chairs for all of us, hating the place, hating it for imprisoning our friend.

From Peter's window, you could see out over all of Midford, the river and the old church.

"Will operations continue as planned?" Peter asked.

"Definitely," I said, meaning to be kind.

"With notable exceptions," said Andrew.

"What about our main objective?"

"It will be pursued," said Andrew. (He meant Paul's father's cat, Tabitha.)

Peter smiled. He knew that when he got back, there would still be plenty for him to do.

"You lot are so funny," said Andrew's mother. "With all your funny talk."

We ignored her. She was a woman, and could not be expected to behave well at a time like this. We were badly awkward for a while. Finally, Andrew's mother got the message and went off to the toilet.

"Quick," said Andrew. "What about the Archives? Are they safe?"

Peter looked from side to side, then pulled the familiar Lever Arch file out from under his pillow.

We congratulated him, and he quickly told us all about rescuing them from the peril of the burning building.

Then, very slowly, as serious as a ceremony-thing, Peter handed the Archives over to Andrew.

"You must keep them," he said. "Until I come back."

"When will you be back?" I asked.

"I don't know," said Peter. "They say soon, but they don't say how soon soon is."

We sympathized. We wanted Peter to come back with us right away.

Andrew's mother returned.

We talked in code with her mocking us until visiting hours were over.

2.

The next time we went to see Peter, he was still in bed, looking just the same. It didn't even look like his bandages had been changed, but they were still clean, so they must of been.

Peter had spent most of the week listening to the Ashes on the radio. He knew the batting and bowling averages of every single England player. (As Gang, we had only ever really played French cricket ourselves. With four of us, there was only enough for a bowler, a batsman, a wicket-keep and one fielder. And that wasn't really much of a game.) With one Test still to go, England had already lost the Series. The Aussies were victorious. But England were still "in with a fighting chance" of winning the final Test.

3.

Then the next time we visited him, Peter was in a wheelchair.

"I don't need it," he whispered to us. "They make me. They say I'll get out sooner if I stay in it."

He was depressed this time. (England had lost.)

"Do we have any clarification of how soon soon is?" asked Andrew.

"By the end of the month," said Peter. (He had been in hospital for two weeks.)

"Come home soon," I said. "Or there'll be no Summer left."

At this, Peter looked very glum.

"I know," he said.

4.

The final time we went to visit, it was Andrew's father who drove us. But he didn't come in. "Give me the heeby-jeebies, hospitals do," he said. "I'll just wait out here for you by the car, and have a couple of Woodbines." (Woodbines were the best cigarette.)

When we arrived on the Children's Ward, we found Peter out of bed and fully dressed. He looked really really stupid in his clothes. Partly because we'd got so used to seeing him in pyjamas, but mostly because the clothes were ones his mother had brought from home. Peter looked like he was dressed up to go to a girl's birthday party. He was wearing a flowery shirt with big collars and a pair of flared blue corduroys. The rest of us were gladder than ever of our khaki uniforms. Peter told us that his mother was treating him like a baby, and enjoying it. He made us promise to collect firewood for a big bonfire at Wychwood, just so he could jump over it and prove that he wasn't at all scared of fire.

126

We promised. The bandages were still there on his head, but smaller.

"When can we have a look?" asked Andrew.

"I'm almost better," said Peter. "There won't hardly be any scars left, the doctor says."

Peter was now allowed to walk around some of the hospital. He had recced the place quite thoroughly, in case he needed to make an emergency exit. Andrew said that Peter should show us around the hospital, as the information could come in handy for future reference. We knew the Children's Ward already, and the way to and back from it. Peter knew other bits: the Emergency Room, the X-Ray Suite and the Dermatology Department. He led us round for a while. Spitfire pilots gave Peter the thumbs-up and said, "Tally-ho." Sometimes different nurses would say "Hello" to him. They smiled and were very twinkly as they asked us our names and we told them. When one of them walked back past us a little while later, holding a bottle full of pee, she remembered all of them exactly. We were very impressed. Her training must of been good. The nurses all told us that Peter had been "very brave". We knew that already. We knew because he was a member of Gang, and everyone in Gang was brave.

After we told him that the Best Father had driven us that day, Peter wanted to see if he could see him. He took us to a window looking down onto the car park. We tried waving and thumping on the glass, but Andrew's father didn't see or hear us. Perhaps it was the cigarette smoke getting in the way of his eyes. Or the traffic noise. He seemed lost in deep thoughts. We admired him from afar. Secretly, Peter was a lot relieved that the Best Father wouldn't see him in his Mummy's Boy outfit. However, we could tell that he was "deeply honoured" that Andrew's father knew all about him being hurt and everything.

The car-park window was in a ward full of old women. "I don't like it here," said Peter, looking around.

We could hear one of the women behind a curtain being talked to by a nurse. The nurse was using a voice like you'd use to a baby or a complete spazz. "Come on Mrs Mrs," she said, "it's time for your bath, now, isn't it?"

Andrew made a sick-o face, which we all understood. "Where do they keep the dead bodies?" he asked.

"They burn them," said Peter. "Did you see the big chimney outside?"

"But before they burn them?" Andrew asked. "They put them in metal boxes and stack them up to the ceiling. Where do they keep the metal boxes?"

"One girl died," said Peter. "They took her away. She was all under a sheet, except for her hand which was dangling down off the side. It was white as anything. Before she died she went blue and coughed for ever. And she had fits, like this." He showed us, twitching like a spastic. A nurse stopped to ask if he was all right. After she was gone, we laughed really hard.

"The girl had cancer," Peter continued. "People sometimes think I do too, because of the bandages on my head. They think I've had brain surgery."

"You need it," I said.

We laughed again.

I felt like Andrew's father. I hated hospitals, too. They gave me the heeby-jeebies. I wanted to be down with him in the car park, smoking Woodbines and talking about how much we hated hospitals.

"Which way did they wheel the dead girl?" asked Andrew.

"I don't know," said Peter. "It happened in the middle of the night. She was six."

Andrew made Peter feel stupid for not following them and finding out where they went.

"I would of," he said.

We knew he was telling the truth. Andrew had always been totally mad about dead things. Once, when we were on our bikes waiting at a crossroads, we had seen a sparrow try to fly under a car. Thunk! We heard it hit the petrol tank or something hollowish on the bottom of the car. When the car had carried on, we saw the sparrow lying in the road. Andrew got off his bike and was about to go and pick it up, when another car whizzed past. Splat! After the second car had gone by, we saw that one half of the bird was completely flat, and its guts and its eye had been squished out. Another car roared by. Then Andrew nipped out into the road and picked the bird up by the wing. The top half opened up like a fan, but the bottom bit was like something that would make even a butcher want to puke up. "It's great, isn't it?" said Andrew. "Just look at it."

"Put it down," I said.

Andrew lifted the bird up and dangled it over his open mouth, like it was spaghetti. Just then, the sloppy bit and the winged bit split apart, and the sloppy bit fell straight into Andrew's big gob.

He spat it out as fast as anything, and carried on spitting and spitting.

We all laughed, especially Paul.

Andrew stepped on the small pile of entrails and said, "Bastard bird."

Another time, when we were really young, perhaps nine, we came across a rabbit that was dying. We were just near the end of Gas House Lane. (See Map.) The rabbit was lying under a hedgerow, and you could hear the loud breathing it made. Its eyes were cloudy like they had cataracts like poor Indian women do. Black bubbly goo was weeping out from under their sides. The fur of its pelt was motheaten-looking. Again, Andrew was the most interested of all of us. He picked the rabbit up by its hind legs. We expected it to buck away, but it had no strength left. As he held it upside-down, its body stretched so long that its ears almost touched the ground.

"You can feel its heartbeat," said Andrew, and held the rabbit out for us to touch.

He was right, its heart was going faster than anything.

Andrew swung the rabbit over his shoulder, like a school blazer on a hot day.

"I'm going to show my father," he said.

We were only down the road, so we went straight round The Pollards. The Best Father was digging up potatoes in the garden. Andrew kept the rabbit hidden till the last minute, then dropped it at his father's feet.

"Where did you find that?" Andrew's father asked, not too surprised at all.

"Over near the Gas Works," Andrew said. "It's still alive."

"Well, why don't you take it up The Park and find a nice big rabbit warren and chuck it in there?"

"What'll that do?" asked Andrew.

The best father explained all about myxomatosis. How it was really cancer. How people in history had deliberately given it to rabbits to make them die because there were too many of them eating up all the crops. If this rabbit was still alive, he said, it could give myxomatosis to lots more rabbits, who would pass it on to even more rabbits. He said that would be a bloody good job, too.

"Do rabbits ever get better from it?" asked Peter.

"No," said Andrew's father. "Once a rabbit has it, it's a goner."

"What about people?" I asked. "They sometimes get better, don't they?"

"Oh, yes," said the best father. "They have a fairly good chance. Now, get that thing away from my potatoes."

We said goodbye and marched off.

Andrew was now carrying the dying rabbit at arm's length. He didn't like the sound of cancer.

(The reason I'd asked the question about people getting better from cancer was because my grandfather had cancer, but I'd been told not to tell anyone about it. He didn't want people knowing about what he called his "private problems". In our house, we didn't even say the word. It was always either the Big C or Grandad's Little Problem. My grandfather had the Big C in his prostate, which is like a valve that turns your pee on and off. I had no idea how the Big C had got in there in the first place. Of course, I'd told all Gang about him being ill.)

As we walked towards The Park, I looked at the rabbit that Andrew was now swinging back and forth with each stride. Now I knew what myxomatosis was, I noticed how the rabbit's eyes did look a little like my grandfather's. He needed drops, sometimes, to get them to open up at all. I had to help him with the drops.

Andrew said he knew where the biggest warren in the whole of The Park was. We all had our own ideas where it was going to be. But Andrew led us to the top of Crackback Hill (where we stood years later and looked out towards Peter in hospital), and then down a little on the other side. There were three big entrance holes in the ground. Grey sand was all over the place, and pilly little droppings as well. Andrew was very happy to be doing two of the things he most enjoyed in the world: obeying his father and killing animals. He dumped the rabbit in the biggest of the holes and cleaned his hands off on his back pockets. "Our crops are safe," he said.

131

With some last strength that it had bravely gathered, the rabbit tried to lollop away from the warren. Maybe it was trying to save its brother and sister rabbits.

Andrew wasn't having any of that. He took a step back and kicked it swiftly in the head.

All of us heard its neck snap.

Andrew swore. He picked up the dangly-dead rabbit by the ear and swore again and again. "It shouldn't have shitting tried to escape," he said.

"You put it out of its misery," I said.

"But we needed it alive to kill more rabbits," said Andrew, very serious. "To keep our crops safe."

Peter looked as if he agreed with me. "Put it down the hole, anyway," he said. "It might still work if it's still warm."

Andrew let the rabbit flop down into the darkness.

"Why don't we see if we can find some more ill rabbits?" said Paul. "Then we can bring them back here and exterminate even more of them."

"I'm going to help my father in the garden," said Andrew in a sulk. "You mustn't tell him about this."

Andrew, in the time since then, had more than made up for the rabbit.

7.

At the end of our last visit, we left Peter staring out of the hospital window, towards where we were going to get into the Best Father's car, and drive home to Amplewick. When we got outside we turned to wave up at him, but he wasn't there.

"How was he?" asked Andrew's father. "Smiling through, I hope."

"He seemed in very good spirits," said Andrew.

"He's coming home next week," added Paul.

"And his bandages are getting smaller," I said.

"Is that right, Matthew?" he said. "Tip-top."

Andrew's father smoked as he drove us back to Amplewick. When we saw an ice-cream van, he stopped and bought us all extra large 99 Flakes.

8.

A week later, Peter came home. His father drove him. Peter sat in the passenger seat of the little Mini. We were outside his house, waiting with his mother. The kitchen had been completely fixed. Peter's father had paid Andrew's father to do it, and he had made it even better than it was before.

The Mini drew up and parked. We could see Peter through the reflections in the windscreen. It was a cold day, compared to the ones just before. The sky was tall and white, rather than low and blue. Most of the Summer had gone. Leaves cracked really loud under the Mini's wheels, like when a cat's spine snaps. We had arrived on bikes. We felt guilty that the holidays had disappeared whilst Peter was in hospital. There were only two weeks left. Not enough time for anything. Peter opened the car door himself, and got slowly out. We were all anxious in case he was now a weakling who couldn't walk any more. Even though we'd seen him at least once a week in hospital, we were still worried that he might have changed since then. Peter carried his own suitcase into the house. It was covered in stickers from places he'd never been, because it had been like that the day he was given it. He went straight upstairs and into his bedroom. We tried to follow him. We wanted to stay and discuss, but his mother sent us away. "He needs to rest, now," she said. "You understand."

We thought Peter would disagree, but he didn't. He just went

133

and sat on the edge of the bed. His bandages made his head look too big for his body, like the foetus of a chicken.

We left him with his mother, who had already started to pull his jumper carefully off.

9.

We didn't see Peter all that week. His parents kept us away. Andrew wanted to return the Archives to him, because, he said, it would be good for him. Paul thought this was a stupid idea, because Peter was confined to barracks. This meant Peter couldn't give an eyewitness account of operations. Paul had wanted to take over writing the Archives until Peter was out of hospital, but Andrew had given this duty to me. I didn't enjoy it as I didn't like writing at all. I never knew what to say, and it felt like homework. I hated the big empty pages with all their narrow lines waiting to be filled with words. I read what Peter had done, and when I could use one of his sentences, I copied it straight out.

10.

Operation Badger took place. Successfully.

11.

I got ill on Monday a week after Peter got out of hospital. It happened quite fast.

In the morning we were meant to meet round The Pollards at ten hundred hours. Then we would go and see if Peter's mother would let us see him, because she hadn't before.

When I went downstairs to have breakfast, my head felt a bit funny, like there was a tennis ball stuffed inside it. It felt spack.

I was all alone in the house. Today was different, in many ways. I wasn't usually left on my own like this.

On most days, my grandmother was in the kitchen when I came down, washing up the breakfast things. They usually had a big cooked breakfast.

Every day I woke up to the smell of bacon and eggs being fried in lard. My grandmother always offered to do "a little something" for me, even though I always said NO! Because I didn't want to feel heavy and putrid and pukey for the rest of the day.

Today, my grandparents had already finished their cooked breakfast and had gone to the garden centre to buy a new rosebush. They had been talking about it for days. They were going to buy an antique rose, either an Old Pink Moss or a Golden Wings. They had shown me photographs in catalogues and asked me which I liked best. (As if I cared about flowers.)

And Miranda wasn't here either. She was away on her stupid German exchange. She was in Baden-Baden-Baden, or somewhere like that.

I still felt sleepy, but not a normal sleepy: I felt sleepy on top of and all around and under sleepy.

Today, the table was laid with the usual blue and white stripy teapot and milk jug and plates and mugs.

Every morning, I could choose what I wanted to eat: cornflakes and milk and sugar, or hot buttered toast and marmalade.

The day I got ill, I had cornflakes. But it wouldn't have made any difference if I'd had toast. But I wish I'd had toast. I liked toast better, really.

It was important to eat quickly. I didn't want to be late for the meeting.

I had a fast routine, to get breakfast over and done with as quickly as possible: I put everything I needed right near my place on the table, then didn't get up until I'd finished.

Everything was more complicated when I had toast: I put the bread under the grill on the cooker as soon as I came down, so it would be ready for when I was ready for it.

The day I got ill, I started out using my fast routine. I put the cornflake packet by my bowl. I got a new bottle of milk from the refrigerator. (I hated weak, watery milk and I hated warm milk.) I moved the sugar bowl to be near me. I poured myself a glass of bright orange orange-juice.

It seemed even brighter than usual this morning. My head went bing-bong, like a doorbell.

I poured cornflakes into a bowl. I poured sugar on top of them. I poured milk all around their edges. Then sat down and quickly began to scoff. (I hated soggy cornflakes and not-hot toast.)

I felt a bit dizzy and didn't know why. I hadn't eaten five mouthfuls before I began to feel pukey.

I took another munch, and then I knew I had to run for the toilet. It was in the upstairs bathroom. I ran.

I didn't make it. I puked up on the carpet of the upstairs landing.

12.

I looked down at my puke, yellow on the flowery brown swirly pattern. There wasn't much of it. The milk looked weak and watery. The cornflakes had gone soggy. Everything was coated in a thin kind of mucous membrane: like when a cat sicks up a bird. Even when I first saw it, I didn't think it looked like ordinary puke.

I wanted to go downstairs and put the milk bottle back in the fridge. I knew that scraping the rest of the cornflakes into the swing bin would make me want to puke again.

All of a sudden, I felt very hot. The stairs telescoped away from me, like in films. I knew I should really clean up the mess, but it seemed much less important than going back to bed.

I went into the bathroom, first: to brush my teeth, to get rid of the sicky taste.

A little bit more puke came up very suddenly as I was walking into my bedroom. I managed to keep it in my mouth and spit it out in my wastepaper basket.

This meant I had to go back to the bathroom, stepping round the splash of puke, and brush my teeth all over again.

Even the effort of just walking had made me sweat. I felt more dizzy, and I knew I had to get back to bed. I put the toothbrush down, still covered in the blue toothpaste foam.

I was getting so stupid that I forgot the puke on the landing, and stepped right in the middle of it. This made me slip and land on my bum. The whole left side of my pyjama bottoms got covered in thin puke.

I got up. The puke now spread over a much bigger area of the carpet, with a leg-shaped splat in the middle.

Again I went back into the bathroom, and I took my pyjama bottoms off, and chucked them in the bath and ran some water over on top of them. The dizziness got bigger.

On the landing this time I made my way carefully around the puke.

I got in my bed. It felt like crawling into comfort. Teddy was there. But straight away I started to feel even worse. My head-dizziness was turning into a headache. My head went bang-bang.

No matter how I tossed and turned, and turned and tossed, I could not get comfortable.

I felt burning hot, so I threw the thin orange blanket off me. Then I felt freezing cold, so I pulled it all around me again.

The pain in my head grew stronger: it was just like a blow-torch blasting away at my skull from the inside.

My neck also began to feel stiff. But at first I thought this was just because I couldn't get comfortable.

Even though I had brushed my teeth twice, the pond-water taste of puke was still running down out of my nostrils and into the back of my mouth. It made me feel like I was going to be sick again.

I got up to go to the bathroom. My head hurt so much I could hardly walk. And now other parts of my body had started to ache as well: my elbows, my ankles.

I stepped round the pile of puke in the landing. The light in the bathroom hurt my eyes.

I knelt down beside the toilet and tried willing myself very hard to be sick. I felt the cold floor of the bathroom tiles against my knees. Nothing came up out of my stomach but a little see-through goo.

I wanted just to lie down there on the floor for a while, and get so I felt strong again. But the light was too bright, so I decided to go back to bed.

I swished some toothpaste around in my mouth, without even using a brush, to try and get rid of the pukey taste.

I was careful not to look into the bath, in case the sight of my sick-covered pyjamas made me sick again.

I stepped over the puke on the landing carpet.

In my bedroom again, I pulled the curtains as tightly shut as I could. Still the room wasn't dark enough for me. The curtains had trains on them, on a white background. They were meant to match my wallpaper, which had the Flying Scotsman and other trains.

I pulled the bedsheet up over my eyes, and folded it a couple of times to make it an even darker blindfold. Teddy was with me. I felt thirsty.

The headache was now so bad that I started to cry with pain. "Stop," I said. "Stop."

The only good thing about my situation now was that I began to feel drowsy again.

When I fell asleep, it was a funny kind: I still felt lots of different kinds of pain all over my body, but it was like a Major-General looking at a map of a big battle from a safe place far behind the lines.

I wasn't there. I felt very calm and in control, like a Major-General would. My grandparents were coming back in an hour.

13.

In fact, they came back even sooner.

My symptoms (I know now, that's what they were) had got worse. Every bone in my body now felt achy. I could feel every joint in my toes. Or it seemed that I could. The headache got better and worse, depending on how much I was able to be drowsy or asleep.

All through being so ill, I kept thinking about one main thing: Is today the day that Peter's mother will let us see him again?

The main reason I wanted my grandparents to come back was not so that I could tell them how terrible I was feeling (and by now it was worse than I'd ever felt in my whole life before), but so that I could get them to pass a message on to the others.

When I heard their car (it was a Morris Traveller) parking in the drive, I knew I was too weak to get up and call my grandparents in. There were more than enough clues scattered and splattered around the house to tell them something strange was going on. Even they weren't spack enough to miss *all* of them.

Outside, it was a brilliant blue sunshiny day.

From downstairs in the kitchen, I heard my grandmother say, "Look at all these cornflakes he's left here. I just don't know."

They were the first clue.

My grandfather came to the bottom of the stairs and shouted

up, "We bought the Golden Wings! Do you want to come and have a look before we plant it?" There was a pause. "Matthew!" he shouted, just at the same time as my grandmother shouted, "It's beautiful!" They were always doing that.

"Matthew?" cooed my grandmother.

Neither of my grandparents liked going up or down the stairs if they could avoid it. I was always fetching them things from their bedroom. I knew where everything was. I even fetched their medicines for them, from the bathroom cabinet. (Miranda did this as well, but they preferred me. I knew.) But by now they knew something was up. I could almost see them looking all bewildered at each other, like geriatrics do.

"Perhaps he's already gone out," said my grandfather hopefully.

"And left his bowl all mucky like that?"

"Perhaps he was in a hurry."

When she got to the top of the stairs, my grandmother saw the second clue.

"Oh dear," she said. She sounded disappointed, not angry.

"What is it?" asked my grandfather, shouting up the stairs like one mountaineer calling to another.

"There's a nasty mess up here. He's been sick, I think."

My grandmother bustled into my bedroom, opening the train curtains and letting in the too-bright light. She had missed the third clue: the pyjama-bottoms in the bath.

"Oh dear," she said, when she saw me in bed. "What's the matter with you, then?"

"I don't know," I said. Speaking was difficult. It felt like the headache was a big, bristly-backed spider, crawling all around the inside of my skull. Sometimes it crouched right behind my face, pushing its specially sharpened legs into my eyes and nose and teeth. Sometimes it just went and hid in a dark corner down by my neck.

"Were you sick?" my grandmother asked, stupidly.

"I couldn't keep it in," I said. Then I delivered my crucial message: "Can you phone Andrew's mother and tell her to tell Andrew that I'm ill and can't come today."

My grandmother put her cool and slippy palm on my forehead.

"You're burning," she said.

"I've got aches all over," I said. "And I'm dizzy."

(See: I told her everything I should have. She was just too stupid and slow to understand what it meant. If she had, everything would have turned out different.)

"You've probably got a stomach bug," said my grandmother. "Or flu. Summer flu. Have any of your friends had flu?"

"No," I said, defensively. We were never ill. Visiting Peter had been the first time any of us had been inside a hospital since we were born.

"Is he all right?" my grandfather called out.

"I think he's got a touch of flu," shouted my grandmother.

"What?" he cried. "I can't hear you!"

"It's flu!"

"Oh," he said. "I'll put the kettle on."

They were so stupid. And slow. Like dinosaurs.

"Is there anything I can get you?" asked my grandmother.

There was a new edition of *Battle* magazine that I knew had arrived yesterday at the Post Office. I thought about using being ill as a way of getting her to buy it for me. But I knew that it would only lie there with me in the dark. My eyes hurt. If I was still ill tomorrow, then I would ask.

"No," I said.

I wanted to be brave and not cry like Miranda would of. But my head had never felt so bad before. I was waiting until my grandmother left the room, so that I could scream a few times into my goosedown pillow.

"Do you think I should see a doctor?" I asked.

My grandmother pushed my hair aside with her claw-like hand. I could smell her sweet powdery smell. It made me want to cough. I knew if I coughed, I would be sick again. And I had nothing left inside of me to be sick with.

"We don't want to go bothering him for no reason, do we?" my grandmother said.

My grandparents always said something like this. My grandfather waited six months before he thought his Big C was serious enough to bother the doctors about. They thought you used doctors only to tell you things were as bad as you thought they were. And, of course, because they waited for ever before doing this, things almost always were that bad. It made me very angry. This was why my grandfather was going to die. He deserved it, I thought.

"No," said my grandmother. "I'll make you a nice cup of tea with some honey in it."

The pain got so bad I couldn't stop myself groaning.

"Oh, m'dut," said my grandmother. "And I'll put some paracetamol in it, too."

She touched my forehead again.

"Ow," I said, as the pain shot through. "That really hurts."

My grandmother stood up. She looked larger and stronger than usual.

"I'll go and get you that paracetamol," said my grandmother, and went back downstairs.

I could hear them whispering in the kitchen. They knew they would have to come up and down the stairs for me, carrying dangerous tea-trays. They might slip and fall.

The black spider in my head started to build a web. The pain no longer moved around. It was a black coating all over everything, both inside me and out.

My grandmother came back in with the tea. She made me sit up and swallow two paracetamol, then drink half a glass of water.

I fell back on the pillow, and tried to go to sleep again. I could smell the hospital-smelling disinfectant my grandmother was using on the landing carpet.

14.

About eleven o'clock, I heard the door-bell ring. It was Andrew, asking what had happened to me, and why I hadn't turned up. The others were outside with him, on bikes. I was too weak to move. Teddy was under my left arm. I heard my grandmother telling them I'd probably be better tomorrow.

My grandmother came in now and again to bring me more honeyed tea, which I didn't drink because I hated it and hated her for bringing me it. I wanted orange juice.

Being as stupid as she was, my grandmother kept making me Earl Grey tea, which always tasted to me like old lady pee. My grandmother knew I hated it. I know she knew. But she kept on in making it. I suppose because she thought it was the best for me. I sweated. I became dry in the mouth. I felt dizzy. I became weak.

"Feeling any better, m'dut?" she would say.

I would groan something back at her.

She put her palm again and again on my head. "The worst will soon be over," she would say. (She was right about that, if nothing else.)

She went away and came back again.

One time when she was downstairs, I had the first of the fits. It was now about three hours since I started feeling ill. Things were getting a lot worse.

I didn't feel all that interested in my body any more. I thought that if I could get rid of the pain, I would be quite happy also to get rid of the stupid life that went with it.

There isn't that much point describing how I felt, because I know that every time I stop describing it, you'll stop feeling it or even thinking about it. That's why I don't like words: they can't tell you about something that never goes away. And they just get boring if they try to. ("Ow," I said. "Shitting hell.") Because I was in the worst pain, ever.

15.

About six o'clock, I had a really bad fit, and conked out completely.

My grandmother was downstairs listening to the *Archers*, and she didn't come up again for another fifteen minutes.

When she couldn't wake me up, even with shouts and slaps, she knew that it was time to bother a doctor.

I looked like I was already dead. The hair was stuck to my dried-out forehead. My skin was grey and slack and clammy.

My grandmother knew that when someone looks like they are about to die, the doctor doesn't mind that much about being bothered.

My grandfather and my grandmother spent about ten minutes having a big argument.

My grandfather said he thought the local surgery would be closed by now. (It was seven twenty in the evening.) He said they should wait and see how I was the next day.

My grandmother just kept saying over and over again, "I think it might be serious." After she said it about a hundred million times, my grandfather realized it might be serious.

He found the number in the local phone directory, dialled, got a wrong number, apologized, hung up, dialled again, got the engaged tone, hung up, dialled again, got through.

When they started to ask about my symptoms, he had to hand the phone over to my grandmother anyway.

"Yes, he's been sick. All over the carpet. Oh, he's burning up.

I gave him some paracetamol for that. He's in bed at the moment, with the curtains drawn. Well, he did complain when I turned the light on, yes. I don't know, he said it ached. I thought it might have something to do with him falling out of a tree a while ago. Fits? I don't think he's had any of those. Fits? Do you mean fits? Well, he seems to be asleep. For about an hour, I think. Yes, I tried to wake him up just now. No, he didn't. What? Right now?"

16.

She put the phone down.
"They're coming round," she said. "They think it's serious."
From now on, everything sped up.
The Doctor arrived ten minutes later.

17.

The Doctor came up to my room alone. His nostrils twitched at the sour smell of the disinfected carpet.

I had met him before: when I had my jabs, and the sugar cube for polio. He was a tall thin man with thick black hair but a grey beard.

Just when he walked in, I started to have the worst fit so far. I was like a little shivering dog.

He switched the light on in the room to see better. I winced away from the glare.

He touched my forehead with his knuckles. He undid the buttons on my pyjama top and listened with a stethoscope to my heart going bang bang bang bang.

He went to the top of the stairs and spoke with authority.

"I want you to call 999, right now, and get them to send an ambulance."

My grandparents stood outside the kitchen door, holding each other like they were on the top deck of a very windy ocean liner.

"What is it?" asked my grandmother.

"What's wrong?" asked my grandfather.

"I'm not sure," said the Doctor, although he was. "But I know we need to get him into a hospital as soon as possible."

My grandfather kept getting the number wrong when he tried to dial. His eyes were so full of girly tears that he couldn't really see anything.

I heard the word hospital and came half awake.

"Will I have to have an injection?" I said.

"Don't worry about that," the Doctor said.

"But will I have to have an injection?" I only repeated myself because I was so ill.

"Try to calm down."

"I don't want to have an injection," I said, then fell back completely whacked on the pillow.

My head went bright with hurting, then black as I fell into a sort of sleep.

18.

"Matthew?" said the Doctor.

I didn't hear.

"Damn," he said, then got a hypodermic out of his bag and gave me an injection in the arm.

My grandmother called up the stairs, "Is he going to be all right?"

The Doctor didn't answer. He was busy trying to save my life.

My grandfather gave the address first of all, before even saying that he wanted an Ambulance, not a Fire Engine or the Police.

The woman at the emergency services had to calm him down, he was being so wibbly-wobbly.

"Come quickly," he said, as if the woman was going to drive the ambulance herself.

My grandmother had come up the stairs and was now in the doorway of my bedroom.

The Doctor was trying to get me to open my eyes again.

"Matthew, wake up!" he shouted. "Matthew, it's very important that you wake up!"

My grandmother had never heard a doctor shout before. Not in real life. The ones on television did. But they weren't real. She was shocked, and her shock made her realize that I might really be dying.

"Is he going to be all right?" she asked.

And then the Doctor said something very important for everything that happened afterwards. He said: "Why didn't you call earlier?"

"We didn't want to bother you."

"Exactly how long has he been like this?"

"I don't know. We were at the garden centre."

My grandmother was cowering in the corner, like she expected the man in the white coat to hit her.

"He's seriously ill," said the Doctor. "We'll take him to Midford General. They'll do what they can there."

"We should have phoned earlier, should we?" asked my grandmother.

The Doctor was kind and didn't say anything.

If I could, I would of shouted at her: I would of shouted, and I would of said: "It's all your fault. I am going to die, and it's all your fault. You have killed me, by being so stupid stupid stupid stupid. You didn't want to bother anyone. You wanted to keep everything quiet. Well, I'm going to be very quiet. I will not speak another word. Ever. I am going to be very dead."

19.

The ambulance arrived. I was put on a stretcher, just like Peter, and carried bumpingly downstairs. Teddy was left behind.

The spider crawled in a big panic all around my head, making gashes in my head with its needle-sharp feet.

I groaned, but did not say anything. I was out completely cold.

A couple of our neighbours, the Pope family and the Jenkinses, came out of their houses to see what all the fuss was about.

They expected the stretcher to be for my grandfather. They were shocked to see through the dark evening that it was me who was on it. Me: Matthew. Stealer of their milk bottles. Smasher of their front windows. Spyer-upon-them through binoculars from trees. Terror of their pets.

I was lifted into the back of the ambulance. The women's hands went over their mouths. The men shook their heads slowly.

The Doctor insisted that my grandparents follow in a separate car. There was, he said, some small risk of infection.

He needed to know if I had any friends I'd been in close physical contact with over the last few weeks.

My grandparents had the numbers for Andrew, Peter and Paul's houses, all written down together.

"And there's also his sister," said my grandfather. "But she's been away in Baden-Baden for six weeks."

"She should be all right, then," said the doctor.

The ambulance man put a needle in my arm, from a clear bottle of saline solution.

I was dead-looking: as grey as the blankets wrapped tight around me.

20.

The ambulance drove off, and my grandparents watched me all the way down Cowfold Lane.

From our house, the Doctor called the others. Andrew and Paul were back at The Pollards. Peter had gone home to his house.

I think the ambulance driver knew that I was going to die. He had the siren on some of the time, but because the roads were nearly empty he cruised along for most of the time in silence.

21.

We arrived at Midford Hospital. We went straight through Accident and Emergency, and up into an isolation ward.

The ambulance men went off to get inoculated.

More doctors took my temperature, listened to my chest, touched my temples, shook their heads.

In a situation like mine, there really wasn't very much they could do. It was all too late.

An hour or so later, around nine, my grandparents arrived. They had scraped someone's car whilst parking in the car park, and had had to go off to get a pen and paper to leave a note.

They stood in the corridor and watched me through the big glass window. My grandmother cried and my grandfather got water-eyed. They were starting to feel really guilty.

"What have we done?" my grandmother asked my grandfather.

"He'll be all right," he lied.

Whenever someone came out of the room, they pestered them for information. Eventually, a Senior Doctor took them into a small office and tried to prepare them for the worst (i.e., hit them with the full horror of the situation, so they'd stop being such bleating nuisances about the place). He left them to cry for a while in his room. There was a poster on the wall of a pregnant woman having a cigarette. My grandparents had no words, they just cried. Miranda was due back from Baden-Baden in two days' time. They thought about having to tell her the terrible news.

22.

I died at 9.27 p.m. that evening. The intervening time was, outwardly at least, uneventful.

Things, however, were going on, in the space between my brain and my skull.

In many ways, I was getting better.

I look back upon that time almost with nostalgia. It was very calm, lying there in the hospital. I lay stiller than at any time in my entire life.

In a way, I was gathering my strength, as many dying people do, for what was to come after death.

The only crisis came at the very end, when my heart stopped pleeping. The doctors and nurses tried, for a short time, to revive me by means of electric shocks. But I was already floating away over their heads.

I died.

Blip.

23.

Although blip is a little melodramatic.

One moment I was in my body, the next I was not.

My grandparents were at my side. I did not hear them tell me we love you and we're sorry and we wish we'd done better by you and oh Matthew forgive us. I did not feel them squeeze my hands (grandmother, right, grandfather, left) or kiss my forehead or stroke my cheek. I did not, as I was leaving my body, pass through their sad hearts. I felt nothing. I was already beyond them. I had become the scab of myself, picked and flicked, with no more thought to where it landed than to how it'd got there in the first place. My only emotion was a desire not to forgive them, and for them not to be forgiven by others. I dropped them as easily as you might drop a grey stone upon a beach of nothing but grey stones.

One final image I had, a tableau, the bed, as seen from directly above, myself, being posthumously attended to, my face, slack, grey.

24.

Then grey turned to white and white to something else altogether.

CHAPTER SIX

Andrew

Ihr wolltet mir mit eurem Leuchten sagen:
Wir möchten nah dir bleiben gerne!
Doch ist uns das vom Schicksal abgeschlagen.
Sieh uns nur an, denn bald sind wir dir ferne!

Was dir nur Augen sind in diesen Tagen:
In künft'gen Nächten sind es dir nur Sterne.

You wanted (to me) with your Light to say:
We'd really love to rest just here,
But Destiny says, "Nay!"
Watch us, for soon we will be far-far-far!

These which are mere Eyes this Day
in future Nights will become Star and Star.

It is a defining characteristic of the innocent that they feel their innocence has already, long ago, been lost. If you had said to me, the day before Matthew's death, that I was an innocent, I would probably have tried, straight away, to beat a retraction out of you. Yet this was to be the moment that we, all of us, finally left our boyhood innocence behind. We had been children, wishing ourselves men; now we were men – albeit very young men – wishing ourselves dead. A great deal was done to prevent our actual deaths, and very efficiently it was done, too. The day that Matthew fell ill, we were fetched away to Midford General Hospital, each in a separate ambulance. Once there, we were examined, blood-tested, questioned and quarantined. The doctors who dealt with us wore latex gloves on their hands and surgeon masks over their noses and mouths. They seemed almost scared of us. This didn't mean, however, that they listened to us or answered our questions as to what was going on.

It turned out that only one of us, Peter, had been in any real danger of developing the condition that killed Matthew. A few antibiotic jabs, and he was protected. But they said they wanted to keep all three of us 'under observation' for twenty-four hours.

They did not observe us very closely, for, as soon as the lights were out, we, acting upon the same impulse, crept from our beds and set off to find one another. Paul and I were first to meet, half-way along one of the quiet, dim corridors. After we found Peter, who had made his way to Paul's room, we went and hid in one of the Ladies' Loos. We knew that here was a place where, even if we were discovered to be missing, no-one would come looking for us. The white-tiled floor was cold against our bare feet. In the corner of the cubicle was a big oblong box with a metal lid – this, we knew, was where women put their jam-rags when they'd filled them with blood. I lifted the lid and looked inside. The box contained a smelly blue liquid, and jam-rags floating in soft red clouds. The only other difference between this and Gents' Loos was the lack of any urinals, or any urinal smell.

'Have you seen Matthew?' I asked.

Neither of the others had.

We then compared notes on what the doctors and nurses had said. It seemed they'd told each of us the same thing, only in slightly different ways. They had said that Matthew was making good progress. They had assured us there was no need to worry. They had insisted everything was being done for Matthew that could be done. They had admitted that he was very ill but added that he had a very good chance of making a full and fast recovery. Because they were wearing uniforms and were taller than us and had stubbly faces and spoke in deep voices, we thought we could trust them absolutely. The uniforms, in particular, reassured us. These, after all, were the doctors who would one day be assigned to look after us when we were brought in, wounded, from our battles with the invading Russkis. Our parents, we knew, were not to be trusted. They had no medical expertise. The doctors would have taken one look at them and seen that they were civilians. There was no operational value at all in telling them the truth. Neither did we put much stock in what the nurses told us. After all, they were only women. We later realized that, even after Matthew had been dead for several hours, we were still being told, 'He's fine. Don't worry. We're taking good care of him.' They lied to us about our best friend. How could they? They were betraying their uniforms.

The cisterns in the Ladies' Loos plipped quietly.

We were whispering.

I said, 'What questions did the doctors ask you?'

'They asked me really stupid questions,' Peter said.

'Like what?' I asked.

'Like, "Did you have any close physical contact with Matthew?"'

'What did you say?' asked Paul.

'"Of course I didn't!" They said perhaps I'd kissed Matthew. They were wrong.' Peter was almost shouting.

'Shh,' I said. 'Or somebody will hear.'

Peter seemed upset. 'But I didn't kiss Matthew. Why did they say that?'

'It was probably a test,' said Paul, wisely.

I could tell that Peter needed to be calmed down. In this time of great trouble, firm leadership was more than anything else required. I decided that our lowest-ranked troops needed some distraction.

'Let's have an explore,' I said.

This rather childish phrase was retained by us long after most of our other pre-Gang language had been ditched. Even so, it was rarely used; and thus, when Peter heard me say it now, he knew that I was appealing to the deepest, most loyal part of him. Of course, I already had a plan formulated as to what *exactly* we were to go looking for. But it is often best to let subordinates believe they have discovered obvious things all by themselves.

We made our way out of the Ladies'. The hospital was very quiet, but that didn't mean there weren't people still about. It meant that the people still about were very quiet people. The nurses hissed past on soft-soled shoes. The patients squeaked to and from the toilets in fresh-rubbered slippers. On most of the wards we passed through, the loudest noise was the rasping sound of someone trying to breathe. We were excellent at not being spotted. We crouched under occupied beds and hid behind slithery curtains. We were the quietest thing of all. If one of the Spitfire pilots woke up and saw us, we would give them the thumbs-up sign. They would smile, give it back, smile some more, and then go back to sleep. Slowly, we made our way down into the basement. I knew where we were heading. I was in the lead. If Paul silently pointed down a corridor, suggesting we might go in that direction, I would shake my head. The name of the department we were heading for was written on wall-signs, square white letters on a green oblong background: PATHOLOGY. I wanted to do some research, for personal reasons. Also, I needed to find out if the other two were brave enough to follow me in there.

We finally found the correct corridor. At the end of it was an office, with a man inside. He was wearing a green surgeon's smock and, as we were soon to see, white Wellington boots. We assumed that he was merely another doctor. He was sitting at a desk under a lamp. Every so often he turned the page of something in front of him. Most likely it was a medical journal.

'Let's go back,' said Peter, as always the first to show he was scared.

'I think there are better places to look,' said Paul.

'No,' I said. 'We have to get past the guard.'

'All right,' said Paul, retracting.

'We need to create a distraction,' I said.

But just as I was about to detail my plan, the doctor got up from his desk, came out of the office and began to walk towards us. We were hiding under a hospital trolley, tucked in an alcove, looking out through the aluminium zig-zags of its supports. The doctor's white rubber boots, which didn't come up as far as proper black Wellingtons, squeaked on the linoleum tiles of the floor. For an awful moment, we thought that the doctor had heard our breathing and was about to check under the gurney.

But he just walked straight past, his feet only inches from our faces. When he reached the end of the corridor, he farted. We had to put our hands over our mouths to stop ourselves laughing out loud. After a contented pause, the doctor's boots squeaked off along the next corridor.

Quickly, we scrambled out from under the trolley and made our way into the Pathology Department.

The mortuary was a long, icy-cold room with metal tables. I examined them carefully. They had raised edges, so the blood wouldn't spill onto the floor. They sloped slightly, so the blood would run into a plug-hole. Underneath each table was a bucket, for collecting the blood. The room smelt of strong thick chemicals – the average hospital smell multiplied and intensified. There were instruments on a trolley with rubber wheels: saws for taking the tops off skulls, pincer-clippers for cutting through ribs. I wasn't squeamish. By now, I had dissected so many animals that the insides of things – their smells and gooinesses – didn't bother me at all. Paul's father's cat, Tabitha, had been just the latest in a long line of experiments, starting with insects and a dead mouse I'd once found still alive in a trap. I was eight. A cat wasn't even the largest thing I'd ever opened up. On one occasion, I found a dead badger in the bushes beside Holy Walk. It was too heavy to lug home. The next day, I returned with my tool kit and set merrily to work. I kept some of its teeth, as souvenirs. The others didn't know everything there was to know about this. I knew more about everything than they did. Especially about important things: the facts of life and death. It was one of the sources of my leadership.

'Let's go before he comes back,' said Peter, chicken.

'No,' I said. 'Not yet.'

As we tiptoed and whispered our way around the mortuary, I could tell that Paul and Peter were far more scared than I was.

One whole wall of the room was made up of oblong locker doors. There were no labels.

'Come on,' I said, and pulled one open.

So easily did it glide that I almost fell over backwards from the surprising lack of resistance.

'Eugh,' said Peter.

When I went round to have a look, I saw a pair of old grey-haired feet with big yellow toenails. They had started to turn black around the edges, like going-off carrots.

'Gosh,' said Paul.

The rest of the dead person was covered over with a white plastic sheet. We went and stood around the head end. I don't know what any of us were expecting to see when I pulled back the sheet. Perhaps a mangled head; perhaps no head at all. The dead person had lots of clumps of white hair, like lambswool caught on a barbwire fence. Their face had obviously been very wrinkly whilst they were alive, but now they were dead it was as if their mother had ironed all the creases out.

'Is it a man?' asked Peter.

'It's dead,' said Paul. 'It isn't either.'

'Let's have a look,' I said, pulling the sheet off the dead person's chest.

It was still impossible to tell. He or she had floppy breasts, with the odd hair standing out, white against the grey.

'It's a man,' said Peter.

'I told you,' said Paul. 'Dead people aren't either.'

I tugged the sheet off completely, revealing nothing – no old, dead, shrivelled penis, no dangly-scrotumed balls.

'Agh!' gasped Paul, stepping back. 'It's a woman.'

'I thought you said dead people weren't either,' I said, pleased.

The area where the dead woman's penis would have been, had she been a man, was almost as clear of hairs as her chest. Even though we could now see all of her at once, it was still not obvious that she was, or had been, female rather than male. I reached out a finger and prodded her right breast. It was cold, like a chicken defrosting on a tray on the kitchen table. It gave no resistance. My finger went deep.

Paul, who had gone to the toe-tag, now read out the dead woman's name. I forget what it was: Margaret or Marjorie or Maude – one of those dinosaur names that are now largely extinct.

Next, I touched her fanny.

'What are you doing?' hissed Peter, almost unable to look. The baby.

'I need to be sure,' I said.

'Sure of what?' he asked.

I pulled the two pieces of skin apart.

'Sure that it is a woman. Sure that when you die, it doesn't just go back up inside you.'

I had a look, but couldn't see anything particularly interesting.

Paul now had no choice. He had to touch the body, too. He couldn't let me be the only one who had done something so important. Tentatively, he reached out a forefinger and prodded her round about her fatty waist.

I grabbed his wrist and pushed his hand as far as I could into the soft dead flesh.

Angrily, he tried to pull away, but I held on and on.

When I let him go, he stared at the place on the woman he'd been touching.

'Now there'll be a big handprint there,' I said. 'Your finger-prints will be all over her.'

'What about yours?' said Paul. 'Yours are in much worse places.'

'I don't care,' I said, which was true.

Peter had backed away. He knew what was coming. Paul said, 'Now Peter has to put his fingerprints on her, too.'

'No,' he said. 'No, I don't.'

Paul grabbed hold of him before he could get away. I ducked under the sliding shelf and trapped Peter's other arm.

'Don't scream,' I whispered. 'Or we'll all be caught.'

Together, we dragged him back to the dead woman. He tried frantically to escape, but together Paul and I were too strong for him. His lips were sucked tight over his teeth, and he was breathing hard through his nose, all in an effort not to yell out.

'On three,' I said calmly to Paul. 'One – two –'

Together, we pressed his hands down into the cold white soft fatty body of the old dead woman. He let out a yelp, as if he were a dog that had just been kicked unexpectedly.

We held him in position for a few seconds, then let go. To our astonishment, he didn't move. His hands remained where we'd placed them.

'I'm not scared any more,' he said. 'It's only a dead person, isn't it?'

His voice was shaking, but we still believed him.

He took the old woman's left wrist in his hand, lifted it up a little then let it slap back onto the stainless steel.

'Wake up! Wake up!' he said, quite lightly.

Not wanting to be outdone, I went up to her head and pulled out a fleecy clump of her hair. It came away very easily, as if it had hardly been attached at all.

'What did you do that for?' asked Paul.

'I'm experimenting,' I said.

'Throw it in the bin,' said Paul, meaning the clump of hair.

'No,' I said. 'I've got a much better idea.'

I went to stick the hair up inside her fanny.

'They'll find it,' said Paul. 'They'll cut her open and find it.'

'It's only hair,' I said. 'People always have hair.'

'Not inside them, they don't,' said Peter.

I twisted the hair round my fingers for a moment, then went and dropped it in a bin beside one of the sinks.

As soon as my back was turned, the other two began to whisper to each other. I also heard the white sheet being pulled back over the woman's body.

'That's all right,' I said in a voice louder than before, deliberately making them jump. 'I'm bored of that one. Let's use another.'

'No,' said Paul. 'I think we should go.'

'Yes,' agreed Peter. 'Before we're caught.'

'Let's find a girl,' I said.

The first two drawers I tried were empty. The third contained an old woman, almost indistinguishable from the other, the only difference being this one had a caved-in mouth (false teeth). The fourth was empty. The fifth was far more exciting: it was a young man. Unlike the others, his skin wasn't a glowy white. It was black and crimson and a dark olive-green. He had obviously been violently killed. His nose was broken, and when I touched his skull, it felt soft and squidgy. There was a lattice of cuts on his face and a blackish bruise striped diagonally across his chest.

'Car crash,' I said, forensically.

Peter looked at me. 'Just like Matthew's parents,' he said.

I pushed shut the fifth drawer, then pulled open the sixth. I flicked back the sheet.

The sixth dead person was Matthew.

However, it took us several moments to come to this extraordinary realization.

At first we were just shocked to have found someone so young and so dead. A life had been ended which had, we assumed, been well worth living. This young man was just like us.

It was only after we had taken in his blond hair, his slightly

165

swollen head, his opalescent-mottled skin, that we realized who he was.

*

'It's him, isn't it?' asked Peter, clearly unsure.

'I think so,' said Paul.

I ripped the sheet off the body and dropped it to the floor.

We had all of us seen Matthew naked before, but never motionless, never lying down. It made a difference. We had taken baths together, got changed in the same cubicle at the swimming pool, undressed for bed round at each other's houses. It made a big difference. He lay there, both himself as we had known him and someone completely different. His face muscles had relaxed, and he seemed to be slightly, secretly smiling. There were some small red marks on his forearms, where the needles they'd used to try and save his life had been slid smoothly in and pulled quickly out. There was something ghostly about dead-Matthew's appearance. We could tell he still had weight, but it was as if he were floating above the steel drawer rather than resting upon it. Matthew's hair was the same bright blond as always, but his skin had changed completely. It seemed like a different substance altogether: like marble or raspberry-ripple ice-cream or ice. We knew that he was solidly *there*, yet we felt the desire to reach over and touch him: just to confirm his presence as a definite fact; and at the same time, we dreaded that very confirmation – and so didn't reach out towards him, didn't touch him. Matthew looked very beautiful, though we would never have allowed ourselves to utter that word at the time. We would rather have said happy or peaceful or just plain dead. However, Matthew's deadness was completely different to the old woman's: his was a live deadness, hers, a completely dead one. We each of us looked at dead-Matthew and saw him as ourself, just as he would have looked at each one of dead-us, and seen himself. This wasn't just the death of Matthew, it was the death of the old Gang. There would be a new Gang, I was certain of that. But it would be very different to the old. It would be cased upon a single thing: the fact of Matthew lying here, dead, and us standing around him, alive.

Our hearts felt like wild animals cornered within us.

'They said he was going to be all right,' hissed Peter. 'They told me he was going to be all right.'

'Don't talk so loud,' said Paul, louder than Peter had been talking.

'He's not really dead,' said Peter. 'He's just pretending. He sneaked down here to wait for us.'

He reached out and prodded Matthew in the arm. Matthew, of course, didn't react; Matthew wasn't Matthew any more.

'Cold,' he said.

'He's dead,' I said. 'They lied to us.'

'Why did they lie?' asked Peter, who was getting hysterical. 'Did we do something wrong? Are we going to get punished? Is it our fault?'

I grabbed Peter and put my hand over his mouth. Paul took hold of his flailing useless arms.

'We need to get out of here,' said Paul.

I could feel my hand becoming hot with Peter's breath and wet with his tears. He shook his head from side to side as much as he could. His eyes were still on Matthew's dead body, so I began to turn him to face in the opposite direction. Paul felt what I was trying to do, and assisted me.

'Can you hold him?' he asked.

'Of course,' I said, quickly putting Peter's neck in an arm-lock.

Paul went and picked up the sheet from the floor. He covered Matthew's body over, just as when we'd found it.

Paul pushed the drawer back into the steel wall. As soon as it was shut, there was no way to tell it from any of the other drawers.

But they contained only dead people, Matthew's contained an entirely dead world.

'All right?' asked Paul.

'All right,' I said.

Peter struggled a bit more. Paul stood squarely opposite him.

'If we let you go, will you be quiet?' he asked.

Peter tried to nod his head.

'If you make a sound,' I said, 'I will strangle you.'

The head shook and shook.

I let him go.

He breathed heavily, but didn't speak. He was humiliated. For a while, he bent over with his hands on his knees. When he looked up, I could still see the red marks of my fingers on his face.

'I'm sorry,' he said.

I let him suffer for a moment, then said, 'That's all right.'

'It's not my fault,' he said.

'We know it's not your fault,' said Paul. 'It's their fault.'

'We need to get out of here,' I said. 'Stay here.'

I did a quick recce of the corridor. The doctor with the white Wellington boots was back at his desk.

I briefed the others, then said, 'Let's see if we can find another way out.'

In ten minutes it became clear that the corridor through which we had entered was the corridor by which we would have to leave. I thought fast, and came up with a brilliant plan.

'Paul,' I said. 'You sleepwalk, don't you?'

I knew he did, because he'd once done it whilst staying round mine for the night. My father had found him downstairs, sitting at the kitchen table, eating an imaginary breakfast with an imaginary knife and fork.

'Not for ages,' said Paul. 'Why?'

I explained my plan. After some reluctance, Paul agreed to go along with it. He was worried he'd get in trouble. I convinced him we'd get in far worse trouble if we were all caught.

We hid out of sight whilst Paul pretended to sleepwalk past the doctor at the desk.

At one stage, it almost looked like Paul was going to stroll right by in front of him without being spotted. But once he'd spotted Paul, the doctor behaved exactly as I'd anticipated. He didn't dare wake a sleepwalker. Instead, he escorted him towards the lifts. Peter and I followed behind the two of them at a safe distance. Paul played his part quite magnificently. Had I not already known that he was shamming, even I would have been convinced. We waited until the lift doors had closed behind Paul and his escort before making our way back up the emergency staircase.

'Will he be punished?' asked Peter, his voice echoing slightly in the tall stairwell.

'This is a hospital, not a school or home,' I said. 'They don't punish people in hospital.'

'Then why were you afraid of being caught?'

'I wasn't afraid,' I said. 'I was just anxious to avoid unnecessary complications.'

'I can't believe Matthew is dead. Do you think it could have been someone else, and we got it wrong?'

I knew there was absolutely no chance of that. Whilst restraining Peter, I'd seen Paul check the name on the toe-tag. Afterwards, he'd looked up at me and sadly nodded his head. (He hadn't even needed to do that: I had seen the change come over him. He was suddenly someone much older, much tougher.)

'It was him,' I said. 'It was definitely him.'

'But why?' said Peter.

'I don't know,' I said. 'That's what I'm going to find out.'

Before Peter and I split up, I grabbed him by the throat and said, 'You mustn't let anyone know you know Matthew is dead.

169

We need to see how long they go on lying to us for. We can't give them any hint we went on an explore.'

I squeezed Peter's neck almost as tight as I could, just to make sure he knew that if he failed to follow orders I would make him suffer very badly and for a long time.

'You can ask them in the morning if he's all right,' I said. 'Like you would of anyway. But if they tell you he's doing well, you have to act like you believe them.'

'I understand,' said Peter. He was clearly the weakest member of Gang.

I had little doubt that Paul, independently, would follow the correct course of action. Yet he couldn't let on that he knew Matthew was dead, because, of course, if he did, then no-one would believe he'd really been sleepwalking. His options were severely limited by this. But safely so.

I let go of Peter's throat and said goodnight.

We made it back to our beds without being spotted.

*

They waited until after we'd had breakfast the next morning before telling us that Matthew was dead. The same doctor spoke to all of us, separately, one after the other. Our parents had been called in to be with us when we received the bad news.

Peter's parents, I later heard, were embarrassed by the whole thing. His mother kept touching his forehead, to check if he had a fever. His father stood in the far corner of the room with his back to Peter, looking out the window.

His mother said, 'You don't have to go into school this week.'

The Doctor said, 'You've had a big shock.'

'And if you don't feel like going in next week, that's fine by us,' said his mother.

The Doctor said, 'It will take you a while to get over this.'

And Peter's father added, 'But the week after that, I should think you'll have to go in.'

Paul's parents held both his hands and told him to cry if he felt like it. They assured him that Matthew hadn't suffered at all. They promised to stay with Paul until it was time for him to go home. When they were told that Paul had been found sleepwalking the night before, they attributed it to his almost supernatural sensitivity. (Paul's mother often tried to force Tarot readings upon Paul.)

'You must have known already,' she said. 'Unconsciously.'

The doctor, however, was very careful not to mention where exactly Paul's sleepwalk had taken him.

My father and mother were much more sensible and much less embarrassing than this. They also said I didn't have to go into school for a few weeks. (The Doctor had obviously prescribed this to all our parents as the most curative thing they could do for us.) I could see that my mother wanted to be weak, to cry and hug me, but that my father was keeping her sensibly in hand. Once the Doctor had finished describing how quietly and peacefully Matthew had died, as if death were an athletic event in which points were awarded for style, my father sat down beside me and spoke, man to man: 'Matthew was a good soldier. One of the best. Remember that time he fell out of the tree. Didn't complain. Knew it was best not to cause too much fuss. He was back up and on his feet again in no time whatsoever. Just like you're going to be. There are always going to be casualties in War. Matthew was given a real tough tittie to suck on. But he took it, like the little man we all knew he was. I'm sure if he were here now, he'd tell you to carry on as per usual. Don't be knocked too far off course by this. It was a tragic error of judgement not to get him to Johnny Doctor sooner. But you have to believe that the grandparents blame themselves far more than you could ever blame them. Matthew was like their own son. I'm sure you're going to see this through in fine style. No blubbing, and all that. We'll make sure he gets a decent send-off.

Full military honours. And then it's off to fight another day, eh? You know it's what he'd want you to do.'

'Yes, Dad,' I said. 'That's what we'll do.'

But I was thinking about what he'd let slip: about how Matthew's grandparents hadn't got to Johnny Doctor soon enough.

'I'm proud of you, son,' said my father, and ruffled my blond hair.

I smiled. The news-breaking Doctor smiled, too, although I noticed that his eyebrows were raised. I spoke to him directly: 'Was it their fault that Matthew died – his grandparents', I mean?'

The Doctor hesitated for a moment before saying, 'They called us as early as they possibly could. Everything that could be done was done. Matthew's condition worsened very rapidly indeed. I don't think it would have made any difference . . .' But he didn't complete the sentence. My mother now took over, flimflammingly.

'You shouldn't think about that,' she said. 'What's important now is just to get you back home as soon as possible.'

The Doctor spoke to them over my head.

'We just have a few more tests to do, and then he's free to go. It shouldn't take more than an hour. Once we're sure he's clear, you can take him home. It's only a few injections. You can wait with him here, if you like.'

My father decided that this time would be more profitably spent stocking up on paint, screws and nails at a nearby iron-monger's. My mother wanted to stay but, between us, we managed to convince her I'd be all right on my own.

'We mustn't baby the boy,' said my father. 'He has to learn to take the knocks, just like the rest of us.'

As we drove home, I sat on the back seat with my fingers in a large brown-paper bag of 3" nails. The harsh-sweet smell of new metal filled the whole car.

*

172

really violent game of War. We could be certain that, once here, no grown-up would tell us to simmer down or to put a sock in it. This was because our screams could not be heard above, or even distinguished from, the squeals of the pigs in the abattoir. The Pond backed right up against the killing shed. Playing War beside Kittenbag Pond was the most actionous thing, ever. To-day, however, there was to be no screaming. After parking our bikes, Peter and I seated ourselves beneath a large laurel bush which was the main piece of cover near the water's edge. The light here was a dulcet brown: the colour of sugar burnt just enough to make it acrid but not so much that it becomes inedibly bitter. Some patches of light came through, egg-custardy. But, for the most part, we spoke our slow words through a roughness of shadow and a cage of beams. I had a couple of cigarettes I'd stolen from my mother's handbag. We sat and passed them back and forth between us, staring out through the gaps in the laurel and out over the reflections in the water. We both felt the same emotions: the same suffocating anger and disgust. But my feelings were the more powerful, because they were the more clearly focused. I knew the names of those towards whom our anger should be directed. I knew the very people who merited our total disgust. We talked a little, but not much. What we talked about is something that neither of us ever felt like mentioning again afterwards. It was the deep kind of talk that young men are sometimes capable of, when they get beneath banter and boasting. Our grief seemed for a while to be burying us. No-one had known Matthew as profoundly as we, for we had been him and he would always remain us. At moments, all we could say to each other was, 'He's dead – I can't believe he's dead.' Yet, there was a focus to our silence, clearly. We sat around our anger as if it were a campfire. With only the odd splutter or crackle. 'Dead,' one of us said. 'Dead.' It made our faces glow hot and red. There were things we would have cast into the flames, had they been within our easy grasp. Our Ganghood had been simultaneously shattered and rededicated. If we stabbed the sticks we had sharpened a little deeper into the earth, lit more matches, used obscenities with greater force and frequency, if we were more attempted-manly than ever before, then we had good reason. No simple expression of anger came our way. At least, not initially. Yet we knew it would come and that, when it came, we would recognize it. That's what we waited for, under the laurel bush at Kittenbag Pond. Each of us looked for it in the other's hunched back and dirtied fingers. For let us say this: we had been special, the four of us. And now, the three of us that remained, in finding a direction for our anger, would find also a new kind of specialness.

'The funeral is on Friday,' said Peter.

'Did you get an invitation, too?' I asked.

'It was on thick card and had black round the edges,' he said. 'They addressed it to my parents, so they're coming along, as well. They spelt our surname wrong.'

'They're so stupid,' I said, but held back from offering the fatal confirmation.

Peter said, 'I suppose that means Paul will be going, too.'

'He must be under interrogation at the moment.'

Both of us knew the terrible fate that had been awaiting Paul once he got home from the hospital. His parents would have been all over him: trying to force him to confess, to let them know what he was thinking, to share the vital information he had.

'He was a good man,' said Peter, interrupting my thoughts. It took me a moment to realize that he meant Matthew, not Paul.

'Yes,' I said. 'We won't see his like again.'

'The best,' said Peter.

I disagreed: I was the best. Next came Matthew. Then Paul. Then Peter. But I let it pass. Now wasn't the time for argument.

Matthew deserved our praises, even if they were a little exaggerated.

When it began to get dark, we cycled home.

*

The day of the funeral was the first unmistakably Autumnal day of the year. Wetness seemed implicit in the lowering sky, though it did not actually rain. Occasionally the fat grey clouds above us thinned out enough to give a hint, a tint, a memory of blue. When the breeze struck our cheeks, it was like the sloppily affectionate lick of a dog you secretly hate.

Matthew was to be buried in Amplewick Churchyard, just across the Gravel Lane from Wychwood. (See Map.) It was obvious to us that Wychwood itself was where Matthew would want to be buried. He had always hated God and all that Sunday school malarky. Eventually his grandparents stopped forcing him to go, and he was able to spend all of every weekend with us.

The families gathered at the front of the church, with graves on either side of them. Our parents, who didn't really like each other, pretended that they did. Paul's father and my father even shook hands, though they didn't speak.

After exchanging a couple of desperate glances with us, Paul was able to take the opportunity of this handshake to escape from his father's grip.

'Greetings,' said Peter.

'Welcome back,' I said. 'How's it been?'

'Hell on earth,' said Paul. 'They haven't let me alone for one single minute.'

(Paul subsequently elaborated on this statement. His mother and father had been worse than ever before. They had practically *demanded* that he start crying whenever they felt he should. But Paul was made of tougher stuff. I'd seen it in his face, back when he'd checked Matthew's name on the toe-tag. Just as before, when he was incarcerated after the Pram Race, Paul held out. They weren't going to break him *that* easily. He treated the whole thing as a training exercise. After parachuting down behind enemy lines, his battalion had been betrayed, encircled and captured. The reinforcements had arrived too late. He'd been taken to the cellars of the local KGB HQ. His parents were the Secret Police. It was their job to break him, by whatever means they could, tough or tender. But he knew he only had to keep shtoom until the day of the funeral. This his allies (us) would be there, and hopefully he'd be able to make some kind of a break for it.)

We stood and looked at each other, silently. Paul was wearing an entirely new outfit, even down to socks and pants. His parents, we later learnt, had taken him on an especial trip to London the day before. His mother had stayed up late into the night: washing and ironing the shirt, taking up the trouser bottoms, taking in the cuffs. They called it 'an important part of the grieving process'. Paul called it 'the worst thing to happen to me in my whole life'. Peter was dressed in a grey tweed suit I'd only ever seen him wearing once before: on a school trip to see *Hamlet* in Stratford-upon-Avon. I was wearing my charcoal-coloured school blazer and trousers. My mother had tacked a black oblong patch of cloth over the school insignia on the breast pocket. The two fabrics didn't match very well, and it was obvious to everyone what she'd done.

The big black funeral cars drew up.

Matthew's grandparents were following the hearse in a big black Mercedes. We saw that Miranda was sitting between them on the back seat. She had come back from Baden-Baden-Baden a couple of days before. I wondered if she'd gone to hospital and been given the same injections we'd had.

The back of the hearse was opened up and the Vicar went to stand by it. 'Pallbearers?' he said.

Matthew's coffin wasn't quite as big as a full-sized one.

His grandparents got out of the Mercedes.

'That's us,' I said, to my fellow Gang-Members.

We moved forwards, ready to take our friend's coffin upon our shoulders. But we were ignored. Our fathers, plus one of the undertakers, had already moved into position.

The others expected me to speak up. 'We want to do it,' I said, half to the Vicar, half to everyone else. 'He was *our* friend. We want to do it.'

The Vicar looked us over, surprised. 'But there's only three of you,' he said.

Everyone had stopped talking. Everyone was paying attention. I looked at my father with pleading eyes. He didn't fail me. The Major-General had promised me a military funeral for Matthew, and a military funeral was what Matthew was going to get. 'We'll need a fourth,' he said. 'About five foot two.'

The men looked one another up and down.

'I'm five foot two,' came a voice from the edge of the group. It was Matthew's grandfather.

'Are you sure?' asked the Vicar.

'I can do this for him,' said Matthew's grandfather, 'if nothing else.'

'Well . . .' said the Vicar. 'If you're sure.'

We were furious. Having Matthew's grandfather assist us was worse even than having to watch our fathers and a complete stranger do the pallbearing.

Letting go of Miranda's hand (her grandmother had the other one), Matthew's grandfather moved into position.

The undertakers pulled the coffin out of the back of the hearse. It ran smoothly on wheels made of grey rubber, like those of the instrument trolley in the Pathology Department. I remembered the smooth drawer in which Matthew had been lying the last time we saw him.

Together, we lifted our friend's boxed body onto our shoulders. I stood front right, with Paul to my left; Matthew's grandfather was immediately behind me, Peter filled the last free space.

The coffin felt heavier than I'd expected, and the corner was already digging in to my collarbone. A little unsteady, we moved off under the Lych-Gate and down the gravel path.

The first bit of the funeral took place inside the church. We walked slowly up the aisle and laid the coffin down on a wooden frame in front of the altar. 'Thank you, boys,' said the Vicar, and then began to tell everyone lies about God and, which was far worse, about Matthew. It seemed as if he were talking not about our friend but about a completely different person: an ideal boy, who had never really existed, but had been designed by a committee of grown-ups and geriatrics. He called him kind, gentle, considerate and happy-smiling (whatever that is). He said that we would remember him best absorbed in his railway set. He said that our Headmistress (Mrs Grassmere, who was there) had described him as one of the most promising students at the school. (We were sure that, before he died, our Headmistress had hardly even known who Matthew was. He had been called in to see her once or twice about playing truant. The only other time she'd ever spoken to him was to tell him never to run along corridors. On his report, she used to write, 'Encouraging but could still do better.' Which is what Mrs Grassmere put for everyone she didn't know. Matthew hadn't been very good at school: he'd come near bottom in everything, apart from Metalwork.) The Vicar said that Matthew had shown a fundamental religious belief in everything he said or did. I wondered if this included feigning illness to get out of Sunday school. He told us that he thought Matthew had gone to a better place. And as I looked around and about me, I couldn't help but agree with that. He was the first of us to make it there, although we'd all come pretty close at one stage or another.

During the sermon, Paul, Peter and I exchanged grimaces, rolled our eyes, stuck out our tongues, and coughed. It was just like being stuck in a particularly dull school assembly.

After the bit of the funeral inside, we picked up the coffin again and carried it back down the aisle.

Matthew's grave had been dug in the far corner of the churchyard, where the new headstones stood in tighter, straighter rows.

Throughout the walk, I felt a ferocious anger at how all the specialness was being ruined by Matthew's grandfather.

The day, rain-threatened, was very close. We all began to sweat. I could sense my father, walking along beside Matthew's grandfather, ready to take over should the old man collapse. The coffin rocked back and forth, like a dining table with one leg shorter than the others: it did this diagonally, along the axis between Paul and Matthew's grandfather. The old man had lied. He was at least a couple of inches shorter than five foot two.

Part of me desperately wanted him to drop the coffin, to fall and die on the spot, killed by the strain of carrying Matthew. If that happened, everyone there would see how old and stupid he was, even though most of them tended in that direction themselves. But then I realized it would be much better for the revenge to come through us, later. We would act in Matthew's name, on his behalf, just as he would have wanted us to.

I thought about Miranda, walking along immediately behind us. I wondered if her eyes were on the gravel or on our backs. When she knew what her grandparents had done (had not done), she too would wish them dead.

We went along at a slow march, like proper soldiers, the only one out of step being Matthew's grandfather.

When we got to the graveside, we laid the coffin down on some green straps that were pointed out to us.

Throughout the last bit of the funeral, we had to keep stopping and praying. As I bowed my head, I stared down into the dirty hole that was Matthew's final resting-place. I thought about when we'd buried Paul (alive, however) only a few weeks before. It seemed to me inevitable that Paul would be thinking the same thing at that very moment. We each of us knew it could easily have been ourself who was dead. The world was definitely out to get us. The only thing that could protect us from being got by the world was Gang. It was my duty, therefore, to protect Gang absolutely. But as the praying finished, and I looked up from the grave, I realized that I had another duty of protection. She was standing directly opposite me, on the other side of her brother's grave. She was sobbing hard, and being comforted by her grandmother: one of the two people most guilty of causing her tears. If Miranda only knew, I thought, how she would flinch away in disgust.

I looked back into the hole, not wanting to be affected by Miranda's girlish tears. The graveyard had once or twice already begun to turn watery at its foundations. But I was determined to prevent its being completely flooded. My father had told me beforehand that tears at the death of a fellow soldier were the only legitimate tears a man should shed. He'd also told me to be brave, and I realized that he was watching to see how martial my behaviour was.

I looked back across the grave. Miranda, for all her crying, was a brave girl. Her cheeks were shiny and pink, and a bit of white snot dangled a moment from her nose before it was collected by her grandmother's hanky. Once or twice, when we were much younger, and he had fallen off his bike, or lost a fight, or laughed too hard, I had seen Matthew cry in a similar way. I couldn't help but be reminded of what we had all lost, what we had so stupidly been deprived of.

I made Miranda a silent promise, across the pitch pine top of her brother's coffin: We will protect you. Anyone who poses a risk to your continued safety will be eliminated. This will be one

CHAPTER SEVEN

Paul

Wenn dein Mütterlein
Tritt zur Tü'herein,
Und den Kopf ich drehe
Ihr entgegen sehe,
Fällt auf ihr Gesicht
Erst der Blick mir nicht,
Sondern auf die Stelle,
Näher nach der Schwelle,
Dort, wo würde dein
Lieb Gesichten sein,
Wenn du freudenhelle
Trätest mit herein,
Wie sonst, mein Töchterlein.

When your Mother
Enters through the door,
And I turn my Head
She is apprehended,
Yet falls not my Gaze
Firstly upon her Face
But upon that Spot
Near the Threshold
There, where formerly
Your koochy-koo Face would be,
When you, with your Exultance
Made your Entrance,
As ever, my diddy Daughter.

We meet at Base Camp Two. For a briefing. By Andrew. Eleven hundred hours. Two days after Matthew's funeral. It is raining. Hard.

The day before, my parents make me stay at home. Andrew and Peter call round on bikes, but my mother sends them away. She lies. She says I am ill. (My parents are still trying to make me crack. They don't succeed.) I stand in the doorway to the kitchen. Andrew sees me. He looks me in the eyes. I look in his eyes. He understands what I mean.

At the briefing we wear our equipment: Army Surplus anoraks, sapper shirts, combat trousers, black leather boots.

Andrew tells us all about what Matthew's grandparents didn't do.

– The bastards, I say.

There is a woman in Flathill whose son is a spastic, a real spastic. When we see her pushing him around in his wheelchair, we can tell she loves it how weak he is. He is always going to be a baby to her. When we look in his eyes, we can see how wild he is to be off, off and away with us. But his mother loves it that he'll never be able to escape.

Grown-ups, apart from Andrew's father, want us to be weak. Except Andrew's father. They want us to behave. Most of all, they want us to be like them.

*

I listen to Andrew. He makes a long speech, which is very convincing. About Matthew. And Matthew's death. Matthew's stupid death. He explains what the doctor let slip. Then he tells us what we should do with Matthew's grandparents. He explains the logic of his argument. How it is our duty to avenge Matthew. How it is only us who can protect Miranda. He leads Peter right up to the conclusion, then gives it him. Straight.

Peter hesitates.

– Kill them? he says. But that's *murder*.

– No, it's not, says Andrew. It's revenge.

I agree.

– But we'll get caught, says Peter.

– Who cares? Andrew says.

– No, we won't, I say, at just the same time. Not if we're careful.

– We have to protect Miranda, says Andrew. And we have to protect ourselves.

– I'm going home, says Peter. He looks very upset.

– Hold on, says Andrew. Let me explain.

– No, says Peter. I'm scared and I'm not doing it.

– No-one is going to do anything, I say.

– Yes, we are, says Andrew.

– No-one is going to do anything that anyone is going to get blamed for, I say, trying to make our position clear, particularly to Peter.

– We'll be caught and sent to prison, Peter says.

He gets up from sitting cross-legged. His face is one big frown. Matthew's dead, he says, not making any sense. We can't do anything.

He goes to the escape hatch and he starts to pull the corrugated iron to the side. He's leaving.

*

188

– Grab him, orders Andrew.

I get hold of his legs. Andrew grabs his arms.

– You're not going anywhere just yet, says Andrew.

Peter stops struggling. He knows it's very futile.

We will let you go, says Andrew, if you promise not to tell anyone what we're planning.

– I promise, says Peter.

– But if you want to come back in Gang, you will have to help us do this.

Peter doesn't speak.

– This is what Gang is for – it's what it was always for, we just didn't know it. Your best friend has been killed, and you say you're not going to do anything about it. Maybe he wasn't your best friend, after all.

– He was, interrupts Peter.

– This is just another covert operation, I say to Peter. We're far too clever to get caught. No-one will ever know – not unless we tell them.

Andrew flinches when I say *covert*. He wants to do something bigger. With more drama.

– The exact nature of the operation has yet to be decided, he says. But it is imperative that initial preparations are made immediately. All forces that were previously to be deployed in taking revenge against Paul's father will now be transferred to this newer, more pressing field of action.

He looks at me and says, Agreed?

– Agreed, I reply, without hesitation. I think we should lose no time at all in making some initial recces.

Peter jabs at the sand of the floor with a broken stick.

– I want to be in Gang, he says. I write the Archives. I saved them from the fire.

– And you are a hero for ever, says Andrew. But maybe we need another fire. A bigger fire.

189

– No, I say.

– What?

– I don't think a fire is a good idea.

– Do you mean burn down their house? asks Peter.

– With them inside, says Andrew. Let them feel what it's like to burn up all over, just like Matthew did.

– We can do better than that, I say. This operation does not have to involve the use of direct force.

Andrew looks at me fiercely.

– I am the Leader. If I decide we are having a fire, we are having a fire.

– It's stupid, I say. They'll know it was us.

Andrew leaps to attack me before he's even begun to shout, Don't call me stupid!

He tries to get his hands round my throat. But I beat them off. Next, he grabs at my sleeves. He wants to pull me off-balance. All the time he keeps repeating, *Don't call me stupid!*, until, after a while, he begins to sound really stupid.

This is a historic moment. We are fighting for who is Leader of Gang. We punch and kick. We both want immediate victory.

But this fight is wrong. I have picked the wrong time for it. Andrew is stronger than me. He will beat me if we fight now. It is a tactical error. He doesn't mind being hit. I do. I blame my father for this. He hasn't taught me about pain like Andrew's father has. My father is responsible.

Luckily, I am rescued because Peter decides to try and escape.

We see him go. We let him go.

It only takes a few seconds before we realize we have to chase him down.

He knows our plan. We can't risk him telling anyone about it.

190

That's just the sort of thing that a weakling like Peter can do to a plan. Ruin it before it's even got started. Andrew knows this, and I know it. We don't want to have to go to prison. Not without first having had our revenge. Peter will put us in danger, immediately. If he blabs. He is a loose cannon.

Andrew lets go of me and I let go of him.

Peter has a headstart.

Andrew is first out of the pit. The soles of his boots are ahead of me, kicking up small waves of sand.

When we get outside of Base Camp Two, we spring North-East towards the hill-top.

– There! shouts Andrew, and he points towards the War Memorial.

Peter is slowed up for a bit because of having to swing the heavy wooden gate open and shut.

We dash towards him.

Out of all Gang, Peter is the best and fastest runner. He ran for the school at 400 yards against another school, and came third.

But this time he isn't just running for the chance to win something, or please the Games Master. (Mr Spate, the second scariest teacher in school, after Mr Butcher.) He is running from fear of us.

And we aren't running just because it's a Games lesson, and if we don't we'll be punished. We are running to stop him ruining everything completely. Our lives. Everything.

Plus, from Base Camp Two to Peter's house is a distance of well over 400 yards. Perhaps four times that. Or more.

Also, Peter has taken off too fast. He is in a terrible panic.

We are different, though. We can pace ourselves like proper runners do. In the Olympic Games, for example.

Andrew is the best out of us two but only at long-distance. Probably because he is so stubborn, and will never give up.

I specialize in all other sorts of running, especially over rough ground. And even more especially The Furze. I have highly adapted techniques for this, which are mostly secret. One is, I put my feet in the gaps where there is sand between the clumps of heather. Another is, I whizz very close past the tree trunks of the silver birches.

When we get to the end of The Prom, Peter is about a hundred yards in the lead.

I am the first through the War Memorial gate, but Andrew is very close behind me.

By now, I know that we will be able to catch him long before he gets anywhere near home.

Peter looks back over his shoulder, sees us, almost stumbles, speeds up, etcetera, etcetera.

We know exactly what he is thinking. Peter always wants most of all to avoid being hit. We are his friends. He will see us again very soon, even if he gets away this time. Either round Amplewick somewhere. Or in school when we go back. He is asking himself if we will hit him more now or later. He knows that most of all we want to stop him telling anybody our plans. He is wondering, if he stops, and promises us never to tell anyone, we will let him off without a serious duffing-up. But he's not sure. He can't decide.

We run fast between the trees, getting closer to Peter with every single second that passes.

Peter decides. Peter stops.

He will take his chances with us here. Rather than spend a

week in hiding, unable to leave the house, and then get duffed up by us in the toilets at school.

We run up and surround him.

– Please, Peter gasps. I won't tell anyone.

I can see that Andrew wants to hurt Peter, just as his father would hurt him. Peter has been disobedient. And so Peter must be punished. Peter must be taught not to be disobedient again. We are all out of breath. We are finding it hard to speak.

– You can trust me, wheezes Peter.

– Can we? asks Andrew, then breathes in deeply. Can we?

Peter nods and gulps.

I feel like I am going to puke my guts up. My mouth tastes of brand-new from-the-dentist fillings. My head is heavy with thick gushing blood.

Andrew yawns, then takes more deep breaths.

I know that, to get to be the Gang-Leader, I will need Peter on my side. If he gets duffed up now, it will be something he will definitely remember. It might be the thing that makes him choose me over Andrew. He is a weak ally to have, and a difficult one to keep under control. But if he thinks I will duff him up less than Andrew, then he will want me to be Leader.

Peter looks at me then Andrew then me again. He wants to guess what we are going to do. He thinks we have decided. I wait until Peter is looking away from me, but Andrew is looking right at me. I nod. He sees what I mean. He understands. And straight away he biffs Peter right in the mouth. Peter tries to cover his face with his hands. He hunches up like an afraid girl, with one foot lifted off the floor. Andrew gets disgusted by this. He wants Peter to fight back. He demands it, almost. And so he hits him some more. Peter doesn't fight back. Andrew aims a couple of hard punches into Peter's kidneys and Peter falls down.

Andrew is so angry he doesn't even notice that I haven't joined in with the duffing-up. But Peter knows. Even as he is lying there in the dirt, Peter, like the big girly coward he is, knows exactly who hit him and how many times, and who didn't.

Andrew doesn't understand this at all. He thinks he's won. But I stand there knowing that everything is mine. It's just like I am half-way to being Leader already, and I ordered Andrew to hit Peter. He did exactly what I wanted.

– Get up, Andrew orders Peter.

I go to help him. A tactical error.

– Let him do it by himself, says Andrew.

Peter takes a bit of a while to stand up. A woman with a stupid dog walks past, giving us all a disapproving look. (She won't look at us like that when we save her from the invading Russkis. She'll cry and say thank you thank you.) She sees that Peter is being duffed up, but doesn't do anything about it. Nothing apart from look all lemon-lips disapproving, that is.

– I won't tell anyone, repeats Peter. Of all of us, he is the only one still out of breath.

– If you do, says Andrew. I will come and track you down wherever you escape to and I will *kill* you.

Andrew gets close to Peter and gives him a little push.

– Never try to run away, he says. You can never get away from me.

– I know, says Peter, weakly.

Now I notice it, the rain has mostly stopped. The clouds above The Furze are the charcoal colour of our school blazers. A wave of rain sweeps towards us, along the avenue of trees. It is a very dramatic moment.

Andrew turns to Peter for one final word.

– This is the most important thing that's ever happened, he says. I'm not going to let a little git like you mess it up.

At that moment, I know Peter is ready.

But Andrew is wise enough not to let me walk home with Peter, on my own. Both of us escort him back. Peter doesn't say anything. I look at him and hope the rain falling on his face will hide his crying from his parents.

We watch him walk in through his door.

We know what he will do as soon as he gets inside. He will go up into his bedroom, sit on his bed, drink orange squash and read his dinosaur books.

Andrew and I look at one another, our blond hair dark in the rain. We know what we are thinking. We share our thought. We are thinking about revenge. Andrew knows more of the facts than me, and has known them for longer, but I saw deeper into them, and was faster to see the things that swam in the depths. He wants a quick revenge. Something obvious. A fire. But I want a perfect revenge. And revenge that we can get away with. This is the big difference between us.

– Goodbye, we say.

We run home separately. I wonder what he's planning and I know he wonders what I'm planning.

For the next few days, we meet but do not discuss. We have only one thing to think about. Each of us is thinking of it on his own, and yet is not on his own in thinking of it.

We enjoy being out in the grown-up world amongst the grown-ups. Everyone else we know is in school.

Some grown-ups ask us why we aren't at school, and if they look as if they will be really hurt by it, we tell them. We say, Because one of our best friends died last week.

We do not feel disloyal to Matthew for using his death as a

195

way to shock. We know he would have wanted us to do this, if he could of told us before he died.

When someone *does* mention what we are thinking about, everybody is surprised, because it is Peter. This seems to be a very strange thing. Peter was so scaredy-cat about the plan before. But this isn't the last time that Peter surprises us.

It is a dry but windy day. We have cycled out to the Tree-Fort. The route we have taken is Hill, not Road.

We are sitting round a small fire. The sticks in it are damp, and they are making a lot of crackly noise and blackish smoke.

Peter speaks up. I've been thinking, he says. I've been reading, too.

Andrew is already bored.

– Books, he says. What can you learn from books?

– What, Peter? I ask.

– You know my favourite book, he begins.

I see him reach into his knapsack.

– The dinosaur one? I say.

He smiles, glad that I know. But we both know, really. It's just that Andrew isn't saying. The blue-covered book emerges in his hands. Peter still has the brittle, flaky dust-jacket. He hides it in a drawer, and it is mended with sticky-backed plastic. He takes his book with him wherever he goes. Even when he goes on holiday.

When he turns the cover, I can see he has written down all the places: Cornwall, Devon, Suffolk and Cornwall again.

He reads out the title, like he is saying the most important thing in the world.

– '*The Death of the Dinosaurs: A Scientific Investigation and Explication*, by Dr Teddy Shawcross, FRGS [Fellow of the Royal Geographical Society]. With some speculations as to evolution. Thirty plates.'

Andrew says, We know all about it. For what Andrew calls *the dinosaur craze* died out ages ago. He lost interest almost as soon as his father helped him collect all the cards given away free in packets of PGTips teabags.

At Primary School, Peter wanted Andrew's Brontosaurus so much that it was one reason for him joining our gang. (It wasn't called Gang in the beginning.)

– No, but listen to this, says Peter. His fingers find the page he means.

– 'One of the dinosaurs most ill-adapted for survival in this new climate was the Brontosaurus. A large, clumsy animal, sometimes exceeding forty feet in length and thirty tonnes in weight, the Brontosaurus lived most of its life half-submerged in water. Its favourite habitat was the deep swamplands which formed such a common feature of the Jurassic landscape. With its long arching neck, surmounted, like a dolphin's, with a blow-hole (in the head), the Brontosaurus could, when necessary, hide itself almost completely under water. This was a particularly handy trick when it came to avoiding the fearsome Tyranno-saurus Rex (See Next Chapter). The Brontosaurus's diet con-sisted mostly of raw vegetable matter: vast trailing pondweed and the leaves of waterside trees. There is some evidence to suggest that the Brontosaurus's elongated neck, like the giraffe's, evolved to help give it an advantage in reaching loftier foliage and more profoundly submerged weeds. Perhaps the most remarkable fact about the Brontosaurus, apart from its sheer size (no animal of similar tonnage has walked the earth either before or since) was its gross stupidity. Despite possessing the body of a veritable Titan, it could boast a brain no larger than that of a common or garden farmyard chicken. Added to this was the handicap of an only rudimentarily developed nervous system.' (Peter stumbles over some of the words.) 'Recent scien-tific research has shown that messages within the body of a

Brontosaurus travelled so slowly that if one had chopped off the very tip of its tail, this cumbersome animal would not have felt anything was amiss until three whole minutes had passed.' (I could see that Andrew was so bored that he was thinking about hitting Peter to make him shut up. But I wasn't bored at all: I knew what Peter meant in what he said. Already I could anticipate what he was going to say in conclusion.) 'Given this massive handicap, a stupidity unparalleled in all creation, it is hardly surprising that the Brontosaurus was one of the very first of the dinosaurs to die out, following the catastrophic event detailed in Chapter Ten. When the earth shook, the waters receded, the temperature rose, and the sky darkened, it was the smaller, more adaptive creatures that were able to survive. In its antiquated slowness and bulk, the Brontosaurus is emblematic –' (Another stumble) '– of an entire genus of "impossible beasts". The only animals alive today with which we might compare the Brontosaurus and its ilk are the blue whales. These marine giants populate, in ever-decreasing numbers, our seven oceans. They, too, may one day pay the evolutionary price of vast size combined with minute intellect. A magnificent specimen of a Brontosaurus skeleton is on view in the Grand Entrance Hall of the Natural History Museum in London. To view it is surely to be awed. The greatest leap the imagination can take is truly to believe that such creatures really existed. Yet the conditions for their demise were exactly those that favoured the ascendancy of *Homo erectus* and, eventually, *Homo sapiens* – ourselves.'

After Peter stops, Andrew waits for a minute, then he says, If we wanted to be in school, we could.

– There's one other bit, says Peter. Let me read it, then I'll explain everything.

Andrew pulls a stick out of the fire and closely examines its orange flame.

– All right, he says. But don't go on for too long.

Peter finds another page, almost at the end of the book. He begins to read again, his voice ringing high and strong off the tree trunks that circle us.

– 'And so we can see that this is the way in which evolution works. Darwin called it "the survival of the fittest". This does not just mean "fittest" in the sense that one might use it of racehorses or athletes. It also means most fit, most adapted, most apt. Those organisms which have outlived the time of their fitness, or have lost their ability to alter themselves so as to remain fit, will inevitably, and rapidly, become extinct. The catastrophic event, whatever it was, necessitated the death of the dinosaurs. But we should not mourn their passing. Extinction is not only Nature's way, it is Nature's very self. For without obsolescence, there would be no renewal. Without decadence, no progress. Without death, no life. And without the death of the dinosaurs, the human race itself could not have come into existence. Darwin's theory of evolution, perhaps the greatest discovery of the greatest age of discovery, gives us a model by which to understand the world we live in today. If we are to survive, we will have to ensure that it is ourselves – and not some other breed of creature – who are fittest.'

Peter closes the book. He looks over at Andrew, trying to guess his reaction. I do, too.

To people that don't know Andrew, it would look just like he is stabbing the fire with his stick.

But Peter and me, who know Andrew the best in the world, can detect the real signs of what is going on. These are the signs that happen when Andrew is thinking his deepest thoughts or making his hardest decisions. His brow is wrinkled. His lips pout. One of the eyelids twitches slightly.

Then, next moment, his mouth goes over to one side of his face. Once. Twice. He takes a quick breath, then lets it squeeze out between his teeth and his cheek. The sound is like a duck farting. Then Andrew relaxes his mouth, and he makes some louder fart-noises. Finally, he spits into the fire where it is whitest.

– They are the dinosaurs, he says. And we are the catastrophe.

– Exactly, says Peter. I knew you'd get it. How I missed it for so long before, I just don't know. Once I realized, it seemed so obvious. They are the dinosaurs; we are the catastrophe.

– No, I say. We aren't the catastrophe. We are *Homo sapiens*. We are what survives and triumphs. If all we are is the catastrophe, then there is no future. We have to be the thing that survives.

– But we all agree, says Andrew, that the dinosaurs should die.

– Yes, I say.

Peter still hesitates.

– Why would you want them to live? asks Andrew.

– He's dying already, Peter asserts.

– Not fast enough, Andrew interjects.

– He has the Big C. We don't need to kill him. And when he dies, she will die as well. They always do.

– But we don't just want them to die, explains Andrew. We want it to be us that kills them. And, at the very end, they must know – they must know that it's because of what they did to Matthew.

– Yes, says Peter, finally giving in. I hate the dinosaurs. I can't think of anything that's too bad to happen to them.

Andrew says, Don't worry. Extremely bad things are going to happen to them.

We know we are staying out too late. Our parents will tell us off when we get home. But none of us wants to leave.

The day after, I go round Peter's before I'm really meant to. At quarter past nine in the morning.

The hall ceiling is still burnt black. Peter's father and mother are out at work. I have two cigarettes which I have stolen from my mother's shoulder-bag.

– We can't smoke those here, says Peter. They'd go mental if they caught me.

– Let's go somewhere else, then, I say.

– I thought we were meeting at Base Camp One, to discuss.

Peter is right. That was the plan we made at the end of yesterday. But I want to talk to him, away from Andrew. I need to make sure of him.

– Not till ten hundred hours, I say. Let's go out back.

Behind Peter's house is a large field. It is full of almost nothing but nettles.

A path in between the tall stingers comes out at a fallen tree trunk. This is where we always go to smoke our secret cigarettes.

– All right, says Peter, and sets off.

I want to say something nice to Peter, first of all.

– That was brilliant, what you said, yesterday, I say. A real breakthrough.

– Well, I suppose, in a way, I've been working up to it for some time.

– But the way you presented it . . . You were very brave to keep going when Andrew interrupted.

– I felt I had to get to the end, at the very least.

– He didn't get it at all to start with, did he?

– I expect he was just considering the full ramifications.

I realize that I have gone too far too fast.

– Of course, I say. But nonetheless, I think you were well aware of those ramifications even as you began.

– Well . . . says Peter, always too modest.

– And I'm sure you know that extinction is a gradual process.

– It is, he says. It's very slow indeed.

We reach the tree trunk and climb it. I light one cigarette with some Swan Vesta matches that I keep handy.

I decide to stop saying anything but to wait and see if Peter says anything himself.

We look out across the field of nettles. They are green and silver in colour. The dew upon their leaves makes it appear as if a hundred million tiny spiders have covered them all over with webs.

The nettlefield is a very secure location. Peter's parents never venture out here.

We could easily wade out to somewhere further off from the tree trunk, and even more secure. We'd probably get stung a couple of times, little white dots itching on our knuckles. (You can treat a nettle sting easily enough by pressing a dock leaf on.) But, for now, the tree trunk is quite secure enough.

I am still waiting. I smoke.

– Paul, says Peter. Why do you think the doctors asked us about kissing? What did that have to do with anything?

I tell him I believe that it is one of the ways people get the illness Matthew got.

– But can the doctors tell if you caught it that way rather than any other?

I tell him I am sure they can't.

– Oh, says Peter. Shall we go and find Andrew?

– Not just yet, I say.

The breeze feels very damp and Autumnish. The tree trunk is rotten, and smells rotten, too.

On the horizon, the trees are starting to turn into stick-figures.

– When did it happen? I ask.

Did what happen? says Peter, too-suddenly.

– The kissing, I say. The kissing you are so worried about.

– I don't know what you're talking about.

Peter moves to drop down off the tree trunk, but then stops.

He doesn't want me to see that he is running away, and if he drops it would be obvious.

– If you tell me about it, I won't tell Andrew.

Peter this time does slide himself off the tree trunk. His landing is bad, and he stumbles forward.

– We didn't kiss, he says.

I wait. I don't speak. I know Peter hates silences. He hates it when he has to speak to make sure that the silence stops.

– We both spat a lot into different cups, then we dared each other to drink each other's spit. It was Matthew's idea. We did it down in one. So, we never kissed.

– Why did you do it?

– To become stronger. Matthew wanted us to think of the most disgusting things we could do, and then do them. That way we'd know we weren't scared of anything.

I am interested by this idea. It sounds good and logical.

– What else did you do?

– Nothing, says Peter. They were experiments – a series of experiments. This was the third.

– When did this happen?

– Just after Matthew fell out of the tree on Pram Race Day. You weren't being allowed out. He told me he wasn't scared of anything any more. He said he would prove it.

I wait to see if there is anything more Peter will say. There isn't.

I drop the finished cigarette onto the wet ground.

– You won't tell Andrew, will you? Not now I've told you. You said you wouldn't.

To make him sweat badly, I jump off the tree trunk and start walking away quite quickly through the nettles.

Peter takes a couple of steps to catch me up, then he shoves me in the back.

– You won't tell him, will you?

I turn round so that we are 'face-to-face'.

– Depends.

– On what?

– On if you agree with me about something.

– About what?

– You know, I say.

– About the extinction? asks Peter.

– Yes, I say. Andrew wants a catastrophic event. I think if he gets one of those, the police will catch us and we'll all get sent to prison. He thinks the way to kill dinosaurs is to burn them to death. But we know different. We know that extinction is a gradual process. The dinosaurs become weaker and weaker. They start to live in a world that isn't very kind to them any more. Things hurt them. Not big things. Little things. Things they wouldn't even have noticed before. One day the dinosaurs realize they might be dying. They fight for a while. But then they realize it's already too late. They give up hope. Their extinction goes faster. It is over quite quickly and quite quietly. The dinosaurs are taken away in an ambulance. We never seem them again. The End.

Peter looks down at the ground.

– I don't want to go to prison, he says. I can't – I wouldn't –

– You don't have to, I say. I put my hand on his shoulder, like a man. And Andrew doesn't have to know about your experiment with Matthew. Not ever.

– I told you, Peter whines. It was his idea.

– I believe you, I say. Of course I believe you. But I don't think Andrew would. I think he'd think you were guilty. I think he might even think you did kiss Matthew. On the lips.

Peter looks as if he is going to cry.

– With tongues, I add.

– It was Matthew's idea, he repeats. I didn't want to do it.

– As long as you promise to agree with me about the extinc-tion, I say. No one will ever know.

Peter looks up at me. His eyes are full of the tears of a grateful weak person.

– I promise, he says. Yours is a better plan, anyway.

– Come on, I say. Let's go and find Andrew.

We go on bikes.

I am pulsating with pride. It's not official, but I know I am now Gang-Leader.

Andrew thinks he's still one hundred per cent in control.

One day soon, he may come to believe that it was him not me who made us change plan. He may lie and say that he never wanted a catastrophic event. But I know, and Peter knows, that we decided this. Here. Now.

I am in control. Because Peter never wants Andrew to know what he did. How he perhaps killed Matthew.

I ride fast. My knees bump against the crossbar.

Peter, like always, can't keep up.

When we arrive at Base Camp One, Andrew is already waiting for us there.

– You're late, he says. Where have you been?

– Peter couldn't get away, I say. His mother was making him drink all his glass of *milk*.

Peter understands my threat, my reference.

– Well, Andrew announces. It's time to discuss.

We sit down.

Andrew begins.

After this, everything goes as I planned.

Andrew gets very angry. He calls us traitors. He issues a direct order for us to obey him. But we don't budge an inch.

When he realizes he is defeated, Andrew tells me I can now be Co-Gang-Leader. He promotes me to Sub-Lieutenant.

Finally, we are agreed:

The Dinosaurs must be extinct before Christmas.

CHAPTER EIGHT

Peter

Wenn dein Mütterlein
Tritt zur Tür herein,
Mit der Kerze Schimmer,
Ist es mir, als immer
Kämst du mit herein,
Huschtest hinterdrein,
Als wie sonst ins Zimmer!
O du, des Vaters Zelle,
Ach, zu schnelle
Erloschner Freudenschein!

When your Mother
Enters through the Door,
In the Candle shine-shift,
It seems almost as if
You too accompanied her
In-flitting behind her,
Just as ever, into my Life!
O you, your Father's woudjkin,
Agh! too soon
Extinguished Joylightbeing!

THE ARCHIVES

THE OFFICIAL ARCHIVES OF ~~THE~~ GANG AS KEPT BY PETER EAST (CORPORAL)

A HISTORY OF ~~THE~~ GANG

We met in Cub Scouts, originally. <u>Andrew</u> was there first and then there was <u>Paul</u>. And after that <u>Matthew</u> and <u>Peter</u> arrived together. It all took about almost a year. Andrew and Matthew were at school together (Oakleaf Junior School) but were not friends because Andrew was a year ahead and because he thought Matthew was stupid.

   In Cub Scouts, we did our badges and played Wide Games. And Bob-a-Job. It was good, mostly. In the Summer there was a <u>Jamboree</u> with lots of other Cubs and Scouts. It was in the county of Devon, England. The Cub Scouts were one hundred years old. It was the <u>Silver Jubilee</u> for Queen Elizabeth II.

   In 1953 <u>Sir Edmund Hilary and Sherpa Tensing</u> climbed <u>Mount Everest</u>, which is the hightest mountain in the world, for the first time ever.

   The first to suggest we form the gang was Andrew.

```
                    N
                 Andrew
                    I
                    I
W_____I_____E
                    I
  Matthew           I           Peter
                    I
                    I
                    S
                  Paul
```

He organized us. We got names: <u>North, South, East and West</u>. Here is a useful diagram:

These were Code Names, and we used them to begin with for a short while. And so the gang was formed of all of us, with Andrew as squad leader.

It was good. We went up Wychwood and <u>played war</u>.

One day, Andrew's Dad gave us a lesson in how to make a brilliant fire. He was the secret head of the gang. He told us we were <u>"a tip-top little army"</u>.

Then we had ranks, instead of East, West, etc.

Andrew was Sergeant. Matthew was Second-Lieutenant. And Peter and Paul were Corporals. We saluted and marched.

The first big Operation was <u>the invasion of Wychwood</u>. It was a hard battle. Many good men died in actionous ways, eg. blown up by mines or jumping onto hand-grenades to protect all their comrades with them. After this we knew we were the <u>best gang ever</u>, because Andrew's Dad told us we were. And so we stopped being the Gang and turned ourselves into Gang.

THE RULES OF ~~THE~~ GANG

1. Be loyal to ~~the~~ Gang.
2. Do not disclose the secrets.
3. No girls.
4. Protect Amplewick from invaders.
5. Be prepared.
6. Do not trust grown ups, except Andrew's Father who is the Secret Head of ~~the~~ Gang.
7. Stay in Amplewick over the Summer holidays for Operations.
8. Make good fires and keep knives sharp.
9. The Motto of ~~the~~ Gang is "Live to Kill, Kill to Live".
10. The Keeper of the Archives will write down everything which happens and nothing which doesn't.

Here is a photograph of ~~the~~ Gang together:

(Photograph Missing)

Here is another photograph:

(Photograph Missing)

This is a photograph of Andrew's tree house

(Photograph Missing)[1]

---

1. (Unfortunately, the photographs were removed from the Archives at some stage and the editor has been unable to trace them. Further reference to excluded material has been avoided, out of a desire not to tax the reader's patience overmuch.)

****

This year the Annaul Amplewick Pram Race was
won by the best team: Andrew's Father, and his co-
runner Mr Grassmere. They came first by a long,
long way. While the race was proceeding norm-
ally, Gang was observing it from our chosen
vantage point i.e., the tree in the garden at
back of The Pollards. When a branch broke,
which had always held firm before, it caused
Matthew to fall down out of the tree. Luckily he
had a soft landing and was not in any serious way
injured. He got up to cheer Andrew's father to
victory.

Afterwards there was home-made lemonade made by
Andrew's mother. Operations were suspended for
the day. It was sunny and hot.

Paul's father was jealous that Andrew's father
had won, and incidentally beaten him. (He had
stopped because he didn't understand what was
going on.)

Everyone knew that he would never beat the
best father in a real race. Paul was forced to go
home. We believe he will be kept imprisoned for
many long and weary days from now. But we know he
will come back. Operations are to go ahead as per
normal.

****

Today these signals were received from Paul in
Morse Code: "Bored. Interogation. Dadmum. Kil.

Week more." We have a plan for when he gets out. It was less sunny than yesterday.[1]

****

THE HISTORY OF MYXAMATOSIS

Myxamatosis is a disease which kills rabbits. It is used by the farmers to keep the pests off the land, so we and everyone else can have food to eat. The disease kills the rabbits by making them so they can't breathe or see. Their eyes go gooey and

---

1. Here the bottom half of a page appears to have been torn out. The remainder is attached by only a single hole to the Lever Arch file. Only one sentence remains: "Meeting of Sub-Section East-West 2. Matthew sugg—" It seems likely, without pushing speculation too far, that what has been excised from the Archives was an entry dealing with the experiment between Peter and Matthew. Earlier references to Sub-Section East-West 2 make it clear that this was Peter's name for the two junior members of ~~the~~ Gang. There seem to have been at least three earlier experiments, one of which took place on a night that Matthew is known — from separate sources — to have slept round at Peter's. The nature of these experiments is, of course, not known. But it seems likely they were of a similar sort to the fatal saliva dare. If we know anything about young men, indeed if we know anything about Matthew and Peter, then these earlier dares were less disgusting than the final one. With young men the tendency towards escalation is almost inevitable. If Matthew and Peter did not, on this occasion, kiss, then it is almost inevitable that they would eventually, at some later meeting of Sub-Section East-West 2, have done so.

they lie down somewhere to die. If you find a rabbit
which is close to death of myxamatosis it is best
to put it down a rabbit-hole while it is still
alive, so that the disease will kill more rabbits.
This will help the farmers and their crops. Other
pests are rats, pigeons, mink, seagulls, red
squirrels, and most of all, foxes. Pests are
animals they are too many of, which eat the crops
and do nothing useful. Even as we speak scientists
are creating new diseases to kill these other
pests and to rid the world of them and their kind.
Rabbits breed very fast, which is why they are not
yet completely extinct from myxamatosis. The kind
of disease which myxamatosis is is a cancer. That
means it is usually fatal. People get cancer too,
i.e., Matthew's Grandfather who fought in World
War II.

(The best father helped with information for some
bits of this essay. P.)

    ****

In the middle of todays operation we were taught
an important lesson. (See above for information
on the operation.) We were ambushed, twice, in
quick succession. To evade the ambusher, Andrew
threw himself into the water, from which it was
necessary for him to be rescued, though he was
never in any real danger of any sort. Andrew is a
good swimmer generally. It was the big surprise of
hitting the water which was the main thing that
made him swallow by mistake. He was soon recovered
from it, and walking around. The operation

continued to The Pollards, where a sniper inflicted heavy casualties on us from the roof where he was hiding. Another lesson was learnt from this. <u>Always to expect the unexpected</u>. Today was maybe the hottest day so far.

****

The action today took place up at Base Camp One. Paul who had been imprisoned by his parents was no longer to be trusted. It was necessary for him to be put through a difficult test of his loyalty. We took him by stealth, up the Furze. He was trapped for a while and interrogated by the Chief Interrogator. At no time was he in any serious danger. Throughout questioning he insisted that he was innocent of all charges. In secret, Gang had considered if a court martial was necessary. Paul bore up under heavy questioning, and did not crack. In the event he was cleared of all charges and we welcomed him back into ~~the~~ Gang with open arms. His rank which was taken away from him temporarily was given back. Paul is a true soldier. It was another sunny day but with some more clouds to the North.

****

<u>A SUBMISSION FROM PAUL</u>

I would like to put on the record this statement: In the last two weeks I have been held captive by enemy forces. During this time I did not do anything wrong. I kept all the rules to the letter.

The pressure on me to talk was great, but I did not waver. Every tactic of interrogation was used against me. Since then, my conduct has been put under investigation and I was found innocent. I felt it was necessary for me to put this statement on record.

Paul South (Corporal).

****

On this day the Archives came under great peril. I was upstairs, minding my own business, reading The Death of the Dinosaurs by Dr Teddy Shawcross FRGS, sitting on my bed, when enemy sabateurs started a fire downstairs, in the kitchen. Alert to all possibilities, I smelt the smoke very early on in the process and went to have a look. Fire was on the walls and ceiling of the kitchen. Without regard to my personal safety I ran back upstairs really fast and got the Archives out from their secret hiding place. I also rescued The Death of the Dinosaurs by Dr Teddy Shawcross FRGS. The fire by now was trying to come under the door, which I had been sure to shut before returning upstairs. I went and hid the Archives in a safe place nearby before alerting the neighbours to the encroaching danger. Fire-engines were on the scene within minutes, as was my mother who had popped out for some milk. She became histerical and needed to be seducted by a fireman. Then my father returned, alerted by a call. In the meantime, the fire was put under control by the efficient deployment of the emergency services. Smoke coming from the back of

the building had looked like bad news for some
time, but damage was estimated as minimal. "You
had a lucky escape," the fireman said to me. The
fireman generally acknowledged that it was me who
had saved the day. My mum made me very embarased by
hugging me in front of everybody. But I was
pleased because I had succeeded in keeping the
Archives safe from the attack of the sabateurs.
The others arrived on bikes after the fire was
already put out.

    ****

I have got back the Archives from Paul. He kept
them very well since I was in hospital. There has
been no new sighting of the sabateurs. But we will
keep looking until we find them. The big operation
against Paul's parents (Operation Badger) has met
with its first big success. A heavy casualty has
been inflicted on them. We buried it out in the park
with full military honours. Before it died, it
gave Andrew a nasty scratch on the hand where he
was holding it down. It put up a strong fight, right
up until the end. Paul was certain we were
justified in our actions. He said, "We need to
teach them a lesson they won't forget." Andrew
kept the flea-collar, so the body could not be
identified if it was ever dug up. He said killing it
had been just like killing chickens which his
father had shown him. None of us were squeamish.
No one was sick behind a tree or looked green. Even
during the post mortem operation. We whistled <u>The
Last Post</u> and marched away. A sunny day.

****

It is with grave duty I have to report that Matthew
today was taken to hospital with a serious
illness. I cannot write much as I have been told to
get ready to go to the hospital, too. Matthew's
disease is something contagious (not myxamatosis)
which I, too, might have. Andrew and Paul will
also be put in quarantine. I am being shouted at.
Will report back later. PS. Sunny but with clouds.

****

We are all back from the hospital. Matthew is
dead. For a long time they were lying and lying to
us about him still being alive. I don't understand
why. We have found out through serious and intense
investigation that Matthew actually died last
night. But when we asked them at that time if he
was all right we were told he was doing very well.
Clearly, there was a conspiracy against us, to
keep us in the dark for some reason. Yesterday we
were tested with needles and a swob in the mouth
and I had to pee into a cold bottle. They asked me
lots of questions. I have confirmation of them
asking the others the same questions. The doctor
wanted to know if I had kissed Matthew. I told him
the truth. No. Never. No. He said he believed me.
Then he explained what the disease was and what it
did to the membranes around the brain, making them
swell up and go all watery. But he was lying about
Matthew, who was already dead. In the night we
made confirmation of this fact. I will not say how
unless I criminate us. We saw that Matthew was

dead and that we had been put under a deliberate
delusion that he was still alive, for some reason.
Andrew went too far, in my humble opinion. He
should not have done it. He wouldn't like it if it
was him. He will read this, in which case I still
think you're wrong. We got away with it, however.
It was a close squeak. Andrew pretended he was
sleepwalking. The guard took him back to bed, and
we creeped through good and quietly. The hospital
at night was a very spooky place. I felt ill
because I had seen my friend dead. I was in shock,
I think, but I was still able to operate with all
my senses alert. Our training came in useful for
being stealthy in this way. Paul was stopped by a
nurse who asked where he was going. Paul said he
was looking for the toilet and got lost. I did not
sleep but I did not cry. I can't believe that
Matthew was really dead. He was too strong to die
just like that in a day. There was an old man in the
bed next to mine and he sounded like he should be
the one who was dying. It was a snore like sawing
through a large piece of wood. I watched it get
light. What I wanted most of all was to talk to
Matthew and tell him I would do anything for him.
And that I was sorry, that he had died. And that we
would never forget him as long as we lived.

    ****

Today we had the first Gang meeting since Matthew
died. Paul was absent. It was Sub-Section
North-East. We talked about Matthew. The funeral
for him is on this weekend. We are going. So are
our parents. Andrew has been punished for what he

did in the hospital. Somebody found out, and there
was an investigation. The Headmistress was told.
Andrew was nearly expelled but this father talked
to the Headmistress and talked her round. He is on
<u>suspension</u> for ten days but no one must know about
the nature of his crime. We are off school for a
different reason, because we have been given
"personal reasons". Andrew was still glad he did
what he did. It meant we found out about Matthew
sooner than they wanted. He was only caught
because they found the scalpel under his pillow. I
didn't have anything to do with any of it. I was
looking the other way all the time. Andrew was
boasting about being so brave. He is a very good
Gang leader. He can do anything. He is less scared
than us of scary things. His father is the reason
for this, we know. Paul has been under
incarceration for some time now. We suspect he is
being tortured so he tells them the vital
information. But Paul will not crack. It rained
today and was cold.

    ****

Matthew's funeral was held at Flathill Church. We
wanted to carry the coffin and they said yes to
begin with but then they changed their minds. In
the end the coffin was carried by our fathers and
another man who drove the hearse. Matthew's
grandmother was crying all the time. She sounded
like Paul's father's cat did, right near the end
when it knew it was going to die. We all looked at
each other, disgusted. (In the graveyard.) <u>Miaow,
miaow,</u> the cat went. Miranda was there. She looked

very sad in black but still very pretty. She looks
just like Matthew with longer hair. We followed
her and the coffin. The Vicar was wearing sandals
so we could see his toes. My mother said it was an
insult. She tried to keep hold of me but I made my
escape. The Vicar didn't say much about Matthew.
Instead he let Matthew's grandfather drone on and
on about how much Matthew meant to them and how he
was the light of their lives and how he had so many
friends. When he said that everybody looked at us.
Then, when they weren't looking, Andrew made a
sick-face at me. I almost started to laugh which I
know was wrong. Then they lowered the coffin into
the grave. It was raining and there were already
small pools of water on the coffin lid, which
spilled off sideways. Everyone walked past and
threw the earth down with a big thunk. Then it was
over and we were taken away. The reception was
held at Matthew's. We drove there in cars in a long
line. The grown-ups stood around and drank
sherry. For us there was lemonade or orange juice
(both from the shops, not homemade like Andrew's
mum's). Grown-ups kept coming up to us and being
all philosophical as if they knew anything at all
about death or Matthew or anything. It made me
very annoyed. Paul talked alot to Matthew's
grandparents. Andrew told him not to, but he
decided to carry on regardless. There were
sausage rolls, egg sandwiches and cake for
afters. I found Andrew in Matthew's bedroom,
looking all over the place for something. We
didn't say anything to each other and he didn't
want me there, so I left. On the sideboard in the

sitting room was Matthew's school photograph from
last year in a new gold frame. Matthew was smiling
because the photographer had said, "Girl's
knickers," just before the camera-shutter went
click. He said that to all the boys. To the girls
he said, "Boy's pants." Matthew hated his school
photograph. He wanted to look big and tough in it,
and not smiling. The background was like a blue
sky full of fleecy clouds. The glass on the
photograph was covered in thumb-prints from where
people kept picking it up to look at it more
closely. Soon the party came to an end and everybody
went home. Andrew told us where and when we will
meet tomorrow. Matthew was my best friend. I'm sorry
that he died, but life goes on, doesn't it?

    ****

When we met at Base Camp One, it was raining and
Andrew revealed his plan to us. It was approved
unanimously, especially by me. I believe that
Andrew is the most tactical genius living in the
world today. When he says jump I jump, immediately
without even thinking about it. His plan is too
top secret to write here. No one apart from us has
the clearance to read about it. Andrew told us we
should be patience because there was no rush now
we knew what we were going to do. Because of course
I wanted to start straight in with whatever I
could. The meeting went on all morning and alot
was decided. Paul agreed with everything that
Andrew said. Gang is safe. Gang will protect
itself. It was strange even though we were talking
about him that Matthew didn't turn up late, like

he sometimes did. I was more surprised not to see
him than if he had really been there, almost. In
the afternoon I went in secret to the churchyard
and told Matthew what was in the offing. I'm sure he
wants us to keep him briefed about all current
operations. With a salute I said goodbye to him.
It was still raining.

    ****

Andrew decided today to make Paul co-leader of
Gang. This was a necessary thing to do because of
the extraordinary circumstances we are in. We
need two leaders to co-ordinate the operation. I
congratulated Paul on his promotion. I do not want
to be promoted as I am more than happy to serve in
the capacity I can. The first part of the plan has
already begun. Andrew gave us an up-to-date
description of the target area. We knew it very
well, because we had been round all the time when
Matthew was alive. But Andrew added some new
details. During the reception he went into some
previously off-limits areas, including the main
bedroom. He mentioned a number of weaknesses all
over the place, which we will exploit in the weeks
and months to come. Part one of the mission is to
infiltrate the enemy camp. This will be a covert
operation, and we will need to gain the enemy's
trust first before we start. Andrew said it would
be suspicious if we all went round one by one, so
we decided to go together asap. More rain and
heavier.

    ****

I am unbearably excited. Just an hour ago, I was
sitting on my bed and reading <u>The Death of the
Dinosaurs</u> by Teddy Shawcross, FRGS. Suddenly
everything became clear as crystal. It is a real
breakthrough in my scientific research. I can't
wait to tell the others. I remembered what the
best father said once about Darwin and the
survival of the fittest. There was a reason why
Matthew died but it wasn't because I did anything
wrong. There were enemy forces involved. This is a
battle for the entire future of our planet. We
thought before that the invasion was coming from
abroad and that it would be Russians, but now I see
that it already has happened, and the invaders are
all around us. They do not have tanks, they have
<u>time</u>. They have lots and lots and lots of time. It
is their main weapon. Slowly they turn from friend
into evil foe. They treat us like babies when we
are babies, but then we grow up into young men and
still they treat us like babies. They are like
Teddy Shawcross says about the Dinosaurs: "Their
greatest failure was their failure to adapt. This
failure had fatal consequences." Yes, I
understand! This is the nature of scientific
research, one day you are stumbling about lost all
in the darkness, and the next it is light and you
know exactly where you are. I can't wait to tell
the others. This will make all the difference. I
am almost happy about it, now I understand why
Matthew died. And we can do something to make it
better. I have to go. My mum is shouting dinner's
on the table. Fishfingers and baked beans. My
favourite. Weather outside bad.

****

When I presented my discovery the others were all
at once very excited about it. Andrew especially.
But I am too modest to write down exactly what.

****

Today we went to visit for the first time our chief
enemies. Miranda answered the door. She is off
school as well. She was bored and thought we were
come to see her. Her friends were all at school. We
have talked about Miranda alot in recent times.
Andrew thinks we maybe can use her in our plan.
Paul seconds this. (He is now a great co-leader.)
We are sure we can't let her into ~~the~~ Gang, or tell
her about Operation Extinction, but we think that
we will use her as a way to get in and out of enemy
territory. Andrew says we should make it look like
we are going to let her join us. Then she will be
really keen and do whatever we say. But on the first
day of the active operation (today) we needed to
get direct access to the enemy commanders. They
were in the living room watching the television
with the sound up too loud. It was a nature
programme about sticklebacks. The room smelt of
biscuits and washing up liquid. "Who is it?"
asked Matthew's grandfather. "It's Matthew's
friends," said Miranda, in explanation. Matthew's
grandparents stood up and said, "Hello. Hello."
They knew all our names, but got us mixed up by
thinking Paul was Andrew and vice versa with me
and Paul. "You look so alike," said Matthew's
grandfather. Then there was a big and awkward

silence and then they asked us to sit down. Next,
Andrew made his speech. "We came round to see if
there was anything you wanted us to do, like when
we were Cub Scouts and did bob-a-job week for you,
only this time we don't want any money, because we
know Matthew used to help you out all the time in
the house, so we thought we might be of some
assistance to you." Matthew's grandparents looked
at each other bewildered. "That's very kind of
you," said Matthew's grandfather, after a long
silent gap of time. "But we're doing quite well on
our own, thank you." "Not that we don't miss him,"
said Matthew's grandmother, looking tearful
towards the school photograph that was still on
the sideboard in the gold frame. The enemy HQ is
light brown in colour, and full all over of
flower-patterns and doilies and lace and tassels.
Everything in it has something on it. There is a
brown clock on the mantelpiece above the gas fire.
Some horse brasses are on the wall, and china
figures of cottages on little shelves. "Would you
like some . . . tea?" asked Matthew's grandmother.
"Yes, please," said Andrew, who drinks tea and
coffee and anything he likes at home all the time
anyway. Paul and me don't, or only round at
Andrew's, but we said, "Yes, please," too, and
followed the plan. "Do you take sugar," asked
Matthew's grandmother, standing in the kitchen
door. "Three," said Andrew. "Four," said Paul.
"Four," I said. "Oh," she said. "And would you
like some biscuits or sweets?" "Biscuits would
be lovely, thank you," said Paul. It was all going
to plan. Then Matthew's grandfather asked about

the weather. "Is it very wet out?" he asked. You could see the rain on the windows right from where he was sitting, so it was a stupid and unnecessary question. Matthew's grandfather talked to us about how terrible the last test match had been. He asked us which football teams we supported, and was disappointed when we said we didn't. "England," said Andrew. "You should support Newton Town," Matthew's grandfather said. "They are your local team." "Did Matthew support Newton Town?" I asked. "Of course," said his grandfather. We didn't know this so it was news to us. Miranda sat on the side listening to our chat. By this time Matthew's grandmother had made the tea and she brought it in on a flowery tray, brown. It was disgusting Earl Gray tea. Then she went back for the biscuits. The teapot was in a knitted cosy, caramel-coloured with zig-zaggy lines and a dark brown bobble on top. "Is it very wet out?" asked Matthew's grandmother. Andrew almost died of frustration. "It's not too bad," said Paul, rescuing the situation from danger. "I was meaning to go to the shops later on, if it clears up," said Matthew's grandmother. "We'll go," said Andrew, eagerly. "That's what we mean. We don't mind if it's raining, just give us your list and we'll be back in two ticks." Andrew was cleverly trying to talk like old people do, so they would trust him more. "You're really very kind," said Matthew's grandmother. "But I think we'll be all right." "I can go with them and make sure they don't get the wrong things," piped up Miranda. "You've just had your hair done," said

Matthew's grandfather to Matthew's grandmother. "You don't want to get it all wet." "All right, then," Matthew's grandmother said. "I'll just need to add a few things more." Andrew winked at us. Mission accomplished. We drank as much tea with as much sugar as possible, and ate all the biscuits. We did other things, too. When we went to the toilet upstairs, we used lots of paper. Andrew took half the pills from an important-looking bottle in the medicine cabinet and flushed them down the loo with his pee, and he turned the light on in Matthew's bedroom and closed the door. When we finished our tea, Matthew's grandmother gave us the list. At the bottom of it added in different colour pen (red not blue) were the words "Sugar" and "Biscuits". This was our first major victory in Operation Extinction. Miranda walked along with us to the shops. She was wheeling her grandmother's basket. She seemed very sad. "I used to go shopping with Matthew," she said. "They didn't trust me or him on our own, but they did together. They always kept us inside the whole rest of the time." We were all nice to her because we had to be. Paul offered to take the basket but she kept hold of it with very tight hands. At the shop she found the things on the list. We watched closely, learning all we needed to learn about their habits. Miranda paid with money out of her grandmother's purse, which was big and fat with pieces of paper. It was raining even worse when we went home with her. "Lucky you didn't go," said Matthew's grandfather, "Your hair would of been

ruined." "Thank you so much," said Matthew's
grandmother. "Would you like some more tea?" We
said yes, and made a second raid on the enemy
supplies. When the time came to say goodbye,
Andrew repeated his speech, more or less. "When
are you going back to school?" asked Matthew's
grandmother. "Next week," said Paul. "But really
only when we want to," said Andrew. "I'm going
back on Monday," said Miranda. "And a good thing,
too," said Matthew's grandfather, then laughed.
None of us laughed at his stupid joke, not even
Matthew's grandmother. Of course none of us,
including Miranda, wants to go back to school. But
we can always bunk off ill, I think, when the time
comes for it to be necessary. Andrew said we could
still come and help at evenings or weekends.
"Don't put yourselves to any trouble," said
Matthew's grandmother. "It's no trouble at all,"
said Paul, intelligently. "You were all very good
friends to Matthew," said Matthew's grandfather.
"And I'm sure he knew what good friends you were."
"He loved playing with you," said Matthew's
grandmother, "He told us all about it." We had a
moment of anxiety before we realized that Matthew
really didn't tell them anything at all.
Matthew's grandparents sat back down in front of
the television. Miranda showed us out. She didn't
ask us if she could join Gang but you could tell
she really wanted to. Andrew toyed with her.
"Perhaps you could come up to Wychwood one day and
cook sausages for us," he said. "But only if we
ask you. Don't come if we don't ask." She smiled
and said goodbye and was annoyed and closed the

door behind us. As we were walking away Andrew
turned to us and said, "Before Christmas. The
Dinosaurs must be extinct before Christmas." I
hope he is right. It rained and got darker for the
whole rest of the day. (From now on they will be
called The Dinosaurs, because Andrew says so.)

    ****

Tomorrow we are back at school, apart from Andrew
who will not go in till next Monday. His father
says so because he listens to what he says. Andrew
is cleverly trying to evade school for as long as
humanly possible. Because of us going to school
tomorrow, it was me and Paul who went round to
continue Operation Extinction today. Andrew gave
us strict instructions, and waited just out of
sight down the road. Miranda looked less sad
today, although I am sure she misses Matthew more
than anyone, even though he used to hit her and
ignore her all the time. It was arranged that Paul
would help Mr Dinosaur in the garden and I would be
in the house with Mrs Dinosaur, in the kitchen in
fact. First, I did the washing up. I used loads of
washing up liquid and poured some down the
plughole while she was looking in the other
direction. I wanted to smash a plate but at the
moment we are still at the infiltration stage of
the Operation, so I knew I must hold back from
dangerous risks and concentrate on gaining the
trust of Mrs Dinosaur. She wouldn't trust me as
much or even at all if I was clumsy. So instead, I
tried to wear her out by asking lots of questions
about where to put things away. Miranda was

hanging around and kept trying to help, but I did
my best to ignore her. I made sure that Mrs
Dinosaur got out of her armchair so often she did
more work with me "helping" than even if she'd
been on her own. The next thing was to fetch a
sewing-machine from the attic. This was a very
useful recce. I saw that there was plenty of room
to hide, and that the ladder could be let down and
pulled up from inside the attic. There was no lock
on the attic door in the ceiling, just a brass hook
to be pulled. I wanted to steal something from the
attic but everything was too big and dusty. There
were suitcases with stickers on from Gibraltar,
Aden, Cape Town and Dubai and other places like
that, old pictures in frames, pots and pans, a
carpet, children's toys, a birdcage on a stand,
empty cardboard boxes and tea chests, candles,
fly-spray, wine bottles full of black liquid, a top
hat, planks of wood and tiny little women's shoes
made of silk and other shiny materials. Mrs
Dinosaur started to use the sewing-machine in the
living room. She thanked me very much for my help.
Miranda was still hanging around. I was glad she
didn't come up into the attic, though she gave me a
little help coming down the ladder. It made me
feel awkward and annoyed because she was watching
me. I knew she wasn't a spy in the enemy camp,
because she didn't have any idea what it was we
were up to. But even without meaning it she was
hampering the smooth and efficient running of the
operation. I wanted to tell her to go away, just
like Matthew always did when she followed and
pleaded with us. "I'll go and tidy Matthew's

room," I said. "You don't need to do that, love,"
said Mrs Dinosaur. "It's really very tidy
already." "I shall clean it, then." "You don't
have to. I cleaned it yesterday. Everything is
just as it was." "Can I have a look?" I asked. "Of
course," Mrs Dinosaur said. Miranda looked like
she was going to follow me, so I warned her off
with a hard look. "I'd prefer to be left alone," I
said, as extra to this. She went into a huff and
went outside into the garden. Matthew's room was
like when he was alive but it felt dead. I looked
through his clothes drawers, which were much
tidier than when he was alive. All his pants were
neatly ironed and folded. His socks were rolled up
into tight little balls. On the top of the chest of
drawers some of his tanks and aeroplanes were
arranged just like the china figures on the
mantel-piece downstairs. When he was alive,
Matthew always put them like they were fighting a
really actionous battle. But now they looked like
they were on a stupid parade for the Queen. His
other armed forces were in boxes underneath his
desk. I decided to rescue a couple of true and good
soldiers from this Life of Hell. I took two who
were heavily wounded. One had lost an arm to
chopping and the other was burnt all up his back. I
put them in my handkerchief in my pocket. Then I
started to make little changes in the room that
Mrs Dinosaur wouldn't notice. Matthew didn't have
as many books as me, but I rearranged them so they
were in strict alphabetical order under their
titles (like mine are at home). I turned his
pillow the other way up. I swopped two framed

pictures around on the wall. One was of Sir Edmund
Hilary and Sherpa Tensing on the summit of
Everest. The other was of Matthew's mother and
father, standing next to a big flat lake in front of
a mountain. It looked like the Lake District. I
was just turning the rug around by 180° when I
heard a voice say, "What are you doing?" It was
Miranda who had come back to pester me even more.
Worse was that I'd just spotted a piece of paper
which had been lying under the rug and which had
Matthew's writing on. I knew it might be of vital
importance. Miranda came into the room and stood
next to me. "Nothing," I said. "What are you
doing?" "They don't want me outside." "I don't
want you here, either." "Can't I help?" "No," I
said. The rug was on the floor at an odd angle. I
moved and put my foot on top of the paper. "What's
that?" said Miranda. "Go away," I said. "You're
hiding something." "No, I'm not." "Show me it."
Miranda was just about to destroy the whole thing.
I hadn't realized she could be so dangerous. I
needed to do something to take control of the
situation which was rapidly running away with
itself. I thought of something fast. "If you
don't go away," I said. "I will tell Andrew never
to let you join ~~the~~ Gang." That stopped her
completely in her tracks. She looked down at the
floor and could see the edge of the paper sticking
out from under my foot. "It's something from my
brother," she said. "I want to see it." I could
see that she was spelling big trouble. I needed to
seize the situation and put it under control. "Go
and stand outside the door," I said. "I'm going to

read it first." "Oh, please let me," she said. I put out my right hand to hold her off while I bent down to pick up the vital note, with my other (left) hand. (This was a manoevre of some hardness.) Experienced from years of fighting with Matthew, she charged me the moment my guard was down. She didn't try to get the paper, like most girls would, instead she pushed me as hard as she could back onto Matthew's bed. The paper was now between my fingers but Miranda was on top of me. After a furious struggle I managed to get free. She was trying to bite my arm. I pushed her onto the bed and sat on top of her, my knees pinning her arms down. Somehow I had managed to keep hold of Matthew's paper, and now I read it. At first I thought it was in code, but then I recognized what it meant. $x2 + y2 = z2$ etcetera. It was a crib sheet for a maths test we were given just before the Summer holidays began in June. "What is it?" squealed Miranda, so loud I was sure even the deaf old Dinosaurs would hear her and come up. "You can see it if you promise to behave," I said, masterfully. She sulked but then she nodded to say yes. I climbed off her and gave her the paper. She understood what the maths meant. "Oh," she said. "I wanted it to be something important. Like a message." We sat side by side on the edge of Matthew's bed. "What was Germany like?" I asked. "It was horrible," she said, and started giggling. "Everyone in the family walked around with no clothes on all the time. Even the father." I looked at her to confirm absolutely that she was telling the truth. "And they had a bird which they didn't keep in a cage. It just flew everywhere pooing on everything. The sofa was horrible. It used to perch there." There is no love lost between us and the Germans. These reports of their degenerateness only added more fuel to the fire. "Can I keep this anyway?" Miranda asked. "I need to show it to the others," I said. She looked very sad. "I don't have much from Matthew," she said. "Shall I show you? In my room." "All right," I said. Her room was across the hall. I'd never been inside it before. It was pink in colour, and the bed was covered in a big quilt. Miranda had a pile of dolls in one corner. There was an oval mirror on her table. From a shelf she got down a box, and was opening it when we heard a shout. It was Mr Dinosaur, calling for us, by name. "Another day," Miranda said. "Give me the paper," I insisted forcefully. She gave it to me. "Don't burn it," she said. We went downstairs. Paul gave me a searching look, because he thought I'd been fraternizing with the enemy. I hadn't, as this record shows. We drank tea, with lots of sugar, ate biscuits and left. Andrew met us at the corner, and we reported the objectives we had accomplished. Paul now knew the garden like the back of his hand, especially where the weedkillers were in the shed. He had put little cuts in the tubers when they planted them, to make sure they went rotten and didn't grow. I told him about what I did, then about Miranda and the naked Germans with the bird. "Good work, men," said Andrew. I showed him the paper which he examined then told me to put it in the Archive. I almost forgot until the end to mention the attic. "What did it have in it?" Andrew asked. I followed my training in remembering everything accurately. I thought about how it smelled and where I was when I looked. When I said about the birdcage, Andrew got very excited. "I have an idea," he said. He explained. It was brilliant. Then we went home. It wasn't raining but it almost was. I spent all evening writing this so it was up to date, which was alot. Now I must get ready for school.

    ****

After school we met at Andrew's and he told us what he had done. When Mrs Dinosaur asked him to put the sewing-machine back up in the attic because she was done with it, he pretended to notice the birdcage. Then he talked to the Dinosaurs about if they loved birds. He was carrying out his ingenious plan from yesterday. "Maybe you should get a bird again," he suggested. He said Mrs Dinosaur kept saying how beautiful her favourite budgerigar's singing was. She called it Bluey, because it had little blue wings but black spots on its neck. Andrew went and brought the cage down from the attic and cleaned it from top to bottom. By the time he was finished the Dinosaurs were talking about how sad they were when Bluey died. "But this one won't die," said Andrew, reassuringly. Then he had tea and left. The birdcage was all he did, but he said it was a major victory. I have homework to do. Maths. It was raining during morning break, and lunch, but had cleared up by the late afternoon.

****

Andrew did excellent work today. He took a
screwdriver to the Dinosaurs house, and while
they were downstairs he changed the fuses on their
bedside lamps to much higher ones. This will make
them possibly dangerous. He has plans to do this
for all the plugs in the house, most especially
the kettle and the television. Also, he took a few
more of Mr Dinosaurs pills from the bathroom
cabinet. Some others he swopped from bottle to
bottle. He drank three cups of tea and ate a third
of a lemon sponge cake. It was a cold and wet
day. We had double Geography. I miss Matthew at
school.

****

[N.B. I decided to go on my own and tell Miranda
that we were keeping control of Matthew's paper.
She stood in the door of the house and started to
cry. She was angry we wouldn't give her Matthew's
last message back. "But he was my brother," she
said. "He wasn't yours, he was mine." But I knew
he was always ours, too.]

****

Andrew reported that today the Dinosaurs had told
him they were going to the pet shop at the weekend
in Midford, to buy themselves a brand new
budgerigar. "But a yellow one," said Mrs
Dinosaur. "Not a blue one, so it doesn't remind us
too much of Bluey." Andrew puts on a very funny Mrs
Dinosaur voice when he tells this story. They are

going to call the new budgerigar, "Sunny."
Because the sun is yellow, and "Yellowey,"
sounded wrong. Lots of rain.

WINTER

CHAPTER NINE

Andrew

Oft denk' ich, sie sind nur ausgegangen!
Bald werden sie wieder nach Hause gelangen!
Der Tag is schön! O, sei nicht bang!
Sie machen nur einen weiten Gang!

Oft I think, they've only just gone!
Soon-as-you-know it, they'll be Home!
The Day is bright. O, do not fret!
They're only out on a longish Trek.

i.

During the next couple of weeks a routine was established. Andrew, still not back at school, went round the Dinosaur House every day. At the weekends, Peter and Paul joined him there. Operation Extinction continued apace. Andrew's ingenuity was remarkable. He took the handyman skills he had learnt from his father and turned them upside-down. Safety devices were converted into death-traps. The substitution of inadequate, or overadequate fuses, was only the first of his endangerments: throughout the house screws were loosened by a turn or two, or three, and nails pulled a quarter inch from flush; the stair carpet was made to slide back and forth, and the dining-room door to scrape against the lintel. When there was nothing more of this sort to be done, Andrew started to create minor discomforts everywhere: he turned the thermostat up in the fridge, causing the Dinosaurs' food to freeze solid; he let air into the radiators, to make them drip and knock; he repeatedly hid the tin-opener behind the cutlery tray in the cutlery drawer; he redid the washing-line with slip-knots; he made sure to leave all jam-jars in the kitchen slightly open, so the fungus spores could get more rapidly to work; he opened the window in Matthew's room slightly, letting the heat escape; he left the lights on in every room he left, in hopes of raising the Dinosaurs' electricity bills. He did everything he could think of. All in all, he was pretty ingenious with his booby-traps.

From the Dinosaurs' point of view, it seemed as if their house was having somewhat of a nervous breakdown – though this was not a term they would themselves ever have used. "Having a bit of a funny turn," that was more their style. They were bewildered, just as they were supposed to be. The kitchen cabinets rattled against the wall, creaking under their tinny load; the cabinet doors no longer fit quite snugly, falling open when the magnets failed to engage; the carriage clock on the mantelpiece, a retirement gift, which had always kept such marvellous time, suddenly started to run slow. (They several times missed the first five minutes or so of the *Archers*.) Some things they didn't consciously notice, or couldn't consciously locate the cause of: their tea started to taste worse than it had (salt in the sugar bowl, soap in the teapot); the morning marmalade was becoming far less of a pleasure (curry powder); Mr Dinosaur's medicines continued to go down astonishingly fast (flushed down the loo).

As the house degenerated, they began to look upon Andrew as their protector. If it hadn't been for him, they thought, things would have been much worse.

In fact, Andrew was such a favourite that it was he, and only he, who was asked to go with the Dinosaurs when they went to buy Sunny. (Miranda had said buying a budgerigar was a stupid idea, stamped her foot, pouted and refused to have anything whatsoever to do with it.) Bet's Pets was located in Midford, on Castle Road. There was a snake displayed in a glass case in the window. Inside, they had a wide selection of tarantulas. When there occurred a difficulty in deciding between two equally lovely yellow birds, Andrew was called upon to judge between them. (After all, the whole thing had been his idea in the first place.) And it was Andrew who, during the drive back from Midford, sat in the back seat of the Morris Traveller with Sunny's cage resting heavily upon his thighs.

During this journey, Mrs Dinosaur was far more flighty than Sunny. She kept asking Andrew if he was sure the little darling was all right. Andrew assured her Sunny was loving every minute of it. To which Mrs Dinosaur replied that she thought Andrew was very good with animals.

He sat with his arms wrapped around his chief weapon of revenge. Beside him, in a bag, was everything that might bring joy to Sunny's (short) life. There was a waterbowl that automatically replenished itself, so it didn't have to be refilled quite so often. There was a little round mirror for Sunny to be puzzled by, and tap with his beautiful beak, beneath which dangled a little bell, which would ring whenever he tapped his own curious image. There was a brand-new swing, upon with Sunny could take his well-deserved rest. There was even that final bird-delighter, without which no respectable cage would be complete – a cuttlefish bone.

After seeing Sunny safely installed, Andrew went off to a prearranged meeting with the others, during which the main point of discuss was to be – Sunny's death.

There had already, on several previous occasions, been no little debate amongst the three of them as to how long they should allow to pass before Sunny's sadly inevitable demise. Andrew, of course, believed that the bird should croak around about the end of the first week. Paul, predictably enough, disagreed. He felt that it was important that the Dinosaurs be given enough time to get used to having Sunny around. If the bird's death was to *mean* anything, then it must be the loss of a much-valued companion. Sunny must become a central part of the Dinosaurs' lives. A week was not long enough for that centrality to be established. Paul believed a month, or perhaps even six weeks, would be the minimum period required. Anything less than that, and the Dinosaurs would merely be losing a new pet.

Andrew arrived at the Gamekeeper's Cottage. Paul and Peter were already upstairs in Paul's brightly coloured bedroom. The confirmation of Sunny's arrival delighted them. But within a few moments, the argument over when the killing should take place had started up again.

Andrew reiterated his conviction that Sunny be assassinated asap. The Dinosaurs, he stated, had become as attached to Sunny as they ever would be before they'd even *left* the pet shop. He said the best way to proceed now was to have Sunny die immediately, then persuade the grief-stricken Dinosaurs to buy another bird to replace him. This second bird, he was prepared to concede, could safely be allowed to survive and thrive for a month or so – in accordance with the logic, emotional and otherwise, of Paul's argument. Yet the second bird must also die sooner rather than later, in order that a third might be procured. The Dinosaurs must be bludgeoned by death after death, for as long as it took. With each new bird's arrival, they would become more fretful, more quickly attached; with each bird's demise, they would be the more deeply grief-stricken. As grief followed grief, their own hold on life would be weakened.

Paul did his best to argue the contrary: that the shocks would every time decrease. And the Dinosaurs, sooner rather than later, would give up on budgerigars completely.

On this issue, Peter stood between them. He even dared wonder, at one point, whether they shouldn't just see if the bird died of its own accord within the first month. Andrew's exasperated reaction to this can easily be imagined: it wasn't enough that Sunny *expire*, he must be *killed* – and he must be killed by *them*. The same argument that applied to the extinction of the Dinosaurs also held true for the murder of the budgerigars.

"If *we* don't kill them," he insisted, "then it doesn't mean anything."

Eventually, Paul decided to make his move. When Andrew went into the bathroom for a pee, he turned to Peter and said, "We have to stop him. I want you to agree with me. I'm

Co-Gang-Leader. If you don't tell him no, then I'll tell him about your experiment with Matthew." To enforce his argument further, he blew a couple of saliva-bubbles.

Peter's head fell. He knew he had to do what Paul said, or else Andrew would find out what had happened and would hate him for ever.

When Andrew came back from the loo, Paul suggested that they vote on it.

The result – for everyone apart from Andrew – was entirely predictable. Two against one.

It had been years since Peter had disagreed so openly with Andrew. On matters of no importance, he had sometimes allowed himself the implied rebellion of hesitation. But, in the end, he had always played Follow the Leader.

As soon as the vote was taken, Andrew knew that there had been a shift in the balance of power. It perplexed him, but there wasn't anything he could do about it. And so, for the moment at least, he decided to concede. With the two others against him, it was his only option.

"We'll leave it a few weeks," he said, allowing himself the secret possibility of *a few weeks* being as few as three.

Paul was wise enough to take this victory and be satisfied with it. He did not press for anything more.

They discussed other things for a while, but in essence the meeting was over.

When the three of them parted, they were as divided in spirit as they had ever been.

Andrew and Paul were now outright enemies. Peter's change of allegiance could mean only one thing: War. The true battles, however, lay ahead. Today had been but an opening skirmish.

When Andrew returned to the Dinosaur House the following day, it was with the clear intent of killing Sunny as soon as he could. To this end, he had procured a handful of rat-poison pellets from his father's shed. These, ground up to a slightly smaller size, would be almost indistinguishable from the lumps of grey feed that made up the solid part of Sunny's diet. Andrew had, overnight, given a great deal of thought to this course of action. Killing Sunny seemed the only way in which he could regain control of the situation, and through that his control of Gang. As always, his strength must derive from his willingness to do more, to do worse, than the others would ever dare. Peter, in the face of this, would be scared back into obedience; Paul, having lost Peter, would have to retreat. As Andrew examined it that rainy morning, the plan didn't seem to have a flaw.

It was with some disbelief, therefore, that upon arriving at the Dinosaurs' Andrew found himself entering a house already awash with grief. Sunny had been found dead not five minutes before he rang the door-bell. And despite Mr Dinosaur's massaging the bird's tiny heart with his thumb, despite his puckering his lips around the holes in Sunny's beak and blowing air into those miniature lungs, no resuscitation had been possible. There the little bird lay, feet up and curled, upon the corn-pattern breadboard in the kitchen.

Andrew was doubly aggrieved: first, he had been prevented from himself killing Sunny, and so the bird's death meant – as he'd said – nothing; second, the others were certain not to believe him when he told them that although Sunny was dead, he had had nothing to do with it. The fact that he had been intending Sunny's death only moments beforehand, and no longer had to run the risk of being caught in the killing act, did not in any way diminish his feelings of indignation. He could only console himself by attempting to console Mr and Mrs Dinosaur, and by doing his level best to ensure that they replaced Sunny as soon as possible. He was, perhaps, a little overeager in putting this idea forward. Now was not the moment to be suggesting another journey to Bet's Pets. Rather, it was best for the Dinosaurs to concern themselves with preparations for Sunny's funeral. Had he been able to take notice of it, Andrew should have been highly gratified as to the damage the bird's death had caused to morale within Enemy HQ.

"Everything I touch," said Mrs Dinosaur. "Everything I touch dies. Everything I love –" The latter sentence, she allowed to complete itself, in accordance with the answer already given in the former.

Andrew was foolish enough to suggest for a second time the swift purchase of another bird – this one almost guaranteed to be immortal.

Mrs Dinosaur began to cry, and Mr Dinosaur said that Andrew should probably come back the following afternoon.

Throughout this touching scene, Miranda stood in the kitchen door-way. The house, though grief-stricken, had – since her return from Germany – been relatively quiet. Although in some ways welcome, this sudden outburst was highly annoying to her. Her grandparents had, in the period after her brother's death, allowed themselves public tears in the only situation that English society tolerates: the funeral. In private, they had been almost equally restrained.

"Why didn't you cry like this for my brother?" she wanted to say. "Why all this for a stupid bird?"

However, once Andrew had gone, she was able to subsume her filial grief into the petty feathered one – and the sobbing partnership she formed with her grandmother was of emotional benefit to both, though wholly understood by neither. And although Mr Dinosaur exhibited a greater outward stoicism, his hidden worries were great. He was, most particularly, concerned over the effect his setback would have upon his wife.

iii.

Outside, the rain had worsened. Andrew did not go home, but climbed up into the high hedge of holly trees that overlooked the Dinosaurs' garden. It was from this safe vantage-point, hidden deep within the olive shadows and pleasantly scratchy leaves, that he witnessed Sunny's funeral – from preparation to ceremony to aftermath.

First of all, Mr Dinosaur came out into the garden, fetched a spade from the shed, and dug a foot-deep wedge out of the turf in one corner of the lawn. He then cut the bottom end off the loamy divot so as to leave a small, budgerigar-sized cavity when it was replaced. He went back inside, after returning the spade to its usual place in the shed. Mrs Dinosaur came out next, carrying what Andrew immediately recognized as the stiff cardboard innards of a pack of fig rolls. It was covered with an embroidered handkerchief. Miranda followed behind her. Without Mr Dinosaur to show them the place, they had to hunt around awhile for the intended grave. (Andrew felt like shouting out to tell them where it was.)

"Has he dug it yet, do you think?" asked Mrs Dinosaur.

"He said he had," replied Miranda.

They were yet to find the hole when Mr Dinosaur re-emerged from the house. He soon put them right. The ceremony as such was so understated that even Andrew might, in another mood, have been touched. If, for example, this had been the burial of a loyal but damaged-beyond-use soldier. But he was still so angry at Sunny for dying unprompted that he could muster no great grief at this juncture. Mrs Dinosaur dropped the cardboard box gently into the hole. The handkerchief, however, she retained. Andrew watched to see whether she would forgetfully use it to dry her eyes, but she did not. Instead, she leaned over, looked down into the grave and said, "Good-bye." Miranda had somewhere acquired a flower, a raspberry-rippled chrysanthemum, which she now placed on top of Sunny. Mr Dinosaur limited his ceremonial to replacing the wedge of turf in as respectful a manner as he could muster. It began to hail. After blowing Sunny a final farewell kiss, and waving the handkerchief at his soon-to-be-sodden sod, Mrs Dinosaur was escorted back inside by her husband and her grand-daughter. She looked older and frailer than ever before, which gave Andrew a moment of intense pleasure.

iv.

After climbing down out of the holly tree, Andrew caught a couple of local cats and threw them over the fence into the Dinosaur garden – in hopes that they would smell Sunny's body and feel moved to dig it up. His ejection from the Dinosaur House, however, had left him the whole afternoon with nothing to do. He certainly did not want to go home, and risk his father. For the first time since Matthew's death, he wished that he were with the others: back at school. He was ashamed of this thought almost as soon as it occurred. The others, he was certain, were most likely to be regretting their confinement at that very same moment. (In this, Andrew was wrong: Peter and Paul were engrossed in a Chemistry practical, attempting to master the fundamentals of chromatography.)

He decided to go and hide in one of the dry places afforded by Wychwood. This would give him the opportunity properly to consider how things had been progressing.

On the bicycle ride, Andrew thought about Operation Extinc-tion's main obstacle: Mr Dinosaur.

255

Although the whole Gang knew that Mr Dinosaur had the Big C, and was bound to die sooner or later, Andrew had been unable to perceive any deathlike tendencies in him. It was very disappointing. To all appearances, Mr Dinosaur was a stupidly healthy old man. He still gardened with a vengeance. Once, though Andrew was ashamed to remember it, they had been play-fighting, and Mr Dinosaur had caught his wrists in a tight finger-grip, from which he was humiliated to find himself unable to escape – however much he wriggled. Matthew had never said exactly in which part of his body Mr Dinosaur had the Big C. But everyone knew that it was somewhere so inaccessible, or vital, that he was not going to have an operation. Instead, there was the bathroom cabinet full of medicines; there was the constant worry that he wasn't eating enough to keep his weight up; there was the ritual cursing of all doctors whenever he lit his pipe.

"A man's got to have a few pleasures," he'd said to Andrew, through the peat-smelling smoke. "Or what else has he got left?"

Andrew had been hoping to see some clear manifestation of Mr Dinosaur's terminality. He was every day expecting the old man's skin to turn crusty and black. He knew that the Big C involved the lavish deployment of lumps, and would have been gratified to see a couple appear on Mr Dinosaur's forehead. He had often fantasized that he would be the only person present when Mr Dinosaur clutched his throat and dropped to the ground with a gargle of agony. This would afford Andrew the opportunity to whisper certain things in his ear, ensuring that the old man's death was as agonized as could possibly be wished.

By now, Andrew had reached Wychwood, parked his bicycle behind the piss-smelling shed and installed himself in a dryish corner. He would stay here, motionless, apart from the odd shiver, for the next three hours.

During this time, he decided to tell the other two that he, and

256

he alone, had been responsible for Sunny's death. There was some small risk they would find out (perhaps from Miranda) that the bird had died earlier in the morning – before he'd even arrived at the Dinosaur House. But Andrew was sure that, if they challenged him, he could easily explain that away. (Say, he'd slipped into the house before the Dinosaurs were awake, and poisoned Sunny's breakfast good and proper.) There were likely to be problems with both Peter and Paul when he informed them – different problems, though deriving from similar sources. Andrew decided to catch them separately, Peter first, then Paul. To this end, he went at three o'clock to hide behind a tree at the entrance to The Close.

v.

The ambush was completely successful: Peter was in a headlock before he had any idea he was under attack. Of course, the moment Peter felt himself humiliated, he could have little doubt as to who he was being humiliated by. "Ow," he said. "Get off!"

Andrew let him go. He didn't want to reawaken Peter's resentment, only to reinspire his fear. "Sunny is dead," he said.

Peter took a moment to realize what this meant. His brain was still thick with the acidic fogs of double Chemistry. "You mean you killed him?" he asked. He began to walk towards home.

"What do you think?" replied Andrew, not answering the question but not lying, either.

"But you said you wouldn't," Peter whined. Secretly, he was both delighted and dismayed: delighted that the conflict between Andrew and Paul was now likely to escalate to such a level of ferocity that they would ignore him completely; dismayed that Andrew was prepared to be so wantonly reckless in pursuing their revenge.

"The opportunity was there," said Andrew. "So, I took it."

Peter trudged on, oppressed by the renewed reality of what they intended. He spared a thought for Miranda. It hurt him to think of her being made sad.

"I'm going to go and find Paul," said Andrew.

"Shall I come, too?" asked Peter.

"No," said Andrew, definitely.

Peter watched as Andrew ran off. He was still thinking about Miranda.

By the time Andrew reached Paul's house, Paul was already home and changed. After a brief word with Paul's mother, they went upstairs. Paul already suspected something was up because Andrew's clothes were soaked through. Before they'd even sat down, Andrew told him, straight out, just as he'd told Peter.

"But we had an agreement," muttered Paul. "You broke our agreement."

"It was a tactical decision," said Andrew. "Peter already knows. He agrees it was the right thing to do, in the circumstances."

Paul sat down heavily on the edge of his bed. He was calculating the effects of Andrew's recklessness. "Gang is dead," he said. "If you are going to act alone, like some mercenary, we may as well all give up now."

"You should have seen them," said Andrew. "They were very upset."

"We can't trust anything you say," Paul whispered. "You're going out of control."

At this point, Andrew felt like confessing the truth – that he hadn't ever been in control of the situation and so hadn't now lost control of it. "Everything is the same," he said. "Things will carry on as per usual. Gang is still Gang. You are still Co-Leader. But I needed to make a decision today, and you weren't there to consult."

"Then you shouldn't have done anything," hissed Paul.

Andrew could see that only the passage of time would reconcile Paul to what had happened. He said, "I'll see you tomorrow." Paul did not respond. Andrew showed himself out.

"Are you sure you're not staying?" asked Paul's father – ready, as always, to be falsely friendly towards Andrew.

"No," Andrew replied. "I have to go."

vi.

Once outside, he walked about twenty yards down the path and then dived into the soaking undergrowth. He rootled himself down into the base of a laurel bush. This – the path – was the route that Paul would take on his way to Peter's. Andrew was pretty sure that, despite the rain, Paul would go by bicycle. After arming himself with two branches, one large and one medium-sized, Andrew squatted down to wait.

The evening was now a Winterish iron-gray. All around Andrew, everything was weighted down with water. Leaves dipped and dripped as raindrops fell on them from higher dipping-dripping leaves. Branches sagged under a burden almost, but not quite, equal to snow.

After about five minutes, Andrew heard the front door of Paul's house slam. It took Paul a couple more minutes to undo the combination lock on his bicycle, wipe the raindrops off the seat, wheel it down the garden path and out the gate. Andrew moved through the thick laurel bush until he was as close to the path as possible. Paul was unlikely to spot him through this gloom, but Andrew didn't want to take any unnecessary risks. Before mounting up, Paul had switched his front (white) and back (red) bicycle lights on. So it was easy for Andrew to see him coming, and to time his attack to the second. He threw the larger branch directly across the path. Paul saw the obstacle, panicked, braked, began to lose balance. Andrew now charged out of the laurel bush, collected water falling to either side of him. As Paul came to a halt, Andrew stuck the smaller branch between the spokes of the back wheel. Paul was immobilized. With a single shove, Andrew knocked Paul off-balance. Paul fell into a puddle on the ground, the bicycle landing on his legs. Andrew stepped on the crossbar, pushing the frame of the bicycle down onto Paul. "Go home," he said. "You are not going to make contact with Peter this evening."

Paul knew that no escape was possible. Andrew pressed down once more, then stepped back. Paul crawled wetly out. Defeated, he picked his bicycle up, pulled the stick out from the spokes, turned it round and rode wordlessly off back home. Andrew removed the larger branch from the path. His second ambush of the day had been even more successful than the first.

vii.

In the final gray of evening, he began to walk home. The path turned into a lane with allotments upon either side. They were completely deserted. No gardener, however obsessive, was prepared to be out on an evening such as this. Andrew sneezed. Under his coat, he was feeling hot and clammy. He cleared his sinuses of snot, spitting it over the hedge onto a row of outgrown cabbage stalks.

As soon as he got home, he had a bath and changed. But it was obvious that he was coming down with something. He sneezed all the way through dinner. When his mother took his temperature, it was 101. He was sent straight to bed.

Rendered doubly anxious by the information leaflets that the nurses in Midford Hospital had given her, Andrew's mother insisted on calling the doctor. He came round at about nine o'clock. After touching Andrew's forehead, taking his temperature and looking into his mouth, he asserted that the boy had nothing more serious than flu. Andrew should stay in bed, drink plenty of hot drinks and not go outside again until fully recovered. Andrew's father gave him a wink while his mother was showing the doctor to the door. "You see," he said. "You'll be up and about in no time."

Andrew's mother came back upstairs, tucked Andrew in, turned the lights out and left him to fall into a feverish sleep.

He dreamt first of birds then of being a bird. He was delighted by his newfound ability to fly, but frustrated that he had simultaneously lost the power of speech. Most annoyingly, he found himself unable to issue orders. For a short time, he was contented with flying high over Amplewick (a view suspiciously like the black and white aerial photograph that hung above the chair in the dentist's surgery). But, after a while, he decided to make a deal with the logic of his dream: he would trade in being able to fly for the greater delight of once again being able to issue orders.

viii.

Andrew woke up the next morning with a nose full of beautifully white snot and a head full of pain. His joints ached. He could not, despite exercising the utmost will, concentrate on anything. There were orders that he knew he needed to issue. Yet he also knew that it would be impossible to get them through. The lines of communication were broken. Neither Peter nor Paul was likely to pass by his house on the way to school. He could only hope that they did nothing without his prior consent.

As it happened, his hope was to be disappointed – though he did not know this until the following day.

CHAPTER TEN

Paul

Jawohl, sie sind nur ausgegangen
Und werden jetzt nach Hause gelangen.
O sei nicht bang, der Tag ist schön!
Sie machen nur den Gang zu jenen Höh'n!

Of course, they've only just gone
And they will come Home ere long.
O, do not fret, the Day is bright!
They're only out Ganging on yonder Height!

1.

Paul was not surprised when Andrew did not turn up at school the following day. (Nor, really, that Miranda, too, had stayed away.) He and Peter were told off for talking during Assembly. It was not until first break that they were able to hide themselves away in a toilet and properly discuss. They talked semi-code, so that any espionage agents loitering outside the cubicle would be unable to comprehend. Paul began –

"The Co-Leader said he spoke to you yesterday."

"He told me the first part of our present Operation had been accomplished early."

"Yes," said Paul, "he gave the same information to me."

Paul was quite desperate that Peter never learn quite how humiliated by Andrew he had been. (Having spent the whole night furious with himself for not having anticipated the ambush.)

Peter, by contrast, was eager to let Paul know that Andrew had rendered him, once again, helpless.

"He gave me a good duffing," he said, not without relish, "and said I mustn't report to you that evening."

Paul saw an opportunity to lie. "After he informed me, I decided it was better to wait before we discussed."

Peter looked at him as if to say, "And . . . ?"

Paul had given a good deal of thought to this matter. "This evening I will pay a visit to the Dinosaur House. I will see what has transpired. You will go home and await orders. I will report back tomorrow, if there's nothing to be done immediately. We can't do anything else. Not whilst we're in here."

Peter had ripped off a couple of sheets of waxy toilet paper, and was not tearing them into smaller and smaller squares.

A smell of cigarette smoke came from the next cubicle.

"What do you think?" said Peter.

Paul didn't really want to answer, but he had to.

"I think it's bad," he said. "Very bad, indeed."

The bell for second lessons went off, startling them as always.

Although they spent most of the day together, Operation Extinction was not alluded to again.

2.

When he arrived at the Dinosaur House, after finishing school, Paul fully expected to find Andrew there. But before he was even over the threshold, Mr Dinosaur had asked him if Andrew was all right.

"What do you mean?" asked Paul.

"Well, it's just we haven't seen him all day," replied Mr Dinosaur.

They went through into the living room and, after saying hello to Mrs Dinosaur, Paul tried to find out what damage Andrew's overprecipitate killing had done.

"I was sorry to hear about Sunny," he said.

The Dinosaurs looked at one another, sharing a glance of commiseration. Then Mrs Dinosaur related the whole story, in grotesque and unnecessary detail. She speculated upon the possible causes of her little one's death: the shock of the move, perhaps, or the sudden change in temperature (Bet's Pets had been terribly cold), or maybe the cake crumbs she'd tipped into the cage as a treat. Incidentally, she mentioned that Sunny's death had passed unwitnessed. She herself had been in the kitchen; Mr Dinosaur (although she didn't call him that) in the garden; Miranda up in her room.

Paul made sure he framed his next question with the utmost subtlety.

"Oh, I thought Andrew said he was already here, when –"

"Oh, no," said Mrs Dinosaur. "He didn't get here until just afterwards. Sunny was still warm, but definitely dead by then."

There seemed to be something in this that gave her perverse pleasure.

At this point, Miranda came downstairs. She did not enter the living room, but took up her customary position in the door-way.

Paul missed some of Mrs Dinosaur's description of the burial, distracted by a head full of calculation. Andrew had lied about killing Sunny. This revelation was both good and bad. It meant a great many contradictory things. Paul's dominant emotion was anger at Andrew for having failed in his first duty: truthfulness. (The Rules of Gang, Rule Seven: Always tell the whole truth and nothing but the truth to other Gang Members.) If they were going to lie to each other, just like grown-ups did, then there was no point in them considering themselves in any way superior to them. Paul was also angry at himself for having accepted Andrew's lie so unquestioningly – despite having had no outside hint that what his friend was saying might be untrue. The resolution rapidly formed within him: Andrew, whatever they had thought of him before, was no longer fit to lead – or even co-lead – Gang. He must immediately be forced into a subordinate position. After he had decided this, Paul turned his attention back to the Dinosaurs.

Despite his experience at Matthew's funeral, Paul still wasn't particularly comfortable with grief. He wanted to talk about other things, but he knew that – tactically – it was necessary to force the Dinosaurs to dwell upon the sad subject as much as possible.

Looking round the room, he could see that the birdcage was already gone. There seemed no point in suggesting they find a replacement for Sunny.

"What did you do with the cage?" he asked.

"I took it upstairs," answered Miranda, from the door-way. "It wasn't very heavy."

Paul ignored her, and asked Mrs Dinosaur, "Have you had any other pets?"

A long history followed, of birds, their little lives and deaths. They had also, once, long ago, had a dog. Paul asked about the dog, seeing such an enquiry as useful.

"Her name was Lady," replied Mr Dinosaur. "She was a lovely dog – a lovely temperament."

"She was a black Collie bitch," said Mrs Dinosaur.

"I don't remember her," interjected Miranda.

"It was before you were born," Mrs Dinosaur replied. "I think we've got a photo, somewhere, haven't we?"

Mr Dinosaur went to the sideboard and pulled out the photograph album.

Paul recoiled. He knew that, once the album was produced, anyone in the immediate vicinity was likely to be trapped for hours.

Mr Dinosaur handed the album to Mrs Dinosaur, who found the page with practised ease.

Lady was a black and white smudge in the lower left hand corner of a family portrait. The Dinosaurs, their daughter (Matthew and Miranda's mother) and her husband (their father) – all were there.

Miranda came close, and bent over Paul to have a look. He was on the sofa and she was behind him. Her long hair brushed against his ear and her sweet scent was all around him. He wanted to choke with disgust. A cross on a gold chain dangled from her neck, dowsing his shoulder-blade.

"She was a lovely dog," Mrs Dinosaur repeated.

"You could always get another one," suggested Paul.

Ideas were forming rapidly in his head. If he could achieve them, Andrew's budgerigar would look like nothing.

"Oh, we're too old for that," said Mr Dinosaur. "I couldn't do the walks any more."

"But we could," said Paul. "We could walk the dog every day."

"And I could, too," said Miranda, not displeased by the idea of walks alone (the dog wouldn't count) with Paul.

"Yes, but –" Mr Dinosaur said. "I think it might be a bit much, what with the yapping and everything. These puppies can be so lively. I'm not sure if I want a little blighter like that bashing up against my knees half the time."

Mrs Dinosaur was still lost in the photograph album, though whether the object of her reverie was her dead child or her dead dog or a co-mixture of both, it was impossible to tell.

"We don't have to get a puppy," Miranda said.

Paul reluctantly saw that an alliance with Miranda was the only way to forward the dog plan. Escalation was everything. If a bird hadn't worked, then a dog might. If they thought a dog too onerous, then persuade them to get a cat. Miranda seemed keen enough to play her part.

"I can ask around," said Paul. "If you're interested."

"Yes," said Mrs Dinosaur, emerging from her memories. "Why don't you do that."

Mr Dinosaur, who suspected his wife of not really knowing what the conversation was about, felt it necessary to say, "I think that might be a little bit premature. After all, they do take a lot of feeding, and they need a great deal of affection."

"And love," added Mrs Dinosaur, thinking of motherhood. Her husband had his garden; she had her photograph album. His surrogates grew; hers could only now be added to when Miranda, reluctantly, brought a photograph home from school.

271

"I'd give it lots of –" Miranda became embarrassed half-way through the sentence, and couldn't say the word. Instead, she said, "that."

Paul knew that nagging was girl's business. Now that he'd set Miranda's heart upon a dog, the best thing he could do was retreat – allowing her the full opportunity to wheedle, whine and whinge. He made his excuses. Miranda showed him out.

3.

The next evening, Paul returned to the Dinosaur House. When he pressed the door-bell, its bing-bong went unanswered. The day was already dark, and there were no lights on either in the living room or upstairs. He assumed the Dinosaurs had gone on an impromptu shopping trip – although he was unable to see how Miranda had beaten him back from school. The Dinosaur car, now he came to think of it, was nowhere to be seen. He looked around the garden, wondering what mischief he might do. A man with a dog walked down the path. Paul would have liked to uproot a few of the plants, but couldn't risk discovery. As he could wreak no havoc, he left for home.

Later that evening, he and Peter met up. They both had theories as to what might have happened. Peter thought the Dinosaurs had found out what was going on and had fled in terror, taking Miranda with them. (He was more concerned about this loss than about their lost opportunity for revenge.) Paul believed that they were engaged in a much less relevant activity. Perhaps, he speculated, one of their elderly friends had died and they had been called away to attend the funeral. Or maybe they had driven off to Midford to purchase the dog, and had decided to make an evening of it. His final possibility was that they had decided to go and live in a home, because the house had become too much for them.

4.

The next day, on his way to school, Paul took a detour past the Dinosaur House. It was with great relief that he saw the car was back and the lights were on. Yet he was unable to investigate further until he had endured another day of state education.

Peter was made a little less anxious by the news, given him during registration, that the Dinosaurs hadn't disappeared. Secretly, he'd been half-hoping they'd gone away somewhere safe. The responsibility of revenge was weighing heavy upon him. Miranda, again, stayed away from school.

She it was, however, who answered the door when Paul called round that evening.

"Hello," she said, as cheerily as she could.

Paul grunted and tried to push past her.

Miranda backed away, afraid that they might touch – something she had fantasized about, but wasn't yet actually ready for.

When Paul made it into the living room, he found that the Dinosaurs had company. A woman Paul had never seen before was sitting on their sofa, drinking a cup of tea.

"And who is this, then?" she asked, putting on an excruciating you-are-a-small-child voice. Her tone, however, was quite open – either Paul or the Dinosaurs were invited to answer. Miranda, for some reason, got in before them.

"This is Paul."

"He's been very helpful," said Mrs Dinosaur.

"They all have," added Mr Dinosaur.

Paul took another couple of steps forward, in a futile attempt to get further away from Miranda, who was crowding him from behind. There was a new smell in the Dinosaur House, heavy and sweet. Paul decided to employ the small child's tone of absolute conversational bluntness. "Who are you?"

"I'm Alma," she said. The use of only her first name suggested friendship militant.

It was only now that Paul noticed Mrs Dinosaur's left hand and how heavily bandaged it was.

"Alma is a Social Worker," said Miranda, loudly, right into his ear.

Unable to tolerate any more of Miranda's from-behind bothering, Paul crossed over to the other side of the room.

"As I was saying," said Alma, turning back to the Dinosaurs. "You can call me at the office any time you want. Just remember: help is at hand. We're not going to abandon you. The Meals-on-Wheels service can be a real boon during times like these."

Paul trained his full observational apparatus upon Alma. She was a dangerous woman. He estimated her decrepitude rating at around forty-five. Her hair was a big barnet of black, apart from one small swish of white. This ran between her left eyebrow and her right ear. Seen from a distance, it looked like combed-in birdshit. Her make-up was heavy and black under the eyes. The new smell in the room was her sicky perfume. Paul could also detect cigarette smoke, both fresh and stale. He saw that there was an unused ashtray on the coffee table in front of Alma. A small pile of leaflets lay there, too.

"You shouldn't have any more trouble with the electronics," said Alma. "We've checked all the plugs." She turned to Mr Dinosaur. "Please be careful what fuses you use. We don't want to risk anything like this happening again. The stair carpet – well, I don't know *how* it got into that state. It was a real deathtrap."

Paul began to realize what was going on. He didn't know a great deal about Social Workers, apart from what his father had told him – which was that they had a "difficult job to do, and did their best in very difficult circumstances". (Paul's father had had quite a few dealings with Social Workers, through his job at the local Comprehensive. At the dinner table, there was often talk

of "liaising" and "behaviour" and "truancy" and "inadequate".)
What Paul did not know was that his father had once reported
Andrew's father to the Social Services. (He had noticed one too
many bruises upon Andrew's legs.) But whatever Paul did or
didn't know, he knew enough to recognize Alma as an important
new enemy for Gang. He was now aware that she, with some
departed assistant, had looked the Dinosaur House over, render-
ing it once again safe and secure.

"We don't need help, thank you very much," said Mr
Dinosaur.

"I can still cook," Mrs Dinosaur said, raising her uninjured hand.

"And I can help," added Miranda. "And so can Paul and his
friends."

"They have been very helpful," Mrs Dinosaur said, not knowing what she said. "They've been round practically every day to
see if there was anything they could do to help."

"What's up with Andrew?" asked Mr Dinosaur.

"He's ill," said Paul, who had heard the news from his form
mistress, Miss Emily Whittle, that day at school. "He has flu.
He'll be better really soon."

Mr and Mrs Dinosaur no longer believed in small, harmless
illnesses.

"I hope so," said Mrs Dinosaur, and left it at that.

Paul felt Alma scrutinizing him, like the experienced espionage
agent she was.

"You were friends with Matthew, then?" she asked.

Paul nodded. He didn't trust his voice. It might come out in
so many tell-tale registers – the squeak of anxiety, the honk of
embarrassment.

"I was very sorry to hear about his death. You must miss him
terribly much."

Paul knew this tactic: Alma was now testing to see if she could
make him cry.

275

"He was our best friend," said Paul.

Alma looked at him very intensely for a couple of moments. Miranda, too, was watching Paul, though for very different reasons.

"Grief is a terrible thing," she said, eventually.

She turned back to Mrs Dinosaur, although part of her attention seemed to hang on around Paul like cigarette smoke.

"You must go to the doctor in three days. Change the bandages every twelve hours. Throw the old ones away, don't disinfect them and re-use them. I know you. But there's plenty more where they came from."

All three grown-ups laughed at this.

"We'll be fine," said Mrs Dinosaur. "Miranda can help with anything difficult."

Alma looked back at Paul.

"And you'll help, too, I suppose?"

He didn't know what to say. Alma seemed to suspect something. He didn't dare appear too keen. "We come round after school," he said. Then, unnecessarily, in a tactical error, he added, "Matthew was our friend."

Alma looked him over once more, as she said, "Well, we'll be keeping a bit closer eye on you than before." Then she turned to Mrs Dinosaur, as if she'd really been talking to her. "I'm afraid we've been very remiss. But what with the cuts . . ."

"We understand," said Mrs Dinosaur.

Mr Dinosaur began to escort Alma to the door.

"Don't you go wasting your time on us," he said. "I'm sure you've got far more needy cases to look after. We'll be just fine."

Alma turned in the door-way.

"Until next week, then," she said.

"Bye-bye, m'dut," Mrs Dinosaur replied, without standing up.

Paul, Miranda and Mrs Dinosaur listened together to Alma being shown out. They were all feeling the way schoolchildren do when the Headmistress leaves the room, and the class is alone again with its Form Teacher. Mrs Dinosaur, not wanting to be too complicit in the feeling of relief, turned to Miranda and said, "Well, she was very helpful, wasn't she?" She indicated the small pile of leaflets lying on the coffee table.

Miranda said, "Yes, but I don't like her perfume."

Mrs Dinosaur looked naughtily pleased. "You can't have everything," she said.

"Or her hair," added Miranda.

Mrs Dinosaur frowned in disapproval – of Miranda, not the hair.

"What happened to your hand?" asked Paul.

"Oh, it was so silly," said Mrs Dinosaur. "It was the kettle."

Mr Dinosaur re-entered the room on this word, and nodded – knowing immediately where the conversation was.

"I just clicked it on and poof! there was a big bang. It gave me quite a shock. I could feel it running through me."

Mr Dinosaur didn't like to hear talk of his wife's accident, and sat down protectively beside her.

"The fuse wasn't big enough, or was too big. I can never remember which is right. When I turned the kettle on it all just went bang! I nearly died of shock. The doctor said I might almost have died, really."

For an instant, but an instant only, Paul felt a whoosh of relief. If Mrs Dinosaur had really died, that would mean that they had really killed her.

"That's terrible," he said.

"The Social Worker said that all our fuses were wrong for what they were on," Mrs Dinosaur explained. "They said we were very lucky something worse hadn't happened."

Mr Dinosaur took his wife by the beloved hand.

"We've not been having much luck recently, have we?" he said. "Never mind. I'm sure we've turned the corner now."

Miranda, who was the only person in the room still standing, muttered ambiguously, "I hope so."

Paul was inflamed for an instant with the hope that she, too, wished death upon the Dinosaurs.

"You'll have to help us keep the house in order from now on," said Mrs Dinosaur, touching Paul with her cold hand. Paul felt sullied, and took the first opportunity to go upstairs and wash. (The fact that he was using the very same soap Mrs Dinosaur used did not alter the vigour with which he scrubbed her imprint off.) He had a quick look in the medicine bottles, and saw that they'd been replenished.

As he was coming back downstairs, he caught the very end of a whispered conversation.

"No, you tell him," hissed Miranda.

"Oh, all right, then," said Mrs Dinosaur. "But you seemed so keen earlier."

"I changed my mind," Miranda quietly said.

Paul waited ten seconds, then finished descending. In silence, he resumed his seat on the sofa. Even had he not overheard their whispering, he would have known that some announcement was about to be made.

"We've decided we would like to get a dog, after all," said Mrs Dinosaur.

"I think that's a very good decision," Paul replied, completely deadpan.

"Well, there's no need to be so po-faced about it," exclaimed Mr Dinosaur. "We thought you'd be happy."

"I am," said Paul. "I am." He caught Miranda looking at him again. There was a meaningful glint in her eye — a glint that he took as the reflection of anticipated mornings together, out in The Park, a dog yapping at their heels, laughter upon their lips. Miranda's motives for desiring this dog could no longer be ignored. She *fancied* him. Paul was too tactically astute not to

278

realize what leverage this gave him. Without the assistance of Miranda, Andrew would never have been able to accomplish the dog. There was a great deal more to be got out of this relationship, or Miranda's desire for it. But Paul nonetheless felt disgusted with himself, in advance, for having to tolerate her girlish glances. He might even have to talk to her at school.

Miranda looked at the floor, then back at Paul. What she saw in him at that moment was an entirely thrilling disdain.

"When are you going to get it?" he asked.

"We're going to the animal home at the weekend," said Miranda. "You can come, too."

Paul muttered something about not being sure if he could.

4.

When he managed to escape from the Dinosaur House, Paul went straight round to Peter's and briefed him on recent developments. He was not as pleased as he should have been.

"The kettle?" he said. "Miranda uses the kettle, doesn't she?"

"I suppose so," said Paul. "But that's not exactly relevant, is it?"

"We're not trying to make her extinct," Peter said. "We're doing it for her, partly. So she can be safe – in future."

"It was you who suggested the course of extinction," said Paul.

"Yes, but I didn't know –" Peter did not or could not finish his sentence.

They were in Peter's bedroom, away from his parents.

"Anyway," said Paul, "that line of attack can no longer be pursued. The Dinosaurs have a new ally. Her name is Alma. She is a Social Worker. I get the distinct feeling that from now on she will keep a close eye on the Dinosaurs. If we change the fuses again, we'll be caught. We have to do other things. The dog is a very good start. But we have to make sure Andrew doesn't assassinate it too soon."

"Definitely," said Peter.

Paul continued, "If we let him have his way it'll be dead the first time he takes it out for a walk. We really need to make sure they become attached to it. Andrew can't just kill it for the sake of killing it. If he gets too keen on killing something, then we'll just have to let him find some ducks, like always."

Peter nodded sagely. Paul knew that he was now running the show. With Andrew out of commission, even if only temporarily, tactical control of the operation had passed to him.

"I have some other ideas, as well," he said. And he went on to detail them to Peter, who agreed that they were very good ideas.

5.

True to their word, the Dinosaurs organized a trip that weekend to the Cat and Dog Home. Paul and Peter turned up, as arranged, at ten o'clock. Miranda, all excitement, was standing on the doorstep.

"They're here," she shouted back into the house. "Let's go."

Fifteen minutes later, when the Dinosaurs had finally finished faffing around, they all piled into the Morris Traveller. Miranda got in first, sitting on the left-hand side. Peter and Paul immediately began to argue about who should sit in the middle. Peter lost, and was shoved in. Paul sat, safely away from Miranda, on the right-hand side.

"Ready?" asked Mr Dinosaur.

The car was about to drive off when Miranda suddenly remembered something she needed to fetch from the house: a hairbrush.

"Can't you do without it?" her grandmother asked.

"No," said Miranda, who these days was utterly indulged.

Mr Dinosaur took the keys out of the ignition and handed them over.

When Miranda returned, carrying the hairbrush, she got in the right-hand side – even though Peter had kept the other door open.

"Shove up," she said.

Paul had to shift over to the middle. Peter pulled the other door shut. Miranda had her wily way.

They set off. In the last few days, the weather had turned. Sleety rain spattered across the windscreen. The bottom of the car tinkled with thrown-up grit.

Paul tried to punish Miranda for the success of her trick by sticking his elbow into her ribs. He got a couple of good jabs in, whilst the car was going round roundabouts. But it soon became evident that Miranda welcomed physical contact of *any* sort. Once he realized this, Paul naturally recoiled. Pleased enough with the victory already achieved, Miranda did not press for a second. There was always the drive home (though Paul was resolved not to be caught by the same trick twice).

The Cat and Dog Home was situated on a road about five miles to the south of Amplewick. One of the bonuses of the trip was that Peter and Paul were able to have a close look at a vast radio listening station that dominated the surrounding landscape. It was a circle of thin steel poles and struts, about eighty feet high and a half mile in diameter. Support wires pulled off from it in very gradual slopes. This was where we (England) listened in to see what the Russkis were plotting. It was a known fact, in the local area, that Soviet nuclear warheads were targeted directly at this map reference.

The Cat and Dog Home was within sight of this important military installation.

The Morris Traveller drew up onto the gravelled forecourt.

As Paul and Peter got out, the sound of woeful-hopeful barking was all around them. Mr Dinosaur went into the front office, emerging a couple of minutes later with a bright-faced young woman in green Wellington boots. There were, she said, about twenty dogs for them to choose from. She led them into a long corrugated-iron hut. They walked along a wet-floored corridor, looking left and right into the cages. Paul was careful to keep the Dinosaurs between himself and Miranda.

One animal, a tragic-faced Bloodhound called Winston, caused the Dinosaurs particular anguish. The optimistic young woman in green Wellingtons informed them that he had been waiting to find a new owner for nine months. The Dinosaurs both looked back into Winston's cage and let out small moans of sympathy. They almost decided to take him. But the Wellington woman, much as she hated destroying the Bloodhound's chances of finding a loving home, felt it necessary to inform these nice people of the likely cost, per week, of feeding and housing Winston. The Dinosaurs shook their heads, moaned anew, said a sad "No," and moved on to the next cage.

Their final quandary fell between Sandy, a neurotic russet-haired Cocker Spaniel, Tripper, a bouncy Dalmatian, and Lizzie, a bashful mongrel Collie bitch.

In the end, they said they'd like to meet Lizzie. Her temperament seemed the most docile, an important factor in this equation.

They went into a small side room whilst the Wellington woman put Lizzie's lead on.

The mixture of affection and terror with which the black Collie greeted them when she was brought through was enough to win the Dinosaurs' hearts for ever. She strained at the leash to get near them, then flinched away when they reached out to stroke her.

"Ahh," was said, again and again – by the Dinosaurs, Miranda, the Wellington woman; even, a couple of times, to join in and not be too conspicuous, by Paul and Peter.

Finally, the Wellington woman said, "I think she's taken a shine to you."

With that, the issue was decided. The dog's lead was handed over to Miranda whilst Mr and Mrs Dinosaur went off to do the paperwork.

The dog strained at the lead, eager to get out of the home. It understood escape.

Paul was very pleased with the choice the Dinosaurs had made. Lizzie was obviously very loving, trusting and stupid. If they'd chosen something sensible, like a guard dog, then he would have felt some remorse at the thought of its inevitable demise. They were never going to get something he would actively enjoy watching die, like a pampered poodle or a lacka-daisical lap-dog.

Miranda let Lizzie drag her along so she bumped into Paul. He stepped aside, polluted again by her touch.

Paul wondered if Peter had noticed the way Miranda was pestering him. Peter, on the other hand, wondered if Paul could tolerate being pestered for much longer. He felt disappointed that Miranda had chosen Paul and not him as the person she most wanted to annoy. It made him feel like trying to attract her attention. The best thing, he thought, would be to cause her a small but unignorable amount of pain. If he could have tripped her over so that she tumbled into a muddy puddle and looked up at him, wet all over, with resentful eyes, that would have been very satisfying.

Mr Dinosaur came out of the office carrying a box full of dog supplies: a bowl, chews, flea powder, a bone. They got into the car and set off for home. To Paul's great relief (initially, at any rate), Miranda had to accompany Lizzie in the very rear of the car – behind the back seats. But Paul soon became aware of the drawbacks of this arrangement. Miranda could look at him whenever she wanted (which turned out to be almost all the time). She could also place Lizzie so that she was right up close behind him. From this position, the dog would prop itself up on its haunches and wetly lick the back of his neck. Miranda would pull her away and playfully scold her, but not until she was satisfied Paul had received a sufficient tonguing. In between attacks, Miranda let Lizzie lick all over her face. Peter's neck was left entirely unmolested, although he tried as discreetly as he could to lean over toward the dog.

As compensation for being humiliated in this way, Paul used the drive home to think over the practicalities of killing the dog. Somehow, they would have to separate Lizzie from both the Dinosaurs and Miranda. The way things were turning out, it seemed likely that whenever Paul walked the dog, Miranda would want to come too. Andrew could hardly be trusted. That left only Peter to volunteer for dog-walking duties. Whatever happened, Lizzie's death would have to look like an accident. Given the opportunity, Andrew would probably choose to decapitate her with a spade whilst the others held her down. Andrew was an expert in killing, and like all experts he had his preferences. In fact, Andrew believed that there was a definite logic behind the method of killing chosen for each animal: squishable animals (frogs, toads) were squashed; flammable animals (squirrels, ducks) were burnt; vicious animals (rats, cats) were dispatched with extreme viciousness; common animals (rabbits, pigeons) were eliminated almost in passing, with no elaborate preparation. Small animals – mice, voles, dormice – a category on their own, were catapulted into brick walls. This was the most actionous way of killing them. There was one wall in Wychwood where these Firing Squads traditionally took place. Exceptions to this logic were, of course, made. Although drownings never satisfied Andrew as much as maimings (perhaps because it was impossible to see what was going on), he was not unaware of the irony of killing ducks by holding them under water. His favourites, undoubtedly, were newts. During bright Summer, he placed these on a slate where they would rapidly roast. During Winter, when they were much rarer, he fed them tail-first through the clothes mangle – so that we could hear their spines crack, link by link, and watch their guts pop out of their mouths. In all of this, Paul and Peter played their part, though with varying degrees of enthusiasm. Peter wished to experiment upon living organisms; Paul enjoyed rebelling against his parents' vegetarianism. Andrew, however, felt it was his duty to kill any- and everything he could get his hands on. Hence rule three of the Rules of Gang, "Live to Kill, Kill to Live."

6.

They arrived back at the Dinosaurs', Paul's neck having been coated in dog saliva only five or six times more. Miranda proposed an immediate walk, a motion that Lizzie (who undoubtedly understood the word) seconded by an enthusiastic display of pawing, jumping, tail-chasing and general jitteriness. Mr and Mrs Dinosaur assented. The idea of such doggy energy being admitted into their house frankly terrified them. Whilst Lizzie was being tired out, knick-knacks could be removed from side-tables to safer shelves, a corner in the living room could be prepared for her with blanket and bowl, and a few nervous looks could be exchanged.

"Have we done the right thing?"

"I don't know."

The youngsters took Lizzie up through The Furze, quite close by Base Camp #1, and then over the road to The Park. Here, Paul finally persuaded Miranda to let her off the leash. Lizzie immediately began to run in circles round the three of them.

They walked on, Miranda doing her best to keep close to Paul, Paul doing his best to keep away from Miranda. Peter was drawn to first one, then the other. Seen from above, their paths followed a plaiting pattern.

When they encountered another dog, a Red Setter, interested in sniffing Lizzie's undercarriage, she became incredibly bashful and screwed her rear-end into the ground. After the trauma of this unwelcome encounter, she was a chastened dog and kept more or less to heel.

Peter, although somewhat embarrassed by Paul's presence, attempted to engage Miranda in conversation.

"She runs very fast, doesn't she?" he said, whilst Lizzie was running. But Miranda replied only distractedly. "Yes, she is." Her attention was elsewhere. What she really wanted was for Paul to look at her, to see her, to take her fully in.

Peter wanted roughly the same thing from Miranda, though he also wanted her to be impressed by the sight of him. He wasn't sure in what way exactly he wanted her to be impressed, he just knew that impressed was what she needed to be.

By now they had almost reached the door of the Gamekeeper's Cottage. Miranda was hoping that she might get invited in for tea. But Paul seemed to have had enough. He said that he had to go in. Peter and Miranda would have to take Lizzie home together.

"Goodbye," said Miranda, longingly.

Paul turned and hurried away without even thinking about replying.

It was only after they had been walking for a full, fully silent minute that Peter finally thought of something to say and worked up the courage to say it.

They were walking into the children's play area, past the swings and slides.

"I'm glad it was your grandmother and not you who got injured."

"How can you say that?" Miranda wailed. "That's a terrible thing to say."

"Why?" asked Peter, genuinely taken aback by her response. "It could easily have been you. You use the kettle, too, don't you?"

"But it didn't have to be her or me. It could have been no-one. It didn't have to happen."

Seated on one of the park benches, a young mother was wiggling her baby's pram with one hand while holding a cigarette in the other.

"Andrew told me about the fuses," said Peter. "They were all wrong, weren't they? Something was bound to happen. I'm just saying I'm glad it wasn't you. It's better that it was your grandmother, who hasn't got so long to live, anyway."

"She's perfectly healthy," said Miranda.

The mother with the pram shouted at them, "Can't you read the sign! You're not meant to bring dogs in here!"

They hurried on.

"Yes," said Peter. "I suppose it would have been even better if it had been your grandfather. Everybody knows he's going to die soon, anyway."

"The doctors say he's responding very well to treatment. He might not die for years yet. Anyway, I don't know why we're talking about this. I don't like talking about it."

"I sometimes wish my parents were dead," said Peter, trying to re-establish some common ground.

"Really?" asked Miranda, her eyes already awash. "Well, you wouldn't if they were!"

She stormed out through the play-area gate, slamming it shut behind her – almost catching both Peter and Lizzie in the process.

Peter shouted after her, "I just want to be your friend."

Lizzie, still off her lead, was confused. She thought this might be something like a game. Her part, she surmised, was to run back and forth between her two new owners. It was unusual that neither of them was calling her name; but maybe this was a version of the running-between game with which she was, as yet, unfamiliar. One had to make allowances for new owners. (Lizzie didn't really think this, she just behaved in a manner which suggested she did.)

Peter climbed over the gate, caught up with Miranda, and for the next five minutes walked alongside her repeating variations on this sentence, "I'm really sorry, Miranda."

Eventually, she couldn't take any more.

"All right," she said. "If you're really sorry just leave me alone. I can walk home on my own. I don't need your help. I'm not stupid or anything."

"I know you're not," said Peter.

"Then let me go home. I'll tell them you stayed at Paul's."

By now, Lizzie had calmed down and was walking to heel – Miranda's heel.

"But we were meant to all go together," Peter said. "They'll be angry."

"Then I'll tell them you came all the way home with me, you just had to hurry off when you got there."

Peter didn't know what to think. Something about the idea of having Miranda lie for him, even in these difficult circumstances, made him vaguely excited.

"They might see," he said.

"They won't," Miranda replied. "They can hardly see the TV, let alone to the end of the garden."

"I don't know," Peter said, doubtfully.

"If you're really sorry," Miranda said.

Lizzie was skulking along with her ears down. Naturally, she assumed that their shouting was her fault.

Peter said, "All right."

Miranda immediately turned and walked away down the hill towards the football field.

"Goodbye," said Peter.

Miranda did not look back.

For a while, Lizzie tried to continue running back and forth between them. But, in the end, she chose to go with Miranda. Things were more exciting with her: she was moving; Peter was just standing still.

Not for long, however. As soon as Miranda was out of sight, Peter ran into the trees.

She followed the path; he, taking a more difficult route, followed *her*.

In her distress, Miranda didn't look back.

Peter watched her all the way back to the Dinosaurs'. He felt annoyed at not having been able to say what he wanted to say. Somehow, he felt protective towards her. He wanted to warn her. He felt like he should tell her that bad things were going to happen but that, in the end, it was all going to be for the best. He knew that if she just listened to him, she would understand. An impulse to go and knock on the door was just taking hold of him, when he felt his throat being grabbed and heard Paul's voice in his ear.

"What did you tell her?" Paul asked.

"Nothing," said Peter.

Paul pulled him away from the Dinosaurs' garden hedge.

"Then why were you having a massive argument right in the middle of The Park?"

"Did you follow me here?" inquired Peter.

"What did you tell her?"

"I told you, I told her nothing."

Peter proceeded to give Paul a version of conversational events that Paul found so annoying he knew it had to be true.

"You only mentioned the fuses once?" Paul asked.

"Only once."

"You didn't say anything more than what you've just said now?"

"I said what I said I did," Peter said.

Paul pushed Peter up against the trunk of one of the holly trees. "You must *never* talk to her about this again," he said. "If you do, we could all end up in prison. In prison. Do you understand?"

Peter said, "Yes." He was petrified. Partly because Paul never made threats like that, and partly because – whilst making the threats – Paul had sounded exactly like Andrew. Peter didn't know if he could cope with two such friends.

Paul let Peter go, and they began to stroll back to Paul's.

"For the moment," said Paul, "we walk the dog as if we were just walking the dog."

Peter did not immediately reply.

"Do you understand?" Paul said.

"Yes," said Peter. "But I don't think Miranda will want to come out with me."

"If we get the dog to ourselves from early on, then that's all to the good. We just need to make sure it's you or me walking it on our own, not Andrew." Paul was on the point of saying, "We can't trust him any more." But he knew that disloyalty on that scale would only be destructive. He must allow Peter to continue believing that, beneath all the surface dissension, there was an essential unity.

"You did very well at the animal home today," Paul said. "And in the car on the way back. Miranda was being very annoying, wasn't she?"

"Unbearable," Peter said.

They turned right before they reached the War Memorial. The rain that had held off so far that day now began to fall. Paul did not speed up, and Peter kept pace with him.

290

He said, "I'm worried we're going to hurt Miranda."

"We won't," said Paul. "She's perfectly safe."

As they continued to walk, Paul couldn't help but think how completely their sphere of operations had changed since the beginning of the Summer. Everything, then, had taken place outside, in sunshine, loudly, bravely. Gang, in its foursquareness, had had a numerical strength. Now, everything seemed unbalanced, wobbling, about to topple. There was going to be a smash. Damage would be sustained. Casualties were inevitable. Their eventual Victory was being tainted by the very means they were using to achieve it. Paul wanted to talk about Matthew. He wanted Peter and himself, between them, to remember things about their dead friend that separately would have been for ever forgotten. But even this had become a tactical activity.

By the time Paul and Peter were safely installed in Paul's bedroom, they had achieved an unprecedented silence. They both fiddled with model cars and trains, pretending to fix things that weren't broken, dismantling things that could never be reassembled. Finally, Peter said, "See you later."

At the bottom of the stairs, Paul's mother attempted to interrogate him about the dog. What kind was it? Where had they got it from? Were they pleased? Peter remembered Paul's cat's death, anticipated the dog's likely fate, mumbled something about it being black and white, fled.

He ran most of the way home. Although it was only Saturday he was ashamed to find himself looking forward to the safety of school.

CHAPTER ELEVEN

Peter

Sie sind uns nur vorausgegangen
Und werden nicht wieder nach Hause gelangen!
Wir holen sie ein auf jenen Höh'n im Sonnenschein!
Der Tag ist schön auf jenen Höh'n!

They've only gone before we came!
And don't want to come Home again!
We'll catch them up, in Sunshine bright!
The Day is bright on yonder Height!

i.

Peter woke to the realization that he and Paul had parted the previous evening without deciding which of them should go round to the Dinosaur House. He strongly suspected that Paul wanted him to take up escort duties. His wish to make peace with Miranda persuaded him further in this direction. And so, soon after finishing his breakfast and bringing the Archives up to date, he set off by bicycle.

That day, everything was swathed in mist, through which the trees – their shapes simplified – appeared to have been cut out of sheet metal. If Peter had stopped and looked at them, some of their intricacy might have been recovered. But the grey mizzle kept his eyes to the wet road.

The first thing that Peter really noticed in the outside world was Andrew's bicycle, leant up against the beige door of the Dinosaur garage.

Peter rang the door-bell. The bing-bong was answered, as he had dreaded, by someone other than Miranda.

"Oh," said Mrs Dinosaur. "You've just missed them. They left ten minutes ago."

"With Paul?"

"No, it was just Andrew came round."

"Do you know where they went?"

Mrs Dinosaur turned and called back into the living room, "Do you know where they went?"

"The Park, I think," came Mr Dinosaur's reply.

Peter was off and running before Mrs Dinosaur had time to echo her husband's words.

Mrs Dinosaur watched as Peter's bicycle slowly toppled over onto the soft lawn. An instinct to pick it up had to be overcome. She couldn't risk getting wet, getting ill. Her husband hadn't been feeling too bright this past couple of days. The effort of driving to the Cat and Dog Home seemed to have taken more out of him than it should. The previous night had been bad. He hadn't been able to keep dinner down at all. There were still flecks of broad beans in white sauce around the rim of the toilet bowl. She felt ashamed for not having made time to clean them off. But her husband needed what she hated to call "nursing". "He just needs a bit of minding," that's how she put it. As if it were merely a continuation of the feeding, clothing, cleaning and agreeing with that had been her delight throughout forty years of marriage.

She closed the door behind her.

"You'll never guess," she said as she re-entered the living room.

Peter was frantic in his pursuit of Andrew. (So frantic, in fact, that he hadn't considered how much faster his pursuit would have been had he not left his bicycle behind.) He imagined the terrible things his friend might, at that very moment, be doing.

Peter's hair was wet, and as he ran his blond cowlick kept banging against his eyelids.

His first sight of Andrew came when he had sprinted about half-way down The Prom. His friend's silhouette was just disappearing over the horizon at the top of The Furze: Miranda's, frailer, was also there; Lizzie's could not be made out.

Peter could see which way they were heading, and cut cater-cornered across the playing fields to intercept them.

As he ran round the base of the hill, Peter could hear Lizzie barking almost constantly. He was reassured by the sound, for it meant nothing fatal had yet happened to the dog.

Peter arrived at the crossroads just as Andrew and Miranda and, yes, Lizzie were turning towards The Park.

"Hey!" Peter called. Neither of them turned round. Lizzie was the first of their party to notice him. She glanced back, but carried on trotting to heel – Andrew's heel.

Peter ran up to Andrew and put his hand on his shoulder, which made Andrew flinch away as if in pain.

"I heard you'd gone," gasped Peter. "I caught up."

Andrew glared at Peter, then said, "It's a nice dog, isn't it?"

One of the things Peter had never been able to understand was why animals loved Andrew so much – even those he was moments away from torturing to death. The whole long walk to the clearing, Paul's father's cat had purred quite happily in Andrew's arms. Lizzie seemed equally besotted with her would-be future killer. The dirt of her paw-prints was all over Andrew's knees.

"We helped choose her," said Peter.

"It was my decision, really," corrected Miranda. "Lizzie's *my* dog."

Peter tugged at Andrew's sleeve, trying discreetly to get him away from Miranda.

"What?" said Andrew.

Miranda looked round. Peter was scared out of the attempt to gain a private word. For several weeks, Miranda's glance had been enough to make him stop whatever he was doing.

"Have you seen Paul today?" Miranda asked.

After an awkward pause, Peter replied, "No."

That was all she'd wanted from him. She turned and walked quickly away.

Andrew, however, stood staring at Peter for a good couple of seconds. Finally, he spoke – just as Miranda went out of earshot. "You fancy her, don't you?"

Peter was so mortified that Andrew had somehow discovered his secret that he couldn't even bring himself to deny it.

"You do," said Andrew, and sprinted off to catch Miranda up.

Peter followed.

Keeping Lizzie safely on her lead, they crossed the busy road that separated The Furze from The Park.

The rest of the walk passed off without incident.

ii.

Peter's anxiety increased again, however, once they returned to the Dinosaur House. In their absence, Paul had arrived. He was sitting on the settee, right beside Mrs Dinosaur. Mr Dinosaur was in his usual armchair, although Peter noticed that, unlike before, he had a brown tartan blanket over his legs. It was horrendous: Andrew and Paul were facing each other, surprised and hostile, at the very heart of their battleground. Paul's position on the sofa was obviously the most advantageous. Settling for a strategic retreat, Andrew took the spare armchair. Miranda kept her usual door-way position. Peter stood awkwardly in front of the fireplace, confirming allegiance to nobody in particular.

"Have a nice walk, did you?" asked Mr Dinosaur.

Lizzie was at his feet, her wagging tail beating out a jungle rhythm upon the leg of the coffee table.

Since there were three young people who might answer, and each of them wanted to see which of the other two would speak first, Mr Dinosaur got no reply.

Eventually, Paul's strength of character triumphed. "She's a very lively dog," he said.

"Lovely, did you say?" asked Mr Dinosaur, leaning a little forwards – not really deaf, not really mishearing, just seeing an easy opportunity further to embarrass a youngster.

"No," said Paul, suspecting the ploy but unable to counteract, "I said 'lively'."

Mr Dinosaur hammed up the falling back. "Oh, I thought you said 'lovely'."

300

Andrew decided this was a battle he had to join.

"She is," he said. "She's a very lively dog."

Missing the point completely, Mrs Dinosaur chipped in with, "Lovely lively Lizzie."

Mr Dinosaur, however, wasn't going to allow himself to lose out here. Infuriation was his home territory. "Not too lively, I hope," he said.

"Oh, no," said Andrew, just before Paul could speak, "just lively enough."

Paul was at first annoyed that he hadn't been quicker in his response, but when he heard Mr Dinosaur's next question, he was almost glad at having been slow.

"And how lively," asked Mr Dinosaur, "would that be?"

Lizzie's sub-table tail-thumping continued, drumming out the long moments it took for Andrew to construct his reply: "Lively enough not to be boring."

He knew it wasn't sufficient.

Mr Dinosaur was good at this kind of thing, good at being really stupid.

"Oh no," the victor said. "She's certainly not boring. Are you, you little tyke?"

Andrew felt like smashing the old man's dentures in right then and there. Both Paul and Peter were aware of his furious impatience. Observing this exchange had been like watching someone tickling the nose of a panther with a very bushy but not very long feather. They needed to get Andrew outside, and fast. If he stayed here much longer, he would do something obvious. Paul looked over at Peter, with the intention of making a quick nod towards the door. But Peter was utterly transfixed by the spectacle of Andrew scratching Lizzie's upturned, teated belly. Paul knew he would have to manufacture their exit all by himself.

"I'm sorry," he said, "but we have to go." Then he turned to Peter, "Don't we?"

Having missed Paul's moments-ago glance, Peter was unprepared. "Yes," he said, then started out on a non-existent explanation. "We have to –"

Paul had anticipated Peter's failure, and quickly made up for it with, "– be somewhere else."

Mr Dinosaur recognized the youngsters' usual tone: evasiveness. "Important things to do, no doubt."

Paul had met Andrew's glare, and was reflecting it back when Miranda unexpectedly put in, "Do you have to?"

Paul looked at her in horror. This ill-timed intervention was just the sort of thing that made him particularly hate girls.

Miranda looked at her grandfather as she said, "You need some help in the garden, don't you?"

For a moment it looked as if Mr Dinosaur had enjoyed annoying the boys enough for one day. But then he decided he might as well make the best of it, while they could still be forced into doing chores for free. "Well," he said, "there's just a bit of digging-over. Weeding-out."

"And Paul could help out inside, couldn't he?" said Miranda.

Mrs Dinosaur said, "I suppose there is always the hoovering."

Andrew looked at Paul. "We can do that," he said. "Can't we?"

As it now seemed inevitable they would have to stay, Paul replied, "You can do the hoovering, I'll go and work in the garden."

Miranda was disappointed, but consoled herself with the thought of watching Paul from her grandparents' bedroom window.

"Come on, Peter," Paul said. "You can help me. I'm sure Andrew can cope by himself."

The two of them went outside, and for an hour or so made the flower-beds as messy as they could.

302

From the sitting room, for a while, came the sound of hoovering. Then, all of a sudden, it stopped.

Very early on, Paul became aware that Miranda was spying upon them. When he passed this information on, Peter started to work much faster.

About half-way through, Mrs Dinosaur, accompanied by Miranda, brought them out some orange squash and biscuits.

"Lovely," said Mrs Dinosaur, inspecting the devastation they had been causing. "I'm sure he'll be delighted when he gets out here again. He's not been feeling himself, recently."

"He's gone upstairs to bed," added Miranda, looking significantly at Peter. "But he's going to be well again very soon."

Peter knew she wanted him to remember what he'd said in The Park, about Mr Dinosaur dying soonest of all.

Mrs Dinosaur paused before adding, "Of course he is."

iii.

When they came inside, they found Andrew putting the Hoover away in the stair cupboard.

"And now we'll really have to go," said Paul.

"Right you are," said Mrs Dinosaur. Miranda whispered good-bye to Paul. Peter's loud, clumsy see-you-later was aimed at Mrs Dinosaur but his heart intended it entirely for Miranda.

She closed the door behind them as they were mounting their bicycles.

Andrew was out through the gate and off down the path before the other two had a chance to speak to him. All they could do was try and catch him up. It was a simple trick. Paul hated him for it. For the moment, Andrew might not have been the Leader but he was in the lead.

After five minutes, they discerned that Andrew, who was about two hundred yards ahead of them, was no longer simply

fleeing but had chosen a destination. He was doubling back –
not towards the Dinosaur House, but in a Westerly direction.
They gained on him slowly but not before it had become clear
that he was drawing them off towards the Tree-Fort, down Road.

Paul caught up with Andrew when they were about half-way
there. He cycled alongside him for a while, assessing the situation.
Andrew had a smirk upon his face, the kind of smirk he always
had when he knew something you didn't – something he knew
you'd want to know.

"Where are we going?" huffed Paul.

"You know where," Andrew replied, and pedalled faster to
get away again.

But Paul wasn't going to let him put any distance between
them.

For a half-mile or so, they engaged in an all-out sprint, leaving
Peter totally behind.

Andrew gave up when he realized that whereas he was straining to escape, Paul was merely doing enough to coast along in
his slipstream.

They came to a slight incline, and Andrew let Paul draw up
alongside him once again. But he was no more communicative
than before.

"Why are we going to the Tree-Fort?" Paul gasped.

"You'll see," said Andrew.

They rode on for another fifteen minutes or so, gradually
reducing their speed so that Peter could catch up.

On arriving at the field, they opened the gate, pushed their
bicycles through and then closed the gate behind them. After
depositing the bicycles up alongside The Door, they made their
way into the great ring of oaks.

Paul allowed Peter to ask the questions. "Why have we come
here?" he said. "We only come here for really important things."

Andrew, still smirking, with his secret knowledge, reached

under his jumper and started to pull something up from under the belt of his trousers.

"Isn't this important enough?" he said, triumphantly plucking forth the Dinosaurs' photograph album.

"Oh, no," said Paul.

"What?" said Peter, out of surprise, not incomprehension.

"I stole it," Andrew crowed, "when Mr Dinosaur went upstairs and Mrs Dinosaur and Miranda brought you out your treats."

Peter still didn't know how to react, and was looking to Paul for guidance.

Paul was stunned. When he finally recovered, it was to shout, "You stupid idiot!"

Andrew ignored this. "We can burn it," he said. "On Bonfire Night. We can stick it in the middle of a Guy and burn it and no-one will ever know. We could even get some money off the Dinosaurs for the Guy." He laughed at the marvellous irony of this.

Peter was half caught up in Andrew's enthusiasm. But Paul's shock was now being replaced by cold calculation.

"They'll miss it straight away," he said. "They always keep it in the same place. They'll never believe they lost it. They'll know it was us that stole it. They'll tell the police."

"No, they won't," said Andrew, rather amazed that Paul wasn't jumping about with delight.

"You've ruined everything. Of *course* they'll know it was us. Who else has been in the house?"

"I don't know," said Andrew. "Lots of people."

"If the police think we stole it, they'll keep us away from the Dinosaurs. We won't be able to make them extinct."

Andrew thought about this for a moment. "If we burn it, they'll be really unhappy," he said. "It'll really help us. They won't want to live any more."

Paul and Andrew had gradually come nearer and nearer to

305

each other. They were now shouting right into one another's faces. Peter stood to their side, ready to try and part them if and when a fight started.

"We have to take it back," said Paul.

"No," said Andrew, "stealing it was a good idea."

"It was the most stupid thing ever."

"What would you have done instead, eh? Nothing. Just helped Mr Dinosaur dig over his vegetables."

"The plan was to kill the dog when we judged it would be worst for the Dinosaurs."

Andrew's impatience made him jump from foot to foot. He thought about punching Paul, but instead decided to say, "It's all too slow. If we do it your way, they'll never die. They have to be extinct by Christmas. That was the promise we made to Matthew."

"We won't be able to do anything if we're in prison."

"The police can't prove we took it. Not if we burn the evidence. We can burn it now. They'll never prove anything. I've got some matches."

"No, we have to take it back before they miss it. We have to take it back right now."

"I'm Leader," said Andrew. "I'm in control. I give the orders."

"No, you're not," said Paul, "Peter and me decided I was the only Leader."

"When?"

"A few days ago."

Andrew flicked a glance at the traitor. His father's was the only way to deal with a rebellion of this direct, undisguised sort: violence. The photograph album dropped to the ground as Andrew lunged towards Paul, fingers spread, aiming for his throat. But Paul knew Andrew too well to be caught out. Ever since he joined Gang, he had followed the rhythms of the Leader's anger. By now, Paul was like the owner of a cigarette lighter with a clapped-out flint – able to tell, just before it catches, exactly when it's going to spark. The dropping of the photograph album gave him an extra second's warning. This, he took full advantage of. As Andrew came towards him, he stepped back and punched him very swiftly and cleanly on the nose. Andrew's hands abandoned the attempted stranglehold. They flew up to cover his face. But, almost as soon as they got there, they began to tense up and curl themselves into fists. Paul, realizing he had to act now or lose perhaps for ever the edge he'd gained, put his head down and rammed himself into Andrew's guts. Like a prop forward in a rugby scrum, he kept driving onwards, whilst Andrew slammed ineffective punches into his lower back.

As soon as the fight started, Peter had decided not to intervene. It was best, he thought, that the Co-Leaders be allowed to battle out their differences. After Paul had knocked Andrew safely out of the way, he'd stepped in to pick the photograph album off the ground.

Andrew could not backpedal for very much longer without being slammed into one of the Tree-Fort oaks. And so, he let his legs buckle beneath him, in hopes that Paul would keep pushing. This would allow him the opportunity to attack him from behind. But Paul, aware that his chances of victory would be much greater in a floorbound scrap than a stand-up slugging match, let himself fall heavily down on top of Andrew. There followed the usual frantic attempts by each to grab the other's wrists. Paul got Andrew's left, Andrew Paul's left. Andrew assumed the fight was now an endurance test. Whose grip would weaken first? That was the issue. He was sure he could win such a contest. Stubbornness was his greatest quality. However, Paul, still physically on top, was determined not to allow Andrew's strengths to come into play. He let go of Andrew's wrist and smacked him a second time and a third time in the face. Enraged, Andrew let go of Paul's left wrist and tried to counterpunch.

Paul dodged this too-predictable move, paused for a second or so before Andrew fell back upon the ground, and then made a grab for both his wrists. The hands landed, the wrists were held, and in an instant Paul found himself victorious. However much Andrew bucked and strained, he could not wriggle his way free.

Peter approached the two of them, the photograph album clutched to his chest.

"Help me!" shouted Andrew, his eyes wide and white like a penned-in bull. "That's an order."

But Peter could see who had won the battle. With Andrew trapped as he was, all Paul had to do was wait. Andrew would eventually have to agree terms for his release.

"I'll have you court martialled!" screamed Andrew.

"By who?" asked Paul, feeling the calm of total triumph.

Andrew tried to spit up at Paul, but the gob fell short and slopped back down onto his own exposed neck. His Adam's apple was sticking out as abruptly as a molehill. His throat seemed to ache and bulge with trapped, humiliated pride. He began to choke. Paul interpreted this as the old 'feigned weakness' trick, a ruse so obvious he was surprised Andrew was even trying it.

"Get off," coughed Andrew.

Paul waited and waited, until he saw Andrew's face turn pink and screw up like a newborn baby's. When he was reasonably certain that Andrew wasn't putting it on, he got ready to let go. He knelt forwards, forcing Andrew's wrists right into the ground. Andrew's upper body was all bunched and hunched up, like that of some spastic in a spazzmobile. Paul then did half a handstand, flipping his legs over until they were clear to one side of Andrew's body. Andrew yelled in pain at the added weight being placed upon his wrists. Paul took a step back from his defeated opponent. His mouth had the iron-filing savour of victory. He considered a kick or two, but Andrew's now obviously genuine coughing fit restrained him. Paul reached over and pulled the photograph album from Peter's grasp.

"We're taking this back," he said. "And you're not going anywhere near the Dinosaurs until I give you a direct order. Do you understand?"

"Yes, sir," replied Andrew, knowing that any other answer would be taken as insubordination – a request plain and simple to be kicked in the stomach.

"I am Leader," said Paul. "You will follow my orders."

"Yes, sir," said Andrew, sneering out his words of obedience. He knew that at some point soon, in some unobserved place between the Tree-Fort and his home, he was going to start crying. His father had many, many times reduced him to this foetal floorbound position. Sometimes his mother was there beside him; sometimes, he stood beside his father, looking down upon her. By losing this fight, Andrew had lost the ability to pass on the pain that he and his mother received. All he could now hope for was an opportunity for revenge, for reassertion. But he knew that a position retaken is far weaker than a position never ceded in the first place.

Paul put the photograph album under his jumper, just as Andrew had done.

"We have to go back," he said to Peter.

Peter nodded obediently, but then his eyes betrayed him by glancing towards Andrew.

"He'll be all right," said Paul. "I didn't do anything serious to him."

Peter, however, knew that Paul had done the most serious thing of all. He had stripped Andrew of the responsibility of Gang-Leadership. If he so chose, Andrew could now turn renegade. Having lost control of Gang, he might now lose control of something far more dangerous: himself.

Paul ran back to his bicycle, Peter came trailing along behind him.

309

Andrew had managed to stand up, but knew there was no point trying to chase the others.

As they rode back towards Amplewick the misty air felt like a seafront wind, coming up off the surf so full of water that it was almost a spray.

Intelligently, Paul made Peter wait up around the corner from the Dinosaur House. They spent five minutes getting their puff back, so they wouldn't arrive suspiciously breathless.

There was no plan, just the overwhelming need to put things back as they'd been before.

"What are we going to say?" asked Paul.

"I don't know," said Paul. "I'm just thinking."

At which point, Miranda came round the corner, pushing her grandmother's wheelie.

She assumed they were just some boys, and therefore to be ignored. She walked quickly past.

Peter said something that was meant to be "Hello" but came out as "Ugghnn".

"What are you doing here?" Miranda asked, a little shocked.

Paul didn't immediately answer.

"We came back," said Peter.

Paul saw he would have to take over.

"We got bored," he said. "I'm sure there's something we could do round yours."

He felt the photograph album pressing very squarely against his chest; the wrinkly, shiny-textured cover felt slidy with his sweat.

"But why were you waiting here?" asked Miranda. "Why didn't you go straight in."

"We were discussing," replied Paul, wanting to raise things to a non-girl level.

"Discussing what?" Miranda pursued. She was enjoying the conversation, even through her fear of seeming stupid. This was the first time in ages she'd been able to get Paul talking. She didn't want to waste the opportunity. If only, she thought, Peter would bog off.

"Discussing private things," said Paul.

"They're all in a panic at home," Miranda said. "They can't find the photos."

Although she didn't seem in any way to be accusing them, Peter still felt alarmed. "Where do they think it might have gone?" he said, hoping to appear helpful.

"Don't be stupid. If they knew where it was then it wouldn't be lost, would it?"

Paul gave Peter a shut-up glare, which worked.

"Do they often lose things?" asked Paul.

"Not really," said Miranda. "And never anything as important as that."

"I'm sure it'll turn up somewhere soon," Paul said.

Miranda admired how calm and grown-up he sounded. "Yes," she said.

"Are you going shopping?" Paul asked.

"We've run out of milk and some other things," Miranda replied.

"We'll come with you," said Paul.

Miranda wasn't going to say no.

After a quick trip round Budgens, they found themselves back at the Dinosaur House.

"Tell them you just bumped into us," said Paul, as they walked up the garden path.

Miranda didn't ask why. Nonetheless, the idea of telling a fib on Paul's behalf was something she found quite exciting.

The boys parked their bicycles, then came inside.

"Back already?" said Mr Dinosaur, who was still in his armchair.

"I bumped into them," said Miranda, then looked across at Paul for approval.

311

"It's definitely not upstairs," said an anxious Mrs Dinosaur as she came into the room. She was flapping her hands, the bandaged and the unbandaged. "Though I don't know how you thought it could've got up there." Only then did she notice Paul and Peter. "Back again?" she said.

"Yes," said Paul, thinking fast. "Can we help look for it?"

"You know, then, do you?" Mrs Dinosaur said.

Peter for a moment misinterpreted these words, and felt caught out.

"Miranda told us," said Paul.

Her first fib not having been sufficiently rewarded, Miranda tried again. "I bumped into them."

This time Paul at least looked at her, though not with the gratitude she'd been hoping for. In fact, he was staring at her like she was stupid. She took immediate revenge.

"Yes," she said, "they were hanging around suspiciously at the end of the road."

"We weren't," said Peter, "we were just there."

"I'm sure I left it on the coffee table," said Mrs Dinosaur. "That's where it was last time I saw it. And now it's completely vanished." She slumped down onto the sofa, then patted her palms on the coffee table. "Just here," she said.

Paul was sure that if anyone looked closely enough at his jumper, they would see beneath it an instantly recognizable outline. He was most of all worried that Miranda, who paid him such close attention these days, would spot it.

"I'm such a silly," said Mrs Dinosaur. "I probably tidied it away somewhere."

"It'll turn up," said her husband. "Things always do."

"I can picture it here exactly," said Mrs Dinosaur.

Despite his anxiety at the possibility of being caught, Paul still took considerable pleasure in observing their distress.

"Where's Lizzie?" asked Peter.

"Oh dear," said Mrs Dinosaur. "We had to shut her in the cellar to calm down. When she saw me crying, she went completely doolally." She put her head in her hands.

"I think you'd better come back later," Mr Dinosaur said firmly. "Now isn't a very good time."

It annoyed Paul that he couldn't carry out his plan. But with Mr Dinosaur ordering them out of the house, he didn't have a choice. He couldn't return the album, even if his life – as possibly it did – depended upon it. In trying to mitigate his wife's distress, Mr Dinosaur was only ensuring it would be prolonged and maximized.

Once outside, Paul and Peter got on their bikes and rode away. At a safe distance from the Dinosaur House, they slowed to a stop. After pulling the photograph album out from beneath his jumper, Paul said to Peter, "You look after this. Keep it wherever you keep the Archives. I don't want to know exactly where. It's Top Secret."

Peter did not put his hands out to receive the thing. "What are we going to tell Andrew?" he asked.

"Are we going to see Andrew?" Paul asked back. "Are we going to talk to him? Is he still our friend?"

"I certainly hope so," said Peter.

"He put us all in danger of being discovered," said Paul sternly. "That just can't happen. It may work out all right in the end, but stealing this was completely rash. We can't let him think he can get away with that sort of behaviour. He has to be kept under control."

Reluctantly, Peter took the photograph album. It was damp with Paul's sweat. Peter put the album in between his vest and shirt, then tucked his shirt in.

"Make sure your parents don't see it," said Paul.

"Don't worry," replied Peter. "I'm an expert in this, aren't I?"

"I'll see you at school tomorrow," said Paul.

"Yes, sir," said Peter, full of trepidation.

They parted.

As he bicycled home, Peter felt the album under his shirt growing heavier and heavier.

He wanted to go to Andrew as an emissary of peace, but the thought of Paul stopped him. With a few well-chosen words, Paul could turn Andrew into his enemy for ever.

Once home, Peter safely stowed the album in the secret hiding-place. Then wrote up the Archives.

iv.

Andrew was nowhere to be seen in Assembly the next morning. Miranda, however, was very much in evidence. Peter saw her first, standing only a few rows in front of them. With a whisper, he alerted Paul to her presence.

"Let us pray," said the Maths Teacher.

Paul bowed his head but kept his eyes on Miranda's face. She was in the middle of a group of girls, none of whom he'd ever spoken to outside lessons. He recognized a few of them. They were her friends. (She was very popular.) One of them, Trisha, spent the Lord's Prayer looking around for someone to make eye-contact with. When she turned towards him, Paul didn't drop his gaze fast enough. Trisha leaned round the back of another of the girls, prodded Miranda, whispered to her and then pointed right at him. It was one of the worst moments of Paul's entire life.

"Amen," said the Maths Teacher.

The Dinosaurs were probably at that very moment alone with Andrew. He could be doing anything he wanted – to them or to Lizzie. (Paul was pretty sure the dog was where he'd start. Warming up, as it were.)

314

Paul had to talk to Miranda. He needed to find out what was going on. Everyone began to shuffle out of the hall. He manœuvred his way quite easily through the press of slow-moving black-uniformed bodies. By the time they were half-way along the main corridor, he had positioned himself alongside Miranda. His approach had been closely observed and loudly commented upon by both Trisha and several other Trisha-type girls. Miranda had steadfastly refused to turn her head to look in his direction: partly out of fear that he wouldn't be there and partly out of an even greater fear that he would.

"Hello," said Paul, unable to delay any longer.

Trisha snorted loudly.

"Hello," Miranda replied.

"Why are you back at school?" Paul asked.

"Because my grandparents think it's better for me."

"Who's going to walk Lizzie?" Paul asked.

"Miranda says she's lovely," Trisha interjected.

"Go away," hissed Miranda. "This is private."

Trisha and her cohorts allowed themselves to fall a couple of paces behind Paul and Miranda. (Mentally, Trisha was already inserting a 4 between these two names, entrapping them within a fat loveheart and finishing them off 4ever with the diagonal slash of an arrow.)

Miranda wanted to nudge up against Paul, so that her friends wouldn't be able to eavesdrop. But she saw that such a move would only make everything worse. "I think Andrew is coming round later," she said, as quietly as she felt she could. "But if he doesn't walk her, I'll do it after school."

Trisha snorted at random, but its effect was as if timed.

"How's your grandfather?" Paul asked.

"He got up this morning. But I think that was only to show me he was all right before I went off to school. He's not very well. I heard him groaning all last night."

315

Paul remembered to say, "I'm sorry."

They had almost reached her classroom.

Miranda knew what would happen if she stayed out in the corridor talking to Paul. Trisha would tell the whole class he was asking her out. When she walked in, they'd all stare at her and know.

"Bye," she said, quickly. Head down, shoulders hunched, she walked without a backwards glance into 3D.

Trisha bumped into Paul as she came past.

"Sorry," she said, then took the opportunity of another snort. (Not a final one: Trisha's day was snortful from beginning to end.)

Paul felt his humiliation fully. So far, he had been able almost completely to miss out on the eternal round of You Fancy Her, She Fancies You. He had achieved this by adopting the simplest of tactics: he ignored all girls completely. His ear did not hear their high, harsh voices; his eye, always downcast, turned away from any hint of white sock. Now, he would have to endure weeks of taunting. Girls would come up to him in the corridor and pretend that they were in on some big secret. They would tell him that he could confide in them, if he wanted someone he could trust. Then they would run away, giggling.

For a moment, Paul thought about bunking off school and going round the Dinosaur House. It was possible to sneak out through the fire doors of the Art Department. Although it seemed a bizarre thing to feel, he wanted to be sure that the Dinosaurs were all right.

The bell rang for the first class of the morning.

Paul was about to head for the Art Department when a teacher, running late, appeared at the far end of the corridor.

Paul took off in the opposite direction before they got close enough to identify him.

Peter was already seated at their desk in class. A despairing look was exchanged. Before they could find out how Andrew had spent his time with the Dinosaurs, they would have to wait out the whole of the long useless day.

v.

Paul and Peter broke from their last lessons like greyhounds from traps. They cycled fast all the way up the long incline to the Dinosaur House.

Andrew's bike was leaning, matter-of-fact, against the garage door. Only one light in the house was on, that of the sitting room.

This time Paul and Peter made no attempt to disguise their out-of-breathness.

When they rang the door-bell, Andrew answered. He was smiling. He didn't say hello, just shouted back into the front room, "You were right. It is them." Paul was relieved. A low shout came from the other room. "Well, bring them in. Don't go letting all the heat out." There was a yapping, and Lizzie appeared in the hall. Andrew reached down and stroked her. Peter felt himself shiver. They followed Andrew into the front room. Everything was the same, apart from the sideboard, which stood a couple of feet away from the wall.

"Hello, lads," said Mr Dinosaur, standing by the far end of the sideboard.

Mrs Dinosaur smiled and said something inaudible.

"It's obviously not here," said Mr Dinosaur to Andrew. "Good suggestion, though."

Andrew took the near end of the sideboard and together they lifted it back into its usual place. The effort of this told heavily upon Mr Dinosaur, a fact which did not escape his wife. "You sit down, now," she said. "We don't want you going knocking yourself up for no good reason."

He looked at her, then at Paul and Peter, then shrugged. "We can't find it anywhere," he said.

"The photograph album," added Andrew, acting as if they didn't know that already.

"It's just completely disappeared."

"A real mystery," Mrs Dinosaur said. "Now sit down." This time, her husband obeyed her. He needed the back of the sofa to steady himself on his swaying way across to the arm-chair.

"No-one has any idea where it went," Andrew said, looking at Paul with real and scary meaning in his eyes.

"We've been looking half the afternoon," said Mr Dinosaur. "That's the third time we've looked behind the sideboard. Heaven knows why."

Andrew stood with his back to the Dinosaurs, and winked. Paul and Peter knew exactly why.

"If it wasn't there the first time, it's hardly likely to have come back since then."

"I just thought it might be under the carpet," Andrew said, over his shoulder.

"I suppose it was worth a try," Mrs Dinosaur replied. "I don't know what I'll do if we don't find it soon."

"Don't worry," Andrew said. "We will."

Paul really wanted to hit Andrew.

Peter was close to deciding never to see either of his old friends outside school again. He couldn't take much more of this subterfuge and double-talk. Somehow it all seemed terribly unheroic. This was Cold War, not World War. They had stolen one of the enemy's most crucial files; not strategically important, but important for morale. Yet Peter was finding it impossible to think of this as a victory.

Mrs Dinosaur asked about school, and Paul began to lie to her in the most natural way possible.

Miranda arrived about five minutes later and was so embarrassed to find the object of her entire day's hopes there in the front room that she ran straight upstairs.

Lizzie's neck was twisted around Andrew's leg as she looked adoringly up into his face.

"She likes you, that one," said Mrs Dinosaur.

Paul found himself blushing terribly, even though he had known exactly which she the old woman was referring to. "We have to go," he said. His head was woozy with adrenalin. To his great relief, Andrew offered no resistance.

"Yes," he said.

"Homework, I expect," said Mr Dinosaur.

Mrs Dinosaur spoke at the same time. "Miranda can walk Lizzie tomorrow, before she goes to school. She'll have to get used to it, sooner or later."

"Maybe I should be getting back to school," Andrew quite unexpectedly said. Lizzie was still adoring his knee. "I can't spend all my time here."

Paul was stunned – all this advantage, all to be given up! Perhaps he, too, should make a concession of some sort. It might just be possible, he saw, to bring Andrew back into Gang without, at the same time, losing any major face.

As soon as they were safely outside, Paul said, "I want to make peace."

Andrew examined him suspiciously, without replying. They wheeled their bicycles up towards Unstable Street.

"At the time," Paul continued, "I didn't think stealing the album was a good idea. I still think it was a bit hasty. But I can also see that we are fairly safe. The Dinosaurs are blaming themselves for being so stupid, which of course will only help to hasten their extinction. So, what I propose is that we follow your original plan."

Andrew was lost for a moment in calculation. "Do you mean,"

he slowly said, "that we make a Guy and burn the photograph album?"

Paul was reassured by the fact that Andrew hadn't just mounted up and ridden off.

"No," he said, daring more. "I think that's too much of a risk."

Andrew took this, still not fleeing. "What then?"

"We burn it. We wait a week first. Just to make sure the Dinosaurs have given up hope. Then we make a big bonfire and burn it."

Andrew wasn't yet ready to let them know exactly what he thought.

"When?" he asked.

Paul, who was at this point improvising, said, "Not on a day we've got school. So perhaps next Sunday."

Peter could no longer hold himself back. "Are you really coming in to school tomorrow?" he asked.

Andrew nodded. He seemed preoccupied with something that wasn't quite the question he and Paul had been discussing.

"All right," he said, eventually. "We have a bonfire on Sunday."

"And until then," Paul clarified, "we don't do anything to the Dinosaurs, or their dog."

"You mean we don't take it for a walk?" Andrew asked.

"I mean," said Paul, "that we don't burn, stab, strangle or in any way harm it."

Andrew almost allowed himself to laugh. He looked at Paul closely, as if to decide one final matter.

"All right," he said. "On one condition."

"Which is?" said Paul, allowing his impatience to enter the negotiations.

"That you don't let anything that happens between now and then change your mind."

Paul searched in Andrew's face for some hint of what this meant. "You're not going to do anything to the Dinosaurs," he said.

"No," Andrew replied.

"Or Miranda," Peter felt it necessary to add.

"No," said Andrew, as if the idea had never occurred.

"All right," Paul said, and put his hand out to be shook.

"Whatever happens," said Andrew, smirking.

They shook on it.

The moment Andrew grabbed his hand, Paul felt a lurch of horror in his chest. And then another. And another. It was as if his heart had been pushed off-balance and was now falling, step by step, down a long dark flight of stairs. He had no idea at all what he'd just agreed to.

Andrew knew when to flee from an advantage already secured. He swung his back leg over the leather saddle of his blue-framed Raleigh racer. "See you at school," he said.

"See you," said Peter.

Paul said, "Yes."

After they had watched Andrew cycle round onto Unstable Street, Paul turned to Peter. "What do you think he's playing at?"

"No idea," Peter said.

vi.

Paul found out soon enough.

He arrived home to find his mother in tears at the kitchen table. His father, whilst clearly furious, was trying to comfort her.

"What's wrong?" Paul asked.

There was a shoe-box on the table in front of them. Paul's father indicated it with a shrug.

321

Paul opened it to see the disjointed, half-decayed skeleton of the family cat.

"I found her in the garden," his mother sobbed. "All in pieces. Just now. Hanging from the clothes line."

Paul's father now found a direction for his fury.

"Do you know anything about this?" he asked.

"But I was at school," said Paul.

"That's not what I meant," Paul's father shouted.

"I don't know anything about it," Paul shouted back. "Why do you never believe me?"

He ran for the stairs, enjoying the drama. False accusations had always amused him.

"Because you never tell the bloody truth, that's why," Paul's father called after him.

His mother's kindly "Oh, leave him alone" was the last thing Paul heard.

Once in his room, Paul found himself laughing. Now he knew the reason for Andrew's one condition. He was immensely relieved that it hadn't been anything worse than this. Andrew must have left the Dinosaurs before lunch and spent the early part of his afternoon preparing this revenge: finding Tabitha's grave, exhuming her, watching the cottage and choosing the safest moment to peg the wet carcass to the clothes line. After that, he must have gone back to the Dinosaur House. It was textbook stuff. Paul admired his friend, and was glad to feel that what he'd done was something he could so easily forgive him for.

Peter, too, had a surprise waiting for him when he arrived home. A pair of girl's blue-towelling underpants had been posted through his letter-box. When he picked them up, three dead sparrows, all badly charred, tumbled out onto the doormat. The name-tag neatly sewn into the knicker elastic confirmed that they were Miranda's. Luckily, his father wasn't yet home from

322

work and his mother had gone shopping in Midford. Peter hurried upstairs, and quickly stowed the underpants in the secret hiding-place, along with the Archives and the photograph album. The sparrows he buried at the end of the garden. Then he went upstairs to have another look at the underpants.

vii.

Peter woke up the next morning dreading school. He could already picture the look in Andrew's eyes, the grotesque knowledge. And so he set off early, in hopes of avoiding Andrew until they were in lessons. But Andrew was waiting, outside the school gates. And there in his eyes was the gleam of knowledge.

"Did you bring them to give back to her?" Andrew asked.

"No," said Peter, scandalized.

"Oh, so you're keeping them?"

"I've already thrown them away."

Andrew said very slowly, "Liar, liar, *pants* on fire."

Andrew laughed in a loud, uncontrolled way. A couple of girls walking in through the gates looked at him, then did the he's-a-loony ear-twizzle. Peter wished his friend was on a hospital bed with straps to hold down his arms and legs.

"Don't tell him," begged Peter. "Please don't tell him when he gets here."

Andrew was offhand. "Tell who? Tell him what?"

"About what you did."

Leaning towards him, Andrew said, "I've done so many things, I don't know which one you're talking about."

Peter gave up on dissuading Andrew. He knew the more he tried, the less likely he was to succeed.

Paul arrived soon afterwards. He, conversely, had been hoping to arrive early, and catch Andrew outside the gates. It was important to let him know that the Tabitha incident hadn't affected their agreement.

"Greetings," said Andrew.

"Greetings," Paul replied.

Andrew looked at Peter and said, "Peter doesn't want me to tell you –" Peter set off at a run through the gates. "– that when he got home yesterday . . ."

Andrew completed the sentence, and then they both laughed.

Paul found it strangely satisfying to hear that Andrew had stolen something off Miranda.

When they had laughed enough, Paul said, "We do nothing until Sunday."

Andrew nodded. "Yes, sir," he said.

Paul turned away, troubled. There was something odd about his friend's voice. It had broken a few months ago, but now sounded higher again.

They went inside, and for the rest of that week they did nothing.

Not nothing, really; just, in effect, nothing. They took Lizzie to The Park, helped the Dinosaurs out around the house, lamented the loss of the photograph album and, whenever possible, left Peter alone with Miranda. His discomfort was delightfully amusing. And because they could find so little else that could bring them together, Andrew and Paul concentrated on exacerbating it.

viii.

Come Sunday, it was clear that the Dinosaurs had given up hope of ever finding the photograph album. Their explanation for its disappearance, as much as they had one, was that it had somehow found its way inside a pile of Mr Dinosaur's newspapers or Mrs Dinosaur's puzzle magazines (blame was equally apportioned).

After this, it had been thrown out with the rubbish. (Andrew, when they got to this point in their obsessively repetitive narration, would always disguised-gleefully suggest an outing to the local tip.) As far as Gang was concerned, their objectives had been achieved: the Dinosaurs' grief at the death of their grandson was renewed. All they had left by way of an image of him was the school photograph upon the sideboard. Mr Dinosaur hadn't been out into the garden for seven days. He spent most of his time dozing in front of the television. Andrew reported a large new bottle of red-and-blue pills in the bathroom cabinet.

With all this taken into consideration, the bonfire had been given the go-ahead.

The three of them met up at Andrew's, on bicycles. Peter had the album in one of his panniers.

It was now just after four o'clock in the evening, and already almost dark. They rode out to the Tree-Fort, three small cherry-coloured lights in a row.

The walk across the field in the twilight made them trip up more than usual. They knew their way, but not all that well. There were molehills and divots.

Paul risked switching on his torch to find The Door into the Tree-Fort.

Once inside, they felt safer. The lights of Midford were a yellow smudge in the sky to the North. They stopped and listened, hard.

"The coast is clear," said Paul.

All of them had brought along fire-making equipment – Swan Vesta matches, candle ends, paraffin cubes, newspaper to scrunch. They took ten minutes to gather the driest kindling, a few thicker sticks and one or two branches. Their breath plumed half-seen in the darkness.

Peter left the album in his pannier until the last minute.

For some reason he didn't quite understand, he had been very careful with the album ever since it had come into his possession. On Saturday night, whilst his parents were out at The Albion, he had dared take it from the secret hiding-place and look through it. He had thought for a while about removing a couple of photographs of Miranda and keeping them hidden away in a different hiding-place, a newer, even more secret one.

Soon, the bonfire was a bright golden blaze in the inky blue and velvety green that surrounded them.

"All right, Peter," said Paul. "I think we're ready now."

Peter walked away from the ring of light. Here was his last chance to save Matthew and Miranda from the flames.

He didn't take it.

He felt humiliated, because he knew that what he was doing was wrong.

"Give it to me," said Paul.

Peter reluctantly handed the album over, half his self-esteem going with it. Andrew reached his hand out, too – and for a moment they were all three of them touching it, stood in a line facing the fire.

This was, on the surface, their moment of closest communion since Matthew's death. But their motives were flying apart, fast as wings or slings.

Peter let go first. From now on, he knew he was completely in the hands of the other two. They could, if they wanted, cast him also into the flames – of parental retribution, legal ignominy.

Paul and Andrew both held on, neither wanting to let go, neither wanting the other to have the glory of casting the Dinosaurs into the flames.

Andrew gave an impatient tug.

Paul did not let go.

Andrew pulled again.

Paul grabbed hold with both hands.

All this had so far taken place in silence. But as they began ridiculously to struggle, a sound began to occur to them.

It was a regular chugging, motorized, slightly coughy, very comic, getting louder, drawing closer.

Peter was first to identify it. "A tractor," he said.

They had always known that the Tree-Fort belonged to someone: a farmer. He had been evaded on many occasions.

They turned, and could now see the whites of the headlights. Still Andrew and Paul held on to the photograph album.

The tractor changed down a gear. The headlights lurched round, only about fifty feet away. They lit up the root of the Tree-Fort, turning the branches of the oaks into a crown of gold. The tractor was heading towards them.

"Throw it on now," urged Andrew.

"No," said Paul. He hadn't time to explain, and probably couldn't have, even given a weekend to write it as an essay. But he felt convinced that this was a ceremony – and as such it had to be correctly performed.

Andrew, it was now clear, cared nothing for such refinements. He just wanted to rip the album from Paul's hands and cast it straightway into the flames.

The tractor was now definitely setting a course that would bring it right past the Tree-Fort.

It seemed impossible that the farmer wouldn't spot the bonfire and, having spotted it, get out to investigate.

The phutty engine now ceased to be comic, becoming bearing-down-upon-them menacing.

Peter asked, "Should we hide?"

Paul gave the album a definitive yank, but Andrew held on.

"He'll see the bikes," Peter shouted, relieved that for once he could without shame give way to panic.

Andrew put all his might into another tug, and found to his surprise that the album had slipped from Paul's grasp.

But Andrew had paid the price for this physical victory. He had lost his balance. He was falling back, directly onto the bonfire.

The heat, which before had been indistinguishable from his excitement and his anger, was suddenly and sharply under him.

This indeed was a serious fire, well-crafted. At its centre, the light was a strong white tinged only fleetingly with yellow.

By now, the headlights of the approaching tractor had turned the Tree-Fort into a bright cathedral of upwards-reaching lines.

Andrew landed with his back on the bonfire. The impact caused sparks to fly out.

For a moment, flames licked up on either side of him.

It was like the splash when you dive into a swimming-pool.

Peter watched, astounded.

Andrew twisted his arms to the right, kicked his legs. He could feel the fire on the back of his head, like his father's hand grabbing at his hair.

With a flick and a turn, he rolled off to one side.

The tractor had now reached the point closest to them.

Neither Paul nor Peter risked looking away from Andrew, but they were both vestigially aware that the engine was still going, hadn't stopped.

Andrew was annoyed to find Paul had grabbed his ankles and was making him continue his escape roll. In all this, he had still somehow managed to keep hold of the album. (In a way, it now felt almost as if he had heroically dived in to rescue it from the flames.)

The Tree-Fort's bare branches slowly faded from white to orange to red. The tractor kept going, on towards a further field.

They had been saved, perhaps, by the brightness of its head-lights – a light with which their small, half-hidden, raised bonfire couldn't compete.

Andrew was all right. Andrew was not on fire. The back of his Army jacket was slightly scorched. The hair on the top of his head had gone slightly crinkly. The air became familiar with the smell of it.

(Andrew loved burning hairs, one by one. Watching the end ball up and travel towards his fingers, whilst the smell made him wince and want to look away.)

Before Andrew had a chance to get up, Paul had placed his boot on his neck.

"Drop it," he said.

Whether from the shock of the fire-fall or the powerlessness of his position, Andrew almost immediately obeyed.

Paul picked up the album, up off the hard ground.

"We're going to do this properly," he said, as Andrew was getting to his feet.

Now they stood, side by side, Gang-like once more, before their bonfire. There was resentment in Andrew, triumph in Paul and foreboding in Peter. But, for a moment, the old unity had come back again. Paul stood in the middle. He opened the first page of the album. There were the old photographs of Matthew's great-grandparents. Paul picked them off the black page with his fingernails, the corners flipping free of the photo corners. He span them into the white heat of the bonfire, where they, as if with a sense of drama, paused a moment, still intact although already doomed, looking out from the pyre, like heretics, like Protestants or Catholics, before flaring, bubbling, twisting, solid-ifying. A chemical smoke, denser and greyer, co-joined with that of the fire in its pure, natural state. Now that Paul had started, had shown the ceremony, the others felt able to join him. Peter tossed in an image of Mrs Dinosaur as a proud young mother, cradling Matthew's own mother in her arms. Andrew threw in the young-married Dinosaurs at the funfair, toffee-apples in their hands. The image-caught past began to flutter down more heavily into the fire. Matthew's girl-mother, dressed as a Red Indian squaw next to an unknown boy-cowboy. Matthew's parents cutting the wedding cake. The Dinosaurs holding their grand-children: him her, her him. Gang watched, as if in the flickering light of a cinema, their friend grow, become familiar, turn final, be consumed. Gang's throwing of the images kept a measured pace throughout. It was only when they got to the final couple of photographs that the full devastation hit. Matthew's funeral hadn't satisfied or got through to them. This different cremation, however, brought them all to the point of tears. Reluctantly, Peter chucked in a Polaroid of puppy-fat Miranda, holding a Christmas cracker and wearing a paper crown. The final image was of Matthew in his school uniform, laughing against a back-ground of brown clouds.

"And now he's really dead," said Paul finally.

"And so are they," added Andrew.

Paul threw the album on top of the crisp remains of its contents.

"Amen," said Peter, without really knowing why.

Paul and Andrew looked at one another, wishing they had something of equal or greater gravity to say. But, recognizing they didn't, they both said, "Amen," as well.

They watched until the pages of the album had burned completely away and only the metal spiral of its spine remained.

Paul fished this out with a stick.

After they had waited a while for it to cool, they buried it at the far end of the Tree-Fort.

Then they spread the bonfire out, letting it die for want of fresh fuel.

All of these actions were performed silently.

Peter felt a new closeness to the other two, but it was one that he would happily have given up to have things back the way they'd been before.

They were all in it together, now.

It just remained to be seen what, exactly, *it* would be.

WINTER, ALSO

CHAPTER TWELVE

Andrew

In diesem Wetter, in diesem Braus,
Nie hätt' ich gesendet die Kinder hinaus!
Man hat sie getragen hinaus,
Ich durfte nichts dazu sagen!

In diesem Wetter, in diesem Saus,
Nie hätt ich gelassen die Kinder hinaus,
Ich fürchtete sie erkranken;
Das sind nun eitle Gedanken.

In this Weather, in this Suicide,
I'd never have sent the Kids outside!
Someone else took them outside,
I durst not naysay it!

In this Weather, in this Suicide,
I'd never have let the Kids outside,
I'd've worried they'd catch their Death;
Vain thought in this Aftermath.

1.

I need to regain control of Gang.

As we are freewheeling back to Amplewick, safe on bikes, where Paul cannot start a proper fight, I tell them my idea.

Paul says nothing. He has lifted both his feet onto the crossbar of his bike and is making it go swoop from side to side. This would be the best time of all to knock him off. Since he is daring me by being so swanky. Paul thinks the bonfire was all his idea. So he's smarming in my face.

Peter is keeping close to my side, hedging.

We must ask Miranda to join Gang, I say.

Paul swoops a little too violently, and I think Hurrah he's going to fall off. But as Paul is good on bikes, he rides through the danger.

Peter goes all thoughtful. But why? he asks. I thought we didn't have girls.

Not before, I say. But now I think she should join instead of Matthew. It means we can keep control of her.

Paul is leading the way – on bikes, at least. I have to shout when I talk to make sure he hears me.

He still hasn't said anything yet, and I need to get him to say something. But then Peter does it for me.

What do you think? he asks Paul.

I can tell that Paul really wants to say, I think it's a stupid idea. He wants to make me feel like nothing.

I think we should meet and discuss, he says. But for now, we don't do anything different at all. We must play a waiting game with the Dinosaurs. It looks to me as if Mr Dinosaur is going to snuff it pdq. I wouldn't expect Mrs Dinosaur to last more than a few months after that.

I say, But then Miranda will need all the training she can get in order to survive.

No, says Paul, we do nothing for the time being.

We separate, cycling off home in the dark to the evening meals that await us.

The road is quiet, and hardly any cars are out. We have made it away from the Tree-Fort without being seen. Operation Bonfire has been a complete success.

I am worried about burnt bits of hair on my head. If my father asks, I will tell him we were practising putting out fires as quickly as possible. He will like that.

2.

I have ruined my coat. I am stupid and inconsiderate and don't know how lucky I am and will go up to bed right now without having any of this lovely supper that my mother has cooked me look at that and just you wait and how did it happen anyway? (I reply, I explain about the fire-putting-out practice.) What am I trying to do, get myself killed? Not that anyone would give a shit anyway. I'm not exactly going to be a great loss to the world, am I? If I keep going on like this my father promises he will come down on me like a ton of bricks so fast I won't know what's hit me. Go.

I go.

I am going now.

From downstairs I can hear the sounds of my father raging at my mother. He is shouting louder and louder. He is banging the walls and doors. I can feel the whole house shake, as if it is about to fall down on top of us. It is like being on top of a tiger's cage containing a tiger and a tiger's rage to be outside the cage.

I know my father is about to come upstairs. I know what he is going to do. But I don't know *exactly* what he is going to do. Which is why it's so awful.

During this time I have been getting ready for bed. I have undressed like a good little boy and put on my pyjamas. I have got into bed and pulled the goosefeather quilt heavy on top of me.

My father's punishment will soon be coming up the stairs and into my bedroom.

I haven't turned the lights off because I know he will just turn the lights back on again.

I don't even think about hiding, like I used to. There is a wardrobe, there is a cupboard – I could hide in either.

By now my mother is probably on the kitchen floor.

I lie and listen. It is like a dream where you know you are in a dream and you know that if you wanted to move you could move but still because you are so afraid inside your dream you can't move.

I know there is no chance he will forgive me before he gets into my room. What my mother is saying won't matter. He would not be making so much furious noise if when he came it was to forgive me.

My father is terrifying. He is like an avalanche down the side of a mountain.

When I think of him he is so big. It is like he is standing between me and the world, and I can't see round him because he's so big and he's blocking my view.

And now I hear the kitchen door slamming.

Footsteps. Loud. Fast.

Coming down on me like a ton of bricks so fast I don't know what's hit me.

341

My father is very trustworthy. He always keeps his promises. (I am about to be buried beneath a ton of bricks.)

Do I know something? My mother is down there in the kitchen right this minute crying her eyes out because she has slaved all afternoon cooking that lovely food and now it's all going to waste and what do I think of that?

(I'm sorry.)

What did I say? My father can't hear me.

(I say, I said I'm sorry.)

I'm sorry, am I? Am I sorry? Well, sorry isn't good enough. My father is going to teach me a lesson. He is going to use the only kind of language that little pieces of shit like me understand.

I am being taught a lesson. I will thank my father for it, one day. I will be bloody fucking grateful for everything he's done for me.

Now my father is giving me a damn good hiding and now it is time to get ready for bed and now I am pissing in the toilet and he is pissing beside me, watching me piss, and I feel his hot splash on my legs, and now I am brushing my teeth with a toothbrush that has been in the yellow toilet water and now I am having my mouth washed out with soap and water and now I am licking the sink clean of foam with my tongue which he pulls out further and now I am lathering up all over my face and arms with shaving foam and now my father is teaching me to shave and trust him with a safety razor.

Half-way through, I think. It's been much worse than this before. This is only average. I can survive this, easily. Secretly, my father must be quite proud of me for the fire-practice. He is only pretending to punish me badly, so as not to look weak in front of my mother. She must always know he is the Best Father.

3.

I dream of Matthew, just like I have before. He is there in the room which I have built inside my head. It is a very safe place, full of comfort. There are pillows and duvets and sheets made into tents. Matthew is at home there. He says it is one of his favourite places, and that he would live there all the time if he could. I tell him the safe place is mine and his, too, if he wants it and he laughs and says that's what they're there for, aren't they?

I ask Matthew if he saw the bonfire. He laughs and says yes. I ask him what he thought. He tells me it was the best thing ever. I ask him if we should have ripped the album up into pieces, like I said I wanted to. He says he would have preferred it that way, but you can't have everything in life – or death. Then he sits down and starts to talk to me about Miranda. He says that my idea was a good one, and that we should invite her to join Gang asap. I ask him whether we should tell her all about our plans. He says that we should try to find out what she thinks first. If it looks like she would be on our side, then we let her know everything. If she threatens to tell the Dinosaurs, then we should kill her. I am pleased Matthew has said this, because it is something I've been thinking about for a long time. I say to him, Would you mind if we killed her? And he says, Not if it meant the Dinosaurs were dead before Christmas. And I say, But that may happen anyway. And he says, But we want to make completely certain of it, don't we?

Then he starts to fade away, like things do in dreams. I know I only have a moment before he can't hear me any more, and I can't see him any more. I shout out, but only in my head and in my dream, I should be Leader, shouldn't I? He shouts back, You are still Leader! You'll always be Leader! Then the dream ends.

343

4.

Our Biology Teacher, Miss Engleheart, says that if you place one frog under a bell jar with an in-tube and an out-tube, and the out-tube goes through white crystals, then we will be able to observe for ourselves the production of carbon monoxide. Or something like that.

I ask, When will we dissect the frog? She tells me, Not until next term. I ask, Will it be the same frog?

Everybody laughs, including Miss Engleheart. She is Jewish and has a bun of hair and thick legs.

5.

I have another dream of Matthew. This time he is angry with me, and asks me why I'm not doing anything for him. He says, Do you want to forget me? And I say, No, never. And he says, Well, you're going the right way about it.

Just then, he winks out of my dream in the blink of an eye. I try to call him back but it's no use at all.

He won't come again until he sees me doing something for him. I will.

6.

We are walking up the garden path of the Dinosaur House, all three of us – together. We are surprised to see Mr Dinosaur in the garden. Paul asks, What are you doing out here? He says, I'm right as rain again.

It is raining.

Paul looks at me, green with sick and frustration.

I do not understand how our plans could go so wrong.

We go inside and Mrs Dinosaur tells us, He's got a new lease of life from somewhere.

Miranda comes in and says, Hello.

Just like that, without warning, Paul asks if she'd like to come round to his house on Sunday.

I am shocked. Paul is following my plan. He is going to ask Miranda to join Gang.

She says, Yes. She smiles her stupid smile.

7.

Matthew is back.

But it is like we're standing so far away from each other that I can only see and can't hear him.

He is smiling, though – I know that for certain. Even though I can't, with my eyes, see it. I know, in my dream, that Matthew will soon be happy again.

Happy enough to come close and talk to me.

He turns and walks away down the beach in Cornwall, which is where I now see we are.

When I try to run after him and catch him up, the sand slows me down.

And anyway, he has dived into a wave and swum away.

8.

At Base Camp One (Wychwood), we show Miranda a few very unsecret things, but she is really excited by them.

Sometimes, when she's not speaking, or squeaking, she reminds me of Matthew. More Matthew dead in my dreams than alive before he died. She has such long hair. It doesn't fit.

We make a fire and Paul asks Miranda about the Dinosaurs. I can tell he is trying to find out how soon they are likely to die, if things go on like they are at the moment. He is considering escalating Operation Extinction. She says, They are very well, thank you.

When we can't take any more of her, we tell her to go home. She is disappointed but obeys.

We get Peter to trail her secretly down the road, just to make double-sure she's gone.

When he comes back, I tell them what I think we should do. Paul says, No. He says, It's still only November. We have plenty of time left. I say, We need to take action – and *soon*. Then I start to tell them all about what Matthew has told me and what he has otherwise meant on his recent visits. They are puzzled. They don't know how to take it. Peter is impressed, I can see. Paul is worried that it might in fact be true. I finish up by saying, The best way to kill the Dinosaurs is to kill Miranda. And then Paul says, Are you stupid? We were doing this to *protect* her from them. He says this as if he were explaining something to a stupid baby. I say, Nothing we do is doing any good. Mr Dinosaur looks like he'll live for ever. But we can't kill Miranda, says Peter. She hasn't done anything wrong. And it's murder. And I say, So is killing the Dinosaurs. What's the difference? And he says, But she hasn't done anything wrong. Paul says, I think we should kill the dog, then see what happens. This is unexpected. I thought he was totally dead set against that. He has flummoxed me for the moment. I feel like I am a dog being thrown a bone.

All right, I say. We'll do it as soon as we can, and still get away with it.

Peter is still thinking too much about what I've said about Miranda. His priorities are all wrong. He is in love, I think – which is a very bad state of affairs.

Paul tries to unify us. We don't do anything to Miranda, he says. He looks straight at me while he is saying this. I say, Yes. I mean, we don't.

9.

No Matthew-dream. Nothing at all.

10.

Miranda is always trying to talk to us at school these days. It's embarrassing. She keeps coming up to Paul to talk about nothing at all. I even heard her mentioning Wychwood to one of the other girls. That's the last thing we want. She was sworn to absolute secrecy, and already it's all been forgotten.

You can never trust women. They'll always let you down in the end. They are the ones who start crying and make so much noise in the hide-out that the Stormtroopers find you. And when you are running away through the forest with only seconds to spare, women trip over obvious branches so the Germans catch up and catch you. And if there is a baby left behind, they will insist you go back to try and save it and get killed.

Peter is stupid with fancying her. Paul is being weakened by his contact with her. It would serve them right if she were to die. Then they would see who their real friends were.

Paul has invited her to Base Camp One again this weekend. I am afraid that he will soon insist on showing her Base Camp Two. There is no firm resolution on his part to do what needs to be done.

We have been going round the Dinosaurs' most evenings this week, but really have helped them live longer. I still swap Mr Dinosaur's pills around whenever I get the chance. But I wish I could do the things I did before. Paul says, No, he says Alma the Social Worker woman is keeping an eye on them. She is often there during the afternoon. I am being held back in everything I want to achieve. On walks with Lizzie, I never get

347

to be alone. Miranda always comes, to be with Paul. And Peter to be with her. Sometimes when they all fall behind and I go ahead round a blind corner, I am able to get a few kicks into Lizzie's ribs. But that's all. The dog still stupidly loves me. I am teaching it to play fetch with a stick. Mr Dinosaur is still working in the garden. Mrs Dinosaur has taken the bandage off her hand. It looks a bit pink, but has healed. I was hoping it would get a dose of gangrene, so she would have to have it amputated. Then she would spill boiling water all over herself when making the tea, and would perhaps die.

11.

At Wychwood with Miranda we are climbing trees. The branches are slippy-off wet but she does not slip. She complains like a girl about getting her hands dirty.

We sit after a while all along a wall. We have edged our way sideways into the middle and it is too high for her to jump down from. Paul is to her left, Peter to her right, and I am to Peter's right. Miranda is trapped between us.

If we wanted to, we could easily push her off. The fall might not kill her, but if we left her wet and cold for a while and sneezed in her face she might catch pneumonia. That would be excellent.

There is mist on The Lake and the horse field behind it is also hidden with cloudy mist. Enemies could be easily hiding in there.

Paul asks Miranda, Do you know what happened with Matthew? And she says, My grandparents told me all about it.

I'm fed up, and I let too much of my anger show. I say, You know it was all their fault.

Paul shhhes me.

Miranda looks across and says, That's not true. The doctor said they did everything they should.

Paul agrees with her, though I know he's lying. I hope he's lying.

They did, he says. But – and stops.

Miranda says, What? What?

He says, They were slow.

Miranda sneezes. A hopeful sign. She says, They're always slow. It's because they're old. They can't help it. They do try.

Peter says, It was a tragedy. He is all solemn, just like the Vicar at Matthew's funeral. I hate him for it. We agreed, it wasn't a tragedy. He is talking like a grown-up. Matthew was a casualty. A casualty in a war. The war between the Young and the Old. Miranda is young, and should be on our side.

Paul says, A doctor told me that if Matthew had been taken to hospital a few hours sooner, he might not have died.

Miranda kicks her heels against the wet brickwork, and bits flake away and fall off into the nettles below.

So, she says.

I try to join in with what Paul is doing.

I say, Doesn't that make you really angry?

Paul's shoulders wince up as soon as I start to speak. But once he hears the whole of what I say, his body relaxes again.

Of course I'm angry he's dead, Miranda says. Can't we talk about something different?

Paul says, Andrew means angry at them not just angry angry.

Our breath chuffs out of our mouths then hangs for a while under our chins, wetting the necks of our pullovers.

Miranda says, I haven't really thought about it all that much. In fact, I've been trying very hard not to think about it. But it's difficult, with my granny mentioning him all the time.

Paul says, Do you think they feel guilty about it?

Miranda says, I'm getting cold. Can we go inside now?

Paul is weak and says, All right. He starts to shuffle along the wall-top, and bumps into her accidentally-on-purpose. Miranda is forced up against Peter who tries to make more room for himself by pushing into me. I don't move. I grab hold of the wall.

Come on, says Paul. He leans round and looks daggers at me. Get a move on.

I say very slowly, We think the Dinosaurs killed Matthew. They saw he was dying and didn't do anything. And that's just the same as killing him. Just as if they put a pillow over his head and pushed down.

Paul and Peter are shouting at me to shut up. Miranda has put her fingers in her ears and is going lah-di-lah-di-lah-di-lah very loudly.

I reach round Peter and poke her leg, so she will listen to me.

She wrinkles up her nose and I can tell she is thinking about sticking out her tongue. She doesn't. She says, Leave me alone.

I shout, They killed him.

She shouts back, They're not dinosaurs, they're not!

Peter is still shoving and shoving. This annoys me. I'm going to move, but only when I'm good and ready. With my left fist I gently smack him in the teeth. He pulls his hands up to his face, then starts to lose balance. His feet come up and he throws his arms forwards. Miranda puts her hand on his thigh and pushes down. But the balance-point has been passed. He teeters for a moment, then falls. He is upside-down. Peter's left foot smacks into Miranda's cheek, and she starts to wobble too. Peter falls – flak! – into a big clump of nettles.

12.

He doesn't make much noise as he lands, not even a thud. Miranda is wailing, even though she isn't unbalanced enough to fall off unless she does something completely stupid like grab hold of Paul. Peter laughs. I am reasonably glad he isn't dead.

Paul steadies himself, and Miranda. He says to me, What did you do that for?

It was an accident, I say. He was pushing me. I just pushed back a bit harder.

Miranda asks, Is he all right?

Peter has rolled, heels over head, out of the nettles, onto the path. He is moving, which is a good sign.

Paul orders me to get out of the way.

I wait for a moment, just to let him know I don't have to do anything if I don't want to.

Then I shuffle sideways until I reach the branches of the beech trees. Using these, I climb slowly towards the ground – still keeping Paul annoyedly waiting.

As soon as she is down out of the tree, Miranda starts crying.

Paul and I run out of Wychwood, racing, through the gate, and round onto the path, where Peter is now sitting up.

I'm fine, he says, before we even ask.

Paul looks at me and says, You will be court-martialled for this.

Miranda arrives and asks, Is he all right?

Peter wants to show us, and himself, that he really is fine. So he stands very slowly and carefully up.

I say, You can't court-martial me.

Miranda says, What are you talking about?

Peter rubs some of the dirt off his bum.

Paul says, Nothing.

And Miranda says, You're stupid. I'm going home.

Peter tries to stop her but she goes anyway.

13.

I am out of Gang, officially. Since I knocked Peter off the wall they will only speak to me at school. When I try to talk to them after lessons, they just walk away. If I ask for the date of my Court Martial, they say, Very soon. But they can't stop me going round to the Dinosaurs'. Once or twice Alma the spy is there. Miranda doesn't speak to me, either. She looks at me as if I was mental or something. The Dinosaurs don't see any of this or any of anything. They still let me take Lizzie out for walks. Miranda comes along the first couple of times. Paul tries to stop me, but he doesn't want an argument about it in front of the Dinosaurs. I just make sure I get to their house nice and early in the morning. Set alarm clock.

14.

Secret-dream of Matthew.

15.

Alarm clock.

This morning Miranda decides not to come out on the walk with me. It is cold and misty. She doesn't ever even speak to me when I am inside the house.

So, here I am. All on my own. Playing fetch with Lizzie. It is a game she likes. I have been training her for this ever since the Dinosaurs got her. What happens is, I throw a stick as far as I can. Lizzie runs after it and brings it back. I do this a few times, so the stupid dog gets really keen on the game. Then I start to hold on to her collar when I throw the stick. This means I can't throw it half as far, but that doesn't really matter. Lizzie watches where the stick falls. Slowly, as the days passed, I've trained her to wait for longer and longer. But as soon as I let her collar go, she dashes off to where the stick fell. Accurately. Lizzie is a very obedient dog.

So, to kill her, I just take her to the road that runs across between The Furze and The Park. (This is the bit where Miranda usually insists we keep Lizzie's lead on.) It is quite busy with cars, with people driving in them to work.

I wait till the road is empty, then throw the stick across to the other side of the road. The fingers of my left hand are tight around Lizzie's leather collar. Her steel name-tag jangles beneath her neck. She pants, her tongue all slobbering out like. I pull her back until we are hidden from the road by a treetrunk. Then I wait for a car to come along.

While I am waiting, I keep saying to Lizzie, The *stick*! Where's the *stick*! It's over there, isn't it? The *stick*. She is so stupid she stays really keen.

Then a car comes along. It is a big one, I can tell from the low engine sound.

At just the right moment, I let go of Lizzie's collar.

16.

She dashes into the road, right in front of the car, which tries to swerve. Doesn't. Lizzie goes through from front to back directly beneath the left-hand wheels. Lizzie is not a small dog. There is a thump, as her skull hits the petrol tank. I hope because of this it will be actionously split open.

The car brakes, ending up in the middle of the road further along.

Lizzie lies there. I can see that she is a dead bundle of wet flesh and fur that is ruffled by the breeze.

17.

I run out from behind the tree, acting all distressed like. A woman gets out of the car. I walk over to where Lizzie twitches. She is not completely dead, but she will be soon. The woman runs up to me and looks down at dead Lizzie.

She's dead, I say. You killed her.

The woman is wearing a long pale Mackintosh coat and has suede boots on with fur round the tops.

It ran out into the road, she says. It wasn't my fault. I couldn't do anything.

She's dead, I say. Her name's Lizzie.

She says, I'm sorry.

I say, It wasn't even my dog. I'm going to get really killed for this.

Oh no, she says. She reaches down and touches Lizzie. Are you sure she's not all right? she asks. She's still warm.

I can smell the woman's choky-sweet perfume.

Another car drives slowly past. A man looking out sees me and a woman and a dead dog.

I say, Her neck's broken.

She says, You shouldn't have been out on the road. You should have kept her on a lead.

I look up at the woman and say, You were driving too fast. You didn't have time to stop.

The woman knows this is true. She also knows that the police station is just a bit further down the road. Everyone knows that.

Another car drives past.

You better get her off the road, the woman says. We don't want you getting run over, too.

I pick Lizzie up, squeezing her windpipe beneath the fur just to make double-sure.

I am about to put her down when the woman says, I'll drive you home. Where do you live?

And I say, I told you before, she isn't my dog. I just walk it for them.

The woman becomes firm and fierce.

She says, Well, I'll take you there.

I carry Lizzie over to the woman's car and get in the front seat. Lizzie's head is a bit sticky, from where her brain is leaking out. It gets all slimy on the knees of my school trousers.

The woman starts the car's engine.

I say, Turn right at The Prom.

She knows what I mean. She is local.

Oh dear, she says. What a way to start the day.

I direct her down the pot-holed road to Cowfold Lane. She parks the car outside the Dinosaurs' house, pulling the hand-brake on without pressing down the button on it. This makes a creaky-wrenching noise. My father says you should never do that, because you'll wear it out really fast and have to pay lots of money to buy a new one. This is going even better than expected. The woman is behind me as I walk up the concrete path to the front door. I try to reach for the bell, lifting Lizzie's body, but the woman gets there first, and gives it a long hard push.

She says, Don't say anything. I'll explain everything.

18.

Miranda opens the door.

The woman says, Is your mother in?

Miranda looks at the dead dog and then at me with about-to-cry eyes. She shouts, You killed her! Oh, you killed her!

The woman tries to say something, but Miranda just turns and runs upstairs.

I carry Lizzie into the living room. Mr Dinosaur is there, half out of his chair.

Oh no, he says when he sees Lizzie's flopping-down head. Oh dear no.

I lie her down on top of the puzzle magazines on the coffee table. From upstairs comes the slam of Miranda's bedroom door.

The woman says, It was my fault. I'm really sorry. I wasn't really concentrating. She just ran out in front of me.

Mrs Dinosaur comes down the stairs and into the room.

The woman says the same thing all over again.

I have Lizzie's brain on my hands as well as my trousers.

Oh dear no, says Mrs Dinosaur. This surely can't have happened.

I hear a door open upstairs, and feet stamping along the landing. Miranda's voice comes down from above. She screams, Can't you see? He killed her! He's completely mental.

The woman is now standing beside Mr Dinosaur, apologizing very quietly. Mr Dinosaur reaches out a hand and strokes Lizzie's head. His eyesight isn't good enough for him to see the stickiness in advance. But he feels it as soon as he touches the slidy fur. He winces a bit, then feels for a drier piece of fur to wipe it off on.

As she's got no reaction shouting from upstairs, Miranda now rushes down and into the living room.

Why don't you listen to me? He *killed* her. She points at me. He did it deliberately. When we were up at Wychwood, he pushed Peter off a really high wall.

I don't say anything because I don't have to.

Mrs Dinosaur says, Really!

Mr Dinosaur says, Just you be careful what you say next, young thing.

The woman says, The dog ran out into the middle of the road.

The boy – I'm sorry, I don't know his name – wasn't anywhere in sight.

After this bout of shouting, the room goes all of a sudden quiet. Together we look down at Lizzie's body.

The woman says, She's a beautiful dog.

Miranda looks evilly at me.

You might think you can fool them, she says, but you can't fool me.

With that, she turns and runs out of the house.

Mr Dinosaur tries to stop her by saying, You come back here right now and apologize. But the slam of the front door is the only answer he gets.

19.

There is another boring bit of silence.

The woman finally puts it out of its misery by saying, I better be getting along to work. I'll leave my number. Or, no, I can give you my business card. I just got them. Silly things. I can't get rid of them fast enough.

Mrs Dinosaur says, Oh dear.

And the woman says sadly, The car came as part of the job.

Mr Dinosaur says, There's no need for that. We're sorry it happened but there's nothing anyone can do about it now.

The woman starts to back towards the door. I'm so sorry about this, she says. She looks at Lizzie one final time. But it really shouldn't have been on the road, she says.

Mrs Dinosaur shows the woman out.

I'm still standing in the same spot.

Mr Dinosaur looks at Lizzie, not at me. Dear old girl, he says to her, but doesn't risk another gooey stroke.

Mrs Dinosaur comes back in and says, She was nice, wasn't she?

357

Yes, Mr Dinosaur says.

Mrs Dinosaur says, We didn't offer her any tea.

She was on her way to work, Mr Dinosaur says.

Yes, Mrs Dinosaur says, but we should at least have offered.

I didn't kill her, I say. She just ran ahead of me and I couldn't catch up to put her collar on.

We know you didn't, says Mr Dinosaur.

Mrs Dinosaur puts her smooth old hand on the back of my head. Her fingers feel cool and hard, like the keys of a piano. It makes me feel sick.

There-there, says Mrs Dinosaur. These things happen. There's no rhyme nor reason to them.

All of a sudden, I feel like telling her exactly what the reason for these things is. I want to say, I am the reason and you are the reason, you and Mr Dinosaur, and Matthew being dead is the reason, and Paul and Peter, and Miranda is also the reason, and all of us together, all of us are the reason.

You better be off to school, Mr Dinosaur says.

Yes, Mrs Dinosaur says. Don't want to be any later than you have to be.

I feel so full of hatred, so grotesque with it, that I have to do something, say something.

Goodbye, Lizzie, I say with a wobbly voice, as if I gave a toss about the stupid animal.

We won't bury her till tonight, Mr Dinosaur says. Miranda should be here. We need to give her time to calm down.

Mrs Dinosaur says, I'm so sorry about what she said.

I say, I'll see you after school.

I show myself out. Behind me I hear Mrs Dinosaur say, Where shall we put her till then?

Mr Dinosaur says, I'll put her in the shed in a minute.

They both sound very deflated and possibly dying.

I close the door with great satisfaction at one of my greatest victories. I can't wait to get to school and tell the others what I've achieved.

20.

They are waiting for me, outside the gates.

Guess what, I say. But they are already pushing me back round behind one of the laurel bushes, where we can talk without being seen.

The trampled-hard ground is covered all over with trod-flat fag ends.

You idiot, whispers Paul. Miranda just told us what you did.

You said you wouldn't do anything, says Peter. You *promised*.

Miranda knows, says Paul. She *knows*.

That doesn't matter, I say.

It does, says Paul.

I try to say something else but they won't let me. They have me pushed up against the wall, both of them together. They are stupidly banging on without listening, like stupid old geriatrics.

How can we let you back in Gang after this? says Paul.

Peter says, The police will get us now. They'll work out what we were trying to do.

I say, I am Gang. You're the ones who've left. I'm the only one brave enough to be in it.

At first Paul and Peter together had me pushed up against the wall. But now that Peter has stepped back, I decide to get away. Paul's hands are pushing my arms back at my side. He isn't expecting a direct attack, which is very stupid of him. I knee him in the bollocks, once, twice. His hands come off me. He doubles up.

Andrew, says Peter. What are you doing?

I push Paul away as hard as I can. He stumbles back into the laurel bush. Its branches slow but don't stop his fall. I kick his ankles.

I am Gang, I say. You're nothing.

Peter just watches, because he knows if he tries to get me I'll just duff him up as well. I feel so strong and in control of everything.

I kick Paul in the guts a couple of times, but not as hard as I could. I still want him to go to school. I don't want him going to the Nurse.

We're all going to prison, Peter says.

For what? I say. Killing a stupid mongrel and burning a few old pictures. And nobody knows we even did that.

You did it, says Peter. You did. Not us.

Suddenly Miranda comes round from in front of the laurel bush, where she's obviously been hiding.

I know, she says. I know what you did.

This is unexpected.

21.

Oh no, says Peter. He gestures at Miranda as if to say, We're all dead.

I realize I don't mind Miranda knowing. I quite want everyone to know. Even the Dinosaurs. The terror of feeling that I am out to kill them, that might be enough to finish them off. They are in a pretty weak state.

Miranda kneels down next to Paul. Are you all right? she asks.

Paul nods and spits, and there is no blood in his spit.

We're in trouble, says Peter.

Shut up, I say.

Miranda stands up again, and comes over to jab her finger into my chest. You are in trouble, she says. If you come anywhere near my family again I'll call the police and have you arrested.

The final bell goes for class. Assembly is already over. The playground is empty. We are late for school.

360

I grab Miranda's jabbing-with finger and twist it back a long way. She squeals and falls down in front of me on her knees to try and stop me bending it any further, breaking it.

Paul is still out of commission, but Peter is ready for action.

Get off her, he says.

Miranda punches my leg but I just twist her finger back a little further.

As quickly and as hard as he can, Peter punches me in the face. His fist lands pretty feebly, just beneath my eye. It's nothing, not compared with what I get at home. But it does knock me slightly off balance. I rock back a few inches on my heels, and that's enough of a movement to snap Miranda's finger. I can feel its small, soft, grisly insides give as she starts to scream. I let go, because there's nothing really much left to hold on to. Her finger now bends both ways. And it's Peter's fault, not mine.

I expect Peter to attack, and he does. His punches are fast and stupidly off-target. I let him think he's winning for a bit, then whop him right in the throat. He steps back, choking. There are a couple of secs during which we all stop right where we are.

Suddenly, Paul is back.

Get him, he says.

22.

Miranda grabs my legs and clings on to my knees. Peter starts to punch me in the guts. Paul takes over full responsibility for my face. I try to land a few decent blows but the three of them together are too much for me. Among all the other minor bangs and bruises, I can feel Miranda biting into my thigh. Then Paul pushes me over, and they are kicking me. Paul and Peter have never kicked me in the head before. Not as if they really wanted to do damage. Peter goes for the face, which I cover up with my hands. Another kick comes in, landing between my fingers, forcing them painfully apart. I feel the nose break. It doesn't hurt. None of it hurts. There is even something sweet about it – about the quick taste of blood in the mouth. Miranda, with her one good hand, is thumping and thumping between my legs. Paul puts a series of sharp, well-aimed kicks together. One rib snaps. Then another. You can hear them easily. I start to laugh. I find it funny, how unexpert they are at this. They're making all this effort and doing all this damage without causing me half the pain my father can cause with just a drawing-pin or even a toothbrush.

Stop, says Paul. Stop before we kill him.

My mouth is full of thick, blood-filled spit.

I say, Kill me, because that's the only way you'll stop me.

Miranda thumps me again.

Now that I can concentrate on her and her alone, she's an easy target. I scissor my legs and kick her up the bum. It's meant to be a joke. She falls away from me, tries to break her fall with her hands, shrieks as she puts weight on her shattered finger, pulls herself into a whimpering ball.

Paul and Peter start kicking me again. I count the number of kicks that get through properly. The number reaches twenty-seven before they stop again. I'm not sure but I think that another rib has gone.

All right, says Paul. He is very out of breath. He says, Let's leave him here.

I can't move.

Paul and Peter help Miranda to stand up. They pick up their books out of the dirt. I watch them, the world at right-angles to the way it usually is.

It really hurts, says Miranda.

We'll take you to see the Nurse, Paul says. I'm sure she can fix it.

She lunges towards me and spits. I hate you, she says. I really hate you.

Boo-hoo, I say.

Leave us alone, she shouts. Leave us alone!

She jabs a little girly kick into my balls.

Come on, says Paul.

They lead her away – defeated, if only they could see it.

23.

For a while I lie on the ground, enjoying my triumph. I know that I am now the only one left on Matthew's side. The others are deserters. They are cowards. They couldn't take this sort of treatment for anything, not even something they really really believed in.

I listen to the cars driving in and out of the school car park. Dinner ladies walk past, arriving to start cooking lunch.

I can't go in to school today. I must go home.

With great effort, I get to my feet. I am the wounded hero half-way through the battle. I need to get to a green tent with a red cross on it in the middle of a white circle. There I will be patched up by a beautiful nurse. She will plead with me not to rejoin the battle and I will smile and smoke my cigarette and say, Of course I won't. But I'll have my fingers crossed behind my back, and when she's not looking I'll rejoin the action just as soon as possible.

I stagger slightly, leaning against the school wall. This is a good detail. I do it once again for effect.

Then I creep to the edge of the laurel bush and look out. No one is around. Only cars. The lollipop lady has gone home.

When the coast is clear, I make a dash across the road.

Soon I am away from the school. As long as I don't meet any interfering old bags, I will be able to get home unimpeded.

I take quiet roads and back alleys. My nose aches and I need to keep my arms in a certain position to stop my ribs from becoming a nuisance, pain-wise.

The walk to school usually takes me twenty minutes. This heroic journey back takes twice as long.

As I shuffle past houses and front gates, I think about how free I am now to attack the Dinosaurs in any way I want to. No longer do I have to wait for Paul to catch up with my ideas. Never again will Peter's cowardice hold me back.

I promise Matthew once again that the Dinosaurs will be extinct by Christmas.

Finally, I make it home.

24.

My father is in the garden. I can hear his hammering.

I sneak along the front of the house, keeping my head beneath the level of the front wall. This is just in case my mother is in the dining room and glances out the window. Really, I expect her to be in the kitchen or back in bed.

I round the corner and go up the cobbled drive. Almost safe now. It is of vital importance that my father sees me before my mother. As long as I can make it to my father, I will get the reaction I want. There will be fury rather than concern. I will be in control.

I am just crawling along behind the Rover 2000 when my mother comes out of the house. She seems to be in a hurry. As she scurries along, she calls out my father's name. She almost never uses his name. It is a detail I have noticed. I wait where I am. I have an idea what is happening.

My mother stands outside the Nissen Hut and talks to my father, quietly.

What? says my father, loudly. He comes out of the shed.

We'd better go, my mother says.

I'll take the car, he says.

She says, I'll come, too.

They are walking rapidly towards me. There is no escape.

The little bastard, my father says. When I get my hands on him, he won't know what's hit him.

My mother looks sideways at him as if to say, He will.

My father is a very impressive man, especially when he is charging towards you in a terrible temper. I have nowhere to hide. My mother is going to get in on my side of the car – the passenger side.

25.

I am about to stand up when they both veer off into the house. My father, I suppose, has gone for the car keys. My mother, if she is being anything like usual, is going for a pee.

I can't believe my luck. If I can keep out of their way until the evening, that will give them time to get some perspective. At the moment they are merely behaving like they *think* they should behave.

I am just sneaking out from behind the Rover when my father smashes out through the door of the house saying, Buggery.

There is no time to dive for cover. My father's legs start off in the direction of the Nissen Hut, but his eyes have already made their way to my bloodied face.

What have you done? he says. We've just had a phone call from your school. They say there's a girl there with a dislocated finger, because of you.

My mother has heard the shouting and is coming outside.

I say, I –

But my father says, And how did you end up in a state like that?

Slowly, my mother edges round the circumference of my father's fury. He continues to shout. He says, You weren't beaten up by a girl, were you?

Despite what they have been saying about me being out of Gang, I have decided not to sneak on Peter or Paul.

My mother puts her hands on my cheeks and looks at my face.

They've broken his nose, she says. My baby.

My father says, Did you let a girl break your nose?

My mother hugs me, and the pain in my ribs is so sharp that I can't help but shriek.

Where are you hurt? my mother asks.

My father comes over for a closer look. I'm going to get to the bottom of this, he says. You're going to tell me exactly what happened. But first we're going to take you back to school.

No, says my mother, we're taking him to hospital.

They need to talk to the boy, says my father.

My mother stands between him and me. Her hands grip my arms, behind her back. He needs to see a doctor, she says.

My father puts his hand on my head and turns it so that I am looking at him straight on, something I usually try to avoid doing. Most often, it gets me into too much trouble.

Does it hurt? he asks.

I don't want to go into school. The Police may be waiting for me there.

A little, I say. Not much. In my ribs.

Where? says my mother, turning round.

I point.

She turns back to my father, about to start pleading.

All right, all right, all right, he says. We'll take the little shit to hospital.

I am grateful that my father is such a great and generous man.

26.

We drive to Midford. A few times my father tries to find out what happened to me.

I just say, It was some older boys.

He doesn't believe me, but I am fairly sure he respects the fact that I am lying.

27.

In the hospital we are told to go and wait in a small grey room with some children. Then I am taken to see a doctor who examines me. He pumps up a black rubber armband around my arm. He uses a stethoscope, so I know I'm not mad like Miranda was. He shines a light in my eyes. Then they do an X-ray of my head and body, which makes me feel very special. I ask, Can I keep it afterwards? They say, Of course you can. We are told to go back to the small grey room to wait for the X-rays to be developed.

28.

As we are walking along the corridor, I see Miranda coming in the opposite direction – and behind her the Dinosaurs. I wonder if my parents will recognize them from the funeral.

Miranda has a white bandage around her hand. The finger I broke is between pieces of wood like extra-large ice-lolly sticks.

When Miranda sees me, she stops dead. It is immaculate. The Dinosaurs bump into her back, then look to see what she has seen. Their eyesight is so bad that they can't make me out.

What is it? I hear them ask.

Miranda says, It's him.

My parents and I are still walking, walking.

Who? says Mrs Dinosaur. Andrew? And then she looks up and sees me. Near. My face has been swabbed clean by a nurse. It smells of school toilets.

Mrs Dinosaur looks scared and angry.

Mr Dinosaur, who has also seen me, steps forward. What have you done to her? he asks.

My parents suddenly become aware of what's going on. I try to keep walking, but my father grabs my arm. Is this the one? he says. The one that beat you up?

My mother says, Oh hello, to Mrs Dinosaur. Mrs Dinosaur does not respond.

My father is shaking me. Look at me when I'm talking to you, he says. I look over his shoulder at Miranda and stick out my tongue. My father cuffs me around the head. Pay attention when I'm talking to you, he says. I stare up into his eyes.

My mother says to the Dinosaurs, I hope she's all right.

It wasn't her, I say to my father. It was some older boys.

Mr Dinosaur suddenly lunges towards me. Did you kill our dog? he says. Did you kill it like Miranda says you did?

I am surprised by this, but I don't let it worry me.

Of course I didn't, I say. Why would I do that? It was just a stupid dog.

Miranda shouts, Liar!

My mother turns to me and says, What's all this about?

The Dinosaurs have taken hold of Miranda and are now hurrying away down the corridor.

Goodbye, my mother calls over her shoulder.

29

And then the questions start. And after the questions, there are more questions. My father and mother ask most of them to start with. The doctors ask a few. Then they fix my nose and my ribs. And then the questions start again. And we drive to my school, where everyone looks at me as I'm escorted like a proper POW through the tea-time playground. And the Headmistress asks me questions. And Alma, the Social Worker woman, arrives and asks me the same questions. And when they let me go home, my parents start up again. But their questions have changed. It is my mother, mainly. At first she asked, What have you done? But now she is asking, Why did you do this?

All the time I'm in school, I don't see Peter or Paul. I think maybe they will get away with it. I am surprised that I don't have to talk to a policeman. I keep thinking they are going to take me to a judge so that I can be sentenced to be hanged from the neck until dead. Or just put in prison for a very long time.

For a while or so, my parents go in to see the Headmistress on their own. I am left waiting out on one of the Chairs of Doom outside. Before they go in, I try to tell my parents about the famous funny smell in the Headmistress's Office. But they won't listen to me. I want to tell them not to breathe in too much, or they will suffocate in there. They tell me not to be so rude. After they come out they look at me all serious like.

You've been suspended, my mother says.

30

I try not to smile. Now I will have plenty more time for Operation Extinction.

CHAPTER THIRTEEN

Paul

In diesem Wetter, in diesem Graus,
Hätt' ich gelassen die Kinder hinaus,
Ich sorgte, sie stürben morgen;
Das ist nun nicht zu besorgen.

In diesem Wetter, in diesem Graus,
Nie hätt ich gesendet die Kinder hinaus;
Man hat sie hinaus getragen,
Ich durfte nichts dazu sagen!

In this Weather, in this Pride,
If I'd've let the Kids outside,
I'd've feared, they'll die Tomorrow;
No need fretting about that now.

In this Weather, in this Pride,
I'd never have sent the Kids outside;
Someone made them all vacate,
I durst not naysay it!

1.

After the terrible incident of Miranda's finger and the big duffing, Andrew disappeared.

We didn't see him at school, because he was suspended. That's what we heard, anyway.

Also, we heard rumours that Alma the Social Worker had been to visit him at home.

We knew Andrew's father hated Social Workers as he hated all meddling Commies. He was on Andrew's side, and would work hard to protect him.

Both Peter and me secretly thought about going round Andrew's house to see him. But even if we did, it didn't feel like anything would change.

For Gang to get back together, like it was before, it needed one of us to give up and say they'd been totally wrong.

And with me being so careful, and Peter so scared, and Andrew so full of pride, there was no-one going to do that.

If it was up to Andrew, we would start Operation Extinction all over again.

Probably, in fact, from his original idea: to burn Matthew's grandparents to death in their house.

After the broken finger, me and Peter decided to stop calling them "the Dinosaurs". For the main reason that we didn't really want them to die any more.

Well, we did – sort of. We just didn't want the Police to be able to get us for it.

If they had died in a big car accident, then we would have been quite happy indeed.

Apart from the fact that Miranda would be put in a children's home, and we wouldn't ever see her again.

Miranda was now Peter's official girlfriend, ever since she'd seen him being so big and brave against Andrew.

He walked around school all day next to her, saying he would protect her from anything.

She was very very scared of Andrew, mostly because she'd seen him in a corridor in the hospital and he'd made the cut-throat sign with his finger and pointed at her grandparents. But also because he was now out on the loose.

Everyone at school knew that it was us who had duffed Andrew completely up, except all the teachers and the Head-mistress.

Miranda didn't want to get us into trouble, so she just told them about how Andrew broke her finger.

She had to say *something* because the School Nurse was asking her too many questions, and the School Nurse was a dragon who smelt of loos.

Peter and me didn't blame Miranda for telling them about Andrew. She was good in other ways, by keeping mum about the most important thing: us.

The Headmistress was told everything by the School Nurse.

Miranda sat there with both of them in the Nurse's Office, and nodded *yes* or *no* whenever the Headmistress looked at her.

"I'd better go and call the parents," the Headmistress said. "He hasn't turned up yet. But that's hardly unusual, now is it?"

The School Nurse bandaged up Miranda's finger, but said that she must go and have it X-rayed to see if it was a break or just dislocated.

Someone from school called Miranda's grandparents, who

drove her to Midford Hospital, which was where she saw Andrew and he did the throat-cut.

Since then, it had been eerily quiet.

Every day before school we went round Miranda's to collect her. After lessons were over we took her back home and stayed there for as long as we could.

We knew for certain that Andrew often prowled around outside the house while we were sitting there inside.

Sometimes we even thought we could hear him, running all about.

On snowy days, we could track where he had been and how he had moved: shuffles behind the hedge, lollops across the lawn.

And everywhere he went, there were little piles of burnt matches left behind.

He made attacks on the house, often with his catapult.

The window in Matthew's room was smashed in, with a small neat round hole.

The TV aerial on the roof was knocked completely sideways. And after that the picture went fuzzy, and the sound sometimes went off – usually in the most important bit: the answer to the question for the star prize of a holiday or a car.

We tried really hard but we could never catch him.

When it came time for us to leave, we would always rush fast out of the front door.

But Andrew was never anywhere near by then.

It was like he now had an extra-special sense, for telling him when to scarper out of there.

Of course, if it hadn't been for Miranda's grandparents and their interfering, we could have rushed faster and more often.

This would have meant we had a lot more chances of catching Andrew out.

We kept on, doing our best. But we couldn't risk scaring

Miranda's grandparents any more than they were, because then they might call the Police.

They knew something was up, but we did our best to keep secret from them what that something exactly was.

Miranda, of course, knew everything.

In the end we knew that even being there and protecting them didn't mean anything.

Andrew would just wait until we weren't around before he made his attack.

And because we weren't around every day during school, he could attack any time then.

In many ways, he didn't need to. Operation Extinction was already nearly a success: Miranda's grandfather got more and more ill every day.

On Monday, he was sitting downstairs in his armchair. On Thursday, he was lying upstairs in bed.

Miranda's grandmother told us he was "feeling a bit under the weather".

She also said that he "will be back on his feet, by and by, right as rain, just you wait and see".

We could hear his coughs as we drank our cups of tea. They were like lightning-cracks in a huge thunderstorm, so fast one on top of the other.

But then it all went quiet, which was possibly worse.

Miranda's grandmother (who was called Estelle) went to the bottom of the stairs.

She shouted up, "Are you alright, m'dut?"

Miranda's grandfather (who was called Bert) shouted back down.

"Nothing to worry about. Just a bit of phlegm. Better out than in!"

He was being brave and stoic, like we would of been. Like even Andrew would of.

When we rushed out of the house on Thursday evening, we didn't catch Andrew – like always. But we found his signs.

He had cut our bike tyres completely up with his Bowie knife. He had also put piles of snow on the saddles, to wet them.

We knew what these signs were meant to say to us – that we were cowards and traitors to Gang.

As we replaced the tyres that evening, we felt very guilty.

2.

On Friday evening, we went round to Miranda's, like the whole week before.

Only this time, Miranda wasn't there. She was round with some other girls at Trisha's house, eating crisps and drinking lemonade.

We were sure she would be safe from Andrew, for she was getting car-lifts there and back.

Peter and me sat on the sofa talking for an hour or so with Estelle.

At one point, Bert had been quiet and not coughing for so long we all thought he might be dead.

"Why don't you go upstairs," said Estelle to me, "and just make sure he's alright?"

The smell started even before I got to the top of the stairs. It was so bad I thought it was coming from the toilet.

But when I put my head round the bathroom door, all I could smell were fake pine-trees.

The medicine bottles were gone from the bathroom cabinet, and it looked very empty and different without them.

As soon as I pushed open the door to Bert and Estelle's bedroom, the smell got stronger.

The heavy curtains with green and yellow flowers on were drawn. One of the bedside lamps gave off a low, brownish light.

A radiator to the right of the door was blasting out the heat, turning the atmosphere muggy.

On the bed, under the covers, Bert was lying flat on his back with his arms straight out in front of him. He was asleep, I think, although it was only a quarter to five.

As I got closer, I could hear his gurgly breathing. The smell was getting worse, and I realized that it was coming from somewhere under his sheets.

Bert's face was pink. His nose looked thinner and sharper than normal. All the veins were visible in it, like red lightning zagging up instead of down. His white hair, usually flat with Brylcreem, stuck out all over the place.

"Are you alright?" I asked, so quietly that I was sure not to wake him up.

His head moved from side to side. He made quiet grunts and loud tasting noises.

I walked back to the door, intending to get out as fast as I could.

I asked again, "Are you alright?"

But somehow Bert heard me. He opened his eyes and worked really hard to lift his head an inch off the pillow.

"Matthew?" he said. "Is that you?"

I didn't reply. I was too embarrassed. Bert had gone mad, and thought I was Matthew.

Bert said, "Matthew?"

I was still stunned, but I could see that here was an opportunity.

"Matthew," Bert said, "Have you come back?"

I tried to remember how Matthew used to speak, and when I spoke I tried to make my voice sound like that.

"Yes," I said. "Yes, I have."

"You're back," said Bert, with tears already in his voice.

I said, "You've already said that."

And he said, "You always were an impatient one, weren't you?"

I was now standing just inside the door. Bert was straining to get a better look at me, over the wooden foot of the bed.

"Come closer," he said. He lifted his hand up.

The thing in the world I wanted least of all was to have to touch him. I was afraid that some of his dyingness would rub off on me, like the lurgy.

His hand strained further out, then dropped, knackered.

Bert said, "I want to see you."

And I said, "I'm sorry, I can't come any closer."

"Oh," he said, as if this was a proper, sensible explanation. He was going back to being the stupid old man we knew and hated. "But you've come back," he said. "That's good."

I felt I was starting to behave, or misbehave, like Andrew would. In thinking how *he* would deal with this situation, I began to get my own ideas.

I said, "I came back to tell you something."

Bert looked tired. Perhaps in some part of his brain, he knew that he wasn't *really* talking to Matthew.

"Oh," he said. "What is that?"

I knew that what I was doing was sort of safe, and that it really wasn't like killing Lizzie or breaking Miranda's finger.

"I came back to tell you how much I hate you."

To me, my voice sounded spookily like Matthew's. It felt almost as if his ghost had climbed inside me, like a diver into a wetsuit.

Bert grunted. His head turned to one side, as if he were trying to block out half of what I was saying by muffling one ear up against the pillow.

"I was young," I said, "and you killed me, because you are part of the War."

"How is he doing? Is he alright?" Estelle's voice, calling from downstairs, terrified me, made me jump.

I stepped out onto the landing.

"Everything up here's fine," I said. "I'll be down in a minute."

"Lovely," said Estelle, ducking back into the living room.

As I re-entered the bedroom, Bert was saying, "Matthew? Are you still there, Matthew?"

"I am," I said.

"Where have you been?" he asked.

"I'm a ghost," I said. "I'm a dead ghost who has to walk around on my own all the time, because I died so young."

"That you did," Bert said. "That you did."

The spooky feeling of half-being Matthew was slowly going away. But this was mostly because I now felt that I really *was* Matthew totally, and that Paul was just letting me use his body to speak out of – like one walkie-talkie uses another.

"And it's all because you were so old and stupid. You didn't care for me enough to save me."

"Don't say that," Bert cried. "That's not true."

"My friends came round, and you sent them away. They asked if you'd called a doctor yet."

"It seemed like a touch of flu, that's all."

"I will never forgive you," the Matthew-voice said. "I will never be happy until you are dead as well. And when you are dead, you will never see me ever again. I will always hide from you and be faster in getting away, so you can never see me. And when Miranda dies, I will fetch her off to somewhere you can't go."

Bert was groaning so loudly now that Matthew was afraid they would hear downstairs. Me, I felt quite differently – I just really wanted to get out of this spooky situation. Matthew was starting to say things worse than I would ever dare – even though most of them were things I thought, too.

"You will suffer for ever," Matthew said. "You will go to hell for what you've done."

"Don't you think I'm not in hell already?" said Bert, his voice suddenly clear – all the thick phlegm for a moment pulled aside, like curtains in a theatre for the encore. "We both are, your grandmother and me. We loved you so much. We'll never forgive ourselves for what happened to you."

"Good," said Matthew. "You shouldn't."

Bert pulled his hands up to cover his face. "Oh God," he said.

More daring than I'd ever have been, Matthew moved in closer.

He was now standing right by the foot of the bed, his hand on the brass ball of the bedpost.

"There is one thing you can do," he said, "which will make me hate you just a little less."

Bert pulled his hands aside. I was afraid he would see it was me, not Matthew.

Matthew knew that Bert's eyes were so old and teary that all he would ever see was a blond-haired blur.

"What can I do?" he said. "Tell me what I can do."

Matthew took a step closer. Then another.

Bert held his arms out, ready to give and get the hug he was all praying and waiting for.

"You can die," hissed Matthew. "Die as soon as you possibly can. Every day longer that you live, I will hate you more."

Bert's hands dropped to the blankets, like sparrows hit by cars. He was sobbing.

A baby, thought Matthew, *a stupid weak big baby*.

When I stepped out from the bedroom, I could feel Matthew sliding out of me. He was staying behind in the bedroom to torture his grandfather some more.

I knew that if I looked back inside, I would see him there – a smear of blond in the air. He would be like a black and white photograph of something moving really fast.

That is how Bert saw him, and would keep on seeing him, from then until he (Bert) died.

I felt very happy as I went downstairs. What I'd done was so much more clever than anything Andrew had ever done.

"How was he?" Estelle asked.

I decided to take a small risk, that she hadn't heard any talk from upstairs. "Sound asleep," I said. "But he was muttering."

"He does that sometimes," she said. "What did he say?"

I pretended not to want to say, then said, "He was talking to Matthew, I think."

"Oh dear," said Estelle. "That's bad."

Peter was looking at me with great interest. Probably he had heard the weeping and wailing from when I was upstairs.

"Why's that bad?" he asked.

Estelle rubbed her lips with her wedding ring, something she often did when upset. "The nightmares stopped a few weeks ago," she said. "I'd hoped they'd stopped for good."

"Sleep is good for him," I said.

She shook her head. "Not that kind of sleep. It's that kind of sleep has made him worse."

I tried to keep Estelle from going upstairs for as long as possible. I told her again that Bert was fast asleep and that it would probably be a bad idea to wake him.

What I did upstairs seemed so dangerous. I didn't know what possessed me.

Yet I did know what possessed me: it was Matthew, and, through Matthew, the spirit of Gang.

I couldn't believe how far we'd fallen apart, like leaves from a normal tree blown sometimes even as far as another country.

3.

When we were safely away from the house, I told Peter what I'd done upstairs. He was shocked, and didn't try to hide it.

"You did what?"

"If we keep going on like this," I said, "Mr Dinosaur will be dead in a week or two."

"Do you think so?"

"But we shouldn't count our chickens," I said. "He's a tough old so-and-so."

Peter seemed too thoughtful for my liking. Still, I myself was euphoric.

What was so good about our kind of extinction was that it was safe. As long as we kept going in the same way we were, we could never be caught.

The main danger was if Bert went into a nursing home, where he would be safe from our gentle attacks.

We had to make sure he stayed in his real home, so he would wear Estelle out as much as he could.

Saturday and Sunday were nothing-happening days.

4.

For Monday, Peter and me agreed to meet outside Matthew's house.

First, we would make sure Bert and Estelle were safe from Andrew. Then we would walk Miranda into school.

There had been a hard frost the previous night. The clouds were grey and almost black in some places. Snow was coming. The ground felt easily cold enough for it to settle.

When we arrived round at Matthew's house, almost together, Estelle told us that Miranda had already set off for school.

It annoyed us that she'd done this without our protection. But right then we were more worried about Bert and Estelle. Without trying to make them scared, we asked if they were staying in or going out that day.

"Oh no," said Estelle, on the door-step. "Bert's still terribly poorly. He had an awful nightmare last night. I won't tell you about it, but it was quite awful."

We left them, as safe as they would ever be, without us around.

It was in Assembly that we saw for the first time that something was wrong: Miranda – she wasn't there.

"Can you see her anywhere?" I asked. Peter looked for her in her regular group of giggly friends. Trisha was at the centre, quieter than usual.

"Nowhere," he said.

The Headmistress came in. We all hushed up.

After Assembly, while we were walking to our classroom, our suspicions were confirmed: Miranda hadn't come to school. We knew this because Trisha came up to us.

"Where is she?" she asked, aggressively. Miranda's other friends were behind her.

"Don't you know?" I asked back, as if I did.

"You better not of hurt her," said Trisha, "you or your friend."

I turned away and Peter followed me.

"I mean it," Trisha said.

Once we were safe in our seats at the back of class, Peter and me whispered to each other. Why had Miranda skived off? What was she going to do on a day as cold and hard as today, when nowhere outside was any fun?

"Do you think she's alright?" asked Peter.

"Stop talking back there," said Miss Whittle.

Our first lesson that day – double Geography – was in our form classroom. The only way we could escape was by asking to go to the toilet. But no way would Mr Butcher (the Geography

Teacher) let both of us go at the same time. He was the worst in the whole school for that sort of thing. (And almost every other sort of thing.) In other words, we were trapped.

Looking out through the steamed-up classroom window, we could see that snow had begun to fall.

Anxiously, we sat through all Mr Butcher's boring talk about alluvial fan deltas, oxbow lakes, terminal moraines, and other kinds of river formation.

I was staring roughly in the direction of Base Camp #2 when it hit me. I *knew*. I knew, and it was spooky.

One look at Peter, and I saw that I couldn't tell him anything. If I did, he would say something out loud – and Mrs Butcher would probably notice and ask what was going on. Even though I knew Peter never blabbed, I didn't want to even risk it.

For eighty-eight long minutes, I gazed out the window and across to The Furze.

The bark of the silver birch trees was white but a different white to the white of the settled snow. It was warm, like silver against blue.

Finally, the bell went.

As everyone was standing up from their desks, I whispered to Peter, "We have to escape."

"Where?" he said.

"I know where she is," I said.

"What?" Peter said.

"And Andrew, too," I said. "Come on."

There was only one method of escaping from Amplewick Middle School.

As Peter and me were skill at skiving off, we decided we would use our old-favourite technique.

During break-time, we fetched our coats, found an empty toilet cubicle and hid in it.

There was a Fire Door in the far end of the Art Department, and it stood right opposite The Furze.

We knew the Art Room would be empty, as Mrs Bosworth only came in in the afternoons. (Mrs Bosworth taught Handicrafts.)

As long as we could sprint without being seen across the narrow stretch of open ground between the school and The Furze, we'd be safely off and away.

Squatting on opposite rims of the toilet bowl, Peter and me waited until we'd heard the last locker door slam shut and the final pair of footsteps echo away.

When we poked our heads out, the corridor was deliciously empty.

We knew that all it would take now was for one teacher to walk into sight, and we would be caught.

The corridor was long and dark, but it gave you nowhere good to hide. Not unless you tried pretending to be a coat on one of the hangers. But your legs and shoes always gave you away to most teachers.

We listened out for a few moments, then set off.

Part of the topness of our plan was that we were, for the first few steps, heading towards the classroom where our next lesson was. To be caught now would be bad, but wouldn't be a complete disaster. We would probably just be told off for being late, and sent on our way.

We made it to the Art Department door with only the sound of our own footsteps and shhhes.

Luckily, the door was unlocked.

We slipped quietly in and closed the door behind us so that it made almost no noise at all.

Because we'd got past the first big obstacle, we relaxed – perhaps too much.

Peter pointed at some stupid drawings that someone in

our class had done, of astronauts in space and rockets blasting off.

We were just laughing at these, when the sound of footsteps coming closer and closer started up.

Quickly, we hid under the nearest desk. This was the one at the front of the classroom: the teacher's desk.

In one way, this was a good move – the desk was the biggest and therefore the most likely to hide us. But in another way, this was disastrous – for it was to this desk that the footsteps made their way.

We pushed ourselves back against the solid wood legs. If the teacher, or whoever it was, sat down, then we were bound to be caught.

"Fucking-shitting," we heard them say. "Shitting-fuck."

They came right up to the desk.

From the green corduroy trouser-legs and scuffed brown brogues, it was easy to identify him: Mr Sacker, the worst teacher in all the school to be caught by.

Just over our heads, Mr Sacker began to rummage about on Mrs Bosworth's untidy desk. His feet were only inches away from our hands.

Mr Sacker smelt of armpits. If he caught you doing anything, he took you to the Headmistress and made double-sure she gave you the punishment the School Rules demanded.

With other teachers, the Headmistress was more likely to be lenient. But she, like everyone else, was terrified of Mr Sacker and his rages.

"Bollocking fuck," Mr Sacker said.

I closed my eyes and employed commando breathing technique. It was necessary to slow my pulse, to remain completely calm. Peter did the same.

All our information about the scene above us was gathered through our ears. But we got more information due to the fact that our eyes were closed. Our training was paying off.

Mr Sacker seemed just about to look under the table and catch us when, "Aha!" he said. "There you are, you little bugger."

Peter and I had been trying not to laugh at hearing a teacher say so many swear-words.

Once he found what he was looking for (probably chalk), Mr Sacker terrified us by rummaging for a few seconds more.

"Not a fucking thing," he said. "Not a sausage."

We had no idea what else he could be looking for.

Then he turned quite suddenly and walked away from the desk.

We could hear him start to hum as he left the Art Room. It was "To be a Pilgrim", the hymn from that morning's Assembly.

Peter and I were so glad that we hadn't been caught that for a few seconds we just sat there and enjoyed breathing as loudly as we felt like (without being shouted at).

Still, the teacher of our next lesson (Metalwork) had probably already noticed we weren't there. We needed to get clean away, and quickly.

"Where are we going?" Peter asked.

"If I tell you," I said, "do you promise not to ask any more questions?"

"Promise," said Peter.

"Base Camp #2," I said.

"Why?" Peter immediately asked, even though he knew asking would make him look stupid in more ways than one.

"No more questions," I said.

We shuffled out from under the desk. I had a quick look, to see if I could spot whatever it was that Mr Sacker had been searching for. No clues.

Peter went over to the Fire Door and looked out across the snowy patch of open ground that was all that stood between us and the freedom of The Furze.

"Coast's clear," he said.

390

I joined him at the door.

"Right," I said, enjoying being total Leader. "In order to avoid being sighted from any of the classroom windows, we will run a diagonal course. You see that tree over there, the one that's taller than all the others?" Peter nodded. "We will head straight for that at thirty-second intervals." Peter looked worried. "I will go first," I said. "If I get caught, you're on your own. Try and make your way to the Metalwork Room as best you can. Good luck." We shook hands. "Keep low," I said, last of all.

I looked left and right as I pushed down the aluminium bar of the Fire Door.

There was always the danger of running straight into the Caretaker. If anyone else came close to being as bad as Mr Sacker to be caught by, then it was Mr Kitson.

All clear.

My breath steamed around my face. The snow that had fallen on the ground between the school and The Furze was chewy and perfect for snowballs. Our footsteps would stick in it to give us away for a long time after we'd gone. But we couldn't worry about that now.

Without looking back, I scrambled my way across the twenty exposed yards.

At every step, I expected to hear a classroom window flying open and an order being barked, "Oi! You! Come back here!"

But I didn't hear anything, nothing but the hushing of my own feet.

It was only when I reached the tallest tree and turned round to look back towards the school that I realized my luck and how fantastic it had been.

Mr Sacker was standing right beside the window of the next classroom along, writing something on the blackboard.

If he'd looked a little to his left, I would have been spotted.

The smallest movement outside was going to catch his eye.

And a schoolboy in a charcoal blazer moving fast against a snowy-white background was more than the smallest movement.

I was desperate to signal Peter. I needed to stop him from setting off.

Until Mr Sacker had turned or moved away from the window, it was entirely unsafe to escape.

But Peter had his orders, and he would obey them to the letter. He would set off *exactly* thirty seconds after I had.

I watched with great worry as the Art Room Fire Door opened.

Mr Sacker had not turned or moved away.

Peter sidewaysed out.

If anything Mr Sacker was now staring directly through the window.

Peter closed the door quietly behind him. I heard it click. Shut. Locked. No way back.

Even worse, Mr Sacker was now rubbing a circle in the steamed-up windowpane.

I saw Peter double-check the second hand on his watch.

For a moment, I thought Mr Sacker might have spotted me – even though I was good and hidden behind the trunk of the tallest tree.

Peter squatted down, ready to dash.

Perhaps Mr Sacker had seen my footprints, left behind in the snow. Perhaps he was deciding whether or not to investigate.

Peter and Mr Sacker were only about ten feet apart.

One second more, and then Peter had set off running towards me.

The game was up. Mr Sacker would catch sight of him before he'd got half-way across the open ground.

(The only question then would be whether I should give myself up, as well, or continue with my mission?)

Peter kept low as he ran, just like I'd ordered him to.

Mr Sacker was still looking out the window.

Just as Peter was emerging from the protection of the angles, I saw a hand go up in Mr Sacker's classroom.

Mr Sacker turned to face his class only a millisecond before Peter burst into sight.

Still, I kept a worried eye upon the classroom.

Peter was two-thirds of the way across.

I saw a head turn, a face looking out of the window. It was a girl. Just for a moment I thought it might be Miranda, arrived late.

Peter was ten feet away from me. But that made no difference. Not if we were going to be reported to teacher by some creepy little girl.

Her hand wiped a small, dark rainbow in the steamed-up classroom window.

Peter arrived breathlessly beside me. "We made —"

"Shh," I said, though our being silent meant nothing now. "You were spotted."

Peter looked back towards the school building.

I pointed out the girl sitting beside the window.

"Who is it?" asked Peter.

"I don't know," I said.

She began to draw something else in steamed-upness on the window.

It was a circle. Then, inside it, a U-shape. A smile. Then a pair of dots. Of eyes.

"I think we're alright," I said.

We waited a short while more, but there was no movement from Mr Sacker.

If the girl was going to sneak on us, she would surely have done so by now.

"Let's move out," I said.

The sandy ground of The Furze was covered with snow that

393

had fallen, frozen, unfrozen, refrozen. It was an icy crust, easily broken, that lay on the top layer of the heather. Some of the snow had unfrozen enough to become bright jewel-droplets on the underneath of branches. These fell off in long lines as soon as you came anywhere near touching them. Everything was cold enough to be quite dry. The ground was frozen just about as hard as it could be, during daylight.

I didn't want to risk catching exposure by staying out too long. We had to keep moving. I led Peter towards Base Camp #2.

"Is Andrew there?" he asked.

"He may already have left," I replied.

"Miranda is with him, is she?"

"Peter," I said, "shut up."

The approach to Base Camp #2 looked no different from normal apart from the snow.

In sub-zero temperatures, the camp lost its operational usefulness. We couldn't risk lighting a bonfire there, and giving away its secret location.

Closer in, and I saw the first signs that something might indeed be up.

Just outside Emergency Escape Route #1, the snow had recently been disturbed by steps.

Two people, I thought as I looked – and one of them being half-dragged.

I felt a wild twist of panic in my stomach, as if a small animal were in there being tortured.

"We'll approach via both Exits," I said. Then I had a thought. "Wait a minute."

I walked the circumference of the Camp, making a close examination of the ground.

Footprints also disturbed the snow outside Emergency Escape Route #2. But it was obvious to a trained tracker that only one person had made them – and it wasn't difficult to guess who.

More interestingly, there were a few small bright splashes of blood.

I continued round until I was back at Exit #1.

Checking again, I made sure I was right that there were *two* sets of footsteps going in.

Peter's eyes followed mine. He had seen the two sets of footprints, one dragged, one not.

"Alright," I said. "I'll take the other Exit. You take this one."

I wanted to keep Peter from seeing the blood for as long as possible.

After dashing back round to Escape Route #2, I went down on hands and knees. The ground was so cold it burned.

I began to crawl through the low tunnel of gorse. The sand here had been violently kicked up, and there were small drops of blood spilled delicately to one side and the other. Some had stuck on the thorns of the gorse, and were now slowly freezing solid. Those on the ground were still wettish.

As I didn't want to get blood-evidence on my trousers, I proceeded very carefully.

Because he didn't do this, Peter got there faster.

I was only half-way along Escape Route #2 when I heard him wailing my name far, far too loudly.

There was something already terrifying in his tone. It was the sound he would have made at the age of five, if he'd spent twelve hours locked in a dark cupboard.

I crawled out into the central clearing, where Peter stood with his hands down by his sides.

The blood was far more obvious here. It trailed in an almost solid smear around the corrugated iron sheet, and a thick slide of it went down into (or came back out of) the pit itself.

A thin breathy steam was curling up round the edge of the corrugated iron, like smoke out from under a chimney-breast.

From where he was standing, Peter could see what was in the pit.

"Look," he said, and stiffly pointed.

I stepped round to stand beside him.

Just before looking down into the pit, I examined Peter's face close-up. I wanted to guess exactly how horrified or delighted I was likely to be.

His nostrils were flared, and he breathed in that animal-like way people do when they think they are about to be sick.

I looked down to what he was looking at.

It was Miranda, that much I could tell. It was Miranda and a lot of Miranda's blood. But there was a confusion. I couldn't tell which way round to look at her, or in fact couldn't see a head at either end. Her shoes had been taken off, and her socks pulled up around her ankles. Her knees, though, looked extra-thin. And her arms seemed bloated and fat. Her skirt covered something bulging. Where her head should have been, there was a sprig of blond hair. Some of her hair had been cut off, and lay half-floating in the blood all around her. Miranda's skin, where I could see it, was veiny blue. Peter was muttering to me, but I didn't pay any attention to him. I was still looking for the head. Her arms lay at strange angles, the joints seeming to go the wrong way. I could tell that her white shirt was resting upon blood, blood that was wet but just hadn't quite had time to soak through yet, or was blood from the heart, too thick to soak through. And her left leg, now that I saw it – it seemed to be bending back upon itself, like it had been totally smashed to bits, inside.

Peter was first to say the actual words. Perhaps saying my name before had made him more used to speaking.

Just before he spoke, I was able to work it out and see what Peter saw. "She's upside-down," he said.

Miranda's clothes were on the wrong way round, the wrong way up. What I thought were arms, were legs, and the legs were arms. The little white socks were on her hands, not her feet. The bulge under her blue skirt must be her head. But that still didn't explain the hair sprouting out of the neck of Miranda's white shirt. It looked just like the hair from her head. Then I looked again at the hair in the blood pool, and I realized what was what.

Paul was still muttering.

I clamped my hand over his mouth. If there were teachers out looking for us on The Furze, such stupidity would give us away.

As soon as his mouth was covered, I heard something else. Another sound. Human. More muffled. Coming from the pit.

Miranda's right arm – no, her right leg – had started to tremble.

The faint sound was of speaking-and-also-crying, like a toddler barging towards you wailing with wild explanations.

Peter stepped forwards, out of my grasp. "Miranda?" he said.

The wail didn't vary, didn't become louder or more urgent.

He turned to me. "She's still alive," he said.

I was already thinking of what we should and shouldn't do. "No, she's not," I said. "Look at all that blood."

He cocked his head, like a robin redbreast on a branch. He was showing me he was listening.

The wailing continued.

"And she's still moving," he said. He pointed at the part of her that trembled.

"I can see that," I said. "But she's dead. When we found her, she was dead."

"We need to call an ambulance," said Peter. "If we call an ambulance, it can take her to hospital, and if they take her to hospital, maybe the doctors can save her."

"How can they save her when she was dead when we got here?"

"But she isn't dead."

"You're wrong."

Peter turned away from the pit. "You go back to school and tell them," he said. "I'll stay here to make sure she's alright."

"You don't understand," I said. "You don't understand what I'm trying to tell you."

"But she's not dead," said Peter. It looked as if I was going to have to smash him, hard, in the mouth.

He had turned into too much of a girl. He needed to be quelled. "If we save her, we'll be alright," he said.

"What we're going to do is this." And I told him. In detail.

Luckily, perhaps, Peter was in such a shocked state that he was almost overjoyed to be ordered about.

This has always been what the Best Father said about the lower ranks: give them something to do, and they'll jump to it, but let the buggers think for themselves, and you're lost.

I reached into the gorse and pulled out a couple of dry and dead branches. Then I demonstrated to Peter the technique we had to employ.

We were going to back out the Escape Routes the way we came, sweeping the ground behind us to get rid of any sign we might have been there.

Miranda, down in the pit, continued to wail. After a minute or two, it became quite easy to ignore – for the kind of sound it was never really varied.

I handed the improvised brush to Peter, and began to sweep away my own traces. He copied me, as trusting as an idiot.

I was frustrated that I didn't have time to look over Escape Route #1 and check he'd done a thorough job.

After a minute or two of rubbing out, we met up again outside the circle of gorse.

"Give me that," I said, then took the branch from his dead hand.

I gave the bloody area around the entrance a decent going over, though it was hard to get the red completely to disappear. Somehow, however hard one tried to flick it underneath, it kept forcing its way to the surface.

When I finished, we backed away down a path.

"Jump sideways," I said.

Peter complied.

We bounded around at random, leaving confusing prints.

I tossed the blood-covered branches off in different directions.

We were safe. Or as safe as the techniques outlined in *Scouting For Boys* could make us.

"To the Dinosaur House," I said.

Peter only nodded. He understood that they were the Dinosaurs again.

"Come on," I said.

We ran through the thick-wooded parts of The Furze.

Luckily, there were no Games lessons in progress on the school playing-fields.

The vast open area of snowed-up grass was entirely empty, apart from the ghostly frame of the never-used cricket nets.

We were able to skirt along the far fence without being seen. As I had anticipated, this was the route Andrew had taken. I could tell this from the single set of swishy footprints that went ahead of us wherever we went, and also the flicks of black blood on the snow-surface. Andrew had done his work with a knife. His trusty Bowie knife, I guessed. And that knife was still with him.

I dragged my feet, and ordered Peter to do the same. It might not be much, but we could try and cover over Andrew's tracks at this particular point.

There was nothing we could do about our own footprints. They would stay as clues until they melted or were covered over.

We made it to the Sports Hall. Things might get a little tricky from now on.

A stray Games Master was often to be found, having a shifty cigarette in the car park.

Lots of people who had escaped from school got this far and then got cocky, and were caught.

Peter was only limply following me now.

Back pressed against the wall, I peered round the corner and saw no-one.

By sneaking from car to car, cover to cover, we made our way past the last bit of the playing-field.

The journey to the Dinosaur House became more dangerous with every corner we turned, with every step we took.

There were about eighty yards between us and the entrance to The Prom. The worst we were likely to meet here was a nosy dog-walker. (Although we *were* walking directly behind the Police Station.)

I decided we had better take this stretch at a run. To give him something to do, I made Peter go first.

He dashed from tree to tree, pausing at every one to check the coast was still clear.

I followed, two trees behind.

Our pulses were racing.

The landscape ahead was more densely populated. We were heading into the suburban streets. Far more likely that here we would encounter PC241.

I told Peter to look ill. (Which wasn't difficult. His face was already greenish.) If anyone asked, I would say that I was taking him home because he felt unwell.

We moved along at a decent whack, but not suspiciously fast. By the time we reached the bottom of Cowfold Lane, we were almost within sight of the Dinosaur House.

It was necessary to approach with extreme caution. Who (apart from Andrew, and even him not a hundred per cent) knew what we were likely to find?

The best way to get close without being seen was to creep along on the other side of the row of thick holly trees. This left us open to observation from houses on the opposite side of the road. But I thought it was worth taking this risk.

It felt good to squat behind the holly trees and know that, if nothing else, we'd made it this far.

Peter nudged me and loudly asked, "What do you think he did?"

I put my hand over Peter's mouth, afraid that he was stupidly going to give us away.

He struggled, unable to breathe.

"I'll let you go," I whispered, "but only if you keep very quiet."

He struggled a bit more, then nodded.

When I let go, he said, "I wasn't talking loud."

"You have no idea how loud you were talking."

"I know exactly," he said.

"Then why are you shouting?" I asked, quite reasonably.

"I am not," he whispered.

"We don't have time to argue," I said. "Let's get moving."

When we came into sight of the Dinosaur House, there was only one indication that anything unusual had been going on: the front door was slightly ajar.

Peter and me approached with extreme caution.

No snow had settled upon the concrete garden path, so there was no indication of how many people had visited the place that morning.

"Do you think he's still here?" asked Peter.

"No," I said. "He's far ahead of us."

Peter did not take my full meaning.

"Is he at home, now?"

I turned on him, irascible. "I don't know where he is, alright?"

Peter chewed the inside of one of his cheeks, like he did when he was very worried.

His face was the colour of a white vest that your mother has washed by mistake with all the dark things.

He had been brave in rescuing the Archives from the fire. But now he faced a real test, and he was falling apart.

"Think about Matthew," I said. "Isn't this what he would have wanted?"

"Miranda," Peter said. "She may still be alive."

"She's dead," I said. "Let's go inside."

We walked up the garden path, leaving no footprints on the snowy lawn. The concrete was drippy with blood. From the out-of-the-house direction of the splashes, I guessed this blood was not Miranda's.

There was an oval smudge of blood on the white paint beside the door-bell. It was the most perfect thumb-print I had ever seen.

Feeling as if I was falling backwards at the same time as standing up, I watched my hand push open the front door.

The frosted glass, covered with the interlocking swirl of sharp-edged leaves, swung slowly to the side.

The house was very silent. For some reason, I half-expected to hear Miranda's dying moaning coming from somewhere inside. This was a stupid, Peter-type thought.

There were more blood-drips on the carpet.

The floral wallpaper on one side of the hall was smeared with a long wavy line made out of blood.

It was like the water experiments we did in Physics, ripples in a clear glass tank seen from the side.

Peter glanced at the phone on the small table, then at me. I knew he was thinking of dialling 999.

"Come on," I said.

Mrs Dinosaur was in the sitting room, half on the sofa, half slumped on the floor. It took me a moment to understand what I was seeing. Aeroplanes were sticking out of her face, as if they

402

had crash-landed into a pulpy moon of blood. The largest of them, an Avro Lancaster B.III Dambuster, had been shoved deep into her mouth. The whole of its front end, including the cockpit and the front turret, was somewhere as deep as her larynx. Some of its machine-gun barrels had snapped off, and were lying on her neck like little plastic twigs. More amazing, though, were the Supermarine Spitfire Mk I and the Hawker Hurricane Mk IIB – one sticking out of each eye socket. Their tail-fins had been very very carefully painted by Matthew – probably the best Airfix modeller out of all of us.

"Paul," said Peter, standing to one side of me, but slightly behind. "Do you see what he did?"

I stepped out into the centre of the room, to get a clear view of Mrs Dinosaur's dead body. It was only then that I saw Matthew's toy box, the contents spilled out onto the carpet beside the sofa. Two more aeroplanes were sticking out of, or stuck into, Mrs Dinosaur – depending on which way you looked at it. A Stuka was divebombing its way into her tummy button area. There was grey material, which I thought was probably guts, around its nose. It had been pushed mostly out again, and now only hung on – just – by a broken propeller. Matthew's pride and joy, a 1:72 scale model of a Messerschmitt Bf 109 G.6 was rammed up inside Mrs Dinosaur's fanny. Her dress hardly covered her, apart from her chest and her neck. The wings of the Bf 109 G.6 stuck backwards, because otherwise they wouldn't fit. The carpet was soaking up the blood that had run out of Mrs Dinosaur's back. Pulling my eyes away from her, I looked around the room for the further details which I somehow knew Andrew would have left.

All at once, something strange happened. I began to know the *exact* things Andrew had done before I'd even seen them. It was as if I were in two places and times at once, both with myself here now and with Andrew at the moment of killing.

I looked over at Matthew's school photograph and, just as I *knew* he would, saw Andrew had drawn a blood-smile over our dead friend's mouth.

This was becoming a little spooky.

I stepped over to the birdcage (Andrew must have brought it down from the attic) and saw that, yes, this was where Andrew had put Mrs Dinosaur's eyes. Sunny was there, too.

There was one way to check this spookiness: I must think about what, together, Andrew and me had done to Mr Dinosaur. Then I must go upstairs and see how right in my knowing I was.

Peter said he wouldn't come. He felt sick.

"You can tell me what you see," he said, standing at the bottom of the stairs. "I'll stay down here and keep an eye out for the Police."

(I did not mention that there were already two eyes out, in the birdcage.)

There was no need for keeping an eye. Obviously, Andrew had been such an efficient killer that there had been no screams.

5.

Mr Dinosaur, as I *knew* he would be, was still in bed. A white sheet, but only a white sheet, covered his body. The blankets and duvet were on the floor. His face was an image. Instead of aeroplanes, Andrew had cut off Mr Dinosaur's fingers and thumbs. Stains came through the sheet, deep red. A body has ten holes: two eyes, two nostrils, two ears, one mouth, one belly button, one urethra, one anus. A body has eight fingers and two thumbs. Andrew had put these two facts together, perfectly. It didn't look as if Andrew had stabbed Mr Dinosaur anywhere unnecessary. In my head I knew that Andrew had just covered his face with a pillow and waited and waited and waited. Sticking

404

out round the edges of the eye-forefingers, were strands of blond hair. Andrew must have saved these. He must have carried them with him from The Furze. He had planned the whole thing. Kill Miranda. Then kill the Dinosaurs. But first tell them Miranda was dead. Show them proof. I could almost hear his voice echoing in the room, "You killed our friend and now we're going to kill you."

Other details had been left, just as they had been left downstairs. Andrew had taken his time. He had done everything that he wanted to do, and done it exactly as he wanted to do it. The floor of the bedroom was covered all over with Mr Dinosaur's pills. I saw that none of them had been crushed. Scattering them, I knew, was the last thing Andrew did before he left the room. The dressing-table mirror had blood-writing on, in capital letters: *EXTINCTION*.

Spookily, I knew as soon as I came out of the bedroom that there was one thing left for Andrew *himself* to do. And I also knew exactly where he was going to do it.

We had to get to the Tree-Fort, and as quickly as possible. For this, we would need our bikes.

I looked once again at Mr Dinosaur's face, all stuck out with fingers.

Time had come to go. Peter was right – at some point the Police would catch up with us. We just had to make sure it didn't happen until we had seen Andrew once again.

Peter followed me out of the house.

"What was it like?"

"You'll never know," I said.

Peter looked at the upstairs windows. He wanted me to think he was thinking about running back in, stomping up the stairs and bursting into the bedroom. But I wasn't fooled. He was a coward. He would never know. Not like I did.

Collect the full set. This was something Peter had never ever done. Even as far back as the PGTips Dinosaur cards, he never got all of anything.

Without warning, I punched him in the neck.

He started to cough, and couldn't speak.

I kneed him in the thigh a couple of times, to give him a dead leg.

He swayed over, off-balance, and left a small dance of footprints in the snow of the front lawn.

When he was able to speak again, he said, "What did you do that for?"

"Because you deserve it," I said. "Why can't you stop being such a complete Peter all the time?"

"I'm sorry," he said. He knew what I meant.

"Don't be sorry," I snapped. "These are your orders. Go home and get your bike without being caught. Meet me at Base Camp #1, in the shed, asap. Stop for no-one. Do you hear me? *No-one.* If you don't do this, I will find Andrew and I will tell him all about your experiment with Matthew, and, together, we will come and get you."

Peter knew by now just how bad being "got" by Andrew could be.

Peter sprinted off towards Unstable Street. I knew, however, that he would slow down as soon as he was out of my sight.

6.

When I got home, I approached stealthily through the trees. I was relieved to see that my mother wasn't outside in the garden. That would have made getting my bike almost impossible.

(The only tactic I might have used would have been to lure her, at great risk to myself, away from the garden by imitating the mewing of an injured cat.)

But, of course, there had been a hard frost the night before. My mother would not be gardening.

My major worry was getting the bike silently through our squeaky gate.

If she came out later to scrape some peelings onto the compost heap, my mother might notice that my bike had been stolen. Then she might probably call the Police. But that didn't matter any more.

I made my way to the far corner of the garden, scaling the fence at a point just out of sight of the kitchen window.

Unseen, I crept along the back hedge. I was very aware of the footprints I was leaving behind.

Keeping low to the ground, I sidled along the garage wall. A quick glance around the corner.

This was the most dangerous point. For a full two seconds or so, I would be clearly visible from my mother's vantage-point.

There was nothing else to be done, apart from take the risk as manfully as I could. On the count of three, I scuttled off.

Slamming slightly breathless into the side wall of the house, I listened out for the call of my mother's voice, the frunk of the front door, the crunch of feet upon gravel.

What I heard, instead, was the plaintive song of a single robin redbreast. I imagined its wounded plumage, brightly crimson against the snow-heavy bough of a holly bush.

Slowly, and using all my training in silent movement, I edged towards the bike.

It was chained, as always, to the metal pipe that took water from the kitchen sink through the wall and down into the outside drain.

Touching the leather saddle of my bike seemed a victory in itself. Already, I had come so far.

My fingers touched the metal of the combination lock. Very carefully, I moved them round from their initial position, 0–0–0–0, to the correct liberating number 1–4–7–7.

(This was comprised of our initials, A–M–P–P, on the basis

407

A=1, B=2, C=3, etc. For letters after J=0, I simply added the two digits together. P for Peter (and Paul)=16 because 1+6=7.)

I felt like a brave commando, setting the timber on a bomb with a Nazi guard patrolling only a few feet away.

My mother suddenly began to sing. She did this all the time, around the house. Particularly phrases from Bach's Masses.

I don't mind Bach. But she never seemed to finish anything, or know more than two lines together. This near drove me mad.

My fingers slipped on the lock, and it clanked down onto the metal of the gears.

My mother kept on singing.

Just as I slid the final digit into place, I heard a glonk sound – and warm water began to steam out of the pipe and into the drain.

I quickly pulled to one side, and waited for the flood to end.

My mother was washing up breakfast and lunch together.

The water was grey, dotted with black tea-leaves.

There was some overspill, which sloshed around the soles of my shoes.

If she was following her usual routine, my mother would now come outside with scrapings for the all-consuming compost-heap.

I had about a minute while she put her coat on.

The combination lock snapped open. I quickly hung it round my neck.

Keeping my head lower than the handlebars, I wheeled the bike towards the gate.

If my mother spotted me once I was outside the garden, I would ignore her shouting and ride away as fast as possible.

The gravel path made a great deal more noise than I would have wished, but that was sadly unavoidable.

By now, my mother would be punching her arms into the arms of her duffel coat.

I was almost at the gate. Still no noise from behind me.

As I lifted the latch I heard, like an echo, the latch of the front door snap up.

I looked back.

The front door began to open. I would be caught. I would be caught.

But just then I heard the telephone begin to ring.

Quite clearly, I heard my mother say, "Bugger!" But the front door closed again.

With no further need for caution, I flung the gate open and slammed it shut behind me.

Putting my right foot on the left pedal, I freewheeled down the hill until I came to the edge of The Park.

As I came out onto Midford Street, I heard the nee-naw of a siren. I had about a moment to wonder which it was – Police, Fire or Ambulance.

In case it was the Police, I dragged my bike back under cover.

An ambulance went past, speeding towards Midford Hospital, just as it did for Peter and for Matthew.

I wondered if Peter – trotting towards The Close – had heard it, too.

The day was still. He was just about within range, provided he wasn't breathing so hard he heard nothing but his own breath.

The sight of the speeding ambulance led me to suspect that Miranda was still alive. (What a tough girl! Her brother would have been proud.)

Still, Miranda had almost certainly not seen us. There was nothing she could tell the Police. Nothing.

Without thinking any more, I lifted my bike up and wheeled it out from behind the bush.

There was almost no traffic on Midford Road, which made me wonder why the ambulance was using its siren.

Once I made it across to Holy Walk, I swung myself up onto the seat, and, after selecting a low gear, set off on the short up-and-down ride to Wychwood.

7.

When I arrived at the piss-smelling barn, I found Peter's bike but not Peter.

However, I had a pretty good idea where he was – and a few moments later he proved me right, by coming through the clanking planks of Initiation.

"He isn't here," said Peter, meaning Wychwood. "I had a look while I was waiting."

"I know he isn't here," I said.

"Did you hear the Police siren?"

"No," I said. "I saw it, and it was an ambulance."

"Where was it going?"

"Towards Midford."

He thought for a moment, and it was as if I were tracking his thoughts like blood and footprints in the snow.

"If she was already dead, they wouldn't have a siren, would they? They'd just take her, like a body."

"Let's be off," I said.

"This time you have to tell me where we're going."

I could see from his stance and his sulk that in this at least Peter was resolute.

"The Tree-Fort," I said.

"Why?" he asked.

"It's where Andrew is."

"How do you know? Did he tell you specially?"

"I just know because I just know."

He looked at his feet.

"Follow me," I said.

What was important now, at this stage of the Operation, was speed not stealth.

I pegged it up Gravel Track, past the churchyard. Peter was close behind.

As we turned onto Church Road, I saw the Best Father reversing out of the drive of The Pollards in his big white Rover 2000.

Instinctively, I hunched up.

"Oh no," I heard Peter say.

Andrew's father spotted us.

We were already past him and on down the hill by the time he'd honked the Rover's horn.

Peter began obediently to slow down.

"Keep going," I ordered. "We haven't got time to stop."

Wobbling slightly, I looked back and saw Peter looking further back, wobbling violently.

There was a real danger that this not knowing what to do, coming on top of everything else, would make Peter lose balance and go arse over tit into the gutter.

Andrew's father honked again. A longer, angrier honk.

I glanced forwards, corrected my course, then turned and looked back again.

The tone of the second honk had worked in my favour. Peter was now panicking, and when that happened he always just ran away as fast as he could.

Behind him, I could see something very bad indeed: the Best Father was turning the Rover 2000 around in a tight circle.

If we didn't take evasive action he would run us down in seconds.

Peter had accelerated so rapidly that by now he was running alongside me.

"Go down Gas House Lane," I said. "If we take the route Hill, he won't be able to follow."

Another glance back. I could see the Best Father's car beginning to catch up with us.

We were almost at Gas House Lane turning when two Police cars shot towards us over the brow of the hill.

They did not have sirens or lights on, but were travelling at great speed.

The white of a face flashed across at me from the passenger seat.

We had been sighted.

As he drove towards them, the Best Father flashed his headlights. The second of the two Police cars slowed down.

"Follow me," the Best Father said.

Skidding wildly, I rounded the corner onto Gas House Lane. Much rougher than the smooth tarmacked road, the track led up past the old Gas Works.

At the end, it became a narrow path between snow-covered hedges.

If we could just make it that far, we could easily outdistance the Best Father and the Police.

There was no way they could follow us by car, and no chance that they would catch us on foot.

Peter took the corner even less tidily than I had, and was very lucky not to end up in a ditch.

Some traffic, probably a tractor or two, had been down Gas House Lane since the last snowfall.

The road surface wasn't quite as covered over as it might have been. Two deepish tracks ran down on either side.

By the time the Best Father had turned in after us, we had got about fifty yards down the farm track. He could now be in little doubt as to our tactics. The Rover 2000 was gaining on us with every second.

Peter struggled to keep up. Worst of all would be if the Best Father managed to catch him, and he blabbed everything.

412

"Come on!" I shouted back at Peter, and was glad to see him start to pedal faster.

We were only fifty, forty, thirty yards from the single-file path. But the Rover was catching us up at a great rate of knots.

The biggest danger now was that we'd be overtaken.

If the Best Father got in front of us, he could easily block the road and bring us to a captured halt.

I heaved my bike over from the right-hand track to the left, then let myself drift back until I was riding exactly alongside Peter.

For a moment, he thought I was giving up. Then, he saw what I meant to do.

If he wanted to overtake us now, the Best Father was left with only one option: to run us down.

If he'd known how deadly serious the situation was, he might have done that.

But because he didn't, he just drove up to within five feet of us, and then kept a steady distance.

With his free hand, he rolled down the side window and leaned out to shout at us.

"Stop at once! I order you to stop at once!"

Peter glanced over at me, terrified by the idea that we were about to disobey a direct order from a superior officer.

"Come on, boys," called the Best Father.

I knew, just from the simple mistaken use of the word *boys*, that the Best Father had turned quisling.

Twenty yards. Fifteen. Ten. All we needed to do now was hold our nerve and keep going.

But just when I thought we were almost safe, my front wheel dropped into a deep pot-hole.

With half my control gone, I found myself wobbling across towards Peter.

Instinctively, he braked to avoid crashing into me.

Just behind us, the Best Father braked, too.

As soon as its wheels were settled in the right-hand track, I managed to get back control of the bike.

But the Best Father hadn't braked fast enough.

The back wheel of Peter's bike received a sharp knock from the Rover's silver chrome bumper.

The Best Father immediately tried to perform an emergency stop, but the car went into a skid.

Peter, shocked by the impact, began to pedal faster than ever.

The Rover skidded from side to side, as the Best Father fought to stop it crashing.

Ahead of us the road turned round to the left, before going into the old Gas Works. But if we kept going in a straight line, we would shoot off up the single-file path.

Peter overtook me just as the two tracks flipped off to the left. Immediately, the snow became thicker under our wheels.

A final glance revealed the Best Father's Rover, safely stopped.

The Police car, too, had halted.

All the grown-ups got out of their cars.

As we cycled up a slow grinding incline, a few angry shouts came after us.

8.

On reaching the top of Greysand Ridge, we turned right. We were in full view of our pursuers, but there was nothing we could do about that.

I ordered Peter to halt for a moment, so that I could inspect my front wheel.

A couple of the spokes were a little bent, but no worse damage had been done.

It was in more than good enough working order to get me where I needed to go.

Around us, the fields were Dalmatian-hued.

"We're in trouble, now," said Peter.

"We were in trouble before," I replied. "It hasn't got any worse."

"Are you sure?" asked Peter.

I ignored him, pushing my bike past him and starting off along the hill-top.

The Tree-Fort was distinctly visible, even from a mile and a half away. But I did not look at it too closely: my head was down, set upon making fast progress.

We rode on, our breath steaming up behind us like the smoke of a locomotive.

The Tree-Fort appeared stark as a crown of thorns upon the brow of the hill.

When I first caught sight of Andrew, I thought he was a particularly dense clump of mistletoe. This grew commonly on Greysand Ridge, favouring the taller trees. But as I cycled closer, I was able to make out the forked human shape. It was, however, upside-down.

I heard Peter give a sharp yell, which told me that he, too, had identified the form within the branches.

We sped up even more.

The sky above us was the same dull white as the fields around us. The footprints of some mid-Winter ramblers were the only thing ahead of us on the path. The day was quiet, but the nee-nawing siren disturbed all distances. The Police car seemed to be only a hundred yards away, whereas the Tree-Fort felt as if it were beyond the vanishing point. Even though they were taking the long way round, it was touch and go whether they or we would reach Andrew first.

Peter reacted badly to the sight of our friend. He began to slow down.

Of course, he had not known what to expect. His connection with Andrew was weaker than mine.

I could no longer be bothered with him.

If Andrew *was* dead, Gang was dead. If Gang was dead, Peter would be less than a friend – he would be an embarrassment.

A narrow road cut across the end of the single-file path. The entrance to the Tree-Fort field was about fifty yards along on the left.

When I swerved out onto the ungritted tarmac, I had no idea how far behind me the Police would be.

I looked quickly over my shoulder. Peter was catching up again. His moment of doubt was over.

I skidded to a halt beside the five-bar gate, jumping off my bike at almost the very same moment.

"Abandon," I said, too puffed to say the whole sentence.

Peter copied me.

I high-jumped the gate, something I have always been particularly skill at.

The Police car was now ahead of the Best Father's.

Peter landed awkwardly in a frozen tractor rut, and I thought he might have twisted his ankle.

I did not want to have to piggyback him the final few yards.

"I'm alright," he said, pushing himself to his feet.

I began to spring towards the Tree-Fort, once again able to afford the time to look up.

Andrew was on the far side of the ring of trees, the North. He was very high up – any higher and the branches would have been too flimsy to support his weight.

I noticed something unusual about Andrew's appearance: his face looked black, and his hair was darker than usual.

Peter had picked himself up. The distance between us was about thirty feet.

Out of their cars got the Police and the Best Father. They ran towards the five-bar gate.

When entering the Tree-Fort, I would inevitably give away the existence of The Door. But that couldn't be helped.

I dashed up to the secret opening and pulled the branches apart.

Only a very little snow fell upon me, for Andrew had already been through and disturbed it.

Behind me, I heard shouts.

I looked back between the tree-trunks.

The Best Father, like the Champion Pram-Racer he was, had already outsprinted both of the Policemen.

I staggered out into the clearing.

Beneath the spot where Andrew was hanging an almost perfect circle of blood had formed.

Running until I stood just outside its circumference, I looked up at his limp body.

His blond hair had been dyed a purply colour by his blood. I still couldn't see the face.

After taking a couple of steps to the side, I saw what he had done.

His throat was cut. The blood was running down over his face, up his nose, around his eyes.

Peter made it through The Door about ten feet ahead of the Best Father. He arrived at my side almost too breathless to look up.

Instead, he gasped and then retched as he saw the circle of blood.

Andrew had tied his legs together around the branch, so he wouldn't fall off even when he lost consciousness.

I recognized the knot that Andrew had used to tie his legs and ankles together.

At the very centre of the blood circle, his Bowie knife had plunged into the ground.

As it dripped from his dangling hand, the blood fell with great delicacy onto the handle of the knife.

The whole thing was perfectly arranged, in a way that I was usually much better at than Andrew.

The Best Father came crashing through The Door.

"Oh Christ," he said, as he looked up at his dead son. "Oh, fuck, what is that?"

The Police emerged a few seconds after him.

Fearing he might be hauled straight off to prison, Peter took his chance to look up.

As soon as he saw Andrew's dangling body, the second Policeman stepped to one side and vomited matter-of-factly against a tree-trunk.

Although he'd held it in all the way until now, Peter couldn't stop himself from puking, too.

The splat of his vomit coincided with the edge of the blood circle. It was like an exercise in maths with sets.

I imagined the scene, as seen from Andrew's angle: circle, circle, circle.

The Best Father had his right hand pressed flat over his mouth, as if – though I knew it wasn't for this reason – trying to stop himself from vomiting, too.

I knew his heart must be filled with unbelievably immense pride.

It was him, as the Major-General, who had told us never to allow the enemy to catch us alive.

And here the enemy were, standing side-by-side with us – and there Andrew was, not caught, never caught.

The Police laid hands upon us. But not roughly, like I expected them to. They grabbed our shoulders and pulled us back, away from the circle of blood.

The Best Father said to the Policeman as he turned away, "Do what you have to with him. Just get him down from there as soon as possible. Before anyone sees him."

The Policeman who had hold of me pointed up at our glorious Leader and asked, "What do you know about this, then?"

I looked warningly across at Peter, who was being held by the other listening Policeman.

The interrogations were about to begin.

I drew a long, deep, cold breath, and gave them the only details they would ever get out of me: Name, rank, number.

The other Policeman grabbed more tightly onto Peter's arms. "What is this?" he asked. "Do you think this is some kind of game?"

Peter, for once, made me truly proud of him: Name, rank, number.

All the rest of the manuscript (apart from The Archives) had been typed out on an old-fashioned typewriter. But the final chapter, a second Chapter Thirteen, was handwritten, hastily. A note had been paperclipped to the first page. It read, "Ignore all previous dispatches." (My father had often talked to me like this, and now I understood where it came from: the Major-General.) The note concluded, "This is the true version." I noticed that the pages were numbered upwards from pg. 375 – as if my father had intended to replace the original Chapter Thirteen with this newer, later version. Perhaps he'd simply run out of time. Or perhaps he'd wanted me to read both versions, anyway. I flipped to the end. At the bottom of the last handwritten page was a serial number, 0197304 – my father's. Probably the last thing he ever wrote. I went for a walk, thinking about what I believed and what I didn't. And then I read –

CHAPTER THIRTEEN, ALSO

Peter (Paul)

In diesem Wetter, in diesem Saus,
In diesem Braus,
Sie ruh'n als wie in der Mutter Haus,
Von keinem Sturm erschrecket,
Von Gottes Hand bedecket,
Sie ruh'n wie in der Mutter Haus.

In this Weather, in this Hide,
In this Pride,
They rest, as after Matricide,
Not Storm-terrified,
By Godhead sanctified,
They rest, as after Patricide,
They rest, as after Fratricide.

saviours. How proud our English women were, common and noble alike, to see their undergarments no longer used for frippery, but in the very instance of life and death. The deprivation of silk and softness was hardly too high a price for our ladies to pay, not when compared with the rich, young, fighting life that their sacrifices had helped preserve.

It has been said, alleged by hidden and by obvious mouths, that we should not have been so much surprised. Perhaps, back in those early months, we should indeed have discerned that our enemy was attempting to clear our skies, in order that his ground troops might more safely and expeditiously land. Perhaps we should more closely have observed and more accurately interpreted these foreboding signs of a forthcoming invasion. Sufficient Wehrmacht forces, or so we thought, could not be mustered upon English soil to pose a serious threat to national sovereignty or integrity. But these are late regrets, and futile as regrets will ever be. In all of this, the horrid aftermath, we must not allow ourselves to forget those early hopes we had. We seemed, back then, in those days Elysian, as close to total victory as is the Führer now. But most of all, in these dark days of our retrenchment, let us not forget one simple fact: *we were betrayed.*

The German Naval Fleet advanced upon us during the night, in a long line, along the whole South-Eastern Coast – from Dover to Lyme Regis, we were to receive assault. Against such mighty force, the Channel, our avowed protectress for so many centuries, could not resist. Two million tons of shipping were engaged in this, the most momentous aquatic advance in all the history of War. The Germans gave the operation the code-name Dog-Fish. The day of the invasion was to be known as D-Day.

As far West as Cornwall, look-outs had been nightly posted, straining their eyes against the darkness. The system of hill-top bonfires worked perfectly, it must be said. Those in Northumberland were alerted only twenty minutes after the first sighting had taken place in Brighton. Ack-ack guns, once alert, sounded out across the whole of Kent and the Southern coast. A heavy battery was laid up above Dover and Portsmouth. By this time, the clear morning skies were thick with the planes of the Luftwaffe, launched from their bases in occupied France. Stukas dropped like hawks from the clouds, repeating the Blitzkrieg tactics which had so devastated Europe. Messerschmitts strafed our airfields with lethal machine-gun fire.

By half past four on this bitter first day, the initial wave of ships had advanced and the first echelons of German troops had come ashore. The motorboat landings alone brought in three divisions. Four battalions of amphibian tanks bloodily accompanied them. Narrow beachheads, and then bridgeheads, had been formed, and then expanded. For the first time, the Nazi jackboot made its hateful imprint upon British soil, or sand. We did not wish to yield a single foot of this ground, but we were forced inexorably back.

Already, even at this early stage, we had suffered some grave and so far irrecoverable losses. Hastings, scene of more than one historic defeat, was ceded. There was confusion in our forces there. The full alert, "Invasion Imminent", was, for some reason, not received. Our codeword, "Winston Churchill", had somehow gone astray. Thus, the coastal defences were unable to perform the doughty deeds that might have been expected of them.

By lunch-time on D-Day, thirteen divisions were ashore. In Hythe, Rye and Eastbourne, the Sixteenth Army, after issuing from ports in Rotterdam and Boulogne, were making inroads. The beaches swarmed with the field-grey uniforms and coal-scuttle helmets of the invader, wave after wave, almost more numerous than those of the sea itself. The Battle of Brighton was well advanced, to our detriment. The swastika flew already over Worthing. The Ninth Army was bringing Hove under heavy shell-fire. A few smaller coastal and near-coastal enclaves, tough in defence, did, for a time, hold out. So many lost, so many valiantly dying for the cause – in East Wittering and Hooe Common, in Peasmarsh and Guestling Green, in Cripp's Corner and Upper Dicker. But it is time to pull our gaze away from these sights, horrifically fascinating as they undoubtedly are. We look instead towards what may seem a small and hardly signifying village: Amplewick.

ii.

It would be a fortnight before the Wehrmacht forces had fought the Battle of Maidstone, had made their way round London, St Albans, Newton, and had reached a point so northerly advanced as Midfordshire.

However, through their extensive network of spies, the German High Command had learned of Amplewick's crucial strategic importance. For here were three of England's bravest lads – or so, at least, it was once thought. (In the event, just two of them emerged with their valour proven and their honour exalted. The other, may his name be for ever cursed, was traitor to us all.)

The Nazis knew that however swiftly the rest of the country was overrun, if they could not cow Amplewick into submission, then all their dominance elsewhere might be to no avail.

Here was where England would stand or fall; here, where the truest hearts were thought to beat.

A surprise attack was therefore made, by parachute and by assault glider. Initially, the Wehrmacht forces were deployed around the small, semi-detached house in which I and my parents lived. Nazi intelligence reports had suggested that, of the three, East was the weakest link, the most easily corrupted – or intimidated. Just after dawn on D-Day, parachutists of the 7th Division were deployed up and down The Close. What slight resistance there was from the locals was swiftly overcome. There were, in fact, no casualties whatsoever.

As I was asleep when the invasion began, I found myself unable to mount any sort of a defence. One of my quisling parents, my father, was sent in to wake me. I have suspected foul play. If anyone woke me, it was usually my mother. But circumstances were such that I found myself unable to act upon these suspicions.

Instead, I was led downstairs, at gunpoint, into the kitchen. It did not take me long to work out from whence the Nazis had been getting their information. Alma, of the German first name, was sitting at the kitchen table. Beside her, speaking intimately into her traitorous ear, sat SS-Kommandant 241. They roped me to the third Formica chair. My mother was then dismissed, with hardly a word. I was left to the tender mercies of the Gestapo. The lights in the kitchen were tormentously bright. Alma-the-Spy wasted no time in beginning her interrogation.

"We know what you've been doing," she said. Was it my confusion, or did her voice now betray a distinct Nazi hiss? "And we know what you've been planning, too."

I said nothing.

Alma-the-Spy continued, "We also know that you are not a bad boy. From what we've heard, you really didn't want any of it to happen."

"I don't know what you're talking about," I said.

Oh, it was a brave enough beginning I made, but would I be able to go on that way?

"Peter," said the SS-Kommandant, "this is very serious, you know."

I knew, of course, that it was serious. The invasion had taken place. Nothing could be more serious than that. For the moment, I was helpless. The Resistance Movement would have to do

379

without me, for the time being at least. But, if I could, I would find a way to get word to the others.

"After we're done here," said Alma-the-Spy, "we're going to Andrew's and then to Paul's. If you tell us what you've been doing, it will help us to make our decisions."

This treacherous woman was obviously referring to their defence plans. It was imperative that they be kept secret – Top Secret. I thought of the Archives, carefully hidden upstairs. I thought of the conflagration from which I had rescued them. It was unthinkable, it was impossible, that I should now so easily, so quickly, be cozened into betraying them, and all that they stood for.

"I don't know what you're talking about," I said.

Alma-the-Spy and the SS-Kommandant looked at each other in despair.

I felt a small surge of hope. The first counter-attack had been made, had been successful.

Alma-the-Spy stood up. It was obvious to me that she was furious, but that she didn't want me to know that she was furious. In other words, she was exactly where I wanted her to be: in the weakest position a grown-up can occupy. If I worked on her a bit more, she would hopefully become so angry that she wouldn't be able to speak at all.

At a gesture, the SS-Kommandant followed Alma-the-Spy out of the kitchen. A single low-ranking SS-Officer was left on guard duty.

Almost immediately, my mother and father were admitted into the room.

"You have to tell them," said my mother. "Whatever it is you've done – we still love you – and we'll forgive you for it – I promise – but you have to tell them."

My father said, "Just you listen carefully to what your mother says."

Sending the parents in: it was an old interrogation tactic, and not one that was going to catch out an experienced soldier such as myself. I said nothing, just sat, arms crossed, eyes down.

The SS-Kommandant came back in. He issued an order to his subordinate: "Take him to the School. The girl and the grandparents are already there. We'll go and round up the other two."

My spirits were momentarily downcast: they had Miranda. And from what the Kommandant had let slip, it was possible they had forced her into collaborating. Of Bert and Estelle, I had expected nothing more and nothing less. They were merely the civilian population.

The SS-Officer took me upstairs, and stood waiting outside the door whilst I got changed out of his pyjamas.

I considered what chances of success an escape bid might stand. There was only one possibility offered to me: a leap from a first-floor window, followed by a dash into the nettlefield. This might, if nothing else, create a diversion – giving Sub-Lieutenant South and Sergeant North a little more time in which to escape, to act. But in their present state of ignorance, they were highly unlikely to make any use of this gained time.

I gave up on the idea, and began to put on my Gang uniform. I tried, whilst dressing, to secrete about my person as many useful pieces of equipment and weaponry as I could. My Swiss Army penknife went inside one of my boots. Into my breast pocket I slipped a metal nail-file and some string. A couple of matches and a strip of sandpaper went into my socks. I could feel them scratching against my anklebone.

"What's keeping you?" said the SS-Officer.

As a final thought, I put my Bowie knife in my front trouser pocket. It was a decoy – if they searched me, they'd find it first and might not look any further.

Thus armed, and as mentally prepared as I could be, I exited my bedroom, was escorted downstairs, into the Gestapo Vehicle and driven to the Internment Camp.

iii.

Alma-the-Spy and SS-Kommandant 241 made their way to the house of Sergeant North. Here, all were abed. This worked to Sergeant North's eventual advantage, as he was woken, like his mother and father, by the Nazi knocking at the front door. (No friendly fist ever rapped upon that entrance-point: all initiates and intimates knew that the side door was the only one they ever used.)

Sergeant North's father, Major-General North, went down, in dressing-gown and slippers, to answer.

North crept to the top of the stairs to eavesdrop. He heard from there the voices of his enemies. They were demanding access to the house, and to his bedroom. North's reaction, as one would expect, was instantaneous. He ran back to his eyrie, swiftly gathered up his uniform and tossed it out of the window to the flags below. Then, carefully and quietly, he took the route his father had taken that day, after he'd shot as sniper from the roof. Never before had North attempted this perilous descent. Given the choice, he would not have chosen to make it barefoot upon a damp and freezing mid-Winter morn. But time was of the very essence, now. He could hear his father downstairs, shouting, "Get out! Get out of my house!"

Welcome as the delay was, Sergeant North couldn't risk capture.

Did he slip? Did he fall a foot or half a foot, then catch himself breathlessly? Did his hands hurt against the freezing drainpipe? These are things that we shall, perhaps, never know. But that he made it to the ground, and made it safely in one piece, of that there can be no doubt. After gathering up his thrown clothes, he ran into his father's Nissen Hut. Here, he dressed himself. Then, just as had Corporal South, he armed himself. Into his capacious trouser- and jacket pockets went a chisel, some nails, a Stanley knife and a cigarette lighter. Wasting no further time, he crept out of his temporary resting-place. He knew that, if they searched for him near by, the Hut would be one of the first places they'd examine. As they were the most likely to be guarded, he couldn't risk going out either down the drive or through the side door of the garden. Instead, he scaled the back fence and made his way across next door's lawn. From there he was able to scramble through a gap in the privet hedge and out onto the road.

Behind him, in his parents' house, the SS-Kommandant put the Major-General under arrest. Alma-the-Spy finally persuaded Sergeant North's mother to take her upstairs. The bedroom, however, was as we already know, empty. The bird, blessedly, had flown. Alma-the-Spy noticed the window was ajar, and guessed the rest. Sergeant North's mother was horrified by the thought of the drop her son had risked, in order to make his escape. There must, however, I am certain, have been at the same time a deal of pride in her heart.

Once out of the next-door neighbour's garden, Sergeant North skirted around until he was opposite the side door of the Pollards garden. Here was where the Gestapo Vehicle had been parked. It was facing towards Crutch Street, as if it had come directly from The Close. Even in his agitated state, this detail was not lost upon the Sergeant. No sentries appeared to have been placed upon the front of the house. With great swiftness and stealth, North made his way across Crutch Street. In seconds, he was ensconced within the rhododendron bush in the middle of the traffic island in front of Amplewick Church. From hence, he could command a decent view of both the house and the Gestapo Vehicle. It seemed, also, a safe enough place finally to dump his bundled-up pyjamas. Hidden deeply here, buried beneath leaves, they would not soon be found. After a few moments to regain his puff, Sergeant North started to work out his plan of action. He was bike-less, therefore his manoeuvres could not be as swift as he might have wished. He could go either to my house or Sub-Lieutenant South's. But he suspected that we had both already been taken prisoner.

There was no time for further thoughts than these, for, across the road, the front door was opening, and the Major-General, handcuffed, was being escorted out. The SS-Kommandant pushed him all the way to the Gestapo Vehicle, after which he unlocked the door and shoved him roughly into the rear seats. Without a moment's hesitation, the SS-Kommandant then strode back into the house.

Against his better judgement, Sergeant North wanted to show himself to his father – to show his father that he was all right. He stood up out of the rhododendron bush, and walked across Crutch Street. He waved his arms above his head, but his father was looking fixedly towards The Pollards. This was a great frustration. It meant that North would have to expose himself to far greater risk. Moving fast and keeping low, Sergeant North crossed Crutch Street. He headed for the right-hand side of the Gestapo Vehicle, so as to keep it between the house and himself. Once there, he tapped on the window to gain his father's attention. What an exchange of glances was then given and received! How infinitely much communication, and all without the possibility of a single word! Sergeant North pointed towards the road up past the Church. "Away," he meant to say, "I'm escaping!" His father nodded and smiled. "Message received and understood."

Just then, the side door to the garden flew open and the SS-Kommandant stormed out. North heard the door slam; the Major-General didn't. Through the windows of the vehicle,

North saw the arrogant Nazi charging towards the car. His father, noting North's alarm, turned and saw, also. In an instant, he understood what he must do – look straight ahead and give no hint at all that Sergeant North was in the general vicinity. The SS-Kommandant was more than half-way to the Gestapo Vehicle. Escape seemed a complete impossibility. There was nowhere at all for Sergeant North to hide – apart, that is, from under the car itself. It was a high-risk strategy, but now, if any, was the time for such. North lay down and rolled himself between the axles of the Gestapo Vehicle. The SS-Kommandant's shiny black boots arrived at the car. The back door was opened.

"You'll be glad to hear that your son is nowhere to be found," said the SS-Kommandant.

"I am glad," said Major-General North, loudly. "He should steer clear of you lot for as long as he can."

Sergeant North heard, and rejoiced: his father knew where he was. The Major-General was, in truth, simultaneously issuing him with an order and giving his blessing to the actions he'd already taken.

"We'll catch him soon enough," said the SS-Kommandant. "And when we do, he'll be for it."

"We'll see," said the Sergeant's father.

The car door slammed. Alma-the-Spy emerged from the garden door. "No sign of him here," she shouted.

"He can't be far away," replied the SS-Kommandant. "I'm going to get another couple of officers. You keep searching."

Alma-the-Spy went back into the garden, closing the door behind her.

Lying beneath the Gestapo Vehicle, Sergeant North listened in on the radio message that the SS-Kommandant proceeded to send. The tenor of it was simple enough: "Send reinforcements immediately." With his orders dispatched, the SS-Kommandant got out of the car. He left the driver's door open. His shiny boots were only inches away from Sergeant North's face. It seemed that he was looking up and down the road, probably scratching his head. He had been foxed by a wily adversary. There was a whiff of sulphur, and a match dropped to the freezing tarmac and tinkled across the asphalt towards Sergeant North. The scent of tobacco came close behind. For one horrifying instant, Sergeant North thought the Kommandant was about to kneel down and look beneath the vehicle. But instead he spoke to the Major-General through the still-open door.

"I don't suppose it's worth asking you where you think he might have gone?"

Proudly, Sergeant North heard his superior officer answer, "No."

"I thought not," said the Kommandant.

Alma-the-Spy came out of the garden door again. "I don't think there's anywhere left to look," she shouted.

"Did you check the shed?" shouted the Kommandant.

"Of course I checked the shed," she shouted back.

"Come on, then," the SS-Kommandant answered. "We'd better go and pick up the other boy. We can drop this one off at the station on the way."

Alma-the-Spy began to walk towards the Gestapo Vehicle. As there was just a slight chance he might be spotted, Sergeant North stayed stock still. The SS-Kommandant dropped his cigarette, ground it under the heel of his jackboot and got in. Alma-the-Spy went round to the front passenger side, opened the door and got in, too. The vehicle's engine started. North shuffled back as far as he could, until his head was just poking out from under the rear bumper. It was almost certain that the SS-Kommandant would merely drive straight ahead. But there was just a chance he'd execute a three-point turn. In which case, Sergeant North might also be executed. The exhaust pipe blew noxious grey gases out a few inches above the Sergeant's head. He heard the handbrake come off. Inside the car, his father held his nerve. This was it. The vehicle moved smoothly off, straight down the road towards Crutch Street. Sergeant North felt it pass from above him, like a storm cloud revealing the sun. He rolled sideways into the gutter. The Gestapo Vehicle indicated left at the crossing, pulled out, accelerated and was gone.

Sergeant North stood up and brushed himself down.

"Andrew!" came an astonished voice. It was North's mother. She had come out of the house to watch the Gestapo Vehicle driving her husband away, perhaps never to be seen again. Sergeant North felt dismayed. His mother ran towards him. "You were under that car," she said.

"I had to escape," Sergeant North replied.

"You must *never* do that again," said Sergeant North's mother. "And you climbed out of that window, didn't you?"

"I'm going now," said Sergeant North. "You must never tell them you saw me."

"No, you're not," said his mother. "You're coming right back inside this instant."

And then Sergeant North did what any loyal and obedient son would have done – he turned and ran away as fast as he possibly could. "Loyal and obedient son," I should perhaps clarify, of the Royal British Commonwealth and Empire. For often the duties we owe our parents, profound as they are, are overbidden and overridden by those placed upon us by the land that bore us, the nation which brought us up, the civilization within which we were educated, and the race which moulded our very soul. To betray any of these sacred duties is doubly to betray those filial. "Come back here!" the Sergeant's mother shouted, not recognizing the higher obedience which caused her son apparently to disobey. But she did not shout very loud, and her call – her re-call – once uttered was not repeated. She felt abandoned, as have so many good mothers, in watching their sons go off – off to War – off, perhaps, to die – off, at the very least, to the greatest uncertainty of Fate they had ever faced.

Is it not likely that the reason Sergeant North chose not to look back was to hide from this woman the tears that were in his own eyes?

She took a single step in the direction her son was heading – a step of nostalgic yearning for the infant which once could not move and the toddler which could never outrun. Then she turned and went back inside her abandoned house, disgracefully reaching for the telephone. Her tears, though genuine, should not really mitigate our condemnation. The mothers of the French Maquis were rarely so eager to collaborate. Indeed, the grand-mothers of Stalingrad were constructed of tougher material.

Sergeant North sped along the Gravel Track beside the churchyard. He was thinking as he ran. If he sprinted, he might perhaps beat the Gestapo Vehicle to Sub-Lieutenant South's house. Then, at least, he might be able to prevent the capture of one ally. He slowed down a little, to a pace that he would be able to maintain all the way to the Gamekeeper's Cottage.

iv.

Meanwhile, I was sitting in the Ante-Chamber to the Main Torture Chamber of Amplewick Internment Camp. With me was my Gestapo escort. We were sitting in silence, the inexperienced SS-Officer having a while ago given up his feeble attempts to force me to disclosure. I had once already followed standard operating procedure and asked to go to the toilet. But I had found myself so closely chaperoned that escape through the Art Room Fire Door had proven quite impossible. However, for some reason, the SS-Officer had neglected to search my person, and so I was still in possession of all my weapons – including the Bowie knife. As I was being escorted back from the toilet to the Ante-Chamber, I did think about seizing the SS-Officer from behind and slitting his throat. Wisely, however, I decided to bide my time. Which did not mean that, at some point in the future, when circumstances demanded it, I wouldn't gladly kill either one or all of my captors.

Moving my eyes only, I examined my surroundings. I was looking for opportunities, for weaknesses. At one end of the oblong-shaped, brown-carpeted room was the door to the Main Torture Chamber, at the other, the door out into the corridor. There were seven chairs in the room: three running along one wall, four along the other. The place of the fourth, mirror-image-balancing chair was taken by a low table covered with neatly stacked copies of the school magazine. The SS-Officer sat in the middle chair of these three. I had positioned myself in the last of the four chairs, the chair nearest the Torture Chamber door. Through this door, I could hear the Chief Torturer making and receiving phone-calls. Unfortunately, she rarely spoke loudly enough for me to be able to make out anything of use. Once, though, she had almost shrieked, and I clearly heard the words, "Well, where is he, then?" This, with its suggestion that the enemy operation was far from going completely to plan, gave me an immense amount of hope. I sat up straighter, and waited for events to develop.

It was into this stable situation that another factor, or group of factors, was, or were, introduced: Miranda. The deliberate cunning of the move, though cunning of a pitifully low order, did not escape me. The person, or persons, who had shoved her into this room, in the presence only of a dozy underling (and East suspected the hand of Alma-the-Spy) were obviously hoping that I would crack. However, I was not to be that easily had. A rueful and not unmelancholic look was all the communication I at first allowed to pass between us. Miranda sat down on the first of the four chairs, the chair furthest away from myself. A long silence ensued.

"You understand, don't you," said Miranda, eventually. (She had been hoping I would speak first. It is possible that, perhaps, she had even been ordered to wait for me to do so.) "I had to tell them. If I hadn't then something terrible would have happened."

To hear that my best girl had turned informer well nigh broke my heart. But, of this, all of my internal conflict, I gave absolutely no outward sign. The low-ranking SS-Officer sipped his mug of tea, and did his paltry level best to pretend that he wasn't listening – in fact, that he wasn't even there at all.

"What you have done," I said, playing a double game, "is tell everyone a load of old lies."

Miranda glanced at the SS-Officer. The implication being she was afraid, for some reason, that I might become sufficiently angry to attack her. East noticed this, and was appalled by just how much I had misjudged this girl. To love her had been my greatest folly, though it was only in this instant of disillusion that I realized how cataclysmically damaging that folly might prove to be. We sat in silence for five minutes, during which time – time in which we did, on the surface, nothing – Sergeant North had made it almost all the way to the Gamekeeper's Cottage, where Sub-Lieutenant South was still ignorantly abed. Eventually, the SS-Officer, acknowledging that the latest of the Gestapo's ruses had failed, moved to a further escalation. He stuck his head out into the corridor, and called out, "You can come in, now." A few seconds later, Bert and Estelle entered.

Of course, the only free pair of chairs in the room were those between Miranda and myself. Naturally, Bert and Estelle were terrified of sitting beside me. They stood, anxiously havering, until the SS-Officer, who had already sat back down in his former position, noticed their discomfort and moved to alleviate it.

Sergeant North made his approach to the Gamekeeper's Cottage with extreme caution. He moved silently through the deepest undergrowth. It seemed likely that the SS-Kommandant, anticipating his next move, would have radioed ahead and ordered the area to be sealed. When North came within sight of the cottage, he saw that a Gestapo guard had indeed been placed on sentry duty outside the front door. All Sergeant North could do now was sit, be patient, and play the observer's role, hoping against hope for an opportunity to spring his comrade. He hid in the bushes beside the path, closer to the cottage than on that day now seemingly so far distant when he'd ambushed Sub-Lieutenant South.

North did not have long to wait: the SS-Kommandant and Alma-the-Spy arrived at a fine canter no more than five minutes later. He watched them swish past, boots at eye-level. There was no chance he would be discovered. This was his territory. He was in his element. The two of them disappeared inside the cottage, leaving the sentry on guard outside.

vi.

Inside the cottage, Sub-Lieutenant South's mother ushered Alma-the-Spy and the SS-Kommandant through into the living room. She had been the only person up and about, and so it was she who had answered the front door. Her husband was still fast asleep, dreaming whatever dreams the guilty dream. After three distressing minutes, South's mother meekly led the representatives of the occupying forces upstairs.

How I wish that this were a scene I could simply skip; that it were possible for me to tell you, in simple terms, the simplest,

391

that Sub-Lieutenant South behaved just as one would trust and expect a loyal member of Her Majesty's Forces to behave. But, sadly for me, sadly for us, sadly, indeed, for England, it is not nor was not so. The sight of the SS-Kommandant entering his bedroom terrified South. He feared, no doubt, the terrors of torture and the privations of imprisonment. In another man, in a truer man, with a truer heart, and a sterner spirit, this momentary quailing would have rapidly passed. The imperative of silence would almost immediately have been felt to be categorical. The challenges ahead would have become but so many bulwarks against capitulation. The resolve to see the thing through, and see it through unto the very end, would have been cast, set, cooled and placed upon a pedestal – solid as statuary, enduring as brass. But Sub-Lieutenant Paul South forgot his training, ignored his conscience, shamed his friends and, worst of all, betrayed his country, Empire, Queen.

"It was Andrew," he said. "He made us do it."

vii.

O iniquity! Here was the moment that our country fell. Here, in this instant, our doom was made manifest. It may be that in future years, when this heinous occupation is removed, when the peace-loving countries of the world have co-joined to remove the Nazi jackboot from our soil, when England once again stands proud and proudly free, an elder and respected brother among all the family of nations – it may be that such a moment as this will be relegated once again to the mere historical: an incident to make a schoolboy shake his head and think, "Thus I would not myself ever have done." But, in our present peril, the thought of this betrayal, there is no other word, is no small retrospective fact: it is the very spur we use to prick our stallion forces into fresh charges and assaults. It is no more and no less than the epitome of our shame, our ire, our need to self-redeem.

viii.

Back at the Internment Camp, Bert was attempting to annoy me into blurting out an angry confession. "We know what you think – that it's our fault that Matthew died; that we could have done more to keep him alive."

"If we'd acted sooner," chipped in Estelle.

"But what good did killing an innocent dog do?"

I sat with my arms folded, gazing at the wall above their heads as if there were something incredibly interesting upon it: a rare butterfly. Actually, I was staring through it at an imaginary version of events taking place elsewhere – a version, it has to be said, that in all but the smallest details was uncannily accurate.

"And now we hear that you were hatching some kind of half-baked plot against us."

"If you've still got it," said Estelle, "we'd be grateful if you could give us back the photograph album. Stealing that was a wicked thing to do, a wicked thing, I tell you."

For the first time, I flinched. I was remembering my own qualms about destroying almost all that the world had left of our heroic friend.

This flinch did not pass unnoticed. The SS-Officer pitched in. "What do you know about the photograph album?" he asked.

But, even though it was now completely futile (Sub-Lieutenant South having started to tell the Nazis everything they wanted to know) I maintained my silence.

393

About twenty minutes after they went in, Sergeant North saw the SS-Kommandant and Alma-the-Spy exiting the Gamekeeper's Cottage. Sub-Lieutenant South followed them, dressed in his Hitler Youth uniform: charcoal blazer and trousers, white shirt, school tie, shiny black shoes. Finally came South's parents, formally accoutred, as if for a rally or an execution. From his very first glimpse of him, Sergeant North could tell that the Sub-Lieutenant was a defeated man. His head was hanging, and his hands, although free, were held as if handcuffed. "Damn you," whispered North. "Damn you to hell." They, the adults, were talking around him, and over him, but also, occasionally, to him. He, for his part, was sullenly and yet obediently responding. As they started along the path towards Sergeant North, they came into earshot.

". . . for an hour or so," said Alma-the-Spy.

"And then what?" asked the Sub-Lieutenant's father, desperately keen to demonstrate his subservience to these figures of invading authority. "You're sure he won't be arrested?"

What a contrast was here on display. Sergeant North could not help but compare the quisling collaboration of South's father with the patriotic resistance of his own.

"Well," said SS-Kommandant 241, "that very much depends."

"On what?" burst out South's anxious mother, then apologized, "I'm sorry. I mean, do you know?"

"I won't go to jail, will I?" put in Sub-Lieutenant South, sounding more like a girl than ever before.

"Paul," said his father. "You'll have plenty of time to talk later. And talk you will." He turned toadying towards the Kommandant. "I'm sorry," he said. "Go on."

"We have to get to . . ." the SS-Kommandant replied. And

then they were no longer audible. The Sergeant suspected that the next words would have been "to the bottom of this", but he had no other assurance beyond a general tendency towards cliché in the speech of all the adults he had ever known. Without requiring more than a second or so internally to debate the matter, Sergeant North set off through the forest in the direction of Amplewick Internment Camp. He, travelling by foot, would get there by much the shortest route. Yet the others, with the advantageous speed of a car, were likely to arrive there before him.

x.

And, indeed, so it proved. Sergeant North, approaching through The Furze, came within sight of the low buildings of the Internment Camp just as Sub-Lieutenant South and his captors were getting out of the Gestapo Vehicle. He watched from a silent distance as they, forming the same four-square escort around South, led the abject Sub-Lieutenant into the Torture Chamber. Also in the car-park, he could see the Morris Traveller of the Collaborators, Bert and Estelle. The Sergeant crept closer, increasing the chance of capture with every further foot. The situation seemed hopeless, and, as you, people of the future, close or distant, already know its outcome, I will not prolong your agony in unnecessary elucidation. There was but one course of action possibly open to Sergeant Andrew North, and manfully he took it. Skirting at a safe and good distance the Internment Camp, he made his way towards the House of the Collaborators, Bert and Estelle.

Inside the Ante-Room to the Main Torture Chamber (which smelt very strange), I was all of a sudden confronted by Sub-Lieutenant South and his escort. At first this sight saddened me, for I knew my comrade to have been captured. Then it gladdened me, for it meant that Sergeant North had so far eluded the Gestapo. Then, for a second time, it saddened me, for, when I looked into the face of Sub-Lieutenant South, I found myself staring into the eyes of a stranger – hang-dog and haunted. My former friend had obviously been coerced into crossing over to the other side.

On seeing my dismay and then my disgust, the Sub-Lieutenant felt the need to say something. "I didn't want to go to jail," he whispered. "They know everything anyway. Miranda told them most of it. And it was *you* that told her. I'm no worse than you. I didn't give the game away."

Citizens of Her Majesty's Great British Empire and Common-wealth, I feel your dismay, I share your wrath, I know your disgust. To have been betrayed is bad enough, but to have been betrayed by such a one, the kind of bright, upstanding, healthy young man upon which our strength has always been founded, to have this mainstay of our intrepid thought and Imperial might – to have, as I say, all this possible majesty collapse so weakly and so fast! It hardly bears the thinking on.

xii.

Amplewick was swarming with SS. It took Sergeant North over an hour to get to the House of the Collaborators, Bert and Estelle. He'd taken the longest, safest route. But even so, he had several times come very close to capture.

Carefully, he double-checked that there was no Gestapo guard outside. Wasting no further time, he went into the garden shed and fetched the petrol can.

After smashing the glass of the back door, he poked his hand through and turned the key in the lock.

He listened for a moment. The house was quiet, seemed empty.

As North emerged into the living room, he felt himself being seized from behind. He struggled like a wild animal trapped, but in the end found resistance was futile. Someone – damn them – had been hiding behind the door.

The Sergeant's first thought, irrational though it might have been, was of Mr Dinosaur. But then he heard himself being addressed by an unmistakable voice.

"Just put the can down, sonny."

It was SS-Kommandant 241.

At first Sergeant North did not react. The stranglehold upon his windpipe tightened. He couldn't breathe.

"Drop it," hissed the Kommandant.

North had no choice. He let the can fall from his grasp.

xiii.

At this moment, all who had gathered or been gathered in the Ante-Room were shuffling through into the Main Torture Chamber. There were not enough chairs, and most of them had to stand. Sub-Lieutenant Paul South stood in front of the Chief Torturer, snivelling. I, by contrast, stood erectly to attention. The Torturer was looking at us down the long bridge of her nose. "Well?" she said. "What have you two got to say for yourselves?" We were ringed by adults. It had always been that way, but for a few brief moments, and but for a few yet briefer moments, it would be that way for ever from now on.

xiv.

It was sad, indeed, for us to see Sergeant North led, handcuffed, into the Torture Chamber.

The SS-Kommandant made a brief report of our Leader's attempted attack upon the Collaborators' house.

"I knew he'd go back there," said the Kommandant, elated. "I just knew it."

"You were correct," said the Chief Torturer.

When I saw North glance at me, I nodded towards the dejected South. The Sub-Lieutenant was looking at his shoes, too ashamed to meet his Leader's eye.

"Traitor," whispered Sergeant North. Sub-Lieutenant South flinched.

After this, North never again addressed South directly.

xv.

I realized that it was time.

Reaching into my front trouser pocket, I quickly produced the Bowie knife. At the same time, I stepped towards the desk, towards the Chief Torturer.

Everyone in the room was frozen in a typical attitude: Sergeant North, defiant; Corporal South, downcast; SS-Kommandant 241, pompous; the Chief Torturer, horrified; Paul's father and mother, toadying; the Conspirators, crumpled; Miranda, afraid.

With another step, I reached the desk. Only now did the Kommandant begin to react. But by then I had stabbed, stabbed the knife down into the table-top.

Grabbed from behind by the Kommandant, I watched as the blade thrummed slightly from side to side. Everyone else was looking at it, too. There were splinters around its shiny tip.

The first person to speak, just before the babble began, the babble that seemed as though it would never end – the first was our Leader, Sergeant Andrew North.

Eloquently, he pointed towards the knife and said, "That is Matthew."

It was our final gesture of defiance. For the time being, anyway.

xvi

I write, of course, as you know, from my temporary exile in the still-free land of Canada. And yet I look out across the mighty Atlantic, oh England, and I yearn towards you with all my heart and soul. As to what will be my own fate, I have no idea. If sufficient time has been and gone, you may already know what I do not. And yet I have a powerful sentiment – almost, dare I say it, a vision – of what may yet come to pass. It is the vision of a once-more-liberated land – land of beauty and of bounty both. And in this vision I am standing once again upon English soil. High up, I am, upon a hill in Amplewick – a hill called Crackback Hill. And there I stand, facing to Northwards – looking out across long fields in the slow slide of the low golden sun. The hedgerows leave their benign temporary grid upon the fields of wide, ungarnered wheat. A hawk is hovering above one of these mice-sparse fields, like the hand of a child told it may select only one chocolate from the Christmas box. In an adjacent field, on emerald grass, sheep are complying with the zigzag of a border collie – itself obedient to the whistles of a humble shepherd. And in a further field, the patient cows distend their stomachs with the rich, thick grass of England. Closer yet, the birds around me cram the air with variable song. A myxomatos-ized rabbit, using the last of its strength, falls down into the darkness of its home warren. Bees constantly visit their blossom-bowers, trysting with stamens, aglow with pollen, then swing off to yet more promiscuities. The badger yawns, awaiting nightfall, his cumbersome emergence and further forage. Owls relish their deep dormancy, safe within oakholes. In a pond near by, the soft bellies of newts are caressed with bubbles, plopping up from the lazy mouths of carp. A cat lopes homeward, shadow five times longer than itself. And overarching everything, a blueness as of eyes and a whiteness as of blossom. The clouds pass easily, entertaining the ground below with the infinite variety of their shadow-shapes. Their cloud-roofs are extravagant, filigree, but their undersides are a line razored in exact parallel to the horizon. This is my vision of a future – a future both gloriously close and bitterly distant. Believe it or believe it not: the Spring will come, and England shall be free once more. I can but hope that I myself will have the posthumous satisfaction of knowing that, in some small way, I helped to bring utopia to pass.

Serial No. ███████

CENSORED

It took me a couple of hours to finish reading back through everything, and a couple of days to recover. I went out for a lot of walks, thinking things through. I went to green, childhood places. Here is a fact: my father never talked to me about these things. All I knew I knew from his manuscript. Here is another fact: my father was a great man. Whatever he did or didn't do, I loved him. He was the best father to me. Just like *the* Best Father. He was a great man, and that was because he never forgot what it was like to be a boy – what it was like to be like me. I didn't want to know the truth. I knew the truth already. My father never betrayed me. Whatever else and whoever else he betrayed, he never betrayed me. He was a great man, and nothing was going to make me think that he wasn't. Nothing. *Nothing.*